THE FOREST OF SOULS

CARLA BANKS

The Forest of Souls

To Northern College
Students

best wishes

Carla Banks
(aka Danuta Reah)

HarperCollins*Publishers*

HarperCollins*Publishers*
77–85 Fulham Palace Road, London W6 8JB

www.harpercollins.co.uk

Published by HarperCollins*Publishers* 2005
1 3 5 7 9 10 8 6 4 2

A catalogue record for this book
is available from the British Library

ISBN 0 00 719210 X
ISBN 0 00 719380 7 (trade paperback)

Set in Sabon by Palimpsest Book Production Limited,
Polmont, Stirlingshire

Printed and bound in Great Britain by
Clays Limited, St Ives plc

For Volodia Shcherbatsevich,
Masha Bruskina and Kiril Trous,
murdered by the Nazis in Minsk,
26 October 1941

And also for Doug.

And what of the wolves, she'd say,
the nine wolves that in the winter's
grey stone dawn would smash
their bones against the door,
hammering like hungry seals
until the door splinters and the baby
is got at – even from the cradle
even from its precious sleep

And listen . . . there are men
As bad as wolves who no door
– no matter how solid the oak –
will keep out.

From 'My Mother' by John Guzlowski

ACKNOWLEDGEMENTS

I would like to thank all the people who have helped me when I was researching this book, especially Anna Gerasimova and Adam Maldzis, First Vice-President, Belarusian PEN, for the help they gave me when I travelled to Minsk; Franklin and Galina Swartz for the help they gave me with my research; the staff at the Museum of the Great Patriotic War, praspekt Francyska Skaryny, Minsk, for copying photographs for me, and for maintaining such a moving and salutary memorial to the events of the 1939–1945 war.

I would also like to thank Eileen Fauset and Jenny Ryan for reading the manuscript and giving invaluable critical comment; my agent Teresa Chris for all the support she has given me during the often difficult process of writing; and Julia Wisdom and Anne O'Brien at HarperCollins, whose editing has helped to make this book what it is.

1

Later in the week, we were given orders to clear the area. That night, they firebombed the houses and left the streets burning. I watched as the work progressed. Towards midnight, a woman with a young child in her arms ran towards the gates. She was stopped by a policeman who seized the child, who was perhaps a year old, struck it against the wall then threw it into the flames. He shot the mother dead.

I very much wish to be home.

The light had faded as Helen worked. She looked up from the page she was studying, her eyes aching from the cramped script. The old library was dark, apart from the pool of yellow cast by the desk lamp on the table beside her. Something had distracted her. She lifted her head, listening. The silence closed around her, the smell of damp, the mustiness of old paper, the chill of the abandoned house. But she knew what she'd heard. It had been the click of the door closing.

There was someone else in the library.

She'd arrived at the old house later than she had planned. She thought she knew the route to the Derwent Valley – thirty minutes, maybe forty-five if the traffic was heavy. It took her less than thirty minutes to get to the far side of Glossop, the small commuter town on the edge of the Pennine hills. The sun was touching the horizon as she reached the top of the Snake Pass and dropped down into the valley at the other side. Last summer, she and Daniel had brought the children out here. They'd flown the kite that Finn, just eleven, had designed and made. 'Chip off the old block,' Daniel had said, proud for once of his studious son.

The road swept round and the valley opened up in front of her. Ladybower Dam lay ahead, the hills reflected in its black mirror. The road wound away to the east under the shadow of trees, the heather moors stretching away beyond. She turned off into the wooded depths of the Derwent valley. The road was narrower here, and her car bumped over the rough surface. The sky had clouded over, and rain began to spatter across the windscreen. The trees closed around her and the road was just the arcs of her headlights in the shadows – ruts and potholes, and a rabbit frozen for a moment in the brightness.

She checked the piece of paper on the seat next to her. The house was about two miles along this road, round the head of the dam. She was driving deeper into the forest and she peered through the windscreen as the car bumped and lurched.

The road turned, and she had to negotiate a gate with a red sign: PRIVATE ROAD. NO ENTRY EXCEPT FOR ACCESS. To her left, silhouetted against the evening sky, she could see the towers of the dam wall above the trees, turreted and massive. Ahead, the road became a track, shadowed by the still, dark trees.

She slowed down more, trying to pick out landmarks. She passed stone gateposts, a high wall, another gate that opened on to a muddy drive, then she was back into the wild. *Past the houses,* the directions said. *Another half-mile up the valley.* It was hard to gauge the distances when she was driving so slowly.

Her headlights picked out the incongruous homely red of

a letter box, and then she saw gates to her left. She stopped and leaned across, trying to read the lettering carved into the stone posts. OLD HALL. She'd made it. She negotiated the turn. The drive bent sharply back and ran steeply up between the trees. And then she was clear of them, and she saw the house for the first time.

It was massive against the darkening sky. The blank windows stared back at her. The stone was patchy with white lichen, and stained where water had run down from the broken gutters and fall pipes. This wasn't a house that was loved. *Or one that loved.* The thought jumped into her mind, startling her.

The rain was a fine drizzle that chilled her skin and seeped through the protective covering of her coat. The door was solid wood, sheltered by a stone canopy. The bell push looked old. She pressed it without much expectation and waited. Nothing happened. She'd thought there would be something more . . . official? More organized. She tried the bell again, then hammered on the wood. *Come on. Come on.* Water dripped on to the stone, splashing her feet.

She was about to knock again when the door opened. She'd heard nothing through the heavy timbers. A man, presumably the caretaker she'd been told about, stood there. He was holding a torch.

'I'm Helen Kovacs,' she said. 'You should be expecting me.'

'Sorry,' he said. 'I was working. I didn't hear you.' He didn't look more than twenty. She'd been expecting someone older. Her head barely came up to his shoulder as she stepped past him. Despite the icy weather, he was in his shirtsleeves. She wondered what it was about young men that made them impervious to the cold.

The smell of the house closed round her, a smell of damp, of mildew, of rot. There was no light. The entrance hall was an echoing dimness. She could just make out a staircase that swept up in front of her to a shadowed gallery.

3

'This way.' He shone the torch in front of him. 'Watch where you're going. Something's shorted the lights. I was just trying to fix them.' He led her through long corridors towards the back of the house, pausing every so often to make sure she was following. In the faint light, she could see dark panelling, damaged in places and rotted away. The ceiling arched above her, and she thought about the tiny semi she shared with Hannah and Finn – that she used to share with Daniel as well – characterless, perhaps, but comfy and warm. She shivered.

'How long has it been like this?'

He paused halfway along the corridor, and pulled a bunch of keys out of his pocket. 'Since the guy who lived here died, I suppose,' he said as he tried a key in the lock of the double doors in front of him. It stuck, and he had to jiggle it to free it. He tried another key. 'I don't go in here much.'

This kind of deterioration took years. The last owner of the house, a reclusive Russian scholar, had died just a few months before. 'It's a pity,' she said, 'that it's been left like this.'

'He was a bit of a nutter by all accounts. Thought the KGB was after him. Shut himself away here. He lived in the back of the house, let the rest fall apart.' The key turned and he gave a grunt of satisfaction as he pushed the doors open and stepped through. He shone his torch around. 'You're right. It's a shame. It must have been beautiful once.'

The library. She was in Gennady Litkin's library. In the twilight, the room was filled with shadows. The high ceiling and the rows of bookcases gave an illusion of space, but as she managed to get a sense of the scale, she realized it was smaller than it seemed. There was a smell of damp and old paper. She looked up. The ceiling was ornate but the plasterwork was damaged. She could see stains and patches, places marking the incursion of water.

She walked slowly down the aisle, looking at the high

shelves and the panelled walls. The shelves were piled with boxes – box files, cardboard boxes sagging at the seams, old shoe boxes, a treasure trove of papers from the past, and one that would probably never be fully explored. As she looked round the shelves closest to her, she realized she had never understood how vast Gennady Litkin's collection had been.

He had died intestate. The collection – books, paintings, letters, diaries, legal documents, photographs – was being archived and would probably end up scattered among various universities and museums. The house was nearly empty now, and once the last details of the estate were sorted out, it would be sold. Even in its dilapidated state, it must be worth a fortune.

She looked at the boxes with growing anxiety. 'Has every-thing been packed up?' She had the reference from Litkin's eccentric filing system to help her, but if the papers had been sorted and stacked, it would be useless. It would take years to go through all of this.

The young man looked at her and then shrugged helplessly. 'I don't know,' he said. 'I'm just here to keep an eye on the place.'

'What's your name?' She should have asked sooner.

'Nick,' he said.

'Nick.' She held out her hand. 'Do you live here?'

He touched her outstretched hand briefly. 'Just until March. They'll have it cleared then.'

'It must be lonely.' He looked very young to be shut away in the isolation of the old house.

'It's not so bad,' he said. 'I've got the van – I go down to the village. I can go into town if I want, but it's all right here. It's a great place for walking.'

'You like that?' she said. She used to go walking a lot before she and Daniel got married, before Finn was born.

He nodded, looking suddenly enthusiastic. 'I did the Pennine Way last summer.'

'That's serious walking.'

He shook his head. 'It's nothing. What I want to do is go to the US, do the Appalachian Trail.'

'Okay,' she said. '*That's* serious walking.'

He grinned. 'You said it.'

She'd have liked to go on talking, but she had work to do. 'I'd better get on.' Officially, she was here to look at the records from a long dissolved mining company. 'I'm looking for the ledgers for the Ruabon Coal Company,' she said.

'Yeah.' He'd obviously been briefed. 'Everyone wants to look at those. It's about the only thing anyone knows about. They're over here. I got them down for you.'

She followed him down the aisle to where two sets of shelves formed a kind of nook. She looked at the boxes that filled the shelves. Some of them were labelled, but the ink had faded. She leaned in closer to try and read the words.

Suddenly, a light came on. She turned round. Nick was balancing a desk light on an empty ledge. Its long neck was too high to fit and it stuck out awkwardly, making its position precarious. He shook his head, obviously unhappy with the arrangements. 'That's the best I can do. You'll have to use this. I'm sorry. I'm working on the lights now.'

'Thanks,' she said. 'I wondered how I was going to manage. Listen, before you go, there's something else I want to have a look at – I'm not sure where to start.' It hadn't occurred to her that Litkin's system might have been disrupted. 'I'm looking for some stuff from the last war. There'll probably be a diary, and some letters . . . I know they're in this library somewhere. Maybe you've seen . . .' Her voice trailed off as she looked round the crammed shelves.

He steadied the light with his hand. 'I don't know. I'm sorry. It's all just, you know . . .' He gestured around him. 'Papers and stuff.'

She looked back at the boxes on the shelves, wondering what to do. Then she noticed something she hadn't seen before. In the light, faint pencil markings on the boxes had become visible. *112.33 OTE*. She knelt down to get closer. 'Look,' she said. 'It's his filing system.' She ran her fingers along the boxes. 'It goes up – the ones I want . . .' She tried to track the numbers on to the next shelf, got lost and then picked it up again. She could feel the tension inside her releasing – the boxes hadn't been put out of sequence or repacked. They were the way he'd left them. She moved along the shelves. What had he said? Third shelf from the top, halfway along . . . Here. A box file marked *120.43 PEKBM*. She pulled it out and looked round for somewhere to put it. The young man watched for a moment. 'I'll get you a table. Hang on.' He disappeared.

But the box was empty. She ran her fingers through her hair, tugging at it in frustration. She'd be lucky to get another chance at these papers. It would take forever to get the ownership status sorted out – she'd had to resort to a manufactured interest in the Ruabon Coal Company to arrange this visit. And she didn't have a lot of time.

She went back to the shelves. The boxes were in shadow She screwed her eyes up in the dim light, trying to read the rest of the inscriptions as she moved along the row, but it was no good, the lettering was too faded. *12_4_KBM*. That could be . . . She lifted the box file out and moved closer to the light. She balanced it on her knee as she opened it. It contained a sheaf of papers, old and stained.

She shifted her balance to stop the box from falling, and lifted the papers out carefully, aware of their fragility. They looked like jottings for someone's accounts – balance sheets, profit and loss. This wasn't what she was looking for. She changed her grip to put them back, and something fell out from between the sheets on to the floor, something that had been slipped into the pile.

It was a book. She felt her heart thump, and she found herself looking over her shoulder around the dark library before she crouched down to pick it up. The cover was stiff card, marbled, and the pages were yellowed and brittle. She turned them carefully. They were covered with a minute script, neatly and economically written, wasting no space. The ink was brown with age. The writing went on and on, and then suddenly ended. The last pages of the book were blank.

She heard the click of the door, and a dragging sound. Nick came into view, pulling a small table. Instinctively, she snapped the book shut. 'It's a bit scruffy,' he said, wiping the top with his sleeve and inspecting it. 'Here.' He pulled the table into the alcove and moved the light from its precarious balance on the shelf. He looked pleased with the result. 'That's better.' Then he looked down at her crouched on the floor. 'Are you okay?'

'Fine.' She stood up, dusting off the knees of her jeans. 'Thanks.'

He hesitated for a minute. 'Do you know how long . . . ?'

'Does it matter?' she said, looking up at him.

'I'm supposed to lock up at nine.' He shrugged. 'Don't worry about it. I'm not going anywhere. When you've done, take the door on your right at the end of the corridor. I'll be in there.' His face was under-lit by the lamp.

'I'll be finished before nine,' she reassured him. 'Thanks.' She put the papers on to the table.

He looked at her working arrangements with some dissatisfaction, and nodded. 'I'll leave you to it, then.' He turned and walked away up the aisle.

She sat down at the makeshift desk and went through the box file carefully. Tucked in among the accounts there was a large envelope that had probably contained the notebook. She looked inside it, holding her breath. There were sheets of paper, folded round something. She slipped them out carefully. The writing on them was dark and recent, and as she unfolded them, she recognized the hand as Gennady Litkin's. She felt a stab of disappointment.

But they had been folded for a purpose. They were wrapped round a thin bundle of letters written on fragile paper that was starting to crumble along the edges. She pulled the shade of the desk lamp down, redirecting its beam. It was a cheap one, and the mechanism that was supposed to hold it in place was faulty. The slightest movement, and it lifted its head slowly, like a wading bird that had been disturbed, expanding its neck in alarm, cautious, checking.

She steadied it, then flattened out the first letter. She didn't recognize the language at first. Russian? She only knew a few words. The script was minute. The first line had to be a salutation: *My dear Captain Vienuolos* . . . It seemed to be an acceptance of an invitation. She scanned down to the signature to see if she could work out the identity of the writer, but it was an indecipherable scrawl: *P* . . . *E* . . . She pulled the lamp closer, and the light flickered. *Who are you? Who were you?* But there was no answer.

She turned to the diary. There was a label on the front of the book, peeling at the edges, and handwritten in ink that had faded. She could barely make it out. The writing was Russian again for a moment, she felt discouraged, then she realized that Gennady Litkin must have written it. She carefully transliterated the letters she could read. There were two words and what looked like dates. The last letter was И. The first one was M, then A. The third letter – she couldn't make it out. The ink had faded. The second word . . . Good, she had what there was. *Ma_y _ro_ _ene_ _ 19_2– _944*. It didn't mean anything.

She opened the book. It was, as Litkin had told her, written in Lithuanian. Even though she'd been studying the language for years, she found the writing hard to decipher, and she remembered that Litkin had said something about making a translation. She looked at the pages of modern notes, suddenly hopeful, but of course, they were in Russian. If Litkin had translated the diary, he had written in his own language. Her

Lithuanian should be sufficient. She applied herself to the diary again.

Her head was starting to ache by the time she'd read the first few pages. She checked her watch. It was after seven. She had been here for almost two hours. She hesitated, reluctant to pull herself away, but she wanted to check on Hannah who had been complaining of earache and a sore throat.

She switched on her phone. The *beep* as it found the network was an intrusion from the 21st century. She keyed in Daniel's number, but his answering machine took the call. She left a message, feeling relieved that she wouldn't have to talk to him. 'It's Helen. I'm just checking that the kids are okay. I'll see you on Thursday.' His usual day for having the children.

She was just getting back to the letters when her phone rang. It was Daniel. 'I was working out front,' he said. 'Any reason why they wouldn't be okay?'

She didn't want to row. 'Hannah felt poorly. And it's not their usual night . . .'

'Right. It isn't. And you dump Hannah when she's ill.'

She felt a stab of anxiety. 'Ill? Has the earache . . . ?'

'She's fine, since you're so worried. They need their routine, Helen. Except when it suits you.'

'I told you. I had to work. Like you do, you know? When you get a late call?'

'Oh, sure, old letters and bits of paper. What does your wife do, Mr Kovacs? Oh, she's got a BA in old shopping lists.' There was a moment's silence, then he added. 'And a PhD in banging the boss.'

Not that again. 'I'm working,' she said. 'Are the kids okay? That's all I wanted to know.'

'I told you. they're fine.'

'Can I speak to Hannah?'

'It's a bad line. She won't be able to hear you.'

'I'll be home by nine. I'll phone when –'

'She'll be in bed.' His voice was cold.

'I know. I'd just like to say –'

'I'll tell her you called.' He hung up.

She felt depressed after the call. She and Daniel couldn't even have a civil conversation about the children. At least it looked as though she wouldn't have to take time off to go to the doctor's with Hannah. She wouldn't have to cancel her meeting with Faith.

She looked at the letters spread out on the desk in front of her, and at the diary. She was about to make a decision. She couldn't finish reading these here. She'd assumed there would be some kind of copying facilities – the word 'library' had conjured up a different image from the one that had confronted her. But no one knew the letters and diary were here, so no one would miss them. She could slip them into her bag and take them away to study at her leisure. It would be okay – she was a bona fide scholar, and she could quietly return them when she'd finished with them. No harm done.

And that was when she heard the sound. It was – it had been – the soft click of the door. 'Nick?' she said. There was no response. She paused with the notebook closed over her finger. 'Hello?' she said.

Silence whispered back. And in the silence . . . Was she imagining it? – the faintest sound of breathing, of something moving through the darkness like silk. She stood up, suddenly uneasy. 'Who's there?' She picked up the lamp to lift it higher, to expand the area of light, but the cord pulled tight. She put it down on the desk and moved slowly back down the aisle, the high shelves looming shadows in the darkness.

Now her imagination was playing tricks, making movements in the dark corners of the room, making soft sounds like footsteps behind her. She spun round, looking back along the aisle to the pool of light that marked the place where she had been working. 'Hello?' she said again.

The aisle was empty, running back into the shadows. But she'd heard . . .

Then there was someone behind her and before she could move something snaked round her neck and pulled tight. Her breath was cut off and her hands clawed futilely at the thing that bit deep into her flesh, feeling the slipperiness of blood under her fingers. *Blood? My blood?* And her legs were starting to tremble as she twisted and struggled for air and there was no one behind her as her flailing arms hit out and the darkness was darker and . . .

And the circle of light from the desk lamp crept up the wall, illuminating the shelves, up and up until the balance mechanism caught, and the light froze, fixed upwards at the stained and ornate ceiling where a plaster cherub, half its face gone, dispensed grapes from fingerless hands and the stains darkened as the rain penetrated and dripped on to the papers spread out below.

2

When Faith was a child, she thought that she lived in a forest. Her grandfather's house, where she spent her childhood, was surrounded by trees, beech and sycamore and chestnut, their heavy leaves shielding it in summer and their branches standing like guardians when the winter stripped them bare. The garden was a playground of green tunnels and damp leaf mould where the sun would sometimes break through and dapple the ground with sudden colour – the vivid green of a leaf, the scarlet of a berry.

The house itself was a place of dark corridors and closed-up rooms, cold and rather comfortless. But she could remember the evenings she spent with her grandfather when he read to her from his book of fairy tales with pictures of witches and goblins, dark paths and mysterious houses in forest glades. And he would tell her stories about his own childhood in a house built deep in a forest, somewhere far away.

And she could remember the way his face would change sometimes as he talked. His voice would falter and then fall silent, and he would pat her hand absently and say, 'That is enough, little one.' He would go to his study and the door would close behind him with the finality of silence . . .

*   *   *

13

Faith woke suddenly, sitting up in bed, the quilt that had tangled round her as she slept sliding on to the floor. For a moment she didn't know where she was, then the confusion cleared. She was in her house in Glossop, where she had lived for just a month. It was still dark. She could see the square of the skylight above her, and the silhouettes of the bedroom furniture emerging from the gloom. She switched on the lamp, flooding the room with warmth and colour. Dreams of her childhood faded from her mind.

Her bedroom was an attic, with slanting walls and odd nooks and corners. It was the first room she'd decorated once she'd bought the house, stripping off the dingy wallpaper and painting everything white, adding colour with throws and blinds so that even on this dark winter morning, the rain beating on the skylight above her head, the room looked warm and welcoming.

She went down the winding staircase to the bathroom. Her head felt muzzy with sleep as she stood under the shower, so she turned the temperature down and woke herself up with a blast of cold water. She wrapped herself in a towel, shivering as she went quickly back up the stairs. A spatter of rain blew across the window.

It was the start of her second week in her new job at the Centre for European Studies at the University of Manchester. She had recently been appointed as a senior research assistant to the director, the eminent historian and political philosopher Antoni Yevanov. It had been a hotly contested post that she had won after a gruelling three-day interview. She knew that a lot of people were surprised when she was appointed – they thought that at thirty-two, she was too young, that she didn't yet have the experience – and the professional knives were out.

She dried her hair. It had grown over the summer, and it hung heavy and dark to her shoulders, so she pulled it off her face and secured it with a clip. She hesitated as she tried

14

to decide what to wear. The day was going to be bitty – she had a meeting first thing, she had an article to complete for an academic journal about the role of statistical analysis in historical research, and there was a departmental meeting at four, which would be the first she had attended at the Centre. She knew the importance of first impressions.

After a moment's thought, she chose a cream skirt and a tailored jacket. She'd be walking a lot today – the corridors of the Centre, the campus – so she opted for shoes with a low heel. She was tall enough to get away with it.

It seemed strange to be back in Manchester. Faith had spent her childhood in the city, brought up by her grandfather who lived in the affluent suburb of Altrincham, but there had been no sentimentality in her decision to return – the opportunity of working with Antoni Yevanov had been incentive enough.

Her attachments to the city were simply a bonus. It was good to be near her grandfather again, and she was working with her oldest friend, Helen Kovacs. The thought of Helen brought a frown to Faith's face as she packed her work bag. Helen was still struggling in the early stages of her academic career – she had left academia after she had graduated, and had only recently returned and completed her PhD. It was hard in the current climate for a woman in her thirties with children to compete against the unencumbered twenty-three-year-olds who were applying for post-doctoral appointments now. Faith's meeting this morning was with Helen, and it would be the first time she'd had to act in her position as Helen's line manager.

Faith and Helen had met at the prestigious grammar school they both attended. It prided itself on its academic excellence and appealed to parents who wanted their children to have a traditional education. The uniform they wore was supposed to iron out any differences of background that the children brought to the school, but the adolescent jungle of status and conformity operated there just the same.

15

Faith, who lived with her immigrant grandfather and had no visible parents, was an object of suspicion. Helen, whose parents were working class and who lived on a modern housing estate in Salford, was a complete outsider. Her father was a builder who was earning just enough to buy his daughter what he believed would be the best education for her. Helen's accent was wrong, her clothes were wrong, she lived in the wrong place and had the wrong parents. The pack turned on her.

The two girls, with the well-honed survival instincts that six years in the school system had given them, had drawn together. They were both bright, they were both athletic, and Faith soon discovered that Helen had a dry wit and a talent for sharp mockery that matched her own. They had seen off their tormentors and established a friendship that had endured into adulthood. They had gone to Oxford together, shared a flat through their student years, seen each other through the ecstasy of first relationships and the subsequent heartbreak. And even though their lives had gone down different paths since then, they had stayed close.

Faith went into the kitchen and put some bread in the toaster. There was coffee left from the night before. She poured some into a mug and put it in the microwave. As she watched the light of the LED, her phone rang. She checked the number. It was her mother. Katya Lange rarely phoned her daughter. Their contacts tended to be Christmas and birthdays and the occasional good-will call that Katya was hardly likely to make at 7.45 in the morning.

Puzzled, she answered it. 'Hello?'

'I'm glad I caught you.' Katya's voice was brisk. 'Listen, Faith, there's a bit of a problem with Marek.'

'What is it? Is he ill?' Her grandfather, Marek Lange, was in his eighties. He was stubbornly independent and would accept almost no help, though Faith had tried often enough to persuade him.

'Nothing like that. You'd be the first to hear. It's this journalist . . .'

Faith sighed. She really didn't want to have this conversation again. A journalist, a man called Jake Denbigh, wanted to interview Grandpapa for a series of articles he was writing about changing attitudes to refugees. Marek Lange, a Polish refugee who had fought on the side of the Allies in the last war, had attracted his interest.

The interview seemed a valid enough enterprise to Faith. She'd read some of Denbigh's articles and she'd heard him once or twice on late-night discussion programmes on Radio 4. As far as Faith could see, the interview would be something her grandfather would enjoy. He was an opinionated man, and would relish the chance to express his views. She thought it would add a bit of variety to a life that was becoming more and more circumscribed by old age, but Katya had been against it from the start.

'I told you what I think,' Faith said now. 'It's up to him. It's nothing to do with me.'

'It's more urgent than that,' Katya said. 'Marek's agreed to do the interview. It's happening this morning.'

'Well – good for him.' Her toast was done. She hunted round for the spread.

'I'm not so sure. I've had a bad feeling about this from the start. I don't trust this Denbigh man, so I looked some stuff up. A few months ago, he got involved in a witch-hunt in Blackburn about a man they said was an ex-Nazi. It got nasty.'

'Oh.' That gave Faith pause for thought. Her grandfather had escaped from Nazi-occupied Poland to join the Polish Free Forces in England in 1943. He had arrived alone, his family and his past lost in the chaos behind him. All that was left were the stories he used to tell her when she was a child, stories about his own childhood, a childhood that had been obliterated as surely as the cities of Europe had been razed

17

in the final destruction of that conflict. His war years in occupied Europe were something he never spoke of, ever.

If Jake Denbigh's focus was Nazis, especially if he was looking for lurid headlines, then Faith shared her mother's misgivings. 'He isn't going to talk to any journalist about it,' she said slowly. 'He wouldn't discuss it with his own family, never mind a stranger.' She sometimes thought it would have been a good thing if he had done, but now it was probably best left where it was, sealed away in his mind.

'I wish I shared your confidence,' Katya said. 'This man is a professional. It's his job to get people talking.'

'I'm not confident. I just don't know what to do. It's still up to Grandpapa in the end.'

'I thought . . .' Katya said, the tentative note in her voice triggering Faith's alarm system, '. . . that maybe you could go over. Sit in on the interview. Then if this Denbigh person tries anything . . .'

Perhaps she should. 'I've got meetings today. It depends what time they've arranged the interview.'

'Eleven,' Katya said.

She was meeting Helen at nine – that would take less than an hour, with luck. She'd pencilled in the rest of the morning for writing the article . . . she could work on that tonight, cancel her plans for the evening. She'd still need some time to prepare for the meeting, but it was do-able. 'Okay,' she said. 'I'll be there.'

She checked the clock as she put the phone down. It was almost eight – she'd better get going. Her meeting with Helen today was a professional thing, part of her new role. If the two women hadn't known each other so well, it could have been tricky.

Helen had left Oxford with a First, but instead of pursuing the academic career she had planned, she had come back to Manchester to marry Daniel Kovacs. This decision had been beyond Faith's comprehension. Helen was pregnant, but that

18

didn't seem to be a good reason to give up her academic carer. Faith didn't like Daniel – he was attractive, but there was a watchful hostility about him, a coldness that made him a strange choice for the warm, vivacious Helen. Despite Faith's misgivings, Helen had been unstoppable. She had asked Faith to be godmother to their son, Finn, who had been born six months later, and this had gone a long way towards healing the slight breach in their friendship.

Their lives had taken different routes after that. Helen had stayed near Manchester, moving with Daniel to Shawbridge, one of the small cotton towns on the outskirts of the city, to live on a road that was not much different from the one where she had grown up. Daniel's work as an electrician was thriving, and Helen became a full-time housewife and mother.

Faith had stayed at Oxford to work on her PhD. She took her duties as godmother seriously, visiting as often as she could, writing letters, sending cards and presents, surprised at how much she enjoyed Helen's baby, who grew up into a bright, serious little boy. Five years later, Helen's second child, Hannah, was born. Faith decided she had been wrong. Helen seemed happy with her life, with her children and with her enigmatic husband.

But then Helen had got restless. She decided that she wanted to take up her career again, and despite Daniel's opposition had embarked on a PhD. Once she had completed that, she had landed a three-year research post at the Centre for European Studies. She had been lucky to get it. Her search for work was confined to Manchester. Even this level of commuting was difficult as Daniel insisted that his work hours made it impossible for him to deliver or collect the children to and from school.

And then, just a few months ago, after twelve years of marriage, she had left Daniel.

Faith pulled her coat on around her as she left the house. It was one of those bleak January days. The wind was whipping the clouds across the sky and blew gusts of rain against her face. She threw her bag on to the back seat and edged out into the rush hour. The grey winter streets made her think longingly of Mediterranean landscapes, of blue skies and warm breezes. One day she was going to work somewhere where the sun shone for more than six weeks a year, somewhere that had warmth, light and space.

Stuck in the stop-go queue into the city, she tried to focus on the meeting she had with Helen in half an hour. Helen was currently working on a paper for a major conference in Bonn, in May. The paper was supposed to be complete by the end of the month – the organizers wanted camera-ready copy in advance – and Helen had fallen behind.

It was understandable. Her life was in chaos. Daniel, outraged by her departure, was fighting her for custody of the children and for the house. He was being as difficult as he could be about child support, and Helen's salary barely covered her expenses. On top of this, the crucial deadline for the Bonn paper had been too much for her, and she had appealed to Faith for help.

Faith ran possible solutions through her mind as she negotiated the roundabout on to the M67. She wanted to manage it so that it didn't become a big issue to Antoni Yevanov. Helen's position at the Centre was vulnerable in the face of ongoing cuts. Her appointment was due for review at the end of her first year, and its continuation depended very much on her successful completion of the paper and the reception it got at Bonn.

The traffic was heavy all the way, and it was almost nine by the time she got to the university. There was a queue for the car park and she was tempted to look for a space on the street, but she wanted a fighting chance of seeing her car again. The rain was falling hard by the time she managed to park. She could feel the rain dripping off her umbrella and trickling down inside her collar as she hurried across campus to the Edwardian façade of the Centre for European Studies. She pushed open the glass doors and entered the lobby, blinking the rain out of her eyes.

The warmth of the building enclosed her with its smell of new carpet and paint. The soothing murmur of activity filled the air, a subdued clatter from keyboards, the distant sound of doors opening and closing, the clunk and hum of the lift. She paused on her way through the lobby to catch her breath, and looked at the display boards. Amongst all the fliers for conferences in Madrid, Paris, and New York there was a glossy poster for the forthcoming Brandt Memorial Lecture. *Antoni Yevanov: 'After Guantanamo – International Law from Nuremberg to the 21st Century'*. She made a note in her diary. She wanted to go to that.

A group of post-grad students were clustered outside the library. They looked across at her and smiled. Faith had given her first lecture the week before, and her face was becoming known. One of them, a tall young man with fair hair, detached himself from the group and came across. He said rather diffidently, 'Faith, have you got any time today? Could I come and see you?'

She gave him a shrewd look, pretty sure what he wanted. She recognized him now: Gregory Fellows, one of the stars of the post-grad intake. He was due to deliver a seminar on his work to the group who monitored and evaluated research carried out under the auspices of the Centre. He was very bright, but most of his energies, Faith had been reliably informed, were focused on his work as a drum and bass artist. She was pretty sure he was looking for a postponement of the seminar. He'd need a good excuse. 'My office time is at three,' she said. 'I can see you then.'

His face fell. 'I wasn't planning on being in all day,' he said. 'I don't suppose you could . . .'

'Three o'clock,' Faith said. He gave her a wry smile of acceptance and she hurried up the stairs, aware that it was

21

already after nine. She unlocked the door of her office, puzzled at Helen's absence. She was only a few minutes late. She phoned Helen's extension, but there was no reply.

Helen worked in one of the small cubicles on the other side of the building. All the research assistants were based down there – one of them might know where she was. Faith went along the corridor, her progress snagging on people who wanted to talk to her, either to set up meetings or to lobby her support for various projects that were being discussed that afternoon. She fielded these as diplomatically as she could, and asked if anyone had seen Helen, but no one had.

Helen's cubicle was empty. The desk was tidy, the computer shut down. There was no coat on the hook, no bag under the desk. A photograph on the side of the computer made a splash of colour. Faith looked at it. It showed Helen, her eyes screwed up against the light, with her arms round her two children, Hannah, small and dark-haired like her mother, and the taller, more solemn Finn.

There was a pile of books on the desk – presumably in preparation for the meeting. Faith glanced through them; they were all standard texts about the role of women in National Socialism, except for one. *The Memorial Book of Mir*. Mir?

But no Helen. She checked the time. It was well after nine. She tried calling Helen's home number but there was no reply. Then she tried Helen's mobile. It was engaged. Faith let out a breath of frustration. She scribbled a note on a yellow post-it and stuck it on the monitor, then went back downstairs to the secretary's office. She wanted to check the teaching schedules.

Trish Parry, Antoni Yevanov's secretary, glanced up when Faith came through her door. 'Can I help you?' Her voice was cool. She had been unfriendly and obstructive from the day Faith arrived. Faith assumed it was to do with the fact that she had been given the job, rather than the internal candidate, but Helen had offered an alternative explanation. 'She's okay with the men. It's the women she doesn't like. She thinks they're rivals for Yevanov's affections.'

'You mean she and Yevanov . . . ?' It seemed unlikely to Faith, though Trish was certainly attractive in a neat, English rose sort of way.

Helen grinned. 'In Trish's dreams,' she said.

'Have you seen Helen Kovacs?' she said to Trish now.

Trish barely looked up. 'Not this morning. She said she might not be in. Something about an appointment.'

'Has she phoned?' It wasn't like Helen to leave people in the lurch.

Trish shrugged. 'She mentioned it yesterday afternoon. Before she left. Early.'

Faith couldn't understand why Helen hadn't contacted her, unless . . . maybe she'd been relying on Trish, and Trish hadn't bothered to pass the message on. 'Did she ask you to let me know?'

'Caroline deals with things like that, not me,' Trish said coolly.

Faith didn't say anything. Technically, Trish was in the right. There was a procedure for reporting absences. She made a mental note to warn Helen not to give Trish ammunition, and looked at her watch. She might as well start work on the article. If she left at ten thirty, she should get to Grandpapa's by eleven, just about.

'Let me know if Helen phones,' she said. 'I'll be in my room.'

'Just a minute.' Trish picked up the phone and keyed in a number. 'Professor Yevanov, I've got Faith Lange here.' She listened, then said, 'She isn't in. Again.' Another pause. 'Are you sure? Faith can give me the –' Her eyes narrowed slightly as they moved to Faith. 'Yes. I'll tell her.' She put the phone down abruptly. 'He wants to see you,' she said.

'Now?' Faith was surprised. Since her arrival, Yevanov had been devoting his time to his ongoing commitments in Europe, and was rarely available. Faith's contact with him had been minimal.

'Of course not. He can see you this afternoon at one.'

Faith raised her eyebrows slightly at Trish's tone. 'One o'clock then.'

As she headed back to her room, she tried Helen's mobile again, but this time it was switched off.

The 999 call came in at 8.45 a.m. The operator listened to the crackling line, and repeated her message. 'Emergency. Which service?' There was no response, just the hiss that told her the line was open. The call was coming through on a cell phone – probably stuffed in someone's bag or pocket without the keypad locked. She wished the people who did this knew about the time and the money it cost when . . .

But now she could hear something. A hitching, gasping sound as though someone was out of breath after running, or . . . frightened, the panicky sound of someone who couldn't get their breath but was trying not to be heard. 'Emergency,' she said again. She kept her voice calm and level. 'Can you tell me where you are? I need to know where you are.'

The gasping breath again, then a voice tense with strain. 'I –' There was a clatter as though the phone had been dropped.

The line cut out.

3

Jake Denbigh came out of the shower drying his hair. He wrapped the towel round his waist and headed for the kitchen area, checking the fax as he passed it.

He switched on the coffee machine and put a couple of oranges through the juicer. His head was aching. He'd been up late the night before – Cass had dropped in. They'd shared a bottle of wine, then opened another, and later she'd experimented with the girder that ran up through the centre of the flat – a warehouse conversion on the river – trying out its potential for pole dancing. Evenings with Cass tended to be strenuous.

He turned on the radio, listening with half an ear as he poured out cereal and pressed the button on the espresso, letting an inch of rich, dark coffee trickle into the cup. The news was typical for the times – trouble in the Middle East, renewed terrorist activity – Jake sometimes thought that if the human race had an overwhelming talent, it was the capacity to make an already difficult life even harder, often in the name of some uncertain glory to come. Jake had no problems with the idea of an afterlife – he thought that a universe that contained Jake Denbigh was a better place than a universe that didn't, but in the meantime, he planned to enjoy the life that he had.

He flicked the switch on the radio to get the local news. A Manchester United story was running as lead, followed by an armed robbery the night before. Nothing that interested him. He took the papers out of the fax and flicked through them – notification that his visa for Belarus was through and his passport was in the post. That was a relief. He'd been worried his plans were going to be held up by the bureaucracy of the last Stalinist state. The rest weren't urgent – he put them in his in-tray for later. He switched on his computer, and got out his tape recorder and mike. He checked the batteries, spares, tape supply and recording levels. He had an interview later that morning.

Jake made his living as a writer and journalist. He'd lived in Manchester for two years now, brought there by a regular slot on a radio programme that was produced in the city, and a weekly column with the local paper, a current affairs piece with a European slant. These days, his interests were shifting more and more towards writing. Broadcasting was good – it got his name out there and he enjoyed it – but it was sound-bite analysis and he was finding its black-and-white simplicity frustrating. He'd published a book on the Rwandan genocides a year ago, looking at the historical impetus behind the horror. It had done well, and now he was seriously researching a second book, this one focusing on the Nazi occupation of Eastern Europe.

He checked his e-mail. There was a message from Cass – she must have sent it when she got back the night before. He frowned. She'd taken a risk sending that from home. Cass lived with someone, and the last thing Jake wanted was for that relationship to go up in smoke for what was, after all, just a casual fling for both of them.

He opened her message and gave a half-smile as he read it: *Was that Pole-ish enough for you?* His current commission was about as Polish as it got. He was writing a series of articles for a monthly journal on immigration into the UK.

The final one, which he was currently researching, looked at the experience of wartime immigrants. He'd put the story of the Jewish immigrants to one side – that warranted an article of its own – and instead focused on the Eastern Europeans: émigré Poles, Russians, Latvians, Lithuanians, Estonians. A motley crew, some of whom had made their escape after the Nazi invasion and fought on the side of the Allies, others who had survived the occupation and had arrived after the end of hostilities. He'd spent the last few days interviewing old men, teasing the information he wanted from the welter of disconnected recollections.

Jake's interest in the occupation of Eastern Europe had begun a few months ago when he'd covered a story about a Lithuanian refugee called Juris Ziverts. Ziverts had been accused of collaboration in the Holocaust, and Jake had befriended the old man. Now, months later, two things stuck in his mind. One was the level of ignorance that existed about the events of Eastern Europe in the last war. The other was the man Ziverts himself.

On Jake's desk next to his computer was a wooden cat. It was black, half-crouching with its tail raised. It was a replica of one of the statues from the roof of the Cat House in Riga. Ziverts had carved it from memory as a memento of the city he had left behind. He had given it to Jake on their last meeting, pushing it towards him with emphatic nods. It was a gift, made in thanks, though what Ziverts thought he had to be grateful for, Jake didn't know.

He stood watching the early light on the water, his eyes narrowed in thought, then he shrugged, and sat down at the desk. The clock on his monitor told him it was seven twenty-nine – a minute before his planned start to the working day. He had an interview at eleven with Marek Lange, a Polish expatriate whose story should be interesting. *Pole-ish enough . . .*

Most people thought of the émigrés as lumpen factory

27

fodder. Jake knew the stereotype – vodka-swilling, brutal and stupid. In fact, they had entered British society at all levels: artists, scholars, teachers, philosophers, entrepreneurs – and criminals. The country they had chosen to make their home was substantially different because they had come here. Lange was the archetype of the entrepreneur, and Jake needed his story. But, as always happened with any project that had gone smoothly, the last bit was proving the most difficult.

Setting up the interview had been hard enough. Lange didn't answer his phone and didn't respond to messages. But something must have got through, because suddenly Jake had Lange's daughter on the phone who had told him brusquely that her father did not want to be involved. Jake had been planning to give up on Lange – there were other people who would fit the profile he wanted – but this opposition aroused his interest. He'd been prepared to persist, but then Lange himself had phoned, apologizing for his earlier silence and agreeing to an interview. Maybe the daughter had been laying the law down there as well, in which case, Jake owed her thanks. He opened the relevant file on his screen and read through the information he'd managed to get hold of:

Marek Lange
Born: 1923
Place of birth: Litva, Poland
Father: Stanislau Lange
Mother: Kristina Lange
Arrived in UK 1943. Joined Polish Free Forces
Marital history: married 1955, divorced, 1961. Ex-wife
    died, 1963
Children: Katya Lange, born 1959

He tapped his fingers on the desk. There was plenty of material relating to Lange's interests after his arrival in the UK, the period he wanted for the article. Jake would have no

28

problems writing a gung-ho profile of a man who'd acquitted himself bravely in the last years of the war and had worked hard and successfully afterwards. But his life before 1943 was frustratingly vague. And this part of Lange's story might tie in very well with the new book Jake had embarked on shortly after his first meeting with Juris Ziverts.

Ziverts' dilemma had opened Jakes eyes to the other refugees, those who had arrived quietly, camouflaged among the thousands who were trying to escape the chaos of Europe and rebuild their shattered lives, those whose papers were in suspiciously good order, and who talked little about their past. These were the people with something to hide and it was their stories that Jake wanted.

Eastern Europe had suffered under the sway of two ideologies: Stalinism and fascism. The storm that had erupted when the two systems collided had been terrifying in its intensity and its brutality. Thirteen million people had died in the war years alone. The millions who had died under Stalin had never been accurately counted, and the majority of the perpetrators had never been brought to book.

Jake didn't want to write about the lost chance for justice – victors' justice, many would have said. He wanted to tell the story of the human cost. His work had given him access to the people who had lived with the Soviet behemoth to the east and the rising darkness of fascism to the west. He needed a hook on which to hang his story, and Juris Ziverts had led him to it: the story of Minsk.

Minsk, a city with a history going back to medieval times, had suffered the worst that both regimes could offer. North of the city, on its outskirts, was the Kurapaty Forest, where 900,000 people had been systematically slaughtered by Stalin's soldiers. And the city itself had been devastated by the Nazi occupation. By the time the Nazis were driven out, a quarter of the population was dead.

Belarus, or Byelorussia, or Belarussia – it was a country

29

with more names than a fugitive. He'd dug around a bit. And he had unearthed a Belarusian émigré living in Manchester. Sophia Yevanova was an invalid who had been housebound for several years. He'd gone to see her with no great expectations. What could an ailing *babushka* have to tell him? But he had come away from their first meeting captivated and enthralled, as had, he suspected, every man who had crossed Sophia Yevanova's path for most of her seventy-five years.

Illness confined her to her room in the spacious old house she shared with her son, the eminent historian, Antoni Yevanov. She was sharp, she was witty, she was unnerving and she was beautiful, and she had woven stories for him that had captivated him for far longer than the hour he had assigned to the meeting. She was from Minsk, and had lived through what may have been one of the most horrific occupations of the 1939–45 war.

At thirteen, she had endured Stalin's terror. At fourteen she had joined the partisans fighting against Hitler's armies. She had ended her war in a concentration camp, but she had survived. And she had made it to England to give birth to her son, the child of her partisan lover who had died in the camps. Jake wanted to tell her story. He wanted to tell the story of the city that she had described with such passion and such regret – the sweep of history focused through the eyes of one woman.

Her son, Antoni Yevanov, was a recent catch for the city's university. It was the articles heralding his arrival that had first drawn Jake's attention to Sophia Yevanova. Yevanov, an expert in international law, had been involved in setting up the war crimes hearings at The Hague. What the mother had experienced in one era, the son was trying to redress in another.

Jake opened his work file and scanned the draft of the chapter he'd been working on the evening before, before Cass's arrival had interrupted him: *The allegiances of the*

Baltic states (Latvia, Lithuania, Estonia) in the Second World War are not as straightforward as those of the western European alliances. The Soviet occupation of these countries was harsh and repressive. The Nazi invasion of 1941 was seen initially as a liberation. This was a major factor behind Baltic collaboration in Nazi atrocities against civilians.

His phone rang. He tucked the handset under his chin, and went on reading. 'Jake Denbigh.'

The notorious 12th battalion of the Lithuanian police carried out massacres of civilians . . .

'Mr Denbigh, this is Katya Lange.'

Marek Lange's daughter. Jake had a good idea what this was going to be about. 'How can I help you, Ms Lange?'

. . . in the Ukraine and Belarus, including massacres in the Pripyet Marshes, Mir, Slutsk, Baranoviche and, notoriously, Minsk.

'I understand you're interviewing my father this morning.'

'That's correct,' Jake said. He deleted 'notoriously' and moved on to the next paragraph.

Sadly, they were assisted in many cases by members of the local police forces.

'I thought I made it clear . . .' He heard her intake of breath. 'My father isn't well,' she said abruptly. 'I don't think this is a good idea.'

He sighed, and gave her his full attention. 'It's just an interview, Ms Lange.'

'About what, exactly?'

'It's about the experience of being an immigrant.' He'd already told her this.

'He had a bad time in the war,' she said. 'Before he escaped. He doesn't like to talk about it.'

'My remit is immigration,' he said. 'I'm interested in what happened to him after he reached the UK.' He clicked open his research notes on Marek Lange and scrolled the list of dead ends he'd encountered while trying to establish what Lange had been doing in occupied Eastern Europe in the years leading up to his escape:

No record Litva – check spelling
Only reference: Litva – Grand Duchy of Medieval Belarus
    and Lithuania.
No record of Lange family as per your profile – NB records
    incomplete – war damage.
. . . cannot trace . . .
. . . no record . . .

'Well, I'm not happy. I've asked my daughter to sit in on the interview. I don't want you to begin until she is there.'

'Okay, your daughter will be there. Thank you for letting me know.' He hung up. Forewarned is forearmed. His appointment with Lange was for eleven. It looked like he'd better get there a bit early.

The Snow Child

This is the story of how Eva was born.

Once upon a time, there was a forest, with birch trees that were bare in the winter and reached their fingers high up into the sky. But in summer, the leaves grew and the branches hung down in fronds. When the wind blew, the branches would wave and the leaves would dance. Then the sunlight made patterns of shadow and gold. And the tree trunks were white, like slender pillars along the paths.

In the forest, there was a clearing. And a man called Stanislau built a house in the clearing, a house of timber. And Stanislau and his wife Kristina lived in the house, where their first child, Marek, was born.

Stanislau planted trees in the clearing, cherry trees and

32

plum trees, and he dug a deep well. The water that came from the well was clear like crystal, sweet and cool.

And Stanislau, Kristina and Marek lived in the forest and they kept chickens, and Kristina had a garden where she grew potatoes and cabbages. Marek gathered mushrooms in the forest, and they all picked the cherries and the plums that Stanislau took into town to sell. They were content.

Except that there were no more children. Marck grew big and strong, a happy boy with fair hair and a ready smile. And then, five years later, in the depths of winter, Eva was born. The last child, a little girl. The night of her birth, there was a storm that made the trees bend, the branches lashing through the air as the wind whooped and swirled.

Stanislau struggled through the forest to the village to find the midwife, and Marek stayed with his mother in the wooden house while the storm raged outside. By morning, the world was still and silent, and Eva lay beside her mother, wrapped in her shawl, and the snow fell for six days.

'You have a sister now,' Stanislau said to Marek. 'You must take care of her.'

The winter passed and spring came to the forest. Marek liked to sing to the baby and tell her stories while she lay in her cradle under the trees and waved her hands, trying to catch the sunlight that danced in the leaves. And the time went by, and Eva began to crawl, and then she could walk, and Marek would take his sister into the forest where he could show her the trees and the birds and the animals that walked the paths, because the forest was vast and quiet – there were not many people, not then. There were foxes and squirrels and rabbits.

And the witch.

He taught her to beware of the witch who lived in the dark places in the forest.

4

The caller had stayed on the line long enough for a trace. The call had come from somewhere in the remote hills on the far side of the dams. It was a lonely place, used by walkers and picnickers in the summer, but isolated through the winter months. The hills tended to mask phone signals. There was only a small area in which a mobile would work reliably. The trace centred on the one building in this area, a house that was marked on the map as 'The Old Hall'.

According to the records, the owner of the house had died recently, and it was empty, under the care of court-appointed executors.

The number of the mobile gave no clues. The house looked like the most promising location. There was a caretaker in residence and the phone was still connected. No one responded when the number was called.

But just after nine, before a car could be despatched, another call came through. This time, someone spoke. It was a male voice, incoherent with panic. 'She's dead! Please, you've got to . . . I didn't . . . She's dead!' He could barely get the words out.

The operator's training took over. Her voice became calm and matter-of-fact. 'Where are you?'

'The library. In the library. She's . . .'

'I need to know where you are,' the operator said again. 'We'll get someone to you. Tell me where you are.'

'It's too late.'

The voice moved from panic to leaden certainty. For a few seconds, he was silent, and they thought they'd lost the connection, then he came on the line again and gave them the location.

The Old Hall.

It was after a car had been dispatched that the full details of the second call were checked. The first call had come through on an unregistered cell phone. It was a pay-as-you-go, and they hadn't been able to link it to a name.

The phone on which the young man, half-weeping, had begged for help was not the same phone. It was later in the day that they managed to get a name for it. It belonged to a woman called Helen Kovacs.

Jake Denbigh checked the A–Z that was open on the seat beside him, and swung his car round the next turning, into a crescent where the houses were set back among the trees and behind tall hedges. He parked and got out of the car, checking numbers on the gateposts.

Marek Lange's house looked neglected. The gate was open, collapsed on its hinges, pushed back against the overgrowing shrubs. The drive was rutted and muddy, last autumn's leaves trodden into the ground. The front of the house was thick with ivy that obscured some of the upstairs windows. The ground-floor windows were under siege from privet and laurel that pressed against the glass. Lange must like his privacy. Jake rang the doorbell and stepped back, looking up at the house. Add a few thorns, a turret or two, and Prince Charming could hack his way through into the enchanted castle where the sleeping princess . . .

The door opened suddenly, and a woman stood there. She

was short and thick-set, and her face was unwelcoming. The princess was out, but apparently the wicked witch was at home. Was this Lange's granddaughter? It couldn't be. This woman must be in her late forties at least. The daughter? Unlikely. He smiled and held out his hand. 'Jake Denbigh. Mr Lange is expecting me.'

'He didn't say anything to me about it.' The woman shrugged. 'You'd better come in.'

Definitely not the daughter. Not the guardian relative at all. He followed the woman – who hadn't introduced herself – across the dim vestibule where the stairway ran up to a half-landing. The house was cold, and he shoved his hands deeper into his pockets. A man was coming down the stairs, moving with a slight shuffle.

'Mr Lange?' It had to be Marek Lange. He was a tall man, well built, but with the stoop of age. He was wearing a cardigan and heavy trousers. He had bedroom slippers on his feet. Jake held out his hand. 'I'm Jake Denbigh. It's good of you to see me.'

The old man settled his glasses on his nose and subjected Jake to a close scrutiny. His eyes were a faded blue and his hair was white, but still thick. His face was severe, but whatever he saw must have satisfied him because he held out his hand in response to Jake's. 'You are early.'

'I thought the traffic would be worse than it was,' Jake said.

Lange nodded once, accepting Jake's explanation. 'You would like coffee?' he asked. He took Jake's coat – which Jake was reluctant to relinquish in the chill – and held it out to the woman, who must be some kind of help, Jake decided. There was no sign of the guardian relative.

He declined the offer of coffee. He didn't trust what might emerge from any kitchen run by the grim-faced woman. Lange opened a door and led the way through. Jake followed him. The room in which he found himself overlooked the back of the house. It smelled of dust and age, but it was large and well proportioned, with French windows looking out over the garden.

The garden was overshadowed by trees, except for a small lawn and a flowerbed close to the window. Lange gestured towards two heavy armchairs that stood on either side of the fireplace, and Jake sat down, running his eyes over the bookcase that filled the alcove beside the chimney-breast. The books were without jackets, and the writing on the spines was faded, but Jake thought he could see at least one that was written in Cyrillic script. The shelves were dusty.

'So . . .' Lange's eyebrows came together as he studied Jake. 'How can I help you?'

Jake had been over this once already on the phone, but he was used to the forgetfulness of old age. 'I'm writing an article about people who came to this country during the war,' he began.

Lange waved this aside impatiently. 'Yes, yes, you already tell me this. People who came to this country during the war – there are many such. So, Mr Denbigh, I ask you again: How can I help you?'

Jake suppressed an appreciative grin and reminded himself that old though Lange was, he had been a ruthless and successful businessman in his day. 'I wanted the experiences of someone who'd built up a successful operation like yours from scratch, in a strange country. I wanted to talk to you about what it was like starting again.'

Lange cleaned his glasses as he thought about this. A book that had been lying on the arm of his chair fell to the floor with a thud. 'Well, maybe I can help you,' he said eventually. 'But it was a long time ago. I have little to tell.'

Or little that he chose to tell. Jake raised a sceptical eyebrow. 'That's not what I've heard,' he said. He leaned forward and picked the book up from the floor.

Lange gave him a sharp look. 'Maybe you had better ask your questions,' he said. 'We will see.'

Jake looked at the book in his hands. It had fallen open and he glanced at the page. *Baba Yaga.* He read on: *Once upon a time, deep in the dark forest where the bears roamed and the wolves hunted, there lived an evil witch*... Okay, that was appropriate. He closed it and looked at the cover. *Russian Fairy Tales.*

But he needed to move on. He wanted to get Lange talking while he had him on his own. He hadn't been convinced by the daughter's claim that Lange had been traumatized by his early war experiences and was unable to talk about them, and now that he had met the old man, he was even less prepared to accept it. Lange's reputation spoke for itself and it didn't look as though age had taken much of his edge. A man like that didn't deal with trauma by hiding from it.

Jake started off with some personal background. Lange had lived in Manchester for almost sixty years. His marriage had ended in divorce and his ex-wife had died over forty years before. Lange steered away from the personal and talked about his work. He'd devoted himself to making a success of his business, making contacts in Europe when the market was there, travelling further afield as the markets changed. Like many men of his generation, he didn't seem to have had much time for family life. 'You've got just the one child?' Jake said.

Lange paused. 'I have a daughter,' he said distantly. Then he smiled for the first time. 'And the granddaughter. Faith.'

He was starting to relax his guard. Jake circled closer. 'Your life must have changed completely when you arrived here. You went into industry – why did you choose that? I'm interested in how people adapt to these circumstances.' He kept his voice casual.

'Industry, yes.' Lange's glance at Jake was sharp. 'The war had led to some new processes. There were opportunities for anyone who cared to take them.'

'It's interesting that you managed to spot them when so

many people didn't. Was it your training? In your home country?'

'I was a peasant, Mr Denbigh, and then over here, I was a soldier. That is training enough for anyone.' He was sitting stiffly in his chair, and his voice had become distant. Jake decided not to push it any further for now.

'Tell me what it was like when you first arrived in Manchester,' he said. 'It must have been very different from the way it is now. I never saw industrial Lancashire. It was all gone before I came here.'

Lange sat in silence as if assessing Jake's request, looking for the hook. 'I have the pictures,' he said. 'First people I work with, first places.' He didn't move from his chair.

'I'd like to see those,' Jake said. Pictures were always useful for triggering reminiscences. They might give him an opening to push Lange further back, to catch him at a moment when he might start talking about his past.

Lange nodded briefly, then got up and left the room. Jake heard him talking to someone and checked his watch. It was after eleven. Had the guardian relative arrived? He heard Lange's voice: '. . . is not necessary, Doreen. I tell you this before.' His tone was peremptory. Then the door opened again and Lange returned carrying a box. He came back to his seat. 'Is so long . . .' he muttered, half to himself as he opened it.

Judging by the dust on the lid, it hadn't been touched in ages. Jake moved his chair across. It contained a few paper wallets, orange-brown with dark stripes, marked 'Kodak'. Jake looked at Lange for permission, then began going through them. Lange evinced no interest. The pictures were disappointing. Black-and-white photos of factories and production lines with the occasional picture of Lange surrounded by different groups of overalled men. Jake began discreetly checking to see if anything more interesting had been slipped in at any time. He could remember his own grandfather's habit of putting loose photographs in with more recent sets.

And his intuition paid off. Tucked away among some negatives that had been undisturbed for so long they had stuck together, were two small prints, grainy monochrome, faded and damaged. He took them out and looked at them. The first one showed a group of people – a family? It looked like a typical peasant family to Jake – standing in front of a small house. It was hard to make out the details. The woman's hair was pulled back from her face and she wore a long dress and apron. She held a young child – about four, maybe – in her arms. Standing next to her, there was a boy who looked as if he might be ten or eleven. Lange? Jake glanced across at the old man. It was hard to tell.

The second one was slightly larger and cut with a deckle edge. He checked the back quickly. It looked as though something had been written on it, but whatever it was, it had faded beyond legibility. It showed a young man in uniform standing in front of a building – the boy from the first photograph? If it was, he was older now, in his late teens or early twenties. This picture was unmistakably of Lange.

He held the first picture out. 'Your family?' he said.

After a brief hesitation, Lange took the photograph. His fingers brushed the woman's face, and then the child's, tentatively, as if the picture was a reflection in water that would disappear at his touch. He stared at it in silence for a full minute, then reached for the box and started going through the envelopes himself, impatiently gesturing Jake to silence.

Jake waited. Lange's reaction to the picture was odd and had aroused his curiosity. He kept his observation discreet, letting his eyes wander over to the French windows and the garden beyond. The rain had stopped, and the day had the brightness of early spring. Unlike the front, the back garden was carefully tended, a strange contrast to the shabby, neglected house. Someone had been working on the rose bed

40

by the window. A spade was propped against the wall, and a fork was dug into the earth. The plants had been pruned, and the remaining leaves shone with health.

'When we are children,' Lange said suddenly, 'we live in a forest. My papa go there because Mama is ill. He has to clear land, build his house. He makes the orchard – cherry trees and plum trees. I am born there.'

'When was that?' Jake knew the answer, but he wanted to hear what Lange would say.

'Many years ago.' Lange's brows drew together as he spoke. 'In the forest,' he said. 'So beautiful. And in a clearing, the timber house and cherry orchard. There was no water, so Papa build a deep well. And Mama got better. And then I was born.' The room darkened as the sun went in. 'It's gone now, the orchard, the forest.'

Jake wanted to let the old man stay in this moment of quiet reflection, but time was short. He pushed on. 'And this one?' he said, pointing to the photo of the young man in uniform. 'This is you?' It must have been taken in '38 or '39 – just before the outbreak of the war. Jake couldn't recognize the uniform.

But the old man seemed not to hear him. His eyes were focused on the photograph that Jake was holding out to him, but his face was blank. 'That winter, everyone is afraid. Fear makes people . . . made *me* . . .' He was looking directly at Jake as he spoke, but who or what he was seeing, Jake wasn't sure. 'I should not have done it,' he said. 'The bear at the gate . . . I was there.' He turned to Jake with a sudden intensity. 'I was *there*. And the little one . . .' Jake couldn't decipher what he said next. At first he thought the old man was speaking gibberish, then he realized that he had lapsed into another language – Polish? But it seemed oddly familiar to Jake.

The photographs dropped from the old man's hand. Jake caught them before they fell to the floor. 'Are you all right?'

He remembered the daughter's warning about Lange's health; he hadn't taken it too seriously up until now.

Lange seemed to have forgotten Jake was there. 'Minsk,' he said. 'It was in Minsk . . .' He was staring at his hand where the photograph had been.

Minsk! Jake held his breath. But then the stillness of the house was broken as the front door slammed and feet tapped briskly across the wooden floor. A woman's voice called from the hallway, 'Grandpapa? Where are you?' The guardian relative. Jake cursed under his breath. There was the sound of bags being dumped, movement, disturbance in the air. The past trembled and shattered in the vitality of the present.

The door opened, and the woman came in. She stopped in the doorway, her eyes taking in the scene. Jake got a quick impression of dark hair, red mouth, cool, tailored elegance. The granddaughter. Lange was levering himself out of his chair. He looked slightly dazed but the expression on his face was unmistakably one of relief.

She went up to the old man and hugged him. 'Grandpapa!' She studied him, her expression anxious and puzzled. Then she turned to Jake.

Jake stood up slowly, trying to hide his frustration at the interruption. *Minsk*. The old man had been about to talk about Minsk. 'Jake Denbigh,' he said.

She looked round at the recorder on the table, the scattered photographs, and her gaze came back to him. 'You were supposed to wait for me,' she said.

Jake shook his head. 'My appointment was for eleven,' he said.

She looked at Lange, who was easing himself back into his chair. He seemed quite composed now. She looked quickly back at Jake, undecided, then moved across the room to sit down on the other side of the fireplace.

'Okay,' she said with an effort. 'I was late. I'm sorry. Please go on.'

42

Jake kept his face expressionless. Something had just dawned on him. His mind had been processing what Lange had said. He hadn't been speaking Polish. The language Lange had used was Russian, and Jake could remember what he had said. He let the surface of his mind take over the interview as he tried to translate what he thought he had heard. 'You said it wasn't difficult, getting started. Tell me about it. Tell me what you did.' He barely heard Lange's reply. The tape was collecting it.

Lange had looked at the photo of himself as a young man in uniform, and he had said: *I should have known. I did know. It was wrong.*

5

Faith leaned back in her chair and listened to the verbal fencing that was going on between Grandpapa and this journalist, Jake Denbigh. When she'd arrived, Grandpapa had seemed confused and upset. Or that's what she'd thought when she came into the room, but he'd greeted her as normal, and now seemed to be enjoying himself, sometimes evading Denbigh's questions, sometimes using them as an opportunity for dogmatic pronouncements.

Denbigh didn't seem unduly put out by these tactics. He was good-humoured and persistent, and gradually this paid off. She watched as her grandfather's interest was aroused, and he began to talk seriously about the difficulties of starting again as an immigrant in a strange country, in a continent that had been ravaged by war.

'Is it easier now?' he was saying. 'There is always suspicion of the stranger. People are people, Mr. Denbigh.'

Before Denbigh could step in, he went off on a tangent about human nature, the urge to fear and reject anything that was different. Denbigh flashed her a quick, amused glance as he caught the thread of Grandpapa's argument and deftly brought it back to the topic in hand. 'Were you made to feel a stranger, Mr Lange? You'd fought for Britain.'

'I was always the stranger,' Grandpapa said.

There was a box of photographs on the table, which interested her. Grandpapa was not a photograph person. As far as she knew, he didn't even own a camera. She picked up one of the wallets and began to flick through it, keeping half her attention on the interview.

They seemed to be business photos – records of official events that must go back years. She hadn't known they existed. She had a sudden vision of Grandpapa's life shut away and hidden in locked desks and dusty boxes, old papers in government offices, crumbling away to nothing, lost, because no one cared, apart from the restless archivists, people like Helen who would search and sift and bring the past to light.

The interview was winding up. Denbigh's questions were moving towards the general now. 'You've always had a reputation as a risk taker. It's one of the things that made you so successful. What makes someone like you walk so close to the line?'

Grandpapa shrugged. 'What is there to lose if the gamble fails? It is only fear that stops you.'

Denbigh looked at Grandpapa. 'One last thing,' he said. 'Eastern Europe was closed to us for decades. Has the new openness reunited you with your past?'

The silence stretched out. She saw that look of blankness she thought she'd seen in his eyes when she first arrived. She took a breath to intervene, but then he spoke.

'I have never left it,' he said.

Denbigh stood up, closing his notebook carefully. He held out his hand to Grandpapa. 'Thank you for your time, Mr Lange. I've enjoyed talking to you.'

'And I you, Mr Denbigh,' Grandpapa said.

'I'll see you out,' Faith said. She followed him out of the room and retrieved his coat from the hall closet, noticing as she did so that the central heating was switched off. No wonder the house was so cold. Irritated, she pressed the button to trip the switch. Grandpapa was taking economy to ridiculous lengths these days. She needed to talk to him about that.

Jake Denbigh was waiting in the hall. She gave him his coat. 'Was that useful?' she asked as she unlocked the front door.

It was a formal query, but to her surprise he took it seriously. He paused in the doorway. 'I don't know. I think so. He's got some stories that I'd like to hear, but I don't think he's going to tell them.'

'Such as?' she said.

'I'm interested in Eastern Europe before the war. I'm working on a book.'

'About Poland?' she said.

He shook his head. 'Belarus.'

'I don't think there's much he could tell you about that.' She racked her brains. 'The Treaty of Brest,' she said.

He looked at her in surprise. 'What?'

She laughed. 'I'm sorry. I was just trying to think of anything I knew about Belarus, and that was it.'

'It's more than most people. What do you know about the treaty?'

'It gave Poland its independence in 1918,' she said, 'and it gave them western Belarus. Byelorussia, it was then.'

'Which wasn't popular with the Belarusians.' He was looking thoughtful. 'Whereabouts did your grandfather come from? Where was he born?'

'Don't you know?' If he'd done his research, he should.

'There was something . . .' He shook his head. 'It's probably nothing. I've had some trouble tracking down the original records, that's all.'

'Well, a lot of them were destroyed. He lived in the east, in the forested part. There wasn't much there. The nearest village was called Litva. I get the impression it was just a tiny place. I don't think it exists any more.'

46

'And he doesn't talk about it?'

'He talks about his childhood,' she said. 'It's the war that he won't discuss. I think a lot of the survivors are like that.'

He leaned his shoulder against the door jamb and looked at her, considering what she'd said to him. 'That hasn't been my experience. I've been talking to a lot of wartime refugees. Most of them want to tell their stories. They feel forgotten.'

She remembered what Katya had told her, about the ex-Nazi in Blackburn, and she wondered what it was he wanted to know. 'Is your book about the war? Do we need another one?'

'Not really,' he said.

'We don't really need it, or you're not really writing about it?'

He laughed. 'Appearances to the contrary, you're very like your grandfather. Okay, I'm working on something that's linked to the war.'

'Which is . . . ?'

He kept his eyes on her but didn't say anything.

'. . . none of my business,' she completed for him.

'It isn't that. It's complicated, that's all.' But she noticed he still didn't tell her what he was writing about.

'It's okay,' she said. 'I'm just . . . concerned about him. He truly doesn't like to talk about the war.'

He nodded. 'That's okay. We didn't.'

'When will it come out? This article?'

'Next issue,' he said. 'I'll send you a copy.' They stood in silence, looking at each other, then he pushed himself upright. 'I've got to go. It's been good meeting you. Really.'

When she'd first seen him in the gloom of Grandpapa's living room, she'd been surprised how young he looked. Now, seeing him in the clear light, she could see the lines at the corners of his eyes and mouth that said thirties rather than twenties. She watched him as he walked down the path towards his car. Despite the cold, he didn't bother putting on his coat. He slung it in the back of the car with his bag, then looked up and saw her watching him from the doorway. He raised his hand in salute, then got in the car and drove off.

She closed the door, shivering slightly in the cold. It was almost twelve. She had to be back for her appointment with Yevanov, but she could spend a bit of time with Grandpapa before she left. It was draughty in the corridor. The door into the study was standing open. That wouldn't help. She went to close it, and heard the sound of someone moving around.

'Grandpapa?' She put her head round the door.

The woman from the cleaning agency was busying herself round the desk. She turned quickly as Faith spoke.

Faith had forgotten it was one of Doreen's days. 'Sorry,' she said. 'I didn't know you were here.'

Doreen pushed the bureau drawer shut. 'I've just done,' she said. 'I didn't like to go while Mr Lange had a visitor. I didn't know you were here.' She came out into the hall, and went to the closet to get her coat. 'He doesn't like the heating on,' she said.

'It's too cold without.'

'I'll be off, then.' Doreen wrapped a scarf round her neck and buttoned up her coat. 'He's been worrying about burglars again. He had a go at me about locking the windows.' Her gaze challenged Faith to make some response.

'There've been some break-ins. You need to be careful.' It wasn't like Grandpapa to be nervous. 'Is everything locked up now?'

'I always leave it right,' Doreen said.

Faith closed the door behind her, then checked her phone in case Helen had left a message, but there was nothing.

She went back into the front room. Grandpapa was still in his chair looking thoughtful. 'I've switched the heating on,' she said. 'You shouldn't have the house so cold.'

He didn't respond, which wasn't like him. The heating

argument was a regular feature of their encounters. 'Are you okay?' she asked.

He didn't seem to hear her. He was looking out of the window at the roses that grew against the glass. She remembered the dream she'd woken up to. 'I used to help you prune those,' she said. 'It was my job, in the summer, remember?'

He shook his head as though he'd been thinking of something else. 'Pruning the roses?' he said vaguely. Then he seemed to come back to the present, and looked at her severely over his spectacles. 'You used to pick them, not prune.'

That was true. One summer – she must have been about thirteen – she'd stripped half the blooms from his prized red rose and woven them into a crown for her hair and carried the rest in a bouquet or pinned to her dress when she went to a party. It had been the party of a girl from school who had tried to bully Helen and Faith. Helen had not been invited. The party was fancy dress, and the girl had been boasting about the Rose Red outfit her mother had bought for her. Faith had decided to go as Rose Red too, only she would have real roses. She smiled, remembering. 'You bought me a present after that,' she said, wondering if he'd remember. He'd never been a man for presents.

He nodded slowly. 'A red ribbon for your hair.' She thought he looked weary. Then he shook himself out of his fatigue and stood up. 'You are staying?' he said. 'We have lunch?'

'I can't. I've got to get back to work. I'll make some coffee.'

She went through to the kitchen, which was cold and silent. There was a sour smell that she tracked down to an unwashed cloth in the spotted damp under the sink. She dumped it in the bin. It disturbed her, the way the house seemed to be sinking into the decay of abandonment. She'd have to try – again – to get some basic maintenance done. She'd tried once or twice, even going so far as to phone a local builder, but Grandpapa had been adamant. 'Not necessary,' he'd said.

She'd lived in this house until she was eighteen. Katya had

brought her here when she was born, and had left her here in Grandpapa's care when she went to live in London. What Katya had been looking for, Faith didn't know. Her mother had been an angry woman when Faith was a child, and was still an angry woman. She had never married, and had had no more children.

She shrugged off the memories and spooned coffee into a jug. She put cups on to a tray, and took it through to the sitting room where Grandpapa was tidying up the table where the photos had been scattered, tucking them into the envelopes and putting them back into the box.

'Don't put them away,' she said. 'I want to look at those.' She put a cup of coffee on the table beside him.

'Is just photos, sweetheart,' he said, frowning. 'From work – long time ago.'

'But I've never seen any photos of you from then,' she said. He was not a man who preserved memories of his life. There was no photographic record of Katya's childhood, and what photos there were of Faith's grandmother, Katya had taken when she had left. 'Come on, hand them over.'

He pushed the box across to her reluctantly, and went on putting away the remainder of the photos, carefully checking each one.

He was right. The photos were dull – pictures of mill buildings, factories, industrial landscapes that had vanished years ago. But there were one or two where a young Marek Lange appeared. They must have been taken in the post-war period. He looked tall and robust, a young man full of energy and dynamism. But his face looked older. Even then, Grandpapa's face had worn that same cold severity with which he met the world today.

He finished putting the photographs away, and sat back in his chair, frowning.

'What's wrong?' she said.

He shook his head. 'I think I have been dreaming . . .' The

cup he was holding tilted slightly, the coffee spilling over the rim.

'Careful,' she warned.

He didn't seem aware of her. 'Winter,' he said. 'So cold . . .'

She mopped at the spilled coffee with a tissue. 'It'll be spring soon.'

'In spring it rain,' he said. 'So cold, that year. They told me . . . I have to do it. I *have* to.'

'What?' she said. 'What did you have to do?'

He looked at her. 'Faith . . .' He shook his head. 'Nothing,' he said. He pushed himself out of his chair. When he spoke again, his voice was firm. 'I must see to the garden.'

After he left the Lange house, Jake drove back into Central Manchester. He called in at the university library to collect a book, then walked down to Oxford Street station for coffee. He ordered an espresso and watched the people passing by outside the window as he went over what he had just learned. The waitress smiled at him as she brought his cup across. She was pretty with dark hair, which made him think of Faith Lange who'd brightened up the gloomy, rambling house.

Why was it that a man of Lange's means had let that beautiful old house deteriorate into such dilapidation? Some old people lived in the past, he knew that. But Lange had – apparently – rejected his own past.

Whatever that past was. After meeting the man, Jake wanted to know.

Faith Lange had told him the same story the few records told, but these were all records that would have relied on Lange for their information. It was possible that a tiny village in agricultural Poland might have vanished, but without any trace, leaving no evidence of its existence? He wasn't convinced. As for the destroyed records . . . not so. It was surprising, once the Iron Curtain had fallen, to find how intact the records were. As you moved further east, further into the areas that had been devastated by the battles that had raged across the land, then the gaps started to appear, but if the story Marek Lange told was true, then there should have been something.

Further east . . . the further east you went, the darker the story became. He lit a cigarette, narrowing his eyes against the smoke as he remembered that tantalizing moment, cut short by Faith Lange's untimely arrival. Lange had spoken Russian. Old people in times of stress sometimes reverted to the language of their childhood. In extreme cases, they could lose the language they had later learned. Something had shocked Lange, and in that moment he had switched, unconsciously, Jake was sure, not to Polish, but to Russian.

And he had been in Minsk at the start of the war. When the old man had named the city, almost as if the word had been torn out of him, a chill had run down Jake's back.

He opened his notebook. As Faith Lange had walked into the room, on impulse he'd slipped the two black-and-white photographs between the pages. He studied them again, the mother and children standing in the doorway of the house, the young soldier in his uniform.

Jake was reminded of a photograph Juris Ziverts had shown him the first time they met, soon after the Latvian government began extradition proceedings against the old man, charging him with war crimes. Latvia and the other Baltic countries had been brutally occupied by Stalinist Russia when Hitler launched his invasion of Poland. Two years later, when the Nazis attacked the Soviets, the stage was set for tragedy. Eastern Europe erupted in a frenzy of killing as virulent anti-Semitism was compounded by a hatred of communists and the 'lesser races'. From the Baltics, from Estonia, from Lithuania and Latvia, the death squads went forth.

And now, after decades of inaction, their governments were trying to make amends. Memories from half a century before were taxed; photographs of men, young and in uniform, were compared with pictures of aging exiles. And the fingers of accusation began to point.

Juris Ziverts lived in a small semi in Blackburn. He had welcomed Jake, ushering him into the front room of his house, a room with a patterned carpet, blown vinyl wallpaper and bric-a-brac on the narrow mantelpiece above the electric fire. There was a fuchsia on the coffee table, its frilled petals looking oddly exotic in the resolutely suburban home. Jake, looking for a neutral topic to break the ice, said, 'That's a beautiful plant.'

The old man's face, heavily bearded, was hawkish, but it lit up at Jake's words. 'You like flowers? I too. Since I retired, I spend my days in my greenhouse.' He poured tea for Jake, his hands trembling slightly. 'I am so glad you have come, Mr Denbigh. There has been a mistake. I'm sure it will all be sorted out . . .' He was trying to make light of it, but his tense face and trembling hands told their own story.

'Why don't you tell me what happened?' Jake had come to the house with no strong views about Ziverts one way or the other, but he was prepared to listen.

'It is . . .' Ziverts' voice wavered, then came back stronger. 'I am Latvian, Mr Denbigh. I was a refugee after the war. My family died, so I came here. I am a teacher. Of maths. I married. I worked in Manchester for forty years, then I retired.' He hesitated and cleared his throat. 'When I arrive,' he continued, 'my English was not good. My name – it was very strange to the people here. They called me George. It was easier, and they meant no harm. So I became George Ziverts.'

Jake nodded. It wasn't unusual for Eastern Europeans to change their names. He knew a Kazimierz who had changed his name to Carl and a Zbigniew who had become John. 'And then . . . ?'

'I fought in the war,' Ziverts said suddenly.

Jake kept his tone casual. 'The German Army?'

'No. Never. But many of us . . . I . . . fought on the side of the Nazis when they drove the Russians out. The Soviets were brutal oppressors – we were glad to oppose them. But I was not a Nazi,' he said. 'We had welcomed in a monster to drive out a monster, and we paid the price. I was never a Nazi.'

Jake listened as he told his story. It was an ugly one, as were so many that came from that time, that place. The investigators claimed to have evidence that the man who was known in Blackburn as George Ziverts was in fact Juka Zivertus, former commander of one of the death squads in Belarus. Zivertus had organized the rounding up of hundreds of civilians, women and children, and had had them machine-gunned by the side of their graves.

'Never!' Ziverts said, his distress making his voice stumble over the words. 'I never did such things. I never knew such things were happening. I fought the Soviets. I killed young men like myself. We have all had to live with that. I am not this man, this Zivertus, but how can I prove it? My family is dead. My friends are dead. They refuse to believe my papers. I don't know what to do.'

Jake thought about this now, as he finished his cigarette, turning the photograph of Marek Lange round and round in his fingers. Had he believed then that Juris Ziverts was innocent? He couldn't remember. He'd thought the case against him was thin to the point of unprovable, and he'd found Ziverts an unconvincing candidate for a war criminal. Perpetrators of such crimes – those who organized or authorized them – tended towards an unapologetic arrogance. They were in no hurry to admit culpability, but neither did they see themselves as having done anything wrong. Ziverts' distressed bewilderment – and his horror at the accusation levelled against him – was not the response of a guilty man. The problem was that there was almost no way to prove guilt or innocence after all these years.

He'd told Ziverts that the whole matter was academic. The

police had no convincing proof and little chance of getting any. 'Don't worry,' he'd reassured the old man. There was no story for him and he hadn't planned on returning – which was a mistake, as it turned out. But Zivert's story had first aroused his interest in Belarus.

Jake felt oddly reluctant to return home and finish off his article with the contribution from Marck Lange. He stared into the distance, remembering how Lange's face had frozen into blankness. The old man had held the photograph, and he'd said . . . Jake relaxed and let the memory form. He was in the room. It was chilly and the light was dim. Lange was motionless, staring at the picture. *Everyone is afraid. Fear makes people . . . made me . . . I should not have done it. The bear at the gate . . . I was there. I was there. And the little one . . .* And then in Russian: *I should know. I did know. It is wrong.*

I should not have done it. Done what? What should he have known, and what did he know? What had the photograph brought so shockingly to Lange's mind? And then Faith Lange had arrived and got her grandfather off the hook. But before she came in, the old man had said something else. *Minsk. It was in Minsk.*

Ghost fingers touched his spine.

He had decided what he was going to do. He left the rest of his coffee and walked down the narrow steps to the street. A train clattered over the bridge above him, making the iron sing. He was going to pay a visit to Sophia Yevanova.

6

The sign on the door said ANTONI YEVANOV, DIRECTOR. Faith took a deep breath. She had never met Yevanov on a one-to-one basis before and would have liked a bit more preparation for this meeting. She'd prefer not to feel rushed and harassed, her mind still picking over the events of the morning. Yevanov had a reputation for impatience and for swift, sharp judgement.

She glanced at her reflection in the glass over a picture. She looked a bit windblown. Her hand moved automatically to smooth her hair – but she was aware of Trish's eyes on her, and suppressed the impulse. She knocked on the door, waited for an acknowledgement, then pushed it open.

The room was spacious and airy. White walls reflected the light from a south-facing window that looked out across the campus, a stunted arcadia in a cityscape of concrete, stone and glass. It was deserted apart from a group of students hurrying out of the driving rain. ·

'Dr Lange.' Antoni Yevanov was coming across the room to greet her. He was tall – well over six foot, and she had to look up at him as he shook her hand. His face was thin, with arched eyebrows and the characteristic high cheekbones of the Slav. She knew that he must be in his fifties, but despite the few threads of grey in his dark hair, he looked younger.

He ushered her towards the desk, and pulled out a chair for her. 'Please sit down.' His movements were quick and vigorous. The room felt cool to her, but he was in his shirt-sleeves and his tie was loosened. She noticed the jacket of his suit slung over the back of his chair, and was enough Katya's daughter to observe the drape of good cloth and fine tailoring.

As she sat down, she took a moment to absorb her surroundings. The wall behind his desk was lined with book-shelves. A map of Europe patterned in reds and greens hung opposite the window. Faith recognized it – it had been the cover of his most recent book.

There were papers spread across the surface of the desk, and the computer monitor was flickering. He also had a laptop in front of him, on which he'd apparently been working before she arrived. A whiteboard beside his desk was covered with lists of ongoing projects.

He waited until she was sitting down, then took a seat in the leather chair behind the desk. 'Dr Lange,' he said again, then with a brief smile, 'Faith. I'm sorry we haven't had a chance to talk before. I realize that your own research is being delayed while you settle in, and I'd like to get things moving there. The software you developed when you were at Oxford gets a very favourable mention in *The Journal of Statistics*. I have some thoughts about the ways in which you plan to move forward with this that I'd like to discuss with you another time. I am delighted that you are joining us. Now, how are you settling in?'

'Very well,' she said.

He asked her about the work the people on her team were doing. She'd spent her first week making sure she was familiar with all the ongoing projects, and was able to bring him up to date.

He nodded when she'd finished, then said, 'And Helen? Helen Kovacs?'

Faith had been hoping to skip over the topic of Helen until they had had a chance to talk. 'She's working on her paper. We have a meeting arranged to talk about it.'

His eyes narrowed slightly. 'I have some concerns about it,' he said. 'Especially as she didn't make it to our meeting this morning.'

'You had a meeting with Helen?' Helen hadn't mentioned a meeting with Yevanov. 'I'd arranged to see her this morning.'

He frowned. 'She didn't make it to your meeting either?'

'No. She left a message with Trish that she might be held up.' It was a poor defence at best, and Yevanov didn't look pleased. She wondered what was going on. There were issues here of which she was unaware.

She remembered Trish's waspish remark earlier when she was on the phone to Yevanov: 'She isn't here. Again.' Helen was letting herself drift into deep water. The academic world was cut-throat. There would be very little slack allowed to anyone who wasn't putting in 100 per cent, no matter what kinds of personal problems they might be dealing with.

He was speaking again, and she made herself concentrate. 'The Bonn conference is a particularly important one. I have made time to attend it myself, and it is essential that any contribution we make from the Centre is of an appropriate standard. I need to confirm the status of the paper with the organizers. I understood that the research stage was complete, and it was simply a matter of writing this up.'

'That's my understanding.'

'So what is the significance of the material from the Litkin Archive?'

'The . . . what?' Faith had no idea what he was talking about.

'The Litkin Archive,' he said again.

She felt completely wrong-footed. 'I don't know anything about it.'

He ran his finger along the line of his jaw, frowning. 'I was hoping you could enlighten me. The archive is a bequest from a Russian collector, Gennady Litkin. It consists mostly of wartime papers from what became the USSR, but there is some material relating to this country. It's a fascinating resource, but completely undocumented. The Centre controls access, and I only found out this morning that Helen had formally applied to look at some papers. It is my responsibility and, normally, these applications come to me, but I've been away, so I don't know what she had in mind.' He picked up a form from his in-tray and studied it. 'Does the Ruabon Coal Company mean anything to you?'

Faith shook her head. 'I'm positive Helen's research was complete. She wanted to discuss her writing schedule with me.' She might as well clear this with Yevanov now. 'I was going to get a few of her teaching hours covered to help her catch up.'

He nodded, as if he agreed with this. 'But the archive?'

'I think she must have been looking for some additional data.'

He raised his eyebrows as he studied the paper in his hand. 'Possibly.' He didn't sound convinced.

'Or maybe it was research for something else,' she said. 'Her PhD was on the decline of the coal industry. She was preparing it for publication.'

He was still reading the form. 'No. She wouldn't have got permission for unauthorized research. There are legal problems over the ownership and, until the papers are properly archived, access to the collection is closely controlled.' He ran his fingers through his hair and tugged it in frustration. 'I explained all of this . . .' He tossed the form back on to the desk in exasperation.

His phone rang. He excused himself and picked it up. 'Yevanov . . . Yes, I am aware of that . . . As soon as she arrives, please . . .'

She glanced at his bookshelves while he was talking. He had books on international law, books on the recent Balkan wars, books on Rwanda, books on Iraq. She saw a copy of *Mein Kampf* and heavy tomes on the Nuremberg trials. He also had, incongruously, some collections of fairy stories and folk tales, including the Russian collection that Grandpapa used to read to her. She went across to the shelves for a closer look.

Russian Fairy Tales. Faded gold lettering on green binding. She heard the phone being put down, and turned. He smiled when he saw the book in her hands. 'You think this is an odd thing for an historian to have?' he said.

She shrugged. 'They're part of history, in a way. They're beautiful stories.'

'They are. And they are very old, probably the oldest records we have.' She gave him the book and he turned it over in his hands, a faint smile on his face. 'Not many people are familiar with them these days.'

'I grew up with them,' she said.

He looked across at her in surprise. 'So did I.' He flicked through the pages. '"Once upon a time, deep in the dark forest where the bears roamed and the wolves hunted, there lived an evil witch . . ."' He raised an eyebrow and looked at the line of books on the shelf behind him: *The Nuremberg Trials*; *The Fall of Srebrenica*; *Inside Al-Qaeda*. 'It's a simple explanation, but I sometimes wonder if we'll ever come up with anything better.' He smiled. 'It's unusual to find someone who knows of these. We have something in common.' He held the book out to her.

She took it and turned the pages, scanning the familiar titles: *The Snow Child, Havroshechka, The Firebird*. 'My grandfather used to read them to me.'

'Your grandfather is Russian?'

'Polish. He was a refugee.'

'Then it's interesting he read you those stories. There is

little love lost between the Poles and the Russians. But we have something else in common. My mother is also a refugee, though she didn't get out until after the war. Those were dreadful times.'

'Is she . . . ?' . . . *still alive*, Faith wanted to ask, but didn't know how to word her query.

'Her health is poor. She's lived in this city for many years, but now she needs caring for – something she does not admit.' His smile was rueful. Then he looked at her, and his face was cool and professional again. 'Don't worry about the meeting this afternoon,' he said. 'Helen's problem will wait for a different occasion. I'm aware of her situation – I'll do what I can. Once again – I'm delighted you have joined our team.'

He stood up as she moved to leave, giving a slight bow. 'Make an appointment to see me . . .' he looked quickly at the board '. . . in a couple of weeks and we can talk about your work.' He held the door open for her. She was aware of Trish watching her as she left the office.

As soon as she was in the corridor she tried Helen's mobile, but the phone was switched off. There was nothing she could do for now. She felt exhausted, as though she'd just run a few miles, but at least her encounter with Yevanov seemed to have gone well. It was odd that he had collections of the same stories that Grandpapa used to read to her when she was small. She had grown up with stories – Grandpapa reading to her during quiet evenings, the long walks together when he told her stories about his childhood: the house that Great-Grandpapa built, the orchard, the trains in the forest, the witch in the wood . . .

The Red Train

This is the story of how the trains came to the forest.

It was spring, and there were men in the forest, strangers.

The sound of axes rang through the air as they cut the trees. They were clearing the land for the railway, Stanislau said. Marek took Eva along the paths to watch as the men worked, watching the tree they were cutting as it swayed and rustled, its branches whispering as it fell until it crashed down to the forest floor. And the men would shout to each other, and the chains would clank as the horses pulled away the tree that had fallen.

Eva would watch and listen. The tree seemed to struggle as the axes bit into its trunk, and then the sigh as it fell was sad, and the leaves of the other trees would rustle in agitation as the fallen one was dragged away. Sometimes the men would call to the children, and they would run back to the house in the clearing.

When the trees had gone, the rails came, long tracks that wound their way through the forest. And the men who built the rails built a bridge that crossed the river – much bigger than the wooden bridge where Stanislau led the horse carrying the orchard fruit to market.

Then the trains came, huge metal engines pulling wagon after wagon after wagon. The wagons were made of wood, apart from the wheels which were iron and sped along the track, making sparks fly up into the air. And the train carried a fire in its heart to make it go, and the fireman shovelled in the fuel and the train moved, sometimes slowly as if the engine was tired of pulling the long line of trucks, sometimes flying along through the forests, the smoke from the engine trailing behind it.

First, there was the sound of the whistle, then the smoke through the trees and the line would start to sing as the train came nearer and nearer and then burst along the track. Da da *dah*, da da *dah*, Marek would sing the song of the train. West to east and east to west, the trains ran night and day.

Eva loved the trains. Before she was old enough to walk the woods on her own, she would dawdle behind her brother, carefully, infuriatingly, holding him back from the things he wanted to do, until he became distracted and she could slip through the undergrowth and into the shadows and make her way through the trees with their shivering fronds that hung down and ran their fingers across her face and tangled in her hair.

She knew the times and the places. She would come to the clearings, the places where the trees had been cut and the ground built up with stones to carry the iron rails. And she would crouch by the line with her fingers on the rail, waiting. And then the iron would begin to hum beneath her fingers, before her ears could hear it, and she would leave her fingers there a bit longer and a bit longer, daring herself, then she would move back to the edge of the trees, waiting as the iron sang. And she would hear the beat of the engine, and sometimes the wail of its horn, and then it would be there, on top of her, in a rush of power and steam and smoke, and she would smell the burning cinders and see the men as they powered the engine, and sometimes they would see her crouched among the trees, and they would sound the horn and wave and laugh, and she would wave back, and then the train was gone, and Marck was calling with frantic anger from the forest behind her: 'Eva! Eva!'

And she would go home with him and help Mama feed the hens, or sort the eggs, or draw water from the well. And the summer wind would blow, soughing in the trees, and she would hear birdsong and the sound of the carts bringing the men back from the fields. Nearby, the hens scratched and clucked, and bees hummed in the flowers that grew round the door.

And away in the distance, to the east, she heard the whistle of the train.

7

Jake parked his car in the road outside the Yevanov house. It was in a similar suburb to Marek Lange's, from the same era, and built in the same style. But there, all similarities ended. Sophia Yevanova's house was surrounded by a well-kept garden that had been planted with a view to year-round colour. As Jake walked up the drive – swept free of autumn leaves weeks ago – he admired the brilliant reds and greens of the dogwood, the yellow of the winter jasmine that climbed up the front of the house among the last leaves of the creeper, whose stalks were now almost bare.

As he stepped through the front door, smiling his thanks to the woman who admitted him, he felt the warmth of the house envelop him. The hallway gleamed with polished wood. Vases of spring flowers on the hall table and windowsills dispelled the winter. 'Good morning, Mr Denbigh.' The woman, Mrs Barker, greeted him with the warmth that befitted a favourite. She led him through to the room at the back of the house where Sophia Yevanova customarily spent her days.

She was confined to her chair, but she sat upright, as though she could rise from it with the ease of a dancer rising *en point*. In fact, she looked like a dancer, with the fine-boned delicacy of a classical ballerina, or like a sculpture or a painting, a work of art ravaged by time.

As Jake was ushered through her door, she put down the tapestry she was working on – every time they had talked, her hands had been restlessly occupied – and held out her hand to him. For all her elegance and composure, he thought she looked poorly – paler and more tired than the last time he'd talked to her. The illness that had imprisoned her must be making its presence felt.

'Miss Yevanova.'

'Mr Denbigh. How good of you to call.'

'My pleasure.' The courtesy was the simple truth. He took pleasure in her company.

Her dark gaze held his, then she smiled. 'I will have tea, Mrs Barker.' She raised an enquiring eyebrow at Jake, who nodded. 'Mr Denbigh and I would like tea – the Darjeeling, I think. Thank you.' The woman withdrew.

Sophia Yevanova laid her tapestry carefully on the table and waited until the door was closed. 'I thought I had told you enough stories to keep you occupied for longer than this, Mr Denbigh,' she said. 'I see I must try harder.'

The last time he'd visited, they had talked about her life in Minsk as a girl, living in the shadow of Stalin's terror. In a way, she was right. There was more than enough in everything she had already told him for a book, but so far, they hadn't talked about the Nazi occupation. They'd touched briefly on the deaths of her fellow partisans, and her response had been unequivocal: 'They are gone. I will not speak of such deaths.'

He looked at the wall behind her chair. An icon hung there, its jewel-like colours gleaming from the shadows. It had been the one thing of value, 'apart from my son', that she had brought out of Belarus. She had smiled when she said that, her eyes going to the photograph on the side table that she kept within easy reach – her son, Antoni Yevanov.

65

She'd told him the story. Passing by the church in Minsk after it had been looted by the fascists as they retreated from the Red Army, she'd seen the gleam of gold in the dirt and rubble, and found the icon – the virgin and child – intact and undamaged. It had been a sign. 'I knew then that God was going to let me live, He was going to let me get away.' She had brought the icon to England, and even in her darkest moments, she had never considered selling it.

He was struck again by the shadows under her eyes, the parchment-like whiteness of her skin. 'You look tired,' he said.

She arched her eyebrows at him. 'If you tell a woman she looks tired, she will assume that you mean she looks old.' He began to speak, but she raised her hand to stop him. 'I *am* old. I am not foolish enough to pretend otherwise.'

'I've got something I'd like you to see,' he said.

'Well then, you must show it to me.' The tea arrived, and she took care serving it. For her, tea was an important social ritual, poured from a silver teapot into white, translucent china.

He took the photographs out of his wallet, and waited until she put her cup down on the occasional table beside her, then passed them to her. She studied the first one, the family standing outside the house, holding it away from her face. 'There were many such,' she said indifferently, handing it back to him.

He watched her carefully as she gave the photo of the young man in uniform the same careful scrutiny. He thought her lips tightened a bit, but otherwise she displayed no emotion. 'Old photographs,' she said. 'You have been doing your research, Mr Denbigh.'

He nodded, not letting his disappointment at her lack of reaction show. He knew from past experience that she would sometimes appear to ignore something he said or something he asked, then return to it later when he'd given up hope of an answer.

'So you are going to Minsk,' she said.

He'd told her about his planned trip. 'I'm leaving after the weekend,' he said. 'Just for a few days. Where should I go?'

She shook her head. 'There is nothing left,' she said. 'Not of my city. I can't advise you.'

'I want to find the old city, what's left. I can bring you back some photos, if you want. I could try and go to the village where you were sent when you were twelve.'

She smiled faintly. 'You are assuming I want to find my past,' she said. 'I left it behind years ago.'

He nodded. He could understand that. 'I'd like to hear more of your story,' he said. 'If you have time.'

'Very well.' The room was silent apart from the sound of the rain. The last time they had talked, she had given him a spare, unemotional account of her childhood in Minsk. Her parents had both been members of the communist party, but life in the city had been hard. There was poverty and deprivation throughout the country. 'My father was a good party member,' she had said. 'He was also a good husband and a good man.' She had ended her story when she was twelve, when her parents had sent her to live with relatives in a village on the outskirts of Minsk, Zialony Luh.

'We lived in the aftermath of the revolution,' she said now. 'It was a terrible war. You know about the history?'

He nodded. 'I've read the books.'

'The books . . .' Her smile mocked knowledge gained that way. In the dull light of the afternoon, her face was a paler shadow among shadows. 'I remember my last weeks in Minsk. It was winter, 1937. So cold. I have never known cold like it before or since. It was as if the world had frozen in the face of what was happening and all that was to come. I remember it was late and I was hurrying to get home. I was walking along the road near the building where the police worked – these were Stalin's police, the NKVD. The building was just ordinary offices. Many people worked there.

'And then I saw it. Narrow openings at the bottom of the walls. They were barred, but there was no glass. They made windows, of a kind, to the cellars. And that night, there was steam rising up, out through the bars, thick in the icy air. The breath of hundreds of people, crammed into the NKVD cellars, waiting . . . People they had arrested. Some people that I knew, maybe. How many were packed down there, I can't imagine . . .'

She looked at Jake. 'Where did they go? The arrests never stopped.'

There was only one answer to that question.

'We knew,' she said. 'But no one talked about it, or not where they thought they might be overheard. But it got so bad in Minsk, the arrests. That was when my father decided to send me to Zialony Luh, on the edge of the Kurapaty Forest.'

Kurapaty. Jake looked across at her, but her eyes were fixed on the distance, as if she had forgotten he was there.

'I had a cousin there, Raina. She was my age, and she was beautiful. These things matter to young girls, even in such . . . The young are very stupid. When I got there, Raina's mother, my aunt, tried to send me back. "It's bad here," she said. But there was nowhere for me to go.' She closed her eyes.

'This is tiring you,' Jake said. 'You need to rest. We can do this another time.'

She looked at him with wry amusement. 'I think you should listen while you can. I may be ashes next time we meet. It is just – it was so long ago, but when I talk about it, it is like yesterday.' She was quiet for a moment, then she began speaking again. 'It was the trucks. I remember the sound of the trucks. They went by into the forest, all afternoon, all evening. My aunt kept the shutters closed tight. "It's cold," she said, and sealed the gaps with rags. But that night, some-thing woke me. I was sharing Raina's bed. I crept out, careful not to disturb her. I wrapped my shawl around myself against the cold, and I pulled away the rags and opened the shutters. And then the sounds I had half heard were clearer. It was a dry sound, over and over: *klop-klop-klop* and quiet. Then *klop-klop-klop* again. And a moaning sound that went on and on in the night, and sometimes a cry that muffled into silence. I knew the sound of gunfire. We all did. But this was so . . . regular, so . . . methodical. And then Raina woke up and she closed the shutters and pulled me back to the bed.' Her face was mask-like, frozen with memory.

'But my aunt couldn't keep the shutters up, and all the time, day and night, the trucks rattled along the road, and we heard the sounds. We were in the forest, Raina and I, the day the guns stopped firing. But that was many weeks later.'

Jake sat back in his chair, letting the tension that had developed in his shoulders relax. As she had spoken, the past had touched the present. He had felt the ice of that winter, seen the steam rising from the breath of the prisoners crammed into the cellars, looked with her into the shadows of the forest.

A knock at the door ended the silence. Miss Yevanova came out of her reverie and picked up her embroidery. 'Yes?' she said.

The nurse, Mrs Barker, came in. 'There's been a message for you,' she said. 'From Miss Harley.' She looked at Jake as she spoke.

Jake made to stand up, but Miss Yevanova waved him back to his seat. 'And she says . . . ?'

Mrs Barker looked anxious. 'It's as she told you,' she said. 'They've . . . taken the action she warned you of.'

'I see.' Miss Yevanova sat very still. Her voice was cool and level, but the colour had left her face. 'It is only what we expected,' she said.

Mrs Barker caught Jake's eye with an implied warning. He gave her an imperceptible nod, and looked again at Miss Yevanova. 'I'll . . .' he began.

She interrupted him. 'There is no need for you to leave, Mr Denbigh.' She turned to Mrs Barker. 'Did Miss Harley . . . ?'

'She said she'd phone as soon as she had any news,' Mrs Barker said. 'And I really think . . .'

Miss Yevanova raised her eyebrows. 'That is all, Mrs Barker.'

She waited until the housekeeper had left, then turned to Jake. He saw that some colour had returned to her face. 'I will tell you another story, Mr Denbigh. And then you will tell me what you think.' He started to speak, but she silenced him with a raised hand. 'Listen. The phone call, the message, was about the son of a close friend – a friend who is now dead. My son Antoni has no children. I think of Nicholas sometimes as the grandchild I do not have. He . . .' She stopped speaking, and sat very still for a moment before she resumed her story. 'I was warned that this was going to happen, but I hoped it would not. There is no easy way to say this. Nicholas has been arrested on a charge of murder.'

Murder? Jake looked at her blankly. 'What happened?'

Her voice had the same dry distance as when she recounted the stories from her past. 'Early this morning, a woman was found dead in a house in the Derwent Valley. It is an isolated location, and Nicholas was working there. It is an irony that I helped him to get the job. I was concerned at once that the police might believe he was implicated – he was there, you see, and they prefer an easy solution. That phone call was from my solicitor. As I feared, Nicholas has been arrested.'

'Have they charged him?'

She shook her head. Her expression was bleak. 'But they will, if they can. He makes a convenient suspect. I have little faith in them.'

It was true enough – they could get it wrong. Jake thought about some of the cases he'd come across. But if they'd arrested this man there had to be more to the story than the simple outline she had given him. He realized that there must be something she wanted him to do, or she wouldn't have told him. 'How can I help you?' he said.

Her gaze was steady. 'Mr Denbigh, you have professional contact with the police, do you not?'

'I have done.' He'd done his share of crime reporting, and he'd kept his contacts up. Cass worked for the local force in a civilian capacity. But he needed to disillusion Miss Yevanova at once about any ability he might have to influence events. 'I can't change what's happening,' he said.

'I'm aware of that,' she said. 'But I would like to know what the police are planning, how their minds are working. I want to know why they suspect Nicholas.'

Was she asking him to investigate the crime? 'Maybe a private detective . . .' he began, but she shook her head impatiently.

'I have every confidence in the solicitor I have instructed. But the police worry me. I want to know what they are thinking, how they are interpreting what they find. Are these questions you could ask?'

It wouldn't be the Manchester force dealing with it. He ran his list of contacts through his mind. He had some ideas about who he could approach. 'Give me the details,' he said. 'I'll see what I can do.'

As he stood up to leave, she handed back the photographs. 'Why did you show me these?' she said.

'I need to know where they were taken. I thought you might be able to help me.'

'The first one is a peasant house. As I told you, there were many such. I have no idea where it might be. But this one –' Her fingers touched the photo of Marek Lange, the young man standing proudly in his uniform. 'I can tell you about this one.' Her face looked sad. 'It was taken in Minsk.'

*   *   *

71

Sophia Yevanova sat watching the fire. The coals shifted, scattering ashes on to the hearth and sending sparks flying up the chimney. The evening was drawing in and the shadows pooled in the corners of the room. She looked up at the icon on the wall, then her eyes went back to the red glow at the heart of the dying fire.

She sometimes thought that all the comforts around her were no more than ramparts she had built against the past, walls that she had braced and strengthened over the years.

Sometimes those years seemed closer than the present. When she had talked to Jake Denbigh, she felt as though she was walking again under the trees of Kurapaty. She had felt the leaf-mould under her feet, and smelled the pine resin on the breeze. Just for a moment, she had been afraid to open her eyes, in case she would find herself back there.

And now the shifting coals were drawing faces in the flames. She watched, and didn't watch, for the face she was afraid she might see and the face she still, after all these years, wanted to see, the face of the man she had loved, the face of her son's father, dead so many years before.

The cushions on her chair had slipped, and her back was starting to ache. She made herself sit up straighter. The discomfort was a useful antidote to fatigue, and she could feel her leg starting to twitch and jump, a sure sign that she was tired.

She heard the sound of doors opening and closing, of people talking in the corridor, Mrs Barker's low voice, and the authoritative tones of her son. She listened to them with a resigned amusement – did they think she was deaf as well as ill? Antoni was asking about Jake Denbigh's visits, something he'd paid little attention to before, and Mrs Barker was telling him, in her muted, self-effacing way, about the events of the day. Antoni would not be pleased. He was not a patient man – but then she hadn't brought him up to be patient.

She heard his footsteps moving along the corridor as he came to greet her. She switched on her light and picked up her sewing. She didn't want him to find her sitting idle in the dark. It would worry him. She sat up straighter, ignoring the stab of pain in her back, and smiled as the door opened.

'Antoni,' she said, holding out her hand.

He took it and looked down at her, his face shadowed. 'You look tired,' he said abruptly. 'I understand that journalist visited you again today.'

'He is a pleasant young man.' She shifted to ease her discomfort. 'I enjoy talking to him.'

He made an impatient sound and went down on one knee to rearrange her cushions, positioning them so that they supported her back. 'Better?' He assessed her with his eyes. 'Good. It's the man's profession to make himself pleasant. Mrs Barker, I can understand, but I thought that you would be impervious to the power of a smile.'

'I will have plenty of time to resist young men with charming smiles when I am in my grave. In the meantime, allow me the few small vices I can still enjoy.' She studied his face as she spoke. He was the one who looked tired. His eyes – suddenly she was looking into his father's eyes, and had to drop her gaze before he could see her expression change – his eyes looked weary and shadowed.

He put his hand on her arm. 'It would be better for you if you didn't see this man again. I can easily arrange it. You don't have to be troubled.'

'It doesn't trouble me,' she said. 'It's Nicholas I'm concerned about.'

He gave a sigh of exasperation. 'Nicholas Garrick is not your responsibility. You paid his hospital bills. You found him work. Don't you think you've done enough?'

She watched the fire. The coals shifted again, and the flames licked up. 'No.'

'There's no reasoning with you,' he said. 'I'll go and change.

I'm free this evening. There's a performance of *Der Rosenkavalier* on Radio 3. Shall we listen to it?'

Back in the days when she was well, they used to go to the opera together. They'd been to La Scala when he had lived in Milan, to the Metropolitan in New York, to the Royal Opera House during his time in London. As her illness confined her more, prevented her from travelling, he would come to her and they would attend performances at the Manchester Opera House. Now, she was dependent on the radio schedules.

After he left, she sat looking out of the window at the night. The rain spattered against the glass and blew across the roofs. Behind her, the hot coals hissed.

Baba Yaga

This is the story of the witch in the woods.

Not far from the house in the forest where Marek and Eva lived, there was a village. After the railway came to the forest, the village began to grow, and slowly the forest around the wooden house began to vanish as the village spread.

And there were troubled times. Men came and took Papa away. They took the fruit from the orchard, and the hens. 'They want to make us Polish,' Marek had said angrily. 'They want to take away our home and our language.' Without the fruit to sell, and the hens for eggs, it was a time of being hungry.

Marek went into the forest when Mama wasn't looking. He would put his fingers to his lips if Eva saw him, and vanish down the paths. He brought back mushrooms and nettles and rabbits, and sometimes a bird. He would pretend to Mama that it was a gift from a neighbour, or that he had found these things near to the house. And sometimes he would slip out early in the morning and then there would be milk for Eva.

Then there came a time when Marek slipped out and came back limping, and there was no milk. Eva was more hungry than she had ever been, and Mama's hands were so white it was as if the light was shining through them. 'Read to me,' she would say, to distract Eva from the empty place that gnawed inside her, so Eva would sit beside her and read to her, her voice halting at first as the letters gradually shaped themselves into sounds, the sounds into words, the words suddenly leaping from the page. She read the story of the firebird, the story of Havroshechka, the story of the snow child who played in the forest too close to the fire. She read the story of Baba Yaga, the witch whose house ran on chicken legs, and whose fence was hung with the skulls of the people she had eaten.

And sometimes, Mama would fall asleep in her chair, the bump, bump of the rockers slowing to silence. Eva would tiptoe to the door and watch Marek until she saw him slip away along the path that led into the forest, and then she would follow him. Now she was older, she could walk further into the forest, but that day Marek was walking fast and she lost sight of him. She didn't mind at first, following him along the path. She would catch up with him soon. The sun felt warm where it shone through the leaf canopy and she swung herself round the trunks of the trees, the silver of the birch and the dark, heavy pines.

A bird took fright, somewhere in the deep glades, and shrieked and clattered its way into the air. The path divided here, and she didn't know which way Marek had gone. That way was to the railway line. She listened. The forest was still. No train, no birds, no rabbits. Just the silence of the forest around her.

The other way . . . She looked along the path. She didn't know this path. Maybe Marek had gone this way. Maybe this was where Marek got the birds and the rabbits and the milk. She walked further, looking at the trees that were starting to change colour, the long fronds brushing against her face as she walked She'd never been this far into the forest before. As her feet pressed into the ground, she could smell the damp earth and the leaf mould. The breeze stirred the leaves and made the shadows dance on the forest floor. The trees whispered to her: *Eva. Eva.*

And she could smell something else, faint on the breeze. It was a sour, rotting smell. It reminded her of the time a rat crawled under the house to die. She stopped. The path branched again ahead of her, winding away through the trees. As she watched, the sun came out above the leaf canopy, and its rays dappled the ground that was golden with the early fall of autumn. The breeze moved the air again and she smelled the scent of the forest, and the birch fronds danced and beckoned. *Eva. Eva.* She turned along the winding path.

It led to a cottage, a house in a clearing, one of the houses in the deep forest that the village hadn't yet reached. It was timber with a picket fence, and along the path, under the trees leading to the house, there were bushes, and the bushes were covered with berries.

The empty place inside Eva came alive. She looked round quickly but the house seemed to be deserted. She ran along the path, and knelt down to look at the bushes. She knew these berries. She could eat them without cooking. And there were enough to take back for everyone. She crammed them into her mouth until the empty place went away and she felt a bit sick. She began to collect berries in her apron.

But the sick feeling wasn't just the berries. It was the smell. The smell was here, in the clearing and it was in her nose, in her hair, in her clothes, in her hands. She was inside the smell, and now she wasn't so hungry, she couldn't ignore it.

She looked at the house again. She could see the white fence glimmering from the shadow of the trees, and the windows were dark spaces behind. She'd never heard of a house so deep in the forest before. She crept nearer. The house was clean, well cared for, and the smell caught in her nostrils and brought tears to her eyes.

She could see movement in the shadows. There was something dark hanging from the beam above the porch. The shape came clearer as she moved closer. She could see a face. The face was watching her, but the eyes were half-closed and sunken. The hair, which was white, was pulled into a neat bun, like Mama's. And the breeze blew, and she almost expected to smell Mama, the smell of lavender and herbs that she knew so well. But the smell that the breeze carried was foul.

And as the forest breathed around her, she knew what it was. She waited, frozen, for the house to stand up on chicken legs and step towards her with deliberate but silent tread. Her hands let go of the corners of her apron, and the berries fell, unheeded, to the ground. She backed away, and again, then turned and ran down the path not stopping, not daring to look back, until suddenly she was past the trees and into the clearing, and she could hear Mama calling her, and Marek had come back from the railway with potatoes and Mama had made soup. She couldn't eat it, though Mama scolded and worried.

Over the next few days, she heard the women talking about the old woman in the woods – '. . . her boy . . . shot in the fighting . . . hanged herself . . .' And they made the sign of the cross, and Mama sighed.

But Eva had seen Baba Yaga's house, seen the fence hung with the bodies of the people she'd killed. And at night, she would lie in bed, tense, listening to the sounds of the forest, trying to pick out the scrape of chicken feet stepping across the forest floor. She could remember the way chickens walked, the way they lifted their feet, the way the tendons moved under the wrinkled skin of their legs, the way their claws stepped on to the ground with slow deliberation. And she knew that Baba Yaga's house was hunting her through the forest, stealthy and inexorable.

She had stolen Baba Yaga's berries and now her bones would hang on that high, white fence.

8

The following morning dawned bright and clear with the promise of an early spring. The sun was rising as Faith left for work, the winter light warming the grey stone and gleaming off the rocky outcrops on the high moors in the distance.

She was worried about Helen. She'd tried contacting her, but no one answered the phone. She'd left messages, but there had been no response. She thought back to the last time they'd talked. Helen had seemed distracted. Daniel was putting a lot of pressure on her. 'He wants his share of the house,' she'd said. 'I didn't want all of this to go through lawyers and the courts. I thought we could sort it ourselves.'

'Why don't you just buy him out?' Faith said. It seemed the simplest way – a clean break.

'I can't take on a mortgage that size. It'll mean moving, and the kids . . . Now he's saying he's going to take me to court for custody.' She sighed, apparently more exasperated than concerned.

'Do you think he means it?'

Helen shook her head. 'He's just making smoke. He thinks we're going to get back together. He'll come round.'

'Are you?' Helen had blossomed since she had left her

marriage. Despite all the worries and all the hassle, she'd seemed brighter and happier than Faith had seen her in years.

'Sometimes I think it would be the easiest way, but . . .' She shook her head. 'It's not going to happen.'

Faith thought about this conversation as she negotiated the traffic. Helen had been evasive about the break-up, about what had been the final trigger. Though Helen hadn't said anything definite, Faith suspected that there was someone else in the picture. She had been astonished when she saw Helen for the first time after the break-up. Despite all the problems, she'd looked years younger. She had been the buoyant, vivacious woman Faith remembered from their university days, but a sophisticated one now, beautifully turned out, her hair styled, her clothes immaculate.

Another time – just after her birthday – Helen had been wearing a new watch with a delicate silver band. 'Present from Daniel?' Faith had asked, though it looked a bit subtle for Daniel.

'No,' Helen had said, caressing the band round her wrist. 'Just a treat.'

A couple of days ago, Faith had met her in the lobby coming back from lunch. She was carrying a bag with the logo of one of the expensive department stores, filled with tiny boxes that looked as though they contained filmy, lacy garments, not workaday cotton.

'I'm sick of the hausfrau image, that's all,' she'd said rather defensively when Faith had raised an ironic eyebrow at her.

Faith put the matter of Helen to the back of her mind, and tried to focus on putting together the budget to finance the research programme that had been approved in yesterday's meeting. But her thoughts drifted to her own family. She'd phoned Katya the evening before, choosing a time when she was pretty sure her mother would be out, and left a message to say that the interview had gone ahead and there hadn't been any problems. But it wasn't the interview that worried

Faith. It was the sense of a gathering futility in Grandpapa's life, epitomized by the slow decay of the house. It was as if he had stopped caring – as if his life no longer had any use or purpose.

His life had always been his work. He hadn't let the reins of business go until he was well into his seventies. And after that, she had been his project for a while – he had supported her though university, helped her out when she was first trying to get established and living hand to mouth on post-graduate grants. But she was independent now, had been for years. Maybe that was it. Maybe for him, life had lost its point.

She was due to see him tomorrow evening. He was making supper for her – he enjoyed making small occasions of her visits. She could talk to him about it, try and find out what was wrong. While she was at it, she meant to put pressure on him about the house – he could at least get it weather-proof. She'd seen the rainwater stains on the ceilings upstairs, and she had felt the chilly draughts from ill-fitting doors and windows. He was going to make himself ill.

Her worries about him occupied her all the way to work. She walked across the campus, the detritus of other people's lives clamouring for attention in her head. *Enough!* she wanted to shout. She needed to focus on the day ahead.

As she approached the Centre, she saw that there were vehicles parked outside, cars and a van. The campus was generally vehicle free and she wondered what was going on. As she got nearer, she saw a man coming out of the main entrance, his arms loaded with files, which he put into the back of the van.

He was in uniform.

She stopped. The writing on the van came into focus. *Police.* And there was a police logo on one of the cars. Someone else was coming down the steps now, carrying a computer. There was a flash of colour from the side of the machine, a bright rectangle of card that flipped over as the breeze caught it.

And suddenly she remembered standing in Helen's cubicle the day before, seeing the photo stuck to the computer, the photo of Helen with Finn and Hannah, Helen squinting into the sun with her hair blowing across her face, Hannah's cheek pressed close to hers.

That was Helen's computer. The police were taking Helen's computer away. And Helen hadn't been around yesterday, had missed her meetings, not answered her phone, not replied to messages . . .

Faith could feel a chill inside her, a tension that twisted her stomach and left a feeling of rising sickness in her throat. She was moving again now, walking faster towards the Centre, breaking into a half-run and stopping as a woman in uniform emerged from the doorway.

'What's happened?'

The woman didn't answer Faith's question. 'Do you work here?'

'Yes. What's going on?' She looked past the woman into the lobby. It was empty and silent.

'And you are . . . ?' The woman's voice was calm. She wasn't going to answer Faith's questions until she knew who she was.

Faith swallowed her impatience. 'I'm Faith Lange. I'm . . .' A man came down the steps past her, carrying a box of files, Helen's files, Faith could recognize the handwriting. 'What's he doing?'

The woman had a clipboard with a list of names. Faith indicated her own, trying to see past the woman as the uniformed man stowed the box in the back of the van. 'I'm a friend of Helen Kovacs. That's her stuff. What's happened?'

'Mrs Kovacs was . . .'

'Doctor,' Faith said automatically. The woman looked at her. 'Dr Kovacs. Helen is Dr. Kovacs.' Helen always insisted on her title, probably because Daniel had been so disparaging of it.

'I'm sorry,' the woman said. 'There's been an incident involving Dr Kovacs . . .' Her eyes checked Faith's face for her response.

'An incident? But she's all right?' She waited for the woman to offer the standard reassurances: *She's fine.*

But she didn't.

Faith tried again. 'She's okay?'

Still the woman refused to pick up her cue. 'I'm sorry,' she said. She paused, and in that pause, Faith understood. 'Dr Kovacs was found dead yesterday.'

Dead. 'But . . .' She needed to explain. Helen couldn't be dead. It was Hannah's birthday on Saturday. Faith hadn't told her about . . . They were supposed to . . . She was aware of a hand on her elbow as the policewoman steered her through the entrance into the Centre.

'Do you need to sit down?'

The policewoman was young, serious, professional. She didn't know that Faith and Helen had been close. In a way, it was easier to hear it like this. She was just doing her job, telling someone that a colleague was dead. She wouldn't be nervous of grief, wouldn't be embarrassed by her own inadequacy. Faith withdrew her arm, and took a deep breath to ensure that her voice would be steady before she spoke again. 'No. Thank you. I'm all right. What happened?'

'We'll need to talk to you,' the woman said. 'Would you mind waiting?' It wasn't a request. 'We've asked the staff to wait in the office.'

Faith wanted to shake the information out of the woman. *What happened?* Instead, she turned away and walked through the lobby. The winter light flooded the high space, the poster for Antoni Yevanov's lecture glowing on the display board – *After Guantanamo* . . . She hesitated at the door of the office, then stepped back. She didn't want to step into the room, listen to the voices falling silent, listen to people who'd hardly known Helen speaking with hushed excitement, listen to the speculation.

Suddenly she was overwhelmed with nausea. She could feel the cold sweat on her forehead and down her back. She went quickly into the ladies and made it into one of the cubicles before she was sick, dry retching long after her stomach was empty. Her legs felt shaky as she stood up.

There was no natural light in the cloakroom, and the mirrors over the row of basins threw back her reflection bleached of colour. The tap water was tepid and she let it run cold before she rinsed her mouth and splashed it over her face.

There was a small yard at the back of the building where the rubbish skips were lined up for collection. She let herself out of the rear entrance, glad to see that no one else was there. It was one of the smokers' refuges, cigarette ends littering the ground and a stale smell of ash lingering in the air. She sat on the low wall by the skips and stared up at the sky. The nausea lingered like a reminder in the pit of her stomach.

Years before, the daughter of one of her colleagues had been killed. A young man had been driving along a straight bit of road, had put his foot down, then swerved to avoid something. His car had clipped the pushchair in which the three-year-old had been sitting. Faith had gone to the funeral. People wept at the graveside, but the bereaved mother hadn't. She had stood there, cradling an infant that someone had given her to hold, and she had watched them bury her daughter. Her stillness was incandescent with a grief that was beyond tears.

Hannah and Finn. They were Helen's world. Faith reached for her phone and tried Helen's home number, but there was no answer. She flicked through the pages of her diary. She could remember scribbling down the number of Daniel's phone at some time. She keyed it in, hoping it was still current. It rang several times before it was answered.

'Kovacs.' It was an abrupt snap.

'Daniel, it's Faith. I just heard about Helen.'

There was a moment of silence, then he said, 'Faith. Yeah, it's . . . I'm kind of, you know . . .'

She didn't know, but she could imagine. No matter what anger there had been between him and Helen, he hadn't wanted the marriage to end. For all the problems they'd had, Helen had felt bad about leaving him. 'What happened? I don't know anything. I just came into work and there were police everywhere.'

'Work.' His laugh was edgy and hostile. 'Well, that's what happened. Work. She's out on a wild-goose chase, something for what d'you call him – *Yevanov*.' He spat the name. 'She's on her own in some old house, and there just happens to be a pervert on the premises.'

A pervert. Did he mean that Helen had been . . . 'Oh, God,' she said.

'I talked to her,' Daniel said. His voice sounded raw. 'Not long before it happened. She wanted to talk to the kids. I was pissed off. I wouldn't let her. And then this . . . *animal* . . . strangled her.'

Faith closed her eyes. She felt sick. 'How are they? Hannah and Finn?'

He was suddenly angry. 'They've just lost their mum. How do you think they are?' And then the anger faded as fast as it had come. 'It's too much, kids that age.'

'Daniel, I'd really like to see them. Can I come round?'

'It's not a good . . .' He began his refusal, then stopped. 'Look, you could help me out – if you want. I'm a bit stuck. I've got a job on this afternoon and I can't leave it. The kids aren't in school – if you want to see them, you could come round and sit with them.'

'Of course. Give me the address and I'll be there.'

He gave her the street name and number. 'Get here for two,' he said, and rang off.

The door into the yard where Faith was sitting opened suddenly. 'Oh. There you are. They're waiting for you.' It was Trish, looking outwardly composed, but there was a suppressed excitement about her and her eyes were bright.

Faith stood up slowly. 'The police?'

'They want to talk to everyone Helen knew,' Trish said. 'Professor Yevanov has promised them full co-operation.'

Yevanov would have little choice but full co-operation. 'Where is he?' Faith asked as she walked back into the lobby. She didn't want to talk about Helen with Trish. She could remember the satisfaction in Trish's voice the day before when she had reported Helen's absence. *She isn't in. Again.*

'He came in with them first thing. Then he went back into town to talk to them.'

Yevanov, with the police? She looked quickly at Trish, but she didn't seem disturbed. 'Why didn't they talk to him here?'

'They need him to look at the archive materials Helen was working on. They want to know if anything's missing.'

That made sense, but she remembered Yevanov telling her the collection was undocumented, and wondered how anyone would be able to tell.

'Miss Lange?' It was the policewoman she'd spoken to earlier. 'We'd like to talk to you now.' She dismissed Trish with a cool smile and directed Faith into one of the small offices that were used by the admin staff.

A young police officer was waiting for her. He apologized for keeping her waiting, then asked, 'Helen Kovacs was a friend of yours?'

Was . . . 'I've known her most of my life.'

'I'm sorry,' he said. 'I need to ask you some questions, okay?'

Faith nodded. 'Okay.'

At first, his questions were general – Helen's routine, her daily contacts – but gradually they began to focus on her marriage. 'What caused the break-up?' he said.

Faith shook her head. 'I don't think it was any one thing.' She explained that Helen had given up a secure job to become an academic. 'Daniel never really understood that, and Helen's work was the most important thing in her life, apart from the kids.'

'He resented it?'

'Yes.' Daniel had resented it a lot. He had never been able to understand Helen's involvement in her work, and she had never been able to compromise. Faith could remember Helen telling her of a massive row with Dan after a weekend with his parents: 'All because I found a trunk of old papers in the attic that had belonged to his grandparents.'

Faith knew about attics full of junk. Grandpapa's was crammed high. 'What kind of papers?'

'His grandparents were Lithuanian. They came over after the war. All this stuff they'd brought with them – it was just mouldering up there. I want to get it translated – I'm learning, but I don't read Lithuanian very well.'

'Couldn't Dan, or his parents . . . ?'

'You're not going to believe this,' Helen said, 'but they don't speak the language. Not at all. And Dan – he was furious. We came to visit, he said. Came to do family things. He said I just vanished all weekend.' She shrugged. 'It didn't bother him until Dinah started complaining. She was just stirring it up. She'd had the kids to herself all weekend – that's what she wants. I swear, Faith, I don't understand that family. We're talking about the kids' history. It's part of who they are. It's important. Anyway, Dinah said I could go back next weekend and go through it all "If it matters so much to you, Helen."' Her voice had parodied her mother-in-law.

A few weeks later, Faith had asked Helen about the papers. Helen's voice had been carefully neutral. 'Dan told his parents to burn the lot. And they did.'

It was shortly after that that Helen and Daniel had split up.

Faith looked at the officer. 'You don't think that Daniel . . .'

He shook his head. 'Mr Kovacs was at home with the children. Tell me about the break-up. Was there anyone else involved? Did she have a boyfriend?'

'I don't think so. Not at the time. She didn't say anything to me.'

'Would she tell you?'

'I don't see why she wouldn't. We talked about most things.'

'And what about later? Did she get involved with anyone after the break-up?'

Faith thought about the shopping trips, the care with her appearance, the secret glow Helen sometimes had. 'I think she did, yes. It was a recent thing.' She forestalled his question. 'But I don't know who it was. She didn't tell me.'

'You didn't ask her? You've been friends for a long time.'

It was hard to explain the almost mischievous secrecy that Helen had maintained. 'It was just – it was like she had a secret, and she wanted me to know she had a secret, but she didn't want to tell me what it was.'

'Why was that?'

'I don't know. Maybe it was just fun. Maybe she enjoyed having a secret lover.' Helen's life with Daniel had always seemed short of fun and frivolity.

'Could she have been involved with someone here?'

'I don't know.' But Faith had wondered about that.

It was as if he had read her mind. 'Did you have any reason to believe she might be involved with your boss? With the professor?'

Antoni Ycvanov and Helen. She remembered the conversation they'd had about Trish, and Helen's certainty that Trish's romance was all in her own mind. She remembered Daniel's recent hostility when Yevanov's name was mentioned. But Daniel had always been jealous of any men that Helen came into contact with. 'That's what Daniel thought,' she said.

He nodded. He already knew this. 'And you?'

'I'm not aware of anything.'

He asked her a few more questions about Helen's relationships with men, then, apparently convinced she'd told him all she could, he moved on.

He showed her a photocopy of some notes in Helen's loose, scrawly hand. She must have written them that evening, the evening that someone . . . Faith studied them closely. There was very little there, just a reference number *120.43 PEKBM* and some initials:

P. E.
Ma_y _ro_ _ene_ _.

She shook her head. They didn't mean anything to her.

'Professor Yevanov said that you were helping Helen with her research.'

'Yes.'

'But you don't recognize this?'

She stared at the page as if the meanings of the jottings would suddenly become clear. There was something . . . no, it had gone. 'I don't know,' she admitted.

'Maybe you need a bit of time to think about it,' he said, handing her a photocopied sheet.

He waited as she slipped the piece of paper into her bag. Then he asked her about her own activities on Tuesday evening, and she wondered if she was a suspect. 'I was at home,' she said. 'Working.' He didn't follow that up.

'One last thing. Does the name Nicholas Garrick mean anything to you?'

She tried the name out in her mind, but she didn't recognize it. 'No.'

'Did Helen ever talk about Nick, or Nicholas?'

She thought again, and shook her head. 'No.'

He asked her a few more questions about Helen's routine, then told her she could go.

She left the building quickly, not wanting to talk to anyone else. It was almost noon. She went straight to the car park and got into her car. She needed to find her way to Daniel's. She needed to see the children.

Jake was now working to a tight schedule. He had his column to finish, he had his interview with Marek Lange to write up, he was leaving for Minsk after the weekend and still had preparations for the trip, and now he'd made a promise to Sophia Yevanova to look into the police investigation, as far as it affected the young man she had taken under her wing, Nicholas Garrick.

The photos he'd taken from Lange's were on his desk. He picked up the one that showed the young soldier. It was a rare photo of pre-war Minsk. He remembered the way Miss Yevanova's face had tensed when she saw it. Was it just a reaction to the image of the city she had left so long ago, or was it something else?

He studied the picture.

The soldier was standing outside a building with a stone edifice. There was a plate on the door post, but it was impossible to see what it said. Jake got out a magnifying glass, but the writing was too blurred to read. He needed to scan the image and enhance it – something else to do before he left. He tossed the pictures into his in-tray and went back to his notes about the murder.

A few phone calls to his contacts the night before had given him the basic facts. The victim, Helen Kovacs, had been an academic in her thirties, an employee, interestingly, of Antoni Yevanov's Centre for European Studies. The husband had an alibi, so that left Garrick. Jake's contacts were unanimous in their opinion that Garrick was the killer, the motive no doubt sexual, and it was all, basically, routine.

There was an anomaly that interested him. Apparently, Garrick had not only been alone in the house with the victim, he'd been covered in her blood when the police had arrived. But according to another report, she had been strangled. So where had the blood come from?

He leaned back in his chair and thought about it. Who would have done the post-mortem? It would have been done over in Derbyshire. He went back to his notes, then checked his directory. Paul Norris. Okay, that worked.

Jake had encountered Norris before. The pathologist liked to see himself as a larger-than-life character who added some colour to the general tedium of disease and death. His colleagues thought he was pompous and self-aggrandizing, and his subordinates generally loathed him. He liked to grandstand, and Jake had found that useful in the past.

He picked up the phone.

'Denbigh,' Norris said, when Jake finally succeeded in working his way through the barriers of the switchboard, Norris's secretary, and a dose of 'on-hold' music. He didn't sound too pleased. 'What can I do for you?'

Jake got straight to the point. 'I'm doing a story about the murder up by the dams.'

'Oh, that one. The body in the library.' Norris's laugh was an explosive bark.

'That one,' Jake agreed, making a quick note. He hadn't known exactly where the body had been found. 'It's one of yours, I assume?'

'Yes, I did the PM last night. I can't talk to you about it. You'll have to wait for the police to do a press release.'

'I heard you'd got your knuckles rapped,' Jake said.

'Nothing of the sort. I make my own decisions. And my *professional judgement* is that I don't talk to the press about the post-mortem.' Norris might be vain, but he wasn't stupid.

'I'm not working on a news story.' Jake knew that Norris would talk eventually. That was why he had taken the call. 'You know the kind of thing I write. It's background for something else. But the police reckon they've got the killer. It's just your job to confirm it, right?'

'*Au contraire*, dear boy. Post-mortems reveal. It isn't my job to confirm the conclusions some little PC has jumped to.'

'The way I heard it, they didn't jump. The conclusion was right there in front of them. This Garrick guy had the victim's blood all over him.'

'And the blood belonged to Kovacs, yes. Bad move to be caught with the stiff. Worse move to have her blood on your hands.' Norris laughed. 'Still, there's more tests to be done.'

'When did she die?' Jake's notes said *Tuesday evening*.

'Time of death, time of death – why do people think we can work miracles? She died on Tuesday night after seven thirty. *That's* when she died.'

That was interesting. 'Why seven thirty?'

'We determined that by the highly scientific method of talking to her ex-husband, who spoke to her on the phone at seven thirty.'

Some time after seven thirty . . . 'According to the information I've got,' Jake said, 'Helen Kovacs was strangled . . .'

Norris gave his barking laugh again. 'Newspaper sources. They never get it right. No, the killer used a garrotte.'

A garrotte? That just meant a ligature. 'You mean rather than manual strangulation?' That still didn't explain the blood.

'Ah, no, there's more to it than that, dear boy. Imagine you're going about your business, you don't know there's anyone else there. Next minute, there's something round your neck and your air supply is cut off. You see how it works? I'm the killer and I'm behind you. You're off balance. Your instinct is to grab for the ligature, not for me. But anyway, I can hold you at arm's length. You can't reach me. And you can't shout, because I've shut off your air supply. It's a favourite stealth weapon, a garrotte. And there's no blood.'

'Except . . . ?' Jake said. This time, there had been blood.

'Ah well, it's the best-laid schemes, isn't it?' Norris said. 'Kovacs' killer used a wire. It cut into her throat.'

'A wire? Any old bit of wire?'

'This one had wooden handles – nicely constructed for the job, otherwise whoever did it would have sliced his own hands off.'

A readily constructed weapon. The killing was pre-meditated. 'So the blood on Garrick came from the cuts to her neck.' Jake thought about it. Even with the botch-up, in the scenario Norris had described the killer wouldn't have much blood on him – maybe none. The blood on Garrick could, as he apparently claimed, have come from his futile attempts to help a dead woman. *Could* have . . .

After he'd finished talking to Norris, he made a few quick notes, then picked up the phone again. This time he called Cass. She was surprised to hear from him. 'What's this? Phoning before you said you would? Got the date wrong or something?'

'I always phone,' he said. 'When did I ever let you down?'

'Have you got a week? Okay, what do you want?'

The trouble with Cass was she knew him too well. 'Just a couple of names.'

There was a pointed silence on the other end of the phone, then she sighed. 'Which case?'

'The woman who was killed over by the dams – I'm working on something that might be linked.'

'It's not ours,' Cass said.

'I know. But they've been interviewing over here – I just want to know who's been involved.'

'Hang on . . .' Her voice faded away, then came back. 'They've had some guys over at the university, and one or two others . . .' He could hear the sound of paper rustling. 'Okay – try Mick Burnley or David Haines.'

Both were detective sergeants, and Jake had had good stuff

from Burnley before now. 'Thanks, Cass,' he said. 'You're great. I'll be in touch when I get back, okay?'

'Not so fast,' she said. 'You promised we'd get together before you go.'

'We did, the other night.'

'That doesn't count,' she said. 'I want to see you this weekend.'

'Cass, I can't. I'm off on Monday, and I've got a pile of stuff to finish. I haven't got a minute. It'll have to wait until I get back.'

The silence lengthened and he suppressed a sigh. This thing with Cass had started out as fun. They'd met when he was working on an article about civilian workers in the Manchester police. She had been an interesting interviewee, excluded from the camaraderie of the canteen culture as a civilian, included in the group as the live-in girlfriend of a detective constable.

Jake had found her an attractive and a witty companion for a drink, someone who was resolutely uninterested in the serious side of the work she did, or the serious side of anything much. The Juris Ziverts debacle had just ended, and he was in the mood for frivolity. Their occasional meetings had drifted into longer evenings, and eventually into his bed. It had been an easy, no-pressure thing at first. But now she was starting to want more.

He waited her silence out. After a minute, she said, 'You're no fun any more. It's always work.'

He kept his voice level. 'The work comes first with me, Cass. It always has.'

'Only when it suits you.' She hung up.

He banged the phone down and went back to his notes, letting his irritation with her, and with himself, distract him. He wanted to be distracted. He had no good news for Miss Yevanova. Everything he'd read, and everyone he'd talked to, said the same thing. Nicholas Garrick was guilty.

*   *   *

94

When the Kovacs' marriage had come to grief, Daniel had rented a house in the Longsight area of Manchester, edging on Moss Side. As Faith drove south, cutting across to Stockport Road, the city became a different world, with red-brick terraces opening directly on to the pavement, and row upon row of empty shops, the windows boarded up or protected by metal grilles. She was having trouble finding her way through the maze of small streets. It was all brick and concrete, no sign of green. She could see alleyways running between the streets, footways empty of traffic, unlit at night, dumping grounds for rubbish and havens for crime.

A group of youths in baggy trousers and hoodies milled around in the road. They fell silent as her car approached, moving apart reluctantly as she negotiated her way through. She was aware of their eyes following her. This was an area where car-jacking, gun crime and drugs were rife. She reached across the passenger seat and made sure the door was locked.

Faith was driving faster than she should, unnerved by the silent observation and the way all activity halted until she, the intruder, had gone. It was like straying off the path in dense forest. One moment, she thought she knew which way she was going, the next, she was lost. Paths seemed to stretch in all directions, then petered out into nothingness. Everything looked the same and offered no clue as to the route back. And in the depths of the forest, the predators were stirring.

She told herself not to be hysterical and glanced down at the map. If she was where she thought she was . . . She took a left turn, and then a right. There were no signs, and she had a feeling she'd gone wrong a few streets back, but as she pulled into the next road, to her relief she saw a large grey van parked half on the pavement, and the words KOVACS ELECTRICAL on the side. Daniel's van. Even in her relief at finding her destination, she wondered how he managed to keep it there without the tyres, the contents, or even the vehicle itself going missing.

The house looked empty – one terrace among many, the windows hidden behind heavy nets that looked slightly grubby and hung unevenly. She'd stopped at a newsagents on the way and bought a computer magazine for Finn and some modelling clay for Hannah. It was a poor apology for the doll she had at home, wrapped for the party Hannah should have been having on Saturday. She put the children's stuff in her bag and then, as an afterthought, took out the radio and put that in her bag as well.

There was no door bell. She banged on the wood and waited. No response. She tried again, and rattled the letter-box.

'Get that, will you?' she heard a voice shout. There was a muffled response and then the voice again, 'I said *you*, Finn.'

The door opened, and Finn was standing there. 'All *right*,' he shouted over his shoulder. Then he looked at Faith. 'Hello,' he said. She could see the change in him at once. His eyes were wary and guarded, an adult look that it hurt her to see in Finn's eyes.

'Finn,' she said. 'Listen, I'm so sorry about your mum.'

'Yeah.' He looked away from her, then at the ground.

'Can I come in?' She and Finn had always been friends, sharing an interest in computers, in numbers, in technology. And Finn was like her in another way – he kept his emotions under wraps.

'People think Finn doesn't care,' Helen had told her. 'They think he's being arrogant or rude. Dan doesn't understand. He's too hard on him.'

The house shook as heavy feet came down the stairs and Daniel Kovacs came into view. 'You'd better come in,' he said. He was a tall man, with a thick-set muscular frame. His face was flushed and his dark hair was sticking to his forehead. His sleeves were rolled up and the hair on his arms was damp with sweat.

'You're busy,' she said.

'No, just – bits and pieces,' he said.

The door opened straight on to the front room. The post was still scattered on the floor. Daniel picked it up and looked round for somewhere to put it. The small room was dominated by the huge eye of a television screen that was switched on with the sound turned down. Football players raced round a green field and the crowd roared in silent accolades.

'Tea?' Daniel was watching her with a frown, as if he wasn't quite sure why she was there.

'Don't bother if it's just for me.'

'I'm making it anyway,' he said. 'Do you want some or not?'

She didn't really want a drink, but it would have seemed stand-offish to refuse. 'Okay. Thanks.'

He disappeared through the door, and she heard the sound of water running and the clash of crockery. The house must be a simple two-up, two-down. Finn sat on the settee, his hands clasped between his knees, his attention apparently on the football game.

She sat down beside him, clearing a space among discarded sweet wrappers, crisp packets and empty Pot Noodle containers, the detritus with which Finn usually surrounded himself. 'Who's playing?'

'Dunno,' he said with a shrug to indicate his total lack of interest – another bone of contention between him and his football-mad father.

Faith picked up the remote and switched the TV off. 'Waste of time,' she agreed, and was rewarded by a quick glance and a half-smile.

'Dad says we can go home at the weekend. If *they* say we can.'

They was presumably the police.

'You'll be glad to get back to all your stuff.'

'Yeah. There's nothing to do here.'

97

She looked round, exasperated by the lack of provision for the children. They needed more than a TV and an endless supply of junk food. Finn was watching her as she picked up a Pot Noodle container and looked round for somewhere to put it. 'At least it's green, right?' he said.

She felt a sudden tightening in her throat as she smiled in response. A couple of years ago, Faith had taken him and Hannah out to an adventure park. She'd unwisely told Finn he could have what he liked to eat, and had watched appalled at the quantities of hot dogs, donuts and soft drinks he had put away. In the end, she had vetoed any further consumption *unless it's green* and had spent the rest of the day in a quasi-legal battle about green candy-floss, green ice cream and green pop. 'Only the packet,' she said. 'That doesn't count.'

The phone rang, and he picked it up. 'Yeah? Okay. I'll get him.' He called through to Daniel, 'Dad! It's Uncle Terry.'

Daniel's voice came from the back of the house: 'I'll take it in here.' Finn put the phone down.

Faith didn't want to push the conversation, just let him take it where he wanted. 'When we go home,' he said, 'I've got this cool new game. Want to see it?'

She nodded. 'Sure.' She and Finn could find their way through most computer games.

'It was a present,' he said.

'From your mum?' She had the feeling she was stepping out on to dangerous ground.

His nod was just a jerk of the head. It could have looked hostile, but she could see the reddening of his eyes and knew he was trying to fight back tears. To Finn, tears were a disgrace. 'I was mad at her,' he said. 'She made Dad go. He didn't want to. She never talked to us. She just did it. Because she . . .' His eyes welled up and he turned away. He was still angry with her. 'Dad said it was all going to be okay. Mum was just, you know . . . she was going to let him come back.

And now . . .' He brushed his hand over his eyes. 'Now it can't ever happen.'

She looked at the boy beside her. He was old enough to understand what was going on, but not old enough to deal with the complexities and the ambiguities of the adult world. She could feel the tension in him. She was trying to formulate her next words when she heard the sound of feet on the stairs, and Hannah exploded into the room.

'Faith!' she said, launching herself at the settee.

Faith scooped her up and hugged her. 'Hannah. You're getting so big!'

'Mummy says I'm a lump. It's my birthday on Saturday,' Hannah announced, wriggling free.

'I know. I've got you something.' She was aware of Finn, suddenly watchful and wary beside her. She got out the modelling clay which was in a bright paper bag. 'Why don't you open it now?' she suggested. 'You can have your proper present on the day.' She looked at Finn. 'I got this as well,' she said, handing him the magazine.

'Thanks,' he said. He made no move to open it, but kept his eyes on Hannah, who sat down on the floor and began opening the bag.

'It can't be my party,' Hannah told Faith as she carefully unpicked the Sellotape. 'We can't have my party till my mum comes back.' Her eyes slid away from Faith's. 'She's coming back on Thursday.'

Faith's throat tightened. 'Sweetheart, she isn't. I'm sorry.'

'She *is*.' Hannah lost patience and tore the bag open. 'She said so. She said . . .'

'Look.' Finn was suddenly beside his sister. 'It's modelling clay. You can make things.' He tried to take the box to open it.

Hannah snatched it back. '*I'll* do it.'

'Take it upstairs,' Finn said. 'Dad doesn't want it all over here.'

'Let her play with it here,' Faith said. 'It'll be okay.' She couldn't see what there was to damage in the dingy room. She watched as the little girl began twisting off strips of brightly coloured clay and started shaping them.

'This is . . .' Hannah put a lump of red clay on the carpet '. . . my mummy. And this is her car.' The next piece was blue and was placed carefully next to the red piece. 'And this is the telephone. And this is me . . .'

Finn scooped up the box and the pieces of clay. 'She's not allowed to play with that down here,' he said, ignoring Hannah's wail of indignation. He wouldn't meet Faith's eye. 'Come on, Hannah. I'll play My Little Pony with you. I've got some chocolate,' he added as Hannah hesitated.

'Here you are. Sorry it took so long.' Daniel came in carrying two mugs, and Finn made his escape with Hannah. Daniel sank down on the settee beside Faith. 'Shit. Sorry, Faith. It's all just a bit . . .'

'I know. How are they coping? Finn looks . . .'

He shrugged helplessly. 'Who knows with Finn?'

'He needs to talk,' she said.

He looked at her. 'He'll talk,' he said. 'To me. When he's ready.'

Their eyes met in a brief struggle. Faith backed down. She couldn't afford to alienate him. 'Finn told me you were moving back to Shawbridge.' To the house that Helen and Daniel had shared ever since they got married.

'Oh. Right, yeah. As soon as I can. Next week, I hope. They've finished with the house.'

The conversation was edgy and difficult. She'd never got on with Daniel; he was not a man who was at ease with women. He'd always seen her as Helen's friend, and lately, presumably, Helen's ally. 'Finn seems to be taking his responsibilities towards Hannah seriously,' she said.

'Yeah, well, he's going to have to help out now.' Daniel

drained his mug and stood up. 'You'll have to excuse me, Faith. That was Terence Lomas. I've got to get moving.'

Lomas was a club owner who put a lot of work Daniel's way. Helen had not liked him. 'He's a crook,' she'd told Faith, 'but he and Daniel grew up together, so he can rely on Daniel to keep his mouth shut.' The Mafia of the streets.

'That's fine. You get off. I can stay for as long as you need.'

He looked embarrassed. 'Listen, I'm sorry, I should have called you back. I've decided to take them with me. I promised them we'd go to McDonald's after.'

'I can stay,' she said. 'It's no trouble.'

'Thanks, but it's on the way. It's not a long job.' He stood up. 'Or it won't be if I get there this afternoon.'

'But now that I'm here, why don't you . . .'

'I *said* I'm taking them with me.' He was standing closer to her than was comfortable.

'Okay, if you're sure.' She kept her voice cool. She didn't want him to see that she found him intimidating. 'I'll be in touch. If there's anything I can do in the meantime . . .'

'Yeah, fine, I'll give you a call. Thanks.'

As she drove away, she could feel the blank eyes of the houses watching her.

From a statement made by Nicholas Garrick:

> *. . . as a caretaker. I've been there for two months. My job is to keep an eye on the house, admit any visitors and see them off the premises when they have finished. I was told that the job would last until March when the collection is being moved . . .*
>
> *. . . Mrs Kovacs arrived at five o'clock. I had forgotten she was coming because the lighting had shorted out and I was trying to fix it. It was unusual for someone to visit the library so late. It was unusual for anyone to visit the library at all . . .*

Nicholas Garrick's life at the Old Hall had followed a simple, undemanding routine. He was more or less camping out in a room at the back of the house, and spent his days carrying out basic repairs and trying to keep the dilapidated electrics and plumbing in some kind of working order. He was reliant on the landline for contact with the outside world. His mobile was unusable as he hadn't been able to keep up with the payments.

He admitted the few visitors who were given permission to visit the archive housed in the decaying library, and made sure they were safely off the premises. In his spare time, he read, went walking or made the occasional foray to the village to visit the pub or to stock up with food. He claimed that he was happy with the quiet and the isolation.

His recent past held a tragedy. Garrick had been driving his parents to the airport and had been involved in a head-on collision with a car that had gone out of control and jumped the central barricade. Garrick had been virtually uninjured. His father had died at the scene, his mother had died a week later. A few weeks after the accident, Garrick had been admitted as a voluntary patient to the psychiatric ward of Manchester Royal Infirmary. When he was discharged, he had dropped out of his university course. The job at the Old Hall had come via the good offices of a family friend, a Miss Yevanova, whose son had overall responsibility for the Litkin Archive.

His account of Helen Kovacs' last evening was minimal. He'd admitted her, he'd set her up with a table and a desk light – the main lighting circuit having shorted out somewhere – and left her to it. He remembered that she'd asked some questions about the archive, about the location of some papers, but he hadn't been able to help her. 'It's just a load of old boxes. I'm not interested in that stuff.' He looked at the notes that Kovacs had left – *120.43 PEKBM; P. E.; Ma_y _ro_ _ene_ _* – and had shaken his head.

But it was his account of the rest of the evening that made his interlocutors take notice, though they kept their response muted, and pushed him on with careful questions. According to Garrick, he had gone back to his room, fallen asleep and not woken until the next morning, when he realized that he hadn't seen Helen Kovacs off the premises. He said he was concerned, because it meant he hadn't done his job properly and she might complain. 'And I'd left a desk lamp plugged in – I don't trust the wiring,' he said.

He had been feeling very ill, but he got up and staggered to the library, where he had found Kovacs on the floor. He'd tried to help her, though he admitted that he knew she was dead. Her phone had been on the floor, by the work table which had fallen over. He had used it to call the police.

When he was pushed about the evening, he admitted that he'd been drinking in his room, and that he'd taken some pills, prescription drugs that he took for anxiety. On further pressing, he admitted that he had received a phone call that had upset him. He told them, reluctantly, that the call had come from Miss Yevanova. It was after that he'd opened the bottle of whisky and taken the Valium.

To the investigating team, it looked open and shut. They hadn't got the confession that they'd hoped for, but Garrick had admitted without prompting that something had happened that evening that had upset him so much he had effectively tried to commit suicide. He denied that was his intent, but the doctors who had treated said that he had taken a dangerously high dose.

There were two anomalies. The first one was the weapon. The wire garrotte that had been embedded in Kovacs' throat was not a weapon of impulse, nor something that would usually be to hand. However, the scenes of crime team had reported that there was still some equipment in the old kitchens. The garrotte could have come from there – it could have been a cheese wire. Garrick would have known the kitchens well. He had told them, with the pride of someone who had done a good job, that he knew the house from top to bottom.

The second anomaly was the first emergency call. Someone had called the police from a location very close to the Old Hall, if not the Old Hall itself that morning. They hadn't been able to trace the phone. It may have been coincidence, an accidental call made at the wrong time and the wrong place, but if so, the caller hadn't come forward.

Coincidences don't sit well with juries.

9

Faith slept badly that night. In a state of semi-sleep, she went over and over the events of the day, drifting between dreams and wakefulness. She was glad when the radio came on at six and she knew the night was over.

Wearily she climbed out of bed and went through her morning routine, putting off the moment when she'd have to decide what to do. She didn't know if the Centre was going to be open today, or if it would still be part of the police investigation. No one had been able to tell her yesterday.

She went down to the kitchen and made herself some coffee, then stood in the middle of the room, holding the cup to her mouth and gazing out of the window. The trees were bare and dead, and the high moors looked bleak and forbidding, but the sky was clear, unlike the day before, when . . .

The cat from next door called from the window sill, interrupting her train of thought. She let it in, realizing that she had been staring at the sky for ages, watching a vapour trail moving across the empty blueness, the silver dart of the plane glinting as the sun caught it. Her coffee was tepid. She put it in the microwave and gave the cat some milk. It bumped its head against her legs for a while, then disappeared into the front room where the morning sun would be warming the cushions.

Faith pulled a stool from under the worktop and sat down, resting her head on her hand. In her mind, she could see a TV screen with silent footballers moving across a green pitch, the crowd waving and shouting in the stands. She saw Finn, his hands between his knees, his head bowed. *She made Dad go. She never talked to us.* She saw Hannah sitting on the floor with her modelling clay. *We can't have my party till my mum comes back. She's coming back on Thursday.*

She had to keep contact with the children. Helen would have relied on her to do that. Later, she would phone Daniel. She didn't know what she was going to say to him, but she would get to see the children over the weekend. Somehow.

The phone rang as she was trying to work out the best way to approach this. It was Katya.

'I've been expecting you to call,' she said. She sounded edgy.

Faith twisted her hair round her finger, wondering if her mother had heard about Helen, if that was why she was expecting a phone call. It seemed unlikely – Katya and Helen had never met, so even if Katya had seen the news stories, she was unlikely to make the connection. 'Why?' she asked.

'Marek.' Katya's voice was sharp with impatience. 'You promised to call.'

'Oh, that.' The interview with Jake Denbigh. It seemed like an eternity ago. 'I did.'

'I don't think a message counts as getting in touch,' Katya said. 'And Marek isn't answering the phone either.'

Grandpapa hardly ever did. 'Try this morning,' she said. 'It's one of Doreen's days.'

'I'll do that later. Well?'

'Well what? I said everything there was to say in the message. The interview went fine, there was nothing about the war and I think he quite enjoyed it. I think it did him good. He needs something like that. I don't think he's looking after himself properly.'

'Oh, Marek's always been a law unto himself,' Katya said dismissively.

After her mother had rung off, Faith went back upstairs, sat down at her desk and switched on her laptop. There was something she wanted to try. She got the photocopy the police officer had given her the day before and looked at the notes that Helen had made: *120.43 PEKBM; P. E.; Ma_y _ro_ene_ _*
She set up a crossword programme that could find whole words from incomplete ones, and typed in the word fragments.

The programme made no sense of the two words together, offered *Macy, Many, Mary Maty, Mazy* for the first one, and nothing at all for the second. She tapped her pen against her teeth. It was only what she'd expected. The programme couldn't really handle proper names.

But the problem nagged at her. Suppose it wasn't a name. Suppose the first word was *many*. Then the last one would end in 's' . . . *Many _ro_ ene_ s*. But *_ro_ ene_ s* wasn't a word. The programme couldn't find any matches. Many . . . many . . . She studied the piece of paper closely. The writing was a scribble. Suppose the 'r' was actually an 'h' – it was possible. The first 'e' was almost closed. An 'a'? She tried the new permutations and got *choiceness, shortness*. She was about to discard it, when she looked more closely at the second 'e'. It was scrawled into the adjacent blank. Suppose it wasn't 'e', but 'd'? She tried again. This time she got *browbands, croplands* – right, that made a lot of sense – and *thousands* . . .

For a moment, she thought she'd made a discovery. *Many thousands*. But many thousands of what? It didn't mean anything. The police would have done all of this anyway.

The phone rang again. She snatched it up, glad of the distraction. 'Faith Lange.'

It was Trish, phoning from the Centre. 'Professor Yevanov asked me to phone you,' she said abruptly.

'Oh?' She'd been expecting a message from the Centre, but not one directly from Yevanov.

There was a pause. 'He wondered how you were,' Trish said, her voice sounding a bit forced. 'He said there's no need to come in.'

'Is the Centre open today?' There was no real reason why it shouldn't be.

There was that same silence, then Trish said, 'Yes, but there's no need . . .'

'Okay,' Faith said. She was puzzled. 'Thanks for phoning.'

After she'd rung off, she thought about what Trish had said. It was kind of Yevanov to offer her time off, but she didn't need it. Helen's . . . death wasn't an illness that needed recovery time – it was a permanent part of her life, something she would have to live with, get used to. She'd planned to go in today as soon as she knew what was happening. She would be more useful in her office instead of sitting at home, unable to concentrate on her work, going over and over events she only half understood, playing detective games with crossword programmes.

It was a relief to get out of the house. She drove quickly, taking the back roads to beat the traffic, and arrived at the university within half an hour. The Centre was tranquil in the winter sun, the windows reflecting the light. The lobby buzzed with the activity of the working day.

She took a deep breath before she went into the general office to collect her post. The clerical assistants knew she had been Helen's friend and greeted her with expressions of shock and disbelief – *Faith, so awful . . . can't believe it . . .* They were sympathetic and concerned. But to Faith, it was like reading from a script. She listened, and responded with her lines. All she felt was distance.

She picked up her letters and extricated herself. Just as she was leaving, one of them said, 'Professor Yevanov was asking for you earlier. We thought you weren't coming in.'

'Okay,' Faith said. She hesitated in the corridor. She'd been planning to go up to her room, but if Yevanov had wanted . . . Maybe he'd told Trish to phone when he found out she wasn't there, and now, of course, he would assume she'd taken up his offer of a day off.

She went along the corridor to Trish's office and tapped on the door before opening it. Trish was talking on the phone. She glanced across at Faith, then looked again. 'I'll get back to you on that,' she said, and put the phone down. 'Faith – I wasn't . . . we weren't expecting you.'

'I understand that Professor Yevanov wanted to see me.'

'Oh, he just wanted to know how you were,' Trish said. 'I'll tell him you've come in, when he's free.'

Before Faith could say anything, she went on, 'Gregory Fellows – he's one of your research students, isn't he? He came in earlier to ask if he could cancel his seminar, after what's happened. He knew Helen quite well.'

Faith shook her head in disbelief. She'd told him on Wednesday that the seminar had to go ahead, and now he was trying to use Helen's death as an excuse.

'I told him that would be all right,' Trish looked up and caught Faith's glance. 'You weren't here,' she said.

'He'll have to uncancel it.' Faith thought about all the ways Gregory could make this difficult. 'Okay. We'll postpone the seminars for a week. He can do it then. I'll let the other post-grads know. And please, unless it's an emergency –'

'Faith.'

The voice came from behind her. Faith swung round. Antoni Yevanov was coming out of his office, looking surprised. 'I didn't expect to see you today. I wanted to talk to you. Are you free now?'

'Professor,' Trish said. 'You have a meeting with –'

He looked impatient. 'John will understand. Tell him I'll

be available in half an hour.' He followed Faith into his office and closed the door behind him. He leaned against it and looked at her. 'How suddenly these things happen,' he said. Then he shook his head. 'Please, sit down.' He waited until she was seated, then pulled his own chair towards her. 'I'm glad you came in,' he said. 'I know that you and Helen were close. I was concerned about you.'

'I've known her . . . it feels like forever,' Faith said.

He nodded. She met his gaze, and he tilted his head in query, an invitation to go on talking.

'She was my oldest friend,' Faith said. 'I'm godmother to her son.' A godmother who had been unable to protect him or even offer much consolation. She had a sudden vision of Finn – not the withdrawn youth from yesterday, but the toddler with huge eyes who had stared at her in solemn interest from his mother's arms.

Yevanov was listening, his chin resting on his hand, his finger curled round his mouth. 'The fairy godmother with no power to grant wishes,' he said. 'Or not the wish you would like to grant.'

He was looking into the distance and she got the impression he was thinking about something else. 'There is something I would like to do,' he went on. 'Which is another reason why I wanted to see you today. I'm away for most of next week and by the time I come back it will be too late. Helen never had the chance to make the impact on the academic world that I'm certain she could have done. She published very little. She had plans for her thesis, but those will come to nothing now. Faith, I would like some kind of contribution to go forward to Bonn from Helen. It mattered a lot to her, and I would like her name to be recorded in their annals. The problem I have is that the paper isn't complete. Ideally, I would like some kind of presentation so that her paper can still appear in the proceedings.'

'And you need someone to finish it.'

His eyes assessed her as he nodded in agreement. 'It would just be a case of putting together the complete paper from her draft, and presenting it at the conference.'

Presenting it. She hadn't thought about that. 'I may not be able to answer all the questions.' If a paper attracted controversy, or even a lot of interest, it could be attacked vigorously from the floor. It was part of the rigour of the discipline. An academic had to be prepared to defend her position.

He shook his head. 'I am sure you could handle it, but I wouldn't expect much discussion. And if you were there, you could do a short presentation on the software you have developed. I have discussed it with the organizers, and they are very keen. They are aware of the circumstances, but I have to confirm this soon.'

'I'll do it. Of course I will. But I'll need access to Helen's data.' The police had taken her computer. She could remember the man carrying it down the steps, the bright photograph flapping in the breeze.

'They've copied her document folder,' he said. 'Trish has the disk. There's one more thing: you will need to work to the original deadline – that can't be altered. It will mean having both papers finished a fortnight today, so I would like to see you to discuss the drafts . . .' He glanced at the board where the ongoing work of the Centre was listed '. . . Thursday next week. Can you manage that?'

Faith thought quickly. Her own work was no problem – she'd just need to update her previous paper and set up a demonstration. She could do it in half a day. Helen's paper might be more tricky. Helen had said that her draft was almost complete. If so, it would just be a case of finishing it off from Helen's notes and checking the references. If not . . . 'I'll need to see exactly how far Helen had got,' she said.

Yevanov's phone rang, and he picked it up with a weary

glance of apology at Faith. Placing his hand over the receiver, he said, 'I will have to take this call. Let me know about Helen's paper by Monday.'

She got up to go. 'I'll get started on it now.'

He waited until she left the room before he resumed his call.

Trish watched her narrowly as she closed Yevanov's door behind her. 'Professor Yevanov said you have the copy of the disk the police left.'

Faith didn't know what Trish had been playing at earlier. She hadn't told Faith that Yevanov wanted to see her. If Faith hadn't decided to come in anyway, then the chance would have gone. Yevanov would have let Helen's paper go. 'It's lucky I came in,' she said.

'He told me it wasn't important.' Trish's face was indifferent. She unlocked the small cabinet behind her desk and took out a CD-rom labelled *Kovacs, 20 Jan*. She passed it to Faith with an odd smile on her face. 'You'll have to take a copy of it and let me have it back.'

Faith had more important things to worry about than Trish's small-minded pettiness, but she couldn't seem to get it out of her head. She remembered the complication she now had to deal with about the post-grad seminars and, instead of going back to her room, she went down to the basement where the technicians' room was housed.

Gregory Fellows did some part-time work for the Centre as a technician to top up his grant, but mostly, the other students had told Faith, because it gave him access to sophisticated music software that wasn't available on the networked system. With a bit of luck, she'd find him there.

The lab was at the back of the building, in an antiseptically clean room that was devoted to computers. It was all hard surfaces – no leather or cloth here, nothing that could harbour dust. The chief technician looked up from his work. 'Morning, Faith. How can I help you?' Faith had made a point of getting to know the technicians as soon as she arrived, knowing that their good will could make life a lot smoother.

As she suspected, Gregory was there. She saw him fading towards the door of the room as she talked to the chief.

'Don't go, Gregory,' she called over her shoulder. 'I need to talk to you.'

'I've got . . .' he began.

'I need to talk to you.'

He subsided on to a bench and Faith went across to him. As she got closer, she saw that he looked ill. He was pale and his eyes were bloodshot and sore. He looked like someone who hadn't slept. She wasn't the only person who was bereaved by Helen's death. This young man – he could only be about twenty-two – had probably never experienced death before, and now a friend of his had been murdered. She modified what she had planned to say. 'I know this has been a dreadful shock,' she said, trying to keep her voice gentle, 'but you have to keep going.'

'Life goes on, you mean?' He sounded angry.

'It does go on. It is. You can't stop it.'

He looked at his hands, but didn't say anything.

'I've postponed the seminars for a few days, okay? You'll be doing yours next Friday.'

She half expected an argument, but he shrugged, then nodded.

She was going to say something else, but the technician arrived with her copies. 'I've done two for you,' he said.

Gregory stood up abruptly. 'Gotta go,' he muttered. He went quickly to the door.

The technician gave Faith an eloquent glance.

Jake spent the morning in his flat, working. It was getting on for midday when he decided to go out for coffee. He picked up a copy of the local paper, and took a table outside

113

in the winter sun. He ordered an Americano and settled down to read.

The headline jumped out at him: NEO-NAZI SON QUESTIONED IN MURDER HUNT. He scanned the article quickly. This was something his contacts hadn't come up with. Nicholas Garrick was the son of David Garrick-Smith, the notorious right-wing philosopher. Garrick-Smith had been killed in a car crash a few months before, but Jake had been familiar with the name for a lot longer than that. You couldn't be in Jake's field and not be aware of the things that lurked under adjacent stones.

Garrick-Smith had been a minor academic with a reputation for eccentricity until he had written a book that had touched the zeitgeist: *Damned Lies: The politics of truth and the politics of persuasion.* It had created a furore. Western governments, Garrick-Smith argued, were being held to a system that was preventing the next stage of civilization. They had been hijacked by the politics of persuasion. The politics of truth were needed to move the human race on.

The power of science, Garrick-Smith claimed, was being restrained by the forces of primitive ideology. The doctrines of freedom and rights for all needed revisiting. For example, science had proven, he claimed, that certain racial groups were more able than others. Nature had produced HIV to reduce population numbers in the poorer parts of the world. The politics of persuasion had cowed people into seeing these ideas as unacceptable. The politics of truth would act on it.

His work had been seized on by the far right, by holocaust deniers and by political parties with a race agenda. Garrick-Smith had refused to repudiate these groups. He wasn't responsible, he said, for the way people chose to use his findings. His commitment was to the truth.

Jake's thoughts were interrupted when the waitress came

out to check the tables. 'You okay?' she said. Jake was a regular customer.

'I'm fine. You?'

'Yeah. I got my results today.' Like most café and bar workers, she was a student working her way through her degree.

Jake smiled at her. 'So how did you do?'

'Better than I expected. Too many parties.' She blew her cheeks out in a comic grimace, and propped one hip against the table, keen to chat. 'Thought I'd go out tonight and celebrate.'

'Have one for me, okay?' He didn't attempt to prolong the exchange. He needed to think. She lingered, making desultory swipes at adjacent tables with her cloth, then retreated. Jake forgot about her and lit a cigarette. He let his mind drift, until it settled on Juris Ziverts.

Convinced the extradition attempt wouldn't come to anything, Jake had kept only a rudimentary watch on the case, and it seemed he had been proven right when Ziverts phoned to say that the charges had been dropped.

And then a tabloid newspaper had broken the story. Three local youths who had been on trial for an assault on an Asian man had been found guilty and each been sentenced to two years' imprisonment. The paper contrasted the treatment meted out to the youths with the 'leniency' which the immigrant Ziverts had been granted. MAN ACCUSED OF WARTIME RACE HORROR WALKS FREE! They published a photograph of the old man, and of his house.

It was bad luck. Ziverts had been the victim of the tabloid's serendipity. He was too old and too ordinary for the story to have attracted much interest – an old man in an old war that happened far away. But British institutions were smarting under accusations of institutional racism, and Blackburn had been stigmatized as a centre of xenophobic hatred. The convicted youths were local. An immigrant who had been treated with leniency for a far worse crime was a gift. Jake went to see the old man. 'I'm sorry,' he said. 'I didn't see this coming. I should have done.'

Ziverts was pathetically grateful for Jake's small gesture of support. He fussed over him, gave him a glass of wine and insisted on entertaining him. 'You must have Latvian hospitality,' he'd said. He brought Jake rye bread and a cheese that he said was a Latvian speciality. 'Janis cheese,' he said. 'We eat it on Midsummer's Night.' The local deli stocked it especially for him. He frowned as he opened the packet. 'This is the last. I went there yesterday and they said they could get no more.' He wouldn't meet Jake's eye.

Jake had thought about writing a response to the tabloid article in Ziverts' defence, but it would only have prolonged the media attention on the issue. The problem was there was no more proof of Ziverts' innocence than there was of his guilt. 'It will blow over,' he reassured the old man. 'As long as no one else picks it up.'

'This already is happening.' Ziverts showed Jake an article that had appeared in a small, right-wing magazine. Jake scanned it quickly with a sense of tired disgust. It dismissed the charges against Ziverts on the grounds that the stories of wartime atrocities were exaggerations spread by the victors. 'Both sides have their guilt,' the writer proclaimed. 'We should not condemn a man for being a patriot.' The writer was David Garrick-Smith.

'I don't think any mainstream papers will touch this,' Jake said. Even the tabloids had been a bit leery of Garrick-Smith by that time.

'There were killings.' Ziverts' eyes were focused somewhere in the past. 'Some of our people followed the Nazis into the east and carried out their murders for them. I have never denied this. Maybe all of us were guilty in some way. And the accusation has been made. I am not "George" any more. I am not even Juris Ziverts. In the eyes of the world, I am the man who killed those women and children.' His face was sad.

Jake knew that he was right. For some crimes, the accusation was enough for judgement to be made.

Ziverts stood up carefully. He had to push himself out of his chair. Jake saw that he now used two sticks to walk. 'I have something to show you,' he said. 'Come with me.'

Jake followed the old man's laborious progress through the house to the back door. Ziverts paused, breathing hard, then stepped carefully outside. The garden was tiny but lovingly tended. There was a greenhouse against the garden wall. He led Jake along the path and opened the door. A damp fragrance engulfed them.

Flowers. They were surrounded by tropical flowers and the air was thick with their scent. He looked at Ziverts in amazement.

The old man's smile was almost wicked in his delight at having surprised Jake. 'I am an old man,' he said. 'I spend a lot of time in my greenhouse.'

Later that afternoon, as Jake was about to leave, Ziverts had given him the carving of the cat. 'For you,' he said. 'I want you to have it.'

That was the last time they met. It was a while since Jake had thought about it. Garrick-Smith's name had reminded him. Garrick-Smith – Miss Yevanova had claimed this man as a friend. She had described Nicholas Garrick as 'the son of a close friend'. It didn't make sense. She had encountered the true face of fascism. She could never have been deceived by Garrick-Smith's sophistry, his insistence on detachment from the consequences of his theories.

And the son? How much was he his father's child? It was interesting that he had changed his name. Was that distance or simply camouflage? And was it in any way relevant to the question of his guilt or innocence? Jake needed to talk to Nicholas Garrick. He wanted to see what his own instincts told him. He picked up his phone, and keyed in the number that Sophia Yevanova had given him, the number of the solicitor she had appointed.

Ann Harley answered her phone at once, which was a relief. He'd had enough the previous day of talking to secretaries and listening to Vivaldi while he waited for someone to put him through. The solicitor didn't seem surprised to hear from him, but she didn't sound enthusiastic. Her voice was cool. 'Miss Yevanova told me she'd given you this number.'

'What's happening with Garrick?' he said. 'Have they charged him?'

'No. He's being released.' She didn't elaborate.

Released? Surprise silenced him. He'd expected her to say that Garrick had been charged. 'Where is he?'

'He's in Derby. They've had him in custody over there.'

'I'd like to meet him,' he said.

'Then that solves my problem.' Her voice was brisk. 'Miss Yevanova asked me to bring him to the house, but I have a client to see. His train gets in at twenty to three. You can meet him at Piccadilly.' She rang off.

Jake looked at the phone and raised his eyebrows. *Nice talking with you, Miss Harley . . .*

He finished his coffee, staring blankly into the distance.

Despite all the evidence, the police had released Garrick.

Faith left work at three to go to her grandfather's. It was an incongruously beautiful day, as if the rain from the day before had washed away the last of the winter and left the way clear for spring. The sun was low, and the fading sky was veiled with small, wispy clouds. It made her think of high summer, when the trees would be in full leaf and the warm breeze would stir the shadows, days when she could sit in her office with the window open, listening to the students as they idled across the campus and sunbathed on the sparse grass.

Last summer, she had sat in Helen's garden, watching Hannah with her friends in the paddling pool . . . *She's coming back on Thursday.* Hannah's voice spoke in her head.

She turned into the road where Grandpapa lived, and pulled into the driveway. The overgrown front of the house banished other thoughts from her mind. She looked at the way the ivy had grown on to the roof and was creeping up the chimney stack. She could see places where the guttering was coming loose, and marks on the stone where water had run down the wall. It looked like a house whose owner had died or had gone away a long time before.

She let herself in through the front door, calling out as she came in, 'Hello? Grandpapa? It's me, Faith.' She was early, and didn't want to alarm him, especially if he was worried about break-ins.

There was no response. It was cold and the air felt damp. She touched a radiator. It was tepid. She sighed with exasperation, and went to the hall cupboard where the heating controls were. But the heating was switched on, and the thermostat set to reasonable level. Maybe the radiator needed bleeding. She added that to the mental *to do* list that was growing longer every day.

Grandpapa was not in the lounge. The study? She pushed open the door. It was dark. The laurels that shielded the house from the road had grown high and no one had pruned them for a long time. She turned on the light, but if was feeble, and flickered as though the bulb was about to go, so she switched it off. She looked round the room in the gloom. It barely seemed to have changed from her childhood memories. The heavy armchairs, the dark wood cabinet, the bookshelves that ran up the wall like a ladder. The air tasted musty, as though it hadn't been disturbed in a long time. Her memories of this room held the smell of leather and pipe tobacco, and the smoky fire in winter.

Doreen had been in here a couple of days before, apparently cleaning. Faith could see no evidence of it. She ran her finger over the table. It was covered with a film of dust. The bureau was open and strewn with papers.

'Grandpapa?' she called again. She went out of the door again and let herself through the wooden gate that led to the back garden. As soon as she came round the corner, she could smell the bonfire. She went through the empty kitchen garden – where he had grown onions and cabbage and broccoli when she was small – to the area at the side of the house where he burned the garden rubbish.

He had a fine blaze going, turning the cold day warm and the clear air hazy. 'So this is where you are,' she said, coming up beside him and slipping her arm round his waist.

He looked at her in surprise. 'Faith! You are early,' he said. He didn't like casual visitors, people dropping in – even with her, he preferred to keep to a schedule.

'I know. I wanted to avoid the traffic.' She picked up the hoe and began pushing half-burned sticks back into the flames. She'd wanted to tell him about Helen. But now as she watched him, she thought that he had enough bad memories. He didn't need this one.

'The garden's looking good,' she said.

He looked round him, pleased. 'I have plans for a pond,' he said. 'Over there, by the rocks. Water lilies in summer.'

'But the house . . .'

He held up a silencing hand. 'I have done it,' he said. 'As soon as weather is better, builder is coming.'

It was like standing on a step that wasn't there. She'd braced herself for a long argument – she had never met anyone who could be as stubborn as he could. If he didn't agree, he didn't argue, he just distanced himself and remained as impervious to argument as granite was to water. But he must have listened after all, and her words had had some effect. He'd called the builder, and even though the house wasn't exactly warm, at least the heating had been on. Maybe she was getting through at last.

The fire shifted, releasing a shower of sparks and a waft of smoke that swirled round her, making her cough. There was a pile of ashes in the middle of the flames that still held their shape, fragile leaves of paper that would crumble to a touch. She wondered what he'd been burning, and looked closer. Pictures. She could see pictures. Then she recognized the gold-and-black pattern of the box. He was burning photographs, the photographs that he'd shown Jake Denbigh.

Instinctively, she reached with the hoe to pull them out of the flames, and they collapsed into dust. 'Grandpapa!' she said.

'What is it, little one?' His voice was mild, but he'd been watching her. He knew what she'd seen.

'Those photos – why did you burn them? I'd have taken them if you didn't want them.' She'd at least have wanted the photos of him as a young man.

He dismissed this with a wave of the hand. 'Just dull, business, factories. They would have burned long ago, but I had forgotten about them.'

She remembered the way he'd gone through them after Jake Denbigh left, one by one as though he were looking for something. 'You should have asked me,' she said.

'If you had not seen them, you would not have known they were there. And then you would not have missed them. Now,' he said briskly, 'you must look at the camellia. It comes into flower.'

He'd planted the camellia the year before, and had been eagerly anticipating its first blooms.

He wouldn't talk about the photographs again. As they strolled down the path together, he outlined his plans for the garden – the pond, new plants for the shrubbery, the progress of the established beds. She could see the place on the lawn where she had had her swing. The bare patch of soil had persisted for years after the swing had gone. She looked at the undergrowth among the trees that had made secret tunnels and hideaways. At the edge of the wild patch, a laurel – grown much larger now – stood. Its centre had died away, making a den where she used to play. The gap under the branches where she used to crawl in was still there.

They were coming to the roses now. The rose bushes were his special pride. The bush whose blooms had ornamented her party dress all those years ago still flowered every summer.

But there was something wrong. She let go of his arm and crossed the lawn to the rose bed. It was empty. The plants had been cut off at ground level, the discarded stems dumped on the lawn, their leaves still green and gleaming, as if they didn't yet know that they were dead.

His roses.

She was aware of him standing behind her, aware of the thin sun barely warm on her face.

'Grandpapa!' she said. 'Your roses . . .'

He looked at the ruined bed in silence, then he turned away. 'It does not matter, little one.'

She watched him as he walked away. It could have been any of a hundred visits from her childhood, not this bright day with its bitter edge, a day when she knew that something she loved was coming to an end.

10

The main forecourt of Piccadilly station was thronged with travellers. The benches were full of people hopefully watching the orange lights of the departures board. Jake checked the arrivals and pushed his way through the crowd. Ann Harley hadn't been quite accurate. The train from Glossop wasn't due in for another five minutes.

The trains were lined up on the platform, and travellers were wearily toting or wheeling their bags as if this last bit of walking was a length too far. Garrick's train, to his surprise, was on time. Jake stood back from the alighting crowd, and watched until he saw a fair-haired young man coming along the platform, a rucksack on his back and a weary stoop to his shoulders.

Jake stepped in front of him as he approached. 'Nicholas Garrick?'

He stopped. 'Yeah?' His voice was wary.

'I'm Jake Denbigh. Miss Harley asked me to meet you.'

Nicholas Garrick was twenty-two, Jake knew that from the background research he'd done. He looked younger. He was smaller than Jake, but well built. He still had the fresh-faced look of youth, and his fair hair was in need of a cut. His face had the tan of someone who spent a lot of time outdoors, but underneath, he looked washed out. There were shadows under his eyes.

'My car's in the multi-storey,' Jake said.

Garrick didn't move. The crowds parted and flowed around the two men. 'You're that journalist, aren't you? I saw you on the TV once.' He hefted the rucksack he was carrying further on to his shoulder.

'Yes. You need a hand with that?'

'I'm okay. I don't need anyone to meet me.' He made to move past Jake, but Jake stood his ground. He intended keeping an eye on Garrick.

'Miss Yevanova wants you at the house,' he said. 'I promised her I'd take you.' Not strictly true, but what the hell.

Garrick looked at him, chewing his lip, trying to decide.

Jake could understand Garrick's edginess. He'd been ill, then he had been put through the mill by the police and dumped on a train more or less penniless and probably unfed. 'Hungry?' he said.

Garrick's eyes were still cautious. 'A bit,' he conceded, then, in a further unbending, 'It's pig-swill they give you in there.'

'Well, it's not meant to be the Hilton,' Jake said with an easy grin. Garrick's mouth twitched in an unwilling response.

Jake took Garrick to a greasy spoon that he'd passed on his way from the car park. It smelled of steam and frying. Jake had a cup of surprisingly good coffee which came in a thick white mug. Garrick ordered an all-day breakfast and the plate arrived piled high – egg, bacon, sausages, beans and fried bread. He didn't speak to Jake at first, or meet his eye. He just concentrated on the food.

'Look,' he said, his voice muffled, 'I didn't mean to be funny with you, but a journalist, you know, talking to Miss Yevanova . . .'

Jake, who was reserving his judgement, was favourably impressed by this evidence of Garrick's concern. 'That's okay. I don't write that kind of stuff.'

Garrick stared at him as if he was preparing to challenge that statement, then his eyes dropped. 'Okay.'

'So what happened?'

'They've let me out for now,' Garrick said. 'The solicitor reckons they're still after me, but I'm okay for the time being. It depends if they find anything else.'

'Will they?'

'Will they what?'

'Find anything else.'

Garrick's return to hostility was instant. 'There isn't anything else to find.'

Jake held his gaze. 'I'm taking you back to Miss Yevanova. Before I do, I want to know what happened.'

For a moment, it looked as though Garrick was going to walk, but he subsided. He looked weary. 'Okay. I get that. Look, it's like I told the police. I left her in the library. I fell asleep. When I woke up it was morning and I realized I hadn't seen her out or locked up or anything. And I found her. It was bad.' His eyes met Jake's defiantly, then his head slumped on to his hand and he rubbed his forehead. 'I liked her. She was nice, friendly, you know? I feel like I let her down.'

'You fell asleep?' Jake didn't attempt to keep the scepticism out of his voice.

'What are you? The FBI?' But Garrick's anger seemed manufactured now. 'I'd been drinking,' he said. Then, as if he realized this cast him in an even worse light, he said, 'Look, Miss Yevanova, I've known her since I was born. My mum liked her . . .' Jake filed that bit of information for later consideration. Maybe it wasn't Garrick-Smith who had been Sophia Yevanova's 'close friend'. Maybe it had been his wife. He tried to remember what he knew about Judith Garrick-Smith. She'd always been a rather colourless figure in the background.

Nick Garrick was still talking. 'She's kind of like my gran, you know? She got me this job. She knew about it because her son's a big wheel, a *professor* . . .' The hostility returned briefly. Garrick-Smith, Jake remembered, had been a professor. 'She said it'd give me a bit of space and a bit of quiet. And I'd be earning something.'

'I thought you were a student,' Jake said.

'I was. I dropped out after the accident.'

Something about Garrick-Smith's death was nudging Jake's mind. 'Accident,' he said neutrally.

'Yeah.' Garrick stopped eating, and pushed his plate away. 'Three months ago. I was taking my parents to the airport . . .' He wiped his hand across his face and shook his head as if to get the memory out of his mind. When he spoke again, his voice was flat. 'My father was killed outright and my mum died a week later.'

'I'm sorry.'

'Why? No one else was.'

The silence lengthened. Jake offered Garrick a cigarette. When Garrick refused, he returned the packet to his pocket without lighting one himself. Garrick took a deep breath.

'That night, she phoned me – Miss Yevanova. We keep in touch, once a week, that's the agreement. She's keeping an eye on me.' His mouth twitched, briefly. 'Look, if Miss Yevanova says, "Don't screw up," believe me, you don't screw up. But she was – I've never heard her like that before, sort of cold and far away. Someone had been talking to her about the war. She didn't say much, but I could tell she was . . . you know, remembering. I know it sounds lame, but she's the only person I've got. And I got to thinking that she's old, and she's ill, and she's going to die soon. And . . .' He was looking down at the table now, his fingers scraping at something that was stuck on the surface. 'I don't want Miss Yevanova to know about this.'

'Do the police know?'

'Yeah. I had to tell them.' He fell silent, then met Jake's eyes. 'I swallowed a load of Valium and washed it down with whisky.'

126

'You tried to kill yourself?'

He shook his head. His face was red. 'No. I didn't mean to take so much. I took some, and they didn't work, so I took some more. I just wanted to get the evening out of the way. I must have passed out.'

That would explain Garrick's hospital admission the day after the murder. But . . . he'd been found on his own with a murder victim, the victim's blood was all over him, and to cap it all, he'd made what looked like a credible suicide attempt, which was as good an admission of guilt as any Jake had ever heard.

'So why did they let you out?' he said.

This time, Garrick's response was less aggressive. 'You think I expected it? I thought they were just going to dump all over me. But that lawyer Miss Yevanova got for me, she found out that there was someone else there.'

'How do they know that?' Someone else . . . Jake's contacts hadn't known that, but Norris had suggested premeditation. A wire garrotte wasn't a weapon of convenience.

'Someone called it in. I called, when I found her. But someone else had done it earlier.'

'From the house?'

'From a mobile. They don't know who it was.'

'And you don't have one?'

'Yeah, actually. Only it doesn't work. I couldn't pay for it. They've taken it anyway.'

Jake could understand now why the police had let Garrick go. They didn't want to waste custody time chasing down this caller. But for the first time, Jake found himself seriously considering the possibility that Garrick was in fact an unlucky innocent. Up until that moment, he'd seen Garrick as a probable, if unlikely, murderer. He looked at the young man opposite him – defensive, prickly, awkward and immature. But a killer? Somehow, Jake couldn't see it. 'Okay,' he said. 'I'll deliver you to Miss Yevanova.'

127

Jake's visit to the Yevanov house was brief. Mrs Barker was expecting them. Her greeting to Garrick was brusque. 'Miss Yevanova is resting,' she said. 'I've prepared your room.' Nick, apparently used to this, hitched his backpack on to his shoulder.

'Thanks,' he said to Jake, and then, after a second's hesitation: 'Sorry if I was a bit . . . you know.'

Jake grinned. 'Being arrested is enough to make anyone a bit "you know".'

As he drove back towards town, he was still puzzling over the conundrum that was Nick Garrick. He'd thought that meeting the man would make things a bit clearer; instead, he was more confused than ever.

Nicholas Garrick dumped his backpack on the bed, and sat down. The room was Spartan – a single bed made up with a blanket and a pillow, a bedside table, a thin grey rug. He could feel the chill creeping along his arms. He checked the radiator. It was hot.

He'd felt cold since that morning. He tried not to think about it. One of the women at the police station had been concerned, bringing him a woolly jumper as he shivered in the interview room. It hadn't helped. The cold was deep inside him.

He felt weary beyond belief. He wanted to lie down and sleep, and maybe when he woke up, it would all be gone. He sat on the floor with his back pressed to the radiator and closed his eyes. The fatigue was like bubbles in his head. Pictures started forming behind his eyelids. His mother was laughing, that bright, nervous laugh she used when his father was angry. And then he could see the lights of the cars, jagged and refracted in the rain and the reflection from the wet road. They were all going too fast – he knew they were going too fast, but they were going to be late. His father's voice carried its familiar tone of bitter resignation: *I should have driven myself.*

And the lights – splashes of red in the rain in front, wavering white and orange in his mirror and on the other side, and the high sides of the trucks as he tried to read the signs. *Where do you think you're going? Judith, whose idea was this?*

But the lights were in the wrong place. That's all he could remember. The lights were in the wrong place. And then it was all very quiet. He could remember the blood, and his father's eyes staring from his ruined face. *You stupid fool.*

The blood. Nick's eyes opened. It had been cold and gelatinous against his fingers. He wiped his hands on his trousers then looked down, expecting to see the thick, black smears. But the police had taken those trousers. They'd taken all his clothes.

The journalist had asked. *Will they?* he'd said. *Find anything else?* And he'd studied Nick with cool, dispassionate eyes.

You were not at fault. That's what they'd told him after the accident, after the investigation. The car had come over the central barrier – there was nothing Nick could have done to avoid it. *You stupid fool.*

He shook his head, trying to disentangle the threads in his mind. It had been easier at the house. It had been quiet there. He had been quiet. He had been able to think. *You just need some time to be quiet*, Miss Yevanova had said. The heat of the radiator was burning him, but he still felt cold.

There was a peremptory rap at the door, and Mrs Barker stuck her head in. 'The professor is home. He wants you in his study.'

The Professor. Nick looked at the woman's disapproving face. 'I don't want to see him.'

Her mouth became a thin line. 'While you're a guest in his house, I suggest you do what he says.'

'I'm a guest in Miss Yevanova's house,' he said. 'I'll see her when she's ready for me.'

She looked at him for a moment longer, then withdrew, slamming the door shut behind her. Wearily, Nick pulled himself to his feet and began taking his things out of his backpack. He wanted to get himself sorted out before Miss Yevanova saw him.

As Jake drove back, the traffic was building up for the rush hour, and it was after five by the time he got into town. He'd intended to go back to his flat and write his column, but he'd had a call from Cass. 'I've got something for you,' she'd said. 'You'll want to see this. I can't talk. I'll meet you at that bar in town. Six thirty.' She meant the bar where they used to meet in the early days of their relationship.

He wouldn't have time to go home. He put his car in one of the multi-storeys, and found a snack bar where he had a tasteless sandwich and a cup of indifferent, tepid coffee. It was just after six when he got to the rendezvous. The room was dim, with a flagged floor and rough wooden tables. The after-work crowd was assembling, and the air tasted of smoke, sweat and perfume.

The tables were filling up. Jake went to the bar where a couple of men were leaning. As he approached, one of them glanced round, making a quick, automatic check of the room. He was a heavy-set man with close-cropped hair and Jake recognized him. It was DS Mick Burnley, one of the officers Cass had named as working on the case. Jake went and stood beside him at the bar. 'All right, mate?'

Burnley's eyes swivelled sideways to observe Jake. He was halfway down a pint, and was watching the TV where a girl dressed in a few whispers of thread writhed to the ground and offered her mouth to the camera. 'Denbigh,' he said. 'Yeah, I'm good. You?'

Jake caught the eye of the girl who was serving behind the bar. 'Becks, and the same again here.' He indicated Burnley's glass.

Burnley seemed happy enough to see him. He stayed at the bar and the two men exchanged small talk while they waited for the drinks. Burnley nodded Jake's attention in the direction of the screen. A silk-smooth bottom was wiggling at the camera now. 'Any closer,' Burnley said, 'and we'll get a back view of her teeth.' He settled against the bar to enjoy the show.

Jake laughed, and leaned against the bar beside Burnley where he could keep a discreet eye on the door. He didn't mind watching sexy women dancing, but it all got a bit samey after a while. He preferred such displays to be up close and personal. Burnley drained his glass and reached for the one that Jake had bought him. 'Cheers,' he said.

Jake brought himself back to the present. 'Busy?' he asked.

Burnley pulled a face. 'We're helping out with a murder enquiry,' he said, 'for a load of hicks in Derby. Now they've let their prime suspect go. Probably smacked his bottom for being a bad lad and told him not to do it again.' He brooded over his drink.

Burnley had brought the subject up. This was good. This was better than good. 'Helen Kovacs?' he said.

Burnley gave him a quick look. 'You know something?'

Jake shook his head. 'Only what's been in the paper.' He needed to be careful here. Burnley might present the stereotype of the red-neck, but he used it to conceal a shrewd mind. 'You reckon he did it then? The caretaker?' He thought about Nick Garrick as he had seen him earlier, demolishing a huge fry-up, then suddenly losing his appetite as he talked about his parents' death; Garrick rising angrily to Sophia Yevanova's defence; Garrick hitching his backpack on to his shoulder, resigned to Mrs Barker's frosty reception. Jake couldn't make up his mind about Nick Garrick.

Burnley looked at his beer, swilling it round his glass. A couple of girls came through the door, dressed for a Mediterranean summer. His eyes followed them as they

131

crossed towards the bar. 'What you've got to remember,' he
said, 'is that most times murder is the simplest crime of the
lot. If you find a dead body with someone covered in blood
and going apeshit, then the chances are you've got the whole
story, or all you need.'

Jake was keeping his eye on the door. If he saw Cass
approaching, he was going to have to intercept her. He didn't
want Burnley to see them together. 'So why did they let him
out?'

Burnley shrugged. 'He came up with an alibi of sorts – it
doesn't amount to much. And there's a few loose ends. They'll
get him.'

'Why would he kill her?' Jake was aware of Burnley looking
at him with sudden suspicion. 'He didn't know her or
anything, did he?'

'I thought you weren't doing a story,' Burnley said.

'I'm not. But I'm interested. I'm interested in anything to
do with Garrick-Smith.' He had, in fact, had an idea for an
article he thought he could sell.

Burnley's eyes narrowed as he thought this over. 'There's
a husband,' he said. 'First place they looked. I was there when
they interviewed him – he lives over near Moss Side. He was
at home all evening with the kids and one of his mates – he
talked to Kovacs on the phone just before it happened.'

'Boyfriend?' Kovacs had separated from her husband.

Before Burnley could answer, Cass came through the door.
She saw Jake and started across, then saw Burnley and her
eyes widened in alarm. Jake jerked his head to indicate a
table over to the left, outside Burnley's line of sight.

Burnley was looking at him with deepening suspicion. 'You
serious about this? Look, mate, if you want all this info, you
go to the press office. Or we can come to an arrangement,
you know? I'm not mithered either way, but I'm not doing
your job for you.' He put his empty glass down on the bar.
'Right. I'm off.'

'Okay,' Jake said. 'An arrangement. I'll be in touch.'

Burnley grinned, and headed for the door. Jake let out his breath. He had been afraid Burnley was going to order another and settle down to a night's serious drinking. He waited until the other man had gone, then went across to the table where Cass was making herself conspicuous by holding a magazine up in front of her face.

'What the fuck is Mick Burnley doing here?' she hissed, keeping the magazine in place. 'He's a mate of Stuart's.' Her boyfriend.

'Having a drink. Relax, he's gone.'

She lowered the magazine slowly and looked round the bar as if she was expecting Burnley, or another of his team to be lurking in one of the dark corners. 'Okay,' she said, sitting up straighter and smiling at him. 'I knew you'd have time to meet before you left.'

He frowned. 'I thought you'd got something I had to see?'

She looked at him from under her lashes. 'Oh, I've always got that.' Registering his lack of response, she sighed. 'Okay. Wait until you see this –' She reached into her bag and pulled out a sheaf of papers.

He took them, keeping his eyes on her face, then looked to see what it was. 'Christ, Cass . . .' She'd copied the Kovacs file for him. Presumably all the papers relating to the case that were held in Manchester were now in his possession. 'You could get into big trouble.'

She shrugged. 'Pleased?'

He wasn't. He didn't want her taking this kind of risk – he didn't need these details. He'd already got what he wanted from Norris, from Burnley and from Garrick himself. 'You shouldn't have done it.'

'Oh, I know you'll be careful with it,' she said.

'Don't do it again, okay? It isn't worth it.'

He bought her a glass of wine, resisting her pressure to get a bottle. The conversation – something that normally

133

flowed with no trouble – was halting. 'What's wrong?' she said in the end.

'Sorry.' He tried to focus. 'I've got the trip on my mind.' But the truth was, he was disturbed that she'd go to these lengths to engineer a meeting. He was touched by the gesture, but he didn't want her taking risks on his behalf. She would now see him as under an obligation to her, an obligation he hadn't asked for and hadn't wanted.

He could feel the pressure of time passing, of unfinished tasks lining up and clamouring for his attention. He wanted to be on his own – he had things he wanted to think through and the noise in the bar and Cass's chat was distracting. It was after eight – he needed to get back.

She was pissed off when he told her. She'd created the sense of obligation he was trying to resist – she'd put her job on the line to get him something she thought he wanted. Against his better judgement, he agreed to meet her the following evening. He walked her to her car and gave her a quick kiss. 'Thanks for this,' he said, indicating the folder. 'See you tomorrow.' He walked to his own car and headed back to his flat.

The feeling of weariness that had dogged him since he had left Nick at the Yevanov house dropped away as he sat down at his desk. He opened the envelope Cass had given him, and spread out the contents. As he skimmed the papers, his eyes snagged on details of the post-mortem report that he really didn't want to read: *contusions of the lower lip . . . petechial haemorrhages . . . blue-grey discolouration of the face indicating incomplete application of the ligature . . . petechia on the surface of the heart and oedema in the lungs which suggests the deceased was trying to breathe and couldn't . . .*

The killing had been brutal. Whoever did it must have held the dying woman on the end of the wire while she struggled for air.

There was a report from the scenes of crime team, and

various witness statements, including one from Sophia Yevanova's son, Antoni. Jake read this one more carefully. Yevanov was divorced, with no children. He apparently had a bit of a reputation as a womanizer. The police had dug out details of an affair with a colleague in Brussels, and some university gossip about his relationship with Kovacs, which he denied categorically. His denial was supported by his secretary, who had dismissed the rumours. There didn't seem to be anything to back it up, but it was interesting to see the way the police mind worked. Yevanov had been at home the night of Kovacs' death, working in his study for the earlier part of the evening. His mother had been taken ill later, and he'd sat with her until around midnight.

What would Sophia Yevanova do if the investigation switched focus from her protégé to her son? Was there any reason why Yevanov would have been secretive if he had been having an affair with Helen Kovacs? She was separated, he was single. He might not want it to become the source of gossip round the university, but it would hardly have been a motive for murder.

There was also the husband's statement. Daniel Kovacs claimed that the separation from his wife was amicable, despite evidence of wrangling over the house, and over custody of the children. However, he had been at home with his kids the night his wife was killed. This was supported by his twelve-year-old son, Finn, and by one of his workmates who had called in around eight. Helen Kovacs had rung the house shortly after seven and left a message on the answering machine. He had called her back, using his mobile, and they'd had a brief conversation which, Kovacs admitted, had been none too friendly. Then he'd had a beer with his friend, watched TV with his son, and gone to bed early.

Jake lit a cigarette and sat back in his chair, summing up the information he'd gleaned from the papers. The husband, the obvious suspect, had been at home, with witnesses, and so had Antoni Yevanov, who may or may not have been involved with Helen Kovacs. Nick had been on the premises, but had no identifiable motive for attacking her, unless he'd succumbed to some kind of psychosis.

Maybe Kovacs had had a lover who had followed her to the isolated house and garrotted her in a fit of jealous rage . . . It sounded unlikely. Maybe an intruder had come to the house . . . armed with a garrotte on the off-chance that he might be caught? Hardly. The scene flashed through Jake's mind in all its farcical inappropriateness: *Would you mind turning your back on me while I put this round your neck . . . ?*

A garrotte was not a weapon of defence or threat, it was a device for killing. It worked by stealth and surprise. Someone had wanted Helen Kovacs dead, and had gone into that library knowing she was there, with that end in mind. The more Jake looked at the case, the more unlikely Nick Garrick looked as a killer. It just wasn't logical.

Add to that the complication of the anonymous call to the emergency services, and he could understand why the investigating team had let Garrick go, pending further enquiries. He wondered what the alibi was that Burnley had mentioned . . . He skimmed the papers again, but all he could find was the phone call that Sophia Yevanova had made to Nick around seven thirty. Maybe that was what Burnley had meant.

He'd done as much as he could. He needed to get on. He checked his e-mail. There was one from Adam Zuygev, his contact in Minsk. *I have located the records you requested.* Jake thought for a moment, then sent back a reply with details of the Lange family, what details he had. He wanted to find out more about Lange's wartime record and more about his background – heart-warming tales of peasant idylls in the forest didn't ring true.

136

Since his meeting with Lange, his curiosity about the old man's vague and sketchy past had increased. Lange had a secret, he was certain of that. A secret that related to the war. The daughter knew about it – why else was she so reluctant to let her father be interviewed? Faith . . . he was not so sure; she seemed to have swallowed the whole war-trauma thing. Lange had concealed himself behind misdirection, and Jake wanted to know why. There might be a Minsk connection. It could add a further dimension to what Jake planned to write.

His eyes ran over the books on his shelves: *The Legacy of Nuremberg; Crimes of War: Guilt and Denial in the 20th Century; The Rape of Nanking; The 10th Circle of Hell.* Plus ça change . . .

Minsk was going to be full of such secrets.

Which reminded him . . .

He picked up the two black-and-white photographs and set up his scanner. Once he had them both copied, he set to work to try and enhance them. The picture of the young soldier was on the screen. He was standing very straight, and the uniform looked new. Jake enlarged the picture and changed the contrast. Shadow washed down the screen and the picture became clearer. He could see more of the features now. It had been unmistakably Marek Lange before, but now he could see that the military seriousness of Lange's expression barely masked the smile that the young man was trying to suppress. The old man he had interviewed in the comfortless house would not have smiled like that. Lange had shown interest, some pleasure in the details of his work, relief and affection when his granddaughter had walked through the door, but Jake had seen nothing like this expression of suppressed joy.

He increased the dpi. Now, the letters on the doorplate were clearer. He couldn't make them all out, and part of the plate was concealed behind Lange's arm, but some of the larger letters were discernible: 'M'? No, it was . . . 'H'. Then 'R'? Possibly. And then 'B'. *HRB*. It didn't mean anything. Maybe Adam Zuygev could help him.

He moved on to the next picture, the family group. The woman had what he always thought of as 'peasant' hair - parted in the middle and pulled severely back. Her head was covered with a scarf. The boy was Marek Lange – the square jaw, the Slavic eyes – they hadn't changed from childhood to youth to old age. He was looking at the girl held in the woman's arms. Here, the smile was given full rein. Jake realized that whatever had happened to him later, Marek Lange had been a happy child. The little girl – he adjusted the contrast again and sharpened the clarity, then again . . . He studied it closely.

He'd only met Faith Lange once, but her face had the same fine-boned delicacy that made Sophia Yevanova so beautiful. It was a memorable face.

And he would have sworn, had he not known it was impossible, that the child in the woman's arms was a young Faith Lange.

Grandpapa wouldn't discuss the roses. He barely seemed aware of them, and by the time they were inside he seemed to have forgotten about them altogether. He refused to let Faith help him prepare the food. 'I make a treat,' he said, which usually meant *draniki*, the potato pancakes from his childhood.

He looked critically at the bottle of wine she'd bought – he used to enjoy fine wines and had kept a small cellar, but these days, he was happy enough with wine from the supermarket. 'I'll do the table,' she said.

He held up his hand. 'You do nothing. Sit.' And he bustled away. She watched him as he went, frowning slightly. He was behaving much as usual, but there was something forced about it. It was as if her visit was a distraction – he was making a lot of it, putting in extra effort because it was taking him away from something else.

Maybe he would talk after they'd eaten. He'd be more relaxed then, he'd have had a glass of wine. He might open up a bit. She looked round, trying to decide what to do. Grandpapa had banned her from the kitchen, but she could restore a bit of order in here. The room was generally untidy – books on the floor or just pushed back on to the shelves, Grandpapa's spare spectacles lying on the table, a pair of slippers asking to be tripped over. Everything looked slightly grubby, as though it all needed a good clean. She made a mental note to call the agency and see if they could find someone more efficient than Doreen.

She straightened things up and put the books back in their proper slots on the shelves. One of them was *Russian Fairy Tales*, and she paused with it in her hand, remembering the morning she'd talked with Antoni Yevanov. She saw his thin, intelligent face light up with interest when she told him she knew them. *They are very old, probably the oldest records we have* . . . She flicked through the pages, recognizing the familiar titles: 'The Snow Child', 'The Firebird', 'Havroshechka' . . . and the one that used to terrify her, the story of Baba Yaga. She pushed the book on to the shelf.

The room looked a bit better. She remembered the disorder in the study and resolved to put in a new bulb and clear those papers away. She went across the corridor. The sound of clattering pans came from the kitchen, and a muffled expostulation from Grandpapa – cooking was progressing as usual. She resisted the temptation to go in. He wouldn't thank her. He'd made it clear he didn't want any help.

There were new bulbs in the cupboard under the stairs. She took one to the study, and, using a chair to stand on, replaced the bulb. She had a troubling vision of Grandpapa balancing on the unsteady surface and reaching up. The bulbs

139

should be replaced before they began to flicker and fade. She seriously needed to speak to the cleaning agency.

But the new bulb flickered as well. The fitting must be faulty. She looked round the room in the odd, disturbing light. It looked as though no one had been in here for a long time. A film of dust lay across everything. Her fingers were grimy from the old light bulb. There was only the desk to show that the room was still used. It was odd to see it open and papers scattered everywhere. He'd always been meticulous with his records. She noticed that the 'secret' drawer, a vertical compartment that masqueraded as a bit of ornamentation, was open. It had always fascinated her as a child, and she used to pester him to release the spring that held it, so she could watch it jump out. He kept his personal papers in there. She could see the long white envelope that contained his will, and the manila envelope where he kept the family certificates. On impulse, she lifted that out and opened it.

There was his marriage certificate. She unfolded it carefully, but the paper was so brittle along the folds, it split. Marek Lange had married Deirdre O'Halloran in 1955. The bride was from Dublin, and the groom had been born in Litva, in Poland. The bride's father had been a shopkeeper. The groom's father, a farmer. She looked at it. This was her past, encapsulated in these few words. And there was her birth certificate. She unfolded it, not sure why she was looking at it. The space for 'father' was blank, as it always would be. When she was in her teens, she had wanted to know his identity, and had been outraged at Katya's refusal to divulge it. She had carried her grievance around with her for a while, and had created a fantasy father in her mind that she had almost convinced herself was real – he was rich, urbane, charming, indulgent and adored her.

She shook her head, remembering. When had that hunger to know disappeared? She tried to recapture it now, and found nothing more than curiosity and a faint embarrassment for

140

her teenage self. Maybe it was when she had grown old enough to realize that her fantasy father was no more than an idealized representation of her grandfather, that she had a father, or all the father she needed. Whoever her real father was, he would be a stranger to her, and she to him.

She put the certificates away, and turned to the mess of papers. They were mostly old newspaper cuttings. Some were yellowed and faded, crumbling along the fold lines as if they hadn't been disturbed for a long time. There were articles about the Nuremberg trials: GOERING, RIBBENTROP, TEN OTHERS TO HANG; NAZI WAR CRIMINALS DIE ON SCAFFOLD. There were more recent articles as well about failed attempts to bring war criminals to trial: ROW OVER 'NAZI' ARREST; AUSTRALIA'S SHAME; EXTRADITION CASE FAILS; THE LAST VICTIMS – VIGILANTE JUSTICE AND WAR CRIMES.

She sat down slowly and picked up one of the cuttings: WAR CRIME SUSPECT DIES AGED 85. It was dated 13 September 2001. She began to read. A Lithuanian who had lived in the UK since the end of the war had been accused of war crimes in Belarus. Belarus? Jake Denbigh had mentioned Belarus. He had been the commander of a platoon in a police unit responsible for massacres in ... her eyes skimmed the list of unfamiliar places – Slutsk, Smilovichi, Borisov, Rudensk – but principally in Minsk. Something cold seemed to touch her skin. She put the cutting down and picked up the next one.

It told a similar story. Karlis Ozols, another refugee from the Baltic states who had surfaced in Australia and made a name for himself as a chess champion, was also accused of war crimes in Belarus. Ozols had successfully resisted all attempts at extradition.

The most recent one was a bit different. THE LAST VICTIMS – VIGILANTE JUSTICE AND WAR CRIMES. It was a feature article that warned against the dangers of misidentification, based around a recent, tragic case. It was sparely written but passionately argued, and she looked to see who the author was.

Jake Denbigh.

She tried to make sense of his name being here. He was interested in Belarus – he'd talked about it. He'd been curious about Grandpapa's origins. Maybe he'd been here looking for . . . what? She read through the article again, but it bore no relation to anything Denbigh had discussed with Grandpapa.

She put the cuttings back in the folder and slipped it into the secret drawer next to the manila envelope. She sat at the desk staring into space. Most of the cuttings had been old, but the recent ones . . . Why had he sought them out, and why had he kept them?

But one thing was clear. Grandpapa was in no danger of being reminded about the war.

He had never forgotten it.

The Bridge

This is the story of the boy on the bridge.

A river ran through the village. Just at the edge of the forest, the river bank narrowed, and the water rushed and foamed over flat rocks and fell into deep pools and brown shallows. The iron bridge, the bridge that carried the trains, crossed the river here. Below the rapids, the water flowed into a calm pool, and in the summer, on the hot days when work was done, the boys from the village used to swim here, and jump from the banks into the cool water. And some of them, not many, used to climb the framework of the iron bridge and leap back into the water. It was dangerous because of the rocks and the currents.

The village girls would jostle Eva and whisper things to her. 'Your brother won't jump. He's scared.'

Marek wasn't scared of anything. He was tall and strong and his face was tanned from the hours he worked on Papa's land. The girls used to watch him when he went past. He wasn't scared of jumping, she knew that.

He was in the yard that evening when she went to get more water from the well. He was splitting logs for the woodpile, his sleeves rolled up, his fair hair damp across his face. 'Hey, little one,' he greeted Eva as she came out with the pail.

'I'm twelve!' she said.

Marek grinned and propped the axe against the block. 'You've got a long way to go.'

Eva turned her back on him and wound the handle to draw up the water. Marek came over and scooped up a ladleful which he tipped over his head. 'It's hot,' he said.

He would probably go to the river in the evening. On these hot and dusty days, most of the boys and the young men in the village swam in the river. 'Marek?' she said.

He looked down at her. 'What is it, little . . .' He grinned again, and stopped himself. 'What is it?' he said.

'Why won't you jump? The girls say you're too scared.'

'Into the river?' he said. 'I do. From the bank.'

'I don't mean that,' she said. 'I meant the bridge.'

When she walked by the river, and looked up at the stone, and the iron girders of the bridge, and the drop above the foaming water, she felt cold. But she knew that if she was a boy, she would do it. She would jump from the bridge, she knew she would.

He rubbed his face, smearing the dirt across it. 'I don't jump because it's dangerous and it's stupid,' he said. 'There's nothing brave about stupid. What would Papa do if I broke my idiot neck proving something to a bunch of girls?'

He was right. Of course he was right. She nodded, and heaved the bucket with two hands. It was too full, and splashed water over her feet.

'Here,' he said. 'Come on.' He took the bucket and carried

143

it into the house. 'Whatever we do, they are never going to like us, Eva.'

It was later that week. Eva finished her chores. The yard where the chickens scratched was dry and dusty, and the sky was a relentless, cloudless blue. She felt sticky and dirty and hot. She walked along the path towards the river. She used to go into the forest when it was hot, go under the shade of the trees where the air was always cool and damp, and the fronds of the birches would brush against her face. But there were dark shadows under the trees, and sometimes – even though she was now twelve and didn't believe at all in such things – sometimes she heard the soft tread of Baba Yaga's house as it searched for her along the paths of the deep glades.

As she got near the river, she could hear the boys shouting, and the sound of splashing as the swimmers leapt into the water. They were in the pool below the rocks, like salmon jumping the rapids, their bodies brown and gleaming where the sun caught them. They were diving into the current and letting the water take them downstream in a great rush into the calmer pool below, and then they were climbing out and scrambling up the rocks to do it again.

The village girls were standing by the bank. Eva saw them, and turned to go the other way. She heard them giggling and whispering to each other as they caught sight of her. She lifted her head, and walked faster.

And then she saw Marek on the bank, watching. He dived into the water, and surfaced blowing and shaking his head. Then he struck out towards the base of the bridge, where the iron towers rested on stone.

He pulled himself out of the water, caught on to the stanchion and hauled himself up. Then he was climbing the ironwork like a ladder, pulling himself towards the parapet. Most of the boys who jumped would jump from the top of the ironwork, where there was a pool close to the bank. The water was deep there, and it wasn't as dangerous.

144

But as Eva stood watching, Marek climbed higher, climbed the parapet wall, edging his way along, holding on to the rough stonework with no more than his fingers and his bare feet, higher and higher above the place where the water foamed and churned.

Marek!

She wanted to call out to him, to tell him to stop, but if she called, if she distracted him, he would fall and be smashed to pieces on the rocks that lay just under the water.

The shouts and the cries died away as the others in the water and on the banks saw what he was doing. Everything went silent.

And Marek reached the middle of the bridge. He was high up and far away, and below him she could see the edges of the rocks as the water sprayed up off them, and in the middle, so small, a pool of calm brown where the water was deep.

Her throat closed up. She could hear the roar of the water and the sound of the birds. He was poised on the edge. She could see his hair like a halo against the sun. And then he leapt high into the air and out over the river, beyond the place where it foamed and swirled. He dropped into the water like a stone.

She heard herself scream and she was running to the riverside. And there was Marek, swimming to the rocks and pulling himself out, wiping the water out of his eyes and laughing.

He was safe. He'd done it.

11

Jake went to see Sophia Yevanova the next morning. He pulled up outside the house and parked behind the BMW that had been there when he dropped Garrick off the day before. The house was silent. The door was opened by Mrs Barker, but before she could greet Jake, a tall, dark-haired man came out of a room across the hall. He saw Jake and came across, looking impatient. 'I will deal with this, Mrs Barker.' His voice was cold.

Antoni Yevanov. Jake hadn't met him before, but he recognized him from the photograph Miss Yevanova kept in her room. He held out his hand. 'I'm Jake Denbigh. I'm here to see Miss Yevanova.'

Antoni Yevanov didn't respond to Jake's proffered hand. He studied Jake in silence. 'Mr Denbigh, I think we need to talk,' he said.

'Is something wrong? Is Miss Yevanova ill?' The man's sombre countenance alarmed him. He remembered what she'd said – only half joking – the last time they'd talked: *I may be ashes next time we meet.*

'My mother's health is no worse than usual,' Yevanov said indifferently, pushing open a door and indicating to Jake that he should go through. He found himself in what was clearly

146

a study, with book-lined walls and a window overlooking a long, well-tended lawn. The garden was deserted.

'Sit.' Yevanov directed him to a chair. Jake ignored the instruction. He was tall, but so was Yevanov, and he wasn't going to give the man the advantage of height if they were in for a bit of horn-locking. He stood with his weight evenly balanced, waiting to see what this was about. Yevanov seemed in no hurry. He glanced through a pile of envelopes that were lying on the desk, and tossed them into the waste-paper basket. Then he turned to Jake.

'You have been devoting a lot of time to my mother, Mr Denbigh,' he said. 'So I assume that your interest has gone beyond the commission you came about originally.'

'Yes.' Jake didn't elaborate. He felt under no obligation to explain himself to Yevanov.

'And your current interest . . . ?' Yevanov's manner was courteous, but Jake could detect the chill underlying his words.

'Is a project Miss Yevanova has agreed to help me with,' Jake said.

'I see.' Yevanov looked out of the window into the garden. 'I want you to understand my concerns,' he said. 'My mother survived a dreadful war. She did that partly by her own determination and will. She learned lessons that may be useful in wartime, but are perhaps not so useful in other situations. She has learned, for example, that the will to make something so can often, indeed, make it so, simply because others will it less.'

He paused and looked at Jake to see if he was following. Jake nodded, still uncertain where this was going, and waited for Yevanov to continue.

'She has a great attachment to the son of a family friend. His parents are dead and the young man is in trouble. She told you about this?'

Nick Garrick. This was all about Garrick. Jake began to

see the way the land was lying. He nodded again, this time letting his previous puzzlement show. 'She told me,' he said.

Yevanov's mouth tightened as if he had heard something he expected but didn't welcome. 'Mr Denbigh, my mother does not understand the way the systems work here – why should she? She has had no contact with criminal law in this country. It would be better if she doesn't attempt to interfere. I am unhappy that she is providing legal support – there is no need. The state will provide what is necessary. I am unhappy that she is prepared to give this young man accommodation. I don't want her involvement to go any further.'

Jake nodded, his mind working quickly. He still wasn't sure where this was going, but he'd done as much as he could in relation to Nick Garrick – if Yevanov's intention was to warn him off, it was too late.

Yevanov turned back from the window and looked at him. 'I am certain she has found, or will find, a way to ask you for help in this matter.'

Jake met the other man's gaze. 'She asked me to use my contacts to find out what was going on,' he acknowledged. 'I suspect she's over-estimated how much I can do.'

Yevanov's expression suggested that, in his opinion, over-estimating Jake's talents would not be difficult. 'I would be obliged if you would resist any attempts my mother makes to involve you, including this.'

Jake wondered what was really bugging Yevanov. Jake's involvement with Garrick had been minimal, and his visits caused no stress to Miss Yevanova as far as he could tell – quite the reverse. The protective Mrs Barker would not have been so accommodating if she had perceived him as inimical to her charge. He kept his response neutral. 'As I said, there would be very little I could do anyway.'

'So why, exactly, are you here today?'

'To talk to Miss Yevanova about Minsk. I'm working on a book.' There was no reason not to tell Yevanov that.

Yevanov's eyebrows arched with carefully measured incredulity. 'What kind of book would that be, Mr Denbigh? Some sort of backpackers' guide?'

'Someone's already written one,' Jake said equitably. He wasn't going to let Yevanov get under his skin. 'I'm working on the story of its recent past.'

'The story,' Yevanov said. 'I see. And this would be about the war?'

'Partly,' he said. 'And the pre-war period. I'm interested in the Stalinist massacres.'

For a moment, Yevanov was distracted. 'Kurapaty,' he said. His eyes measured Jake with more interest. 'Not many people know about that.'

'That's something I'd like to change.'

Footsteps moved along the corridor outside, and a door slammed in the distance. Jake's attention was drawn to the garden beyond the window, where an overalled figure was pushing a wheel barrow across the lawn.

Yevanov's gaze followed his, and as Jake glanced back at him, he saw the man's expression set in cold anger. He looked back to the garden, and realized that they were watching Nick Garrick, who was emptying the contents of the barrow on to the flower bed.

'Very well,' Yevanov said. His voice sounded almost indifferent. 'My mother is tired this morning. She asked me to tell you that she will be available tomorrow, if you wish.' He turned away from Jake and stood in the window, watching Garrick as he worked. And everything about him told Jake, as clearly as if he had spoken it out loud, that Yevanov didn't want Nicholas Garrick in his house, or anywhere near him.

Faith had a busy weekend ahead, for which she was thankful. Instead of the plans she'd made – helping with Hannah's party, having a drink with Helen, walking in the hills if the weather was fine – she was going to work. She

149

was glad of the task that Antoni Yevanov had set her. It had the same effect that organizing a funeral must have, the organization and the planning giving the bereaved something to focus on as they came to terms with the loss. Faith was not religious. She didn't share her mother's Catholicism. For her, the conference at Bonn would serve as a memorial for Helen.

She sat at her desk in the dormer window and watched the light creeping across the rooftops and gleaming from the slates. She couldn't devote the whole weekend to this. There were other things she needed to do. She needed to think of a way of seeing Hannah and Finn, and the problem of Grandpapa nagged away at her mind.

As she loaded Helen's disk and began to search through the files, she thought about the evening before. Grandpapa had seemed okay when she'd left, but she could remember the food he'd put in front of her, the *draniki* blackened on the underside, the grated potato still half raw. He hadn't seemed to notice. And he'd been distracted and edgy. He hadn't let her draw the curtains, and his eyes had kept wandering to the darkness of the window that looked out on to the garden. The night had been stormy. She could hear the sound of the trees soughing in the wind, and the branches of the creeper scraping against the window.

But he'd been cheerful enough, making disparaging comments about the wine and telling her off for worrying about him. *I am old*, he'd said. *And there's nothing anyone – not even you, little one – can do about it.* She'd felt uneasy about leaving him, but he'd seemed almost glad to get her off the premises, refusing to let her clear up, rushing her with concerns about driving back late, and agreeing in a hurried way to another evening the following week.

Her laptop beeped. It had finished searching. She looked at the list of files and began to check them more closely to see which one contained Helen's draft. She'd expected it to

150

be clearly marked, but none of the obvious titles had appeared.

Helen's files were full of interesting miscellany: interviews, memorials, collections of jokes, rhymes, folk wisdom, old recipes. There were articles and commentaries that clearly related to the paper that she had been working on, but nothing Faith tried could locate the draft that she was looking for. She wondered what was going to happen to all this material Helen had collected. Presumably it would go in the archives at the Centre for future researchers.

The thought of the archives reminded her of Helen's visit to the Old Hall. Yevanov said that she'd gone to look at some ledgers from an old mining company, the Ruabon Coal Company. She put 'Ruabon' into the search box, and tried a search with wild cards, but it didn't find anything useful. There was nothing about Ruabon on Helen's disk either.

She eased the back of her neck with her hand and stretched, not certain what to do next. She went down to the kitchen and switched on the coffee machine. The cat emerged from some corner where it had been sleeping, stretched, and began twining round her ankles. Faith made herself some coffee and sat on a stool by the window. The cat leapt up on to her knee and curled up, purring. She stroked it absently.

Her first pet had been Katya's old dog, Mooch, a threadbare spaniel who had died when she was seven. She'd cried for three nights for Mooch, and then Grandpapa had brought her a kitten from one of the factories he visited. It was a tiny, spitting thing with needle claws. 'She has a bad foot, see?' Grandpapa had said. 'The cats there, they work. She can't work, so she will die. She needs you to look after her, little one.'

The phone rang and she picked it up. 'Yes?'

'Is that Faith? Faith Lange?' It was a man's voice, unfamiliar.

'Yes.'

'It's Jake Denbigh. We met at your . . .'

'I remember,' she said. 'How are you?' She could picture him leaning in the doorway as they talked, looking at her with speculative interest. He'd said that he wanted to talk to Grandpapa again – he'd asked for her number so he could get in touch.

'I'm fine. Listen, I'm sorry to disturb you at home, but I was just going through my notes from the other day and I found . . .'

She thought about the cut-down rose stems scattered on the grass. 'I don't think it would be a good idea for you to talk to my grandfather again, not just now,' she said quickly, surprising herself.

'No, it's something else.' There was a moment's silence. 'Is Mr Lange ill?'

'He's okay. He's just a bit tired.'

He read her meaning in her tone rather than her words. 'I'm sorry if he isn't well,' he said. 'Look, I found something of your grandfather's in among my things. I must have picked it up by mistake. I don't want to trust it to the post. I could take it round, but . . . Oh hell. To be honest, that woman who looks after him scares the life out of me.'

Faith laughed, but she could understand what he meant. Doreen's unmoveable grimness could be unnerving. 'I thought journalists were – I don't know – intrepid, or something.'

'The word you're looking for is *chicken*,' he said. 'I'm going away, so it'll have to wait until I get back, but can I drop them off with you? Next weekend sometime?'

He hadn't told her what it was, this *something* he didn't want to trust to the post. 'What is it?' she asked.

'Didn't I say? Sorry. It's just a couple of photos. Old ones – that's why I don't want to post them.'

'Old photos?' She thought about the ashes on the bonfire, and then she remembered Grandpapa going through the photos once, twice, then sitting there looking lost and puzzled.

He couldn't find what he was looking for, so he had burned the lot.

'I think it's his family,' Denbigh was saying. 'We were looking at them when you got there the other day. I'm sorry I . . .'

'His family? You mean me, my mother?'

'No.' His voice had changed slightly. 'His family, you know, from . . . Poland. I could send them back by courier, I suppose.' He sounded doubtful.

Old photographs. She could see the flames licking round the paper, the paper curling up and blackening, the pictures darkening into nothing. 'No. Don't do that,' she said, a bit too quickly. 'He's bad about answering the door,' she improvised. 'It's best if you give them to me.'

'I can do that,' he said. 'Let me buy you a drink to make amends. I'll be back on Friday. Why don't I . . .'

'I'd really like them before then.' She wanted to see the pictures. 'When are you leaving?

'It's tricky. I'm going up to London tomorrow evening. I'm flying from Heathrow first thing on Monday. And I'm . . .' There was a pause, then he said, 'Are you doing anything tonight?'

Tonight. Today was the day when Hannah should have been having her party. Faith had promised Helen that she'd help out. Tonight, the two of them should be sitting down with a bottle of wine to recover from the impact of fifteen five- and six-year-olds. She could hear Helen's voice, speaking in her head. *We'll collapse with a bottle and talk about the joys of children . . .*

'No,' she said. 'No, I'm not doing anything.'

'Okay – look, I'm pretty much booked up until about eight, but I could meet you somewhere after that.'

She thought quickly. She didn't want to go into Manchester on a Saturday night, but she didn't want to leave the photos with him. She had a sudden vision of him making the short detour to Grandpapa's on his way to the motorway and pushing the photos through the letter box. 'Okay,' she said. 'Where should we meet?'

'Do you know central Manchester? There's a club in Barton Arcade, near the TV Centre that's quieter than most. It'll get busy later, but we should be okay early on.'

'I know it.' It would mean driving, but she wanted those photos. They agreed to meet later.

She drank the rest of her coffee, and went back to work.

Jake hung up. That had been interesting. He'd wanted an opportunity to talk to Faith Lange, to try and get more information about her grandfather's background. She might plead ignorance, but she'd lived with Lange right through her childhood. There was probably no one who knew the old man better. She would have picked up the random bits of information that people let drop over the years, and those random bits were the ones that Jake could use to build a larger picture.

He'd expected some problem explaining why he couldn't just return the photos directly to Lange, but to his surprise, she had jumped at the idea that Jake should give them to her. His antennae were twitching in earnest now.

Faith Lange hadn't known anything about those photos – she apparently had no idea they existed. And Lange had buried them away, pushed them in among some pictures he surely wouldn't have looked at again – almost as if he couldn't bear to acknowledge their existence. *Minsk,* he had said. *It was in Minsk . . .* And Sophia Yevanova had confirmed it: *Oh yes, this was taken in Minsk.* He wanted to see Faith's reaction when she looked at them.

Unfortunately, he was now double-booked for the evening. He picked the phone up again and called Cass's number. He got her answering service, which was a relief. He didn't want to get involved in any arguments. 'Hi,' he said. 'It's Jake.

154

Something's come up to do with work – I'll have to cancel tonight. Sorry for the short notice. I'll call you when I get back.'

Faith went back to her search of Helen's files, but she found it hard to concentrate. Photos. Jake Denbigh had found photos of Grandpapa's family, on the day of the interview. If it hadn't been for the fact he had taken them away – and she wasn't sure she was convinced by his explanation that they had got mixed up with his notes – they would have burned with the rest. She looked at her watch impatiently, but it wasn't quite midday.

She set up a keyword search designed to flush out the elusive paper, but after half an hour she had run out of key words to try. She hadn't found anything that looked remotely like a draft. Okay, she was going to have to do this the hard way. She started opening individual documents and skimming them. After a further hour, her head was aching. It wasn't there.

That was ridiculous. Helen had talked about a draft. She had promised to give Faith a copy at the meeting that they'd never had. Where would it be if it wasn't on her computer? Her head was aching and her shoulders felt stiff from the time she'd spent over the keyboard. She stared out of the window as she thought. In the distance, she could see the line of the high moorland. The horizon looked blurred as though it was raining on the hills. It was up there where Helen had gone, chasing her obsession with old papers, looking for . . . *Many thousands . . .*

Faith tapped her fingers on her desk in frustration. The only other place to look was among Helen's papers at home, which at least gave Faith the perfect excuse to contact Daniel.

She tried the number of the house in Longsight, but there was no reply. Daniel must have taken the children back home – he'd said he wanted to do that as soon as possible.

She tried the Shawbridge number, and got him straight away. 'Kovacs.' His voice sounded wary and distant.

There was a pause on the other end of the line when he realized who it was. 'Faith,' he said slowly. 'I'm a bit busy . . .'

'I know you must be,' she said. 'I won't keep you. How are you? How's Finn, and Hannah?'

'They're coping,' he said. 'Look, I've got to . . .'

'I'll be quick,' she said. She explained about Yevanov's plan for Bonn. Recalling Daniel's hostility the last time they'd spoken, she avoided using Yevanov's name and just talked about the Centre. 'I want to do this. But I need her notes – I think she'll have kept those at home.'

'Does it matter?' he said. 'Now?'

'It mattered to Helen.'

'Yeah.' His voice was heavy. There was silence on the other end of the line and she waited tensely until he spoke again. 'There's a whole room full of stuff,' he said eventually. 'I don't know what to do with it.' He seemed to have forgotten about being in a hurry. 'Books, papers. I dunno. It'd take you a week to go through that lot.'

'I know what I'm looking for,' she said. 'It won't take me long. I could help you sort it all out if you want.'

'Maybe.' There was silence again. 'Look, come across tomorrow. Come about eleven, okay? I'll be around then.'

'Eleven. Fine. If you want to go out, I could keep an eye on Hannah and Finn for a while.'

'That's okay,' he said. 'They're out for the day tomorrow. They're going to my mum's.'

She was committed to the visit now. And she suspected that if she tried to change it, he'd just say he wasn't available. 'I'd like to see them,' she said.

'Another time. Look, I've got to go.' He hung up.

Faith sat back in her chair after she'd put the phone down. It looked as though Daniel planned to cut her out of the children's lives. She had been Helen's friend, and she was

156

probably now the target of all the anger he'd felt towards his wife. She wondered what to do. She could just go across tomorrow, check through Helen's papers and try and arrange another visit – but she felt a nagging anxiety about Finn. His silence and his strange hostility didn't look like something as healthy as grief. There was something wrong, and she wanted to find out what it was.

Maybe his grandmother . . . ? But Helen had never liked Daniel's parents. Faith could remember her talking about it. 'Maybe it's just a daughter-in-law thing,' she'd said. 'But since I had the kids . . . Dinah drives me up the wall. Finn's got to be a proper boy, a miniature Daniel, and Hannah's got to be a proper girl. She buys Hannah those frilly dresses that make her look like a big doll. Which Hannah loves, of course. And she got her that foul pink pony she's so keen on. And its all guns and footballs for Finn.' It hadn't sounded so very dreadful to Faith – but it had mattered a lot to Helen.

Maybe if she turned up at the house early – she could go across in the morning, say she had to go into work and was calling in on her way . . . Daniel would accept that. He was used to Helen's working pattern which extended into evenings and weekends. But would that give her any more of a chance to talk to Finn? Most people would advise her to leave it, wait for the dust to settle, then try again.

She kept telling herself that the important thing was to step carefully, to keep Daniel sweet, to safeguard her contact with the children. A few days wouldn't hurt. She could ruin everything by rushing it.

She was seeing him on Sunday. The children wouldn't be there, but it might give her a chance to talk to him, to get him to see that she posed no threat to him or to his relationship with his children – she just wanted, for their sake as much as hers, to be allowed to be part of their lives.

12

Faith dressed carefully for her meeting with Jake Denbigh. She wore a black skirt, well-tailored but close fitting, and a white silk jersey. She put her hair up and was pleased with the image she presented.

The night was cold, so she wrapped herself in a wool coat she'd picked up in Paris three years before, and drove into central Manchester. As soon as she stepped out of the car, the icy cold hit her. She huddled into her coat, watching a group of young women flocking arm in arm in happy anticipation of the night ahead, their exuberance already fuelled by 'happy hour' cocktails. They were dressed in skimpy tops and tiny low-slung skirts with expanses of flesh exposed to the winter night. She wondered if the cheap cocktails also provided a form of insulation.

As she turned off Deansgate, the street was suddenly empty. The buildings rose up around her, the anonymous concrete of multi-storeys and warehouses that were in darkness now. The streetlights cast a cold white light. Something more than the cold made her shiver as she hurried to the next street where the arcade was.

The club was discreet and subdued, a small sign outside the door announcing its presence. It was a members-only venue. She gave her name to the doorman, and went down the stairs to the bar. Jake Denbigh was waiting at a table in a small booth. He stood up to greet her, 'Faith. Good to see you.' His eyes were approving as he looked at her. He took her coat and asked her what she wanted to drink.

She asked for a spritzer, and he went to the bar while she took stock of her surroundings. It was quiet with people scattered in the various booths around the room. The bar glowed in a warm light that reflected off an impressive array of bottles and glasses. Subdued music blurred the background noise. 'This is a nice place,' she said as he put her drink in front of her.

'That's why I joined,' he said. 'Most evenings, you can get a quiet drink here. It'll be heaving later on, but we'll be fine for a couple of hours.'

She tasted her spritzer, taking the opportunity to study him. He looked much the same as she remembered him from Grandpapa's: short, curly hair, observant eyes and an attractive smile. He obviously favoured the studied casual dress she'd seen before, open collar, soft jacket. The wine tasted strong. She'd have to be careful.

'How are you?' he said, lifting his glass.

It wasn't a question she could answer honestly to someone she barely knew. 'I'm fine. Did you get your article finished?'

He nodded. 'It comes out next week, and there's a potted version of the whole series in *NS* in a fortnight. I'm preaching to the converted – the idea is that immigration is a good thing, if you handle it right. I should have tried selling it to the *Sun*.'

She raised a disbelieving eyebrow. 'That sounds like a strategy for success.'

He grinned. 'So far, my ambition has always outstripped my achievement, but I'm working on it.'

He seemed to have done well enough to her. 'What's your next project?'

'Belarus. I'm flying out early on Monday.'

She remembered their brief talk as he was leaving Grandpapa's, when he'd talked about writing a book. 'Of course. The Treaty of Brest.'

'Right.' He smiled at her.

He used that smile. Journalists had to be good actors – they had to present a convincing and sympathetic public face so that people would talk to them, and she had the feeling that all she was seeing – all she had seen so far – was Jake Denbigh's public face. 'I thought you were leaving tomorrow.'

'I'm driving up to London tomorrow. I've got to fly from Heathrow – there were no flights to Minsk from Manchester until later in the week. It's not exactly Benidorm.'

'But why Belarus?' It seemed an odd and obscure location. She wondered where she would go if she was researching the recent history of Eastern Europe. Russia certainly. The Ukraine? Georgia? There were a lot of places that were vital and influential. Belarus was a relic.

'I've got a commission for a travel article,' he said. 'Package tours à la Lukashenko, that kind of thing.'

'I didn't know you wrote travel articles – I thought you wrote about politics.'

'Travel in Belarus is politics,' he said. 'It isn't a tourist destination.'

He clearly didn't want to talk about it, and she wondered why. 'Okay, but you still haven't told me: why Belarus. What?' she added, to his amused glance.

'I think I've already said it. You're a lot like your grandfather. How is he, by the way?'

It was a deft change of subject. She hesitated, remembering the cut-down roses. 'He's okay, thanks. He's fine.'

He studied her face, as if he'd picked something up from her tone. 'That's good. I'd like to talk to him again when I get back.'

Faith stirred the ice in her glass to disguise her hesitation. She wasn't sure she trusted Jake Denbigh's interest in Grandpapa. 'It might be better if you call me first,' she said.

'I'll remember,' he said, a careful non-promise. His next question surprised her. 'You're very close to your grandfather, aren't you?'

'He brought me up. He's more like my father, really. So, yes, we're close.'

He reached into the inside pocket of his jacket, and got out a small envelope. He passed it to her. 'Here.'

The photographs. She looked at him, then opened the envelope. There were two photos. She took them out and studied them. The first showed a family standing outside a timber house, a woman, a small child and a boy. The boy was Grandpapa – she recognized him at once. He was smiling at the little girl who was gazing at the camera with wide-eyed solemnity. She must be Eva. The woman would be her great-grandmother . . . *and a man called Stanislau built a house in the clearing, a house of timber. And Stanislau and his wife Kristina lived in the house, where their first child, Marek . . . And then, five years later, in the depths of winter, Eva was born. The last child . . .*

The house in the forest.

'My grandfather used to tell me about this,' she said. 'He used to tell me stories about his childhood. I grew up with it – and with his family, what they were like, how they used to live, what they used to do. Look. That must be his mother, my great-grandmother. She was called Kristina. And that must be his sister, Eva. She was five years younger than he was. He used to look after her.' She thought about the stories he used to tell of the two children in the forest, the crackle of the fire in his study and the smell of leather and pipe smoke.

'You've never seen them before?'

She blinked as Jake's voice interrupted her thoughts. For

161

a moment, she had forgotten where she was. 'No. He didn't bring anything out of there with him.' She looked at the photos. 'Or almost nothing.' She remembered the way he'd searched through the box after Denbigh had left, and she remembered the pile of ashes in the bonfire. He hadn't been burning pictures of his working days. These were what he'd tried to burn. She was certain of it. He hadn't been able to find them, so he'd destroyed everything.

'They didn't make it?' Jake said.

She shook her head. 'I don't think so.'

'I thought your grandfather came from around Minsk. Or spent some time there.'

She looked at him blankly. 'Whatever gave you that idea?'

'Something he said just before you arrived. It makes a kind of sense if his family lived in east Poland. That's the bit that was taken from Byelorussia under the treaty, and reclaimed by Stalin after the outbreak of war. I wondered if he was Belarusian, or if his family were.'

'No, he's Polish,' Faith said automatically. But her mind was turning the problem over. Grandpapa always said that he had been born in Poland, but he'd never said anything about his family, or their affiliations. And he had never had much to do with the Polish community in the UK. 'He's never really talked about it,' she said. She could see he was going to ask something else, so she said quickly, 'I liked the article you wrote.'

He looked at her in query.

'The one about war crimes, about vigilante justice.' She'd hoped he might be taken by surprise and let slip something more about his interest in Grandpapa, but he didn't say anything, just waited for her to go on. 'My grandfather had a copy,' she explained.

'Right. I sent it to him. I usually send something to people I'm going to interview.'

'Why that one?' She felt relieved in a way she couldn't

162

quite explain that Grandpapa had not sought out the article for himself.

He shrugged. 'Refugees' stories – he needed an idea of the kind of thing I was doing.'

'What happened to him? The man you were writing about? Where is he now?'

'He's dead.' Just for a moment, his face was bleak, then he shrugged. 'Juris Ziverts was an old man.'

That generation, the people who had experienced and survived the war, were disappearing. Men like Grandpapa. 'Is that why you're going to Belarus?' He still hadn't answered her question.

'No. Not entirely. I'm not quite sure myself yet . . .' His eyes moved round the room, and he nodded to someone by the bar. The club was getting busier, and the music was louder. She had to lean towards him to hear properly. 'I'm following up a bit of research I did for something else – there's a lot of stuff come out about the USSR in the past ten years or so. Belarus is one of those places no one knows much about. I got interested. It's no big secret, but it's all a bit unformed in here –' He touched his head. 'I don't like to talk about things until they're clear.'

After that, the conversation drifted on to other things. She told him about the different universities where she had worked. 'You have to follow the grants,' she explained when he asked her why she'd moved around so much. She told him about her research into the statistics of human behaviour. 'So much history depends on the memories of the people who were there. But if you ask three different people, they'll all tell you the truth as they know it, and they'll all tell you something different. That's why I prefer working with numbers. You know what you're dealing with.'

He was interested but sceptical. 'You mean people do things because the statistics are right?'

'In a way. It's more complicated than that – people are made by the times they live in, of course.'

He thought about this for a while. 'So, in theory, you could predict what's going to happen . . .'

'If you can get the numbers right. Yes.'

He wanted to know more, but he was steering the topic back towards the war. She didn't want to discuss Grandpapa with him, so she switched the conversation round to him, and after a couple of attempts to turn it back, he gave a resigned smile and started answering her questions. He told her about his various career paths before he settled into journalism. 'Journalism suits me,' he said. 'Writing is what I do best, and I like to be in charge of my time.'

He'd done a lot of interesting things – he'd gone backpacking in Europe when he left university and kept himself afloat with various jobs: teaching English, working in restaurants, even joining a travelling circus once. He came out of that with fluent Spanish and a nodding acquaintance with spoken Russian. After that, he'd travelled further afield – 'Travelling was the only thing I wanted to do' – and had funded himself by selling articles about anything he could to anyone who would pay him. 'That's me,' he said when he'd finished. 'What about you?'

'We've already done me,' she said.

'We've done your past. Now we get to do the present.' He looked at her with that querying tilt of his head that she'd noticed before. 'You can tell me to mind my own business if you want, but you looked a bit down when you came in – is it your grandfather? Is there something wrong?' He offered her a cigarette.

She didn't often smoke, but she felt like one this evening. She leaned forward as he lit it for her. 'Thanks. No, truly, there's nothing.' And there wasn't anything, other than her own sense of unease. 'It's . . .' She probably wouldn't have said anything, but the wine had relaxed her. 'You know the woman in that house on the moors?'

He was lighting his cigarette and she couldn't see his face. 'The murder?' he said.

'Yes. I worked with her. She was a friend of mine.'

'Christ. That's . . .' She couldn't read his expression. 'I'm sorry.'

'I've known Helen since I was at school. I just can't accept what's happened. I keep thinking things like *Oh, I'm meeting Helen,* or *I must tell Helen about that.* And then . . .' She shook her head.

'Of course you can't accept it,' he said quietly. 'Why should you?'

'Because it's happened,' she said. It had happened. It was real. She suddenly knew that she would never see Helen again, and felt her throat start to thicken. For the first time, she knew she would be able to cry for her, but she couldn't – not here, not now.

'And there's nothing you can do to change it,' he said. 'I know.'

She shook her head. She didn't want to talk about it. There was a moment's silence, then he changed the subject. 'I've just realized,' he said. 'You must work with Antoni Yevanov.'

The paralysis that had gripped her throat loosened, and when she spoke, her voice was steady. 'Yes. Do you know him?'

'I know of him,' he said. 'Who doesn't? What's he like to work with?'

'I don't really know,' she said. 'I've only been there a couple of weeks.' She shrugged. 'Demanding. He sets high standards. Which is what I wanted.'

He'd read Yevanov's last book and asked her about it, leading the conversation further away from the Centre, from Helen, looping round finally to the war crimes tribunal at the Hague.

'You're interested in war crimes. Why?' She'd heard him

on radio programmes, talking about the impetus behind the Rwandan massacres, about Srebrenica, about the torture of Iraqi prisoners. And the article he'd sent to Grandpapa – that was about war crimes.

He was studying his glass, which was almost empty. 'It's the conundrum that interests me,' he said slowly. 'We condemn it, but we never recognize the capacity in ourselves – there's never been a culture that won't carry out atrocities, if the circumstances are right. We've done our share and we'll do it again, if . . .' He shrugged.

'If the numbers fit,' she said. 'Is that why you're so interested in my grandfather? Because he can tell you something about the Nazi occupation?'

He gave her a quick glance, then went back to swirling the remains of his wine round his glass. 'No,' he said. 'There's more than enough known about that.'

'So why?' she persisted.

His face was expressionless as he emptied his glass. 'I thought he might know something about Minsk,' he said. He gave her a quick smile. 'He might be able to give me a postscript to my Lukashenko story.'

'And if he doesn't?'

'Then there goes my postscript.' He checked his watch. 'You know, I only remembered when I was on my way here that you live out at Glossop. Are you driving?'

'Yes. That's why I've been . . .' She gestured towards the glass of wine she had been conserving all evening.

'If I'd remembered, I'd have met you somewhere closer,' he said. 'I'm sorry.'

'That's okay. You're the one who's going away tomorrow.' But he'd reminded her about the passing time. It was getting on for ten, and she wanted to avoid the chaos of closing time. 'I'd better be getting back,' she said reluctantly. She'd been enjoying the evening and could have sat there talking to him for longer.

'I'll walk you to your car,' he said.

They walked back along the canal. The moonlight glittered off the water. 'It's beautiful at night,' he said, 'when you can't see the graffiti and the rubbish.'

'Do you like living in Manchester?' She'd never been drawn to the inner city. Her childhood had been in the suburbs.

'It's okay. It's convenient, it's central, there's an airport on the doorstep.' He shrugged. 'You have to watch your back a bit. It's worse than London from that point of view.'

She'd been thinking more about what made a place home. 'I like space around me,' she said. 'This is too . . .' she gestured up at the high buildings that were walling them in '. . . confining. That's why I decided to live in Glossop.'

He shook his head. 'It's always the city for me.'

They met the crowds again once they were on Deansgate. People were rowdier now, amiable enough, but with an edge to their exuberance that was fuelled by the alcohol they had drunk. She could hear the sound of singing, and the sound of breaking glass. A police car cruised slowly along the street.

It took ten minutes to reach the multi-storey where she'd parked. Their footsteps echoed in the cold air as they followed the strip of walkway up to the second level. The lights were yellow and flickered slightly, making a low, metallic buzz. There was a smell of urine and the air tasted of oil. She was glad of his company. It wasn't a good place to be alone.

'This is mine,' she said, as they reached her battered Polo. 'It's put in a few years.'

'At least it's still here,' he said.

She laughed, but she wouldn't be the first person to return to her parking space and find her car gone. This was why she hadn't bothered to get herself something better when she came back. Why provide thieves with expensive cars?

He waited until she was sitting at the wheel with the engine

167

running, then he leaned forward as she wound down the window. 'Thanks for this evening,' he said. 'I suppose I ought to apologize for abducting those photos.'

'That's okay.' If he hadn't picked them up, she might never have seen them. 'Have a good trip. Enjoy the package tours.'

He grinned. 'It'll be interesting,' he said. 'I'm not sure about the rest. Watch out for maniacs on your way back. It's Saturday – they'll all have had a skin-full. Is your passenger door locked?'

'It's always locked,' she said, but she reached across to check. She looked up at him. 'Goodbye, then.'

He leaned down and gave her the briefest of kisses, his hand lightly touching her arm. They looked at each other in silence, then he said, 'I'll call you when I get back, okay?'

She could see him watching her as she drove away.

It was almost eleven by the time Jake got home, and he was too wide awake to think about sleep. He'd enjoyed the evening, even though he hadn't found out much more about Marek Lange. Faith Lange was protective of her grandfather, but Jake had noticed some interesting anomalies in her account of her childhood with him. Jake could pick the topic up with her when he got back. He might have a better idea then of what he was looking for.

He began to sketch out a diagram on a piece of paper. Marek Lange was linked via Minsk to Sophia Yevanova. She in turn was linked to Nicholas Garrick and through him, to the right-wing fanaticism of his father, David Garrick-Smith. On the edges of this was the murder of Helen Kovacs.

Jake looked at the schema he had drawn. He couldn't see any patterns forming, any links of which he had been unaware. He couldn't even tell if these were true connections, or just the connections that happenstance threw up all the time.

After a moment's hesitation, he wrote Faith's name in on

the edge of the diagram, then put a question mark beside it. She was in that web somewhere.

He was looking forward to seeing her again – and not just because she gave him a route to Marek Lange's background. He wanted to get to know her better. He realized he was moving into dangerous ground – if he found out something interesting about Lange, he was going to follow it up, no matter what it was. He gave a mental shrug. Sometimes, behaving like a shit was just part of the territory. He'd resigned himself to that years ago.

He checked his messages. There was one from Adam Zuygev, his contact in Minsk. He listened to the message:

Hello, Jake. This is Adam. I will be at the office on Monday until four o'clock. Phone me when you arrive and we can arrange to meet. There is a protest rally that afternoon, which means that the police will be arresting people. This will be at a distance from your hotel, so we should have no difficulty.

Okay, forewarned was forearmed. Protests, arrests, beatings and disappearances were part of the daily round in Belarus. He wasn't there to get tied up in current politics, but he wondered if it would be worth taking a look at the rally and risking some photographs. On the other hand, he didn't want to spend his brief visit in jail. It was too late to phone Adam back. He made a note to do it the next day.

There was a message from Cass as well. She was more succinct. *You're a shit, Jake.* Fair enough.

He could do with getting some sleep. He'd arranged to visit Sophia Yevanova in the morning, and he was driving to London overnight. His plane left at six a.m. on Monday, so he would need to be at the airport by four. He was going to go short of sleep tomorrow. But he wasn't tired, he felt restless and dissatisfied. He looked at Juris Ziverts' carving, a wooden replica of one of the two cat statues that adorned the pointed towers of the Cat House in Riga. About a hundred years ago, the owner of the house had had a dispute with one of the guilds across the road and had turned the cats round, pointing their raised tails at the guild building, to great scandal and consternation in the city. 'To bare the backside at authority, see?' Ziverts had said, his hawkish face lighting up with his smile. But Juris Ziverts was dead.

Jake tried not to think about the old man too often. After the tabloid article had come out, the police had come under pressure to reopen the case. The evidence against Ziverts was so thin and so unreliable that the case would almost certainly have been thrown out of court, if it had ever got there, but the fact of the investigation was enough to prove his guilt in the eyes of some people. Ziverts had died a few weeks after Jake had first met him. The hostility in the press, the graffiti on the wall of his house, and finally, a series of vandalisms culminating in the wrecking of his greenhouse and the flowers to which he had devoted so many years, had left him a broken and broken-hearted man.

Jake had written his article. His editor hadn't wanted to publish it. 'We don't defend old fascists,' he'd told Jake. Jake had threatened to take the article elsewhere, publicizing the fact that his own paper refused to publish it. It had been a gamble, and one that had come close to costing him his job. In the end, it had appeared with an editorial disclaimer. Jake wasn't sure what good it had done. None, he suspected. As suddenly as the furore had erupted, it vanished. No one cared.

There was no point in thinking about it. As he'd said to Faith, there was nothing he could do to change it. He poured himself a larger whisky than was probably wise and switched on his computer. He read through his notes, making himself focus on the story that Sophia Yevanova had told him a few days before, of her evening walk past the building where the NKVD held prisoners awaiting death.

170

In his mind, he could see the street on that winter's night, the sidewalk shining with frost, the air frozen to stillness. And in the light from the pre-war lamps, cold and intermittent, a young girl hurried from light to shadow, light to shadow, not wanting to pass the barracks-like building with the gratings in the ground. He could see the steam rising from them, drifting away into the night air. And he could see the girl hunch herself over as she tried not to think about what that rising cloud of human breath meant.

His eyes moved back to the diagram he had drawn. Marek Lange. Sophia Yevanova. Nicholas Garrick, child of a warped man with a warped ideal.

The ghost fingers reached out, insubstantial, dead and gone.

The message light was flashing on the phone as Faith let herself in through the front door. She dumped her bag and hung her coat up. She felt a bit flat now the evening was over, and found herself wondering what Jake Denbigh was doing at this moment. Probably much the same as she was.

She realized she was starving and went into the kitchen. The bread was a bit stale so she put a slice in the toaster, and cut herself some cheese. She'd only had one drink with Jake, so she took a bottle of wine out of the fridge and poured herself a generous glass.

The blinds were open and she went across the room to close them, pausing to look out at the small paved yard and the squares of light that marked her neighbours' houses. She shut the blinds and felt the security of the house close around her.

The phone rang, making her jump. It was well after eleven – late for a casual call. She picked it up. 'Hello?'

'Faith?' It was Jake Denbigh. 'I'm just checking you got back safely.'

It was an oddly old-fashioned courtesy that touched her. 'Yes. Thank you. And you?'

'Well, I had to wade through wall-to-wall drunks, but they were yuppie drunks, so that's okay.'

She laughed. 'What time are you leaving?'

'Not till late. My flight leaves at the crack of dawn, so I'll drive down overnight.' His tone was light, but there was an undertone of something else, as though he was very tired.

'Long day,' she said.

'I've had worse. Listen, I'll call when I get back, okay?'

'Okay. Have a good trip.'

After he'd rung off, she sat in the chair by the phone, enjoying her wine and thinking about Jake Denbigh. It was a long time since she'd met a man who really interested her.

The message light caught her attention with its insistent flash. She pressed the button and wandered back to the kitchen as she listened to the messages. There were two from friends, expressing shock and sympathy about Helen. The third one started with silence, then Grandpapa's voice spoke. She put her glass down and came back quickly to the phone. It wasn't like him to call. It definitely wasn't like him to leave a message.

Faith . . . I . . . You are there? I . . . Doreen doesn't . . . The silence came back, along with the hiss of the machine, then his voice spoke again. *Camellia is flowering. You must come and see.*

There was a click and the message ended. She stood in the hallway staring at the answering machine. He'd never been good with them, rarely leaving messages at all. She couldn't work out why he had phoned. *Doreen.* He'd said *Doreen doesn't.* Doreen doesn't what?

She looked at her watch. It was getting on for midnight, far too late to call. It would take an hour to drive, and she was probably over the limit with the glass of wine she'd just had. She bit her lip in indecision. The best thing she could do was go to bed and phone him first thing.

But she lay awake for a long time, her mind going over and over the message and her ears alert for the sound of the phone.

13

Faith woke with a headache and a sense of nagging worry. Grandpapa. She checked the time on her radio. It was just after eight, too early to phone him – he was rarely up and about before nine. She listened to the regional news as she showered. There was a terrorist threat that was affecting the London trains, another football scandal was brewing, and the police claimed to be close to making an arrest in connection with a recent armed robbery. Helen's murder wasn't mentioned.

Her mind flashed back to the evening before. She'd been sitting in the bar with Jake, and she'd told him about Helen. Just for a moment, he'd gone very still. She hadn't noticed at the time – maybe the wine had been stronger than she realized – but she could remember it now.

She puzzled over it as she dried her hair, but she couldn't come up with any answers. She didn't know enough about Jake Denbigh to work out what his agenda was, but it was a useful reminder to be wary in any further contacts with him.

By the time she was dressed – jeans and a sweatshirt, her weekend uniform – it was nine o'clock. She dialled Grandpapa's number, waiting for him to answer. The phone rang eight times, nine times, ten times. She could feel the tension in her fingers.

'Hello?' Grandpapa's voice. Relief flooded her.

'It's Faith,' she said. 'You phoned last night. I was worried.'

'Phoned?' He sounded puzzled.

'You left a message, remember? Something about Doreen, and the camellia.'

'Camellia. Yes, she is flowering. You must come and see.'

'I will,' she promised. 'But what was it about Doreen?'

'She doesn't come,' he said, his voice sounding puzzled again.

'Yesterday? She didn't come yesterday?'

'Yes. I don't know . . .'

'Grandpapa, it was Saturday. She doesn't come at the weekend. She'll be there tomorrow.'

There was silence as he thought about this. 'Saturday. I had forgotten.' She was relieved to hear him laugh. 'When you are my age, little one, this day, that day, who knows? Just . . . foolish old man.'

'Are you all right?' she said. 'I can come across today if you want.'

'Fine, I am fine. No. You come on Wednesday. I will make the treat.'

That meant *draniki* again. This time, she intended doing the cooking.

'I'll come on Wednesday anyway. Why don't I drop in today? I want to see the camellia.'

'And the old man in his dotage?' He was always quick to spot any over-protectiveness, any attempt to manipulate him.

'Okay,' she said. 'I want to come across because I'm worried about you and I want to make sure you're all right.'

'And you have made sure,' he said with finality. 'I will see you on Wednesday.'

'Grandpapa . . .'

'Wednesday.'

He wasn't going to budge. She sighed, letting him hear her exasperation. 'Wednesday, then. I'll come straight from work. I'll be there by six.'

She felt better after speaking to him. His stubbornness was infuriating, but it was also reassuring. Going across to Altrincham would have taken a large chunk out of the day. She went out into her back garden, waving at her neighbour who was trying to dig the frozen earth. She could hear the *clunk* of his spade hitting the ground as she stood there enjoying the winter morning. The air was clear and she could see the hills and the glitter of frost in the high valleys. Having the Peak District on her doorstep was one of the things that had drawn her to Glossop.

Even though she'd spent her childhood in Manchester, she'd never discovered the Derbyshire Peak until Helen had introduced her to the beauties of its remoter parts, to the dark rock edges and the bleak moorland.

They'd spent a week together in the Peak the summer they finished at Oxford, walking in the hills, staying in hostels and small B&Bs. It had been a glorious week of blue skies, remote hills, the freedom of youth and the optimism of a new life ahead. Helen had glowed for those few short days. It was afterwards that Faith realized she must have been in the early stages of pregnancy. She had married Daniel later that summer, and that autumn, Finn had been born.

Faith still had a stone she'd found on that holiday. It was green and striated, washed smooth by a long-gone river. It had stood on her windowsill in her room at Oxford, it had lain on the hearth in her first flat, and now it was part of her garden, back in its native setting.

She touched it lightly, her fingers brushing over its polished surface. It was a Derbyshire stone, but it looked as alien against the millstone grit as it had among the mellow stones of Oxford.

She wasn't due at Daniel's until after eleven. She suspected that this was to give him time to get the children safely packed off to his mother's. She'd considered arriving early, but had decided to keep to the arrangement. For now, she had to play by whatever rules he set.

She spent an hour cleaning the house, then set off for Daniel's. Shawbridge, a run-down town on the outskirts of Manchester, wasn't far from Glossop. It didn't have the cachet of other commuter towns – Marple, Wilmslow, or even Glossop itself. Helen used to say that it would come into its own one day when everywhere else had priced itself out of the market, but as far as Faith could see, that day was still to come.

The house was on the edge of the town on a quiet cul-de-sac. Faith parked against the grass verge, outside the familiar thirties semi. Daniel's KOVACS ELECTRICAL van was parked outside, as she'd seen it on a hundred visits. The low hedge behind the wall and the dark-stained wood of the front door were all disturbing in their familiarity.

She pressed the doorbell. Before, if she'd been coming to see Helen, she would have pushed the door open and called out her greeting. Now, she waited. Finally a shadow moved in the glass and the door opened.

'Oh, it's you.' Daniel hesitated, then stood back to let her in. For a moment, she'd thought he was going to leave her standing on the doorstep.

'How are you?' she said, stepping inside.

He didn't answer, but turned away towards the back of the house where the sitting room was located. She followed him through, noticing that everything was pristine and orderly, the surfaces gleaming, the floors vacuumed. Daniel had always liked everything just so, in contrast to the easy-going disorder that Helen favoured. 'In here,' he said.

The sitting room was silent and empty. She looked round for evidence of Hannah's toys that used to be strewn across the carpet, or of Finn's latest project, but the room looked unlived in. She noticed a new TV in the corner, the huge, flat-screen model she'd seen in his house at Longsight. On the table, there was a cardboard box stuffed full of papers.

Daniel pointed to it. 'There,' he said.

'Do you want me to take it?' she said. 'I can sort through her papers here. There might be some stuff you want to keep.'

'Take them,' he said. 'I just want it all out of the way.'

'What about her books? Do you want me to have a look at those?'

'No need,' Daniel said. 'I got a dealer to take them.'

Faith turned her face away to hide her expression. Helen had spent a lot of time and care putting together her library, and now it was gone, just like that. It was as if Daniel was trying to destroy every vestige of her academic identity. He had never liked or understood Helen's work. He'd resented her non-earning years at university and he'd always resented the way her work intruded into their time together.

'We could have used them . . .'

'Yeah, well, I don't have time for that. I've got a lot to take care of here.'

Faith bit back her comment. She and Daniel had never got on, but he was right. He had too much to deal with. She could have helped him, but he'd made it clear that her offers were unwelcome. 'What's happening now?' she said.

He sighed. 'I dunno. First they say they've got him, then they let him go. There's an inquest in a couple of days, then we can have the . . . you know.' The funeral. He didn't want to say the word.

'You'll let me know, won't you? When it is?'

He didn't look at her. 'It's just for family. We don't want a load of work people turning up.'

'I'm not "work people",' Faith said. 'I've known Helen since she was a child. I'd like to be there.'

'Yeah.' He was silent for a moment. 'Well, do you want those papers or don't you?'

The abrupt change of topic threw her. She'd wanted him to go on talking about Helen. It would give her a chance to discuss the children. 'I'll take them with me,' she said. 'There might be some stuff the university can use.'

'Do what you like with them,' he said. 'I don't want them.' He moved towards the table as if he was going to carry the boxes to the car and get rid of her.

'Wait,' she said.

He stopped and looked down at her. He was a big man with a solid, muscular build. His face was expressionless. 'What?'

She made an inarticulate gesture. 'Helen. She's dead. We both care and we aren't talking about her.'

'What's to say? Everything got to be work with her in the end. She got herself killed chasing after work. Her family, my family, it was all fucking – sorry – it was all work.'

At least he was talking. 'Your family came from Eastern Europe, didn't they?'

'My grandparents were Lithuanian,' he said. 'Came over after the war. Do you know, when she met me, when we got together, she started learning Lithuanian.' His face was a mixture of incomprehension and exasperation. 'She said if we ever had kids, it'd be part of their heritage. You know the stupid thing? I don't speak a word of it and neither do my folks. But she wouldn't let up. She tried to get my dad to tell her the stories his dad used to tell him. As if he could remember. Then there was that stuff about all those old letters and things she found in my Dad's attic. "It's history," she says. "It's Hannah and Finn's past." I got my dad to burn them.' He rubbed a hand across his face. 'They were my nan and granddad. They weren't . . .' He hunted round for words. 'They weren't someone's thesis. They weren't history. Everything had to be work.'

'I'm sorry.' Faith didn't know what else to say. The silence hung awkwardly. Before he could turn the talk back to business, she said, 'How are Hannah and Finn?'

179

He looked at her, then looked away. 'They're with my folks,' he said.

'I know. I just want to know how they are.'

'They're okay.'

'Daniel . . .' He'd opened up a bit. Maybe he'd listen. 'I'm Finn's godmother. I've known both of them since they were born. They've lost their mother, and I'm worried about them. I'd like to see them and I think they'd like to see me.'

'Oh, do you?' He turned towards her and stood facing her, standing square, his arms folded. Suddenly he was hostile. 'Well, I'm their dad and I decide who they see and who they don't.'

'I know that. I do. But what's so terrible about me seeing them? I don't understand. Helen would have wanted me to . . .' As soon as the words were out of her mouth, she knew she'd made a mistake.

His face went cold. 'Helen would have wanted? Don't *you* tell me what Helen would have wanted. She wanted a lot of things. And she didn't think about the kids then.' He moved towards her, his finger pointing at her. 'I remember you,' he said. 'I can remember when we first met. You were there with all your posh school and your fancy voice and all that Oxford shit. "Oh, Helen, it's all so amazing, you can't leave now."' His mimicry was cruel. 'You didn't want her to have anything to do with me. You looked at me like I'd come round to collect the bins, like I was a bit of rough that Helen needed to get out of her system. And it was all *Faith's got to be godmother, Faith's coming to stay, Faith this, Faith that.* You were always fucking there. I was sick of it then and I'm still sick of it.' There was something deliberate about his anger, as though he was working himself up on purpose. His proximity was designed to intimidate her as he moved closer, making her aware of his heaviness and the bulk of his muscle. She could see his arms tensing.

'That was a long time ago.' Faith didn't try to deny what

he had said. She *had* thought from the time she first met him that he wasn't good enough for Helen, that he would hold her back, keep her tied to her roots instead of letting her escape into the wider world. And she'd been right. Helen had been born on a Manchester estate and she'd died living in a run-down cotton town a few miles from where she was born.

'You don't change, do you? I'm telling you – stay away from my children. I'm not having you filling their heads with all your shit. Take all this fucking stuff, all this –' he gave a contemptuous gesture towards the box on the table – '*paper* away with you and don't come back.'

He moved towards her and, for a moment, she thought he was going to hit her. He saw her flinch, and a look of satisfaction crossed his face. He picked up the box, carried it to the door and threw it on to the path. 'You want that stuff?' he said. 'You get it.' He came back to where she stood frozen by the table. 'Right,' he said. He was panting. 'Get out.'

He grabbed hold of her arm. She jerked herself free. 'Don't touch me.' She could taste acid in her throat. She moved deliberately, picking up her coat and her bag. She didn't want him to see how much he had frightened her. She turned back to him as she reached the door. 'If you try that sort of stunt with the children,' she said, 'you'll be in trouble. I'll make certain of that.'

'Right,' he said. 'I'd like to see you try.' He slammed the door on her, making her stagger, leaving her to pick up the damaged boxes and the papers that were spilling out on to the ground.

Sophia Yevanova's house looked welcoming in the bright winter morning as Jake pulled into the drive. He saw Antoni Yevanov's BMW parked outside the house and prepared himself for another confrontation, remembering his dismissal the day before. The prospect depressed him. He had no desire to cross swords with the professor again so soon.

But he was taken straight to Miss Yevanova's room. Her eyes were shadowed and her face was pale, but she greeted him warmly, her hand outstretched in welcome. 'Mr Denbigh. I am delighted to see you.' She inclined her head to Mrs Baker, who was waiting by the door. 'We will have tea later,' she said.

She waited until the door closed, then turned to Jake. 'Please, sit down. Now, what news do you have?'

'I sent some papers through to your solicitor,' he said. He'd hesitated about using the papers that Cass had given him. He doubted, from his quick skim, if there was anything there that Ann Harvey didn't already know. 'And I've talked to people who've been working on the case. I don't have good news,' he said. 'But it's not all bad.' He explained the police stance, and the anomalies that were – so far – keeping Nick out of custody.

She gazed out of the window when he had finished speaking, her hands falling still. 'In the absence of another witness . . .' she said, almost to herself. She looked at Jake. 'And that witness will not come forward. We know that. It would be an unhappy outcome if Nicholas were to go through life with the shadow of *unproven* hanging over him.'

As Juris Ziverts had. No charges had been brought against the old man, but he had been judged and found guilty in a wider court, and he not been able to live with that.

Sophia Yevanova was watching him. 'That, too, is a life sentence,' she said.

Jake nodded. 'I know, but it doesn't have to be like that.'

'It's . . . unfortunate I chose that evening to call him. My mind was on my own concerns. If he had not been unsettled, then he would not have behaved the way he did. This is why the police suspect him.'

The overdose. Jake hadn't been sure if she knew about that.

There was a sheaf of papers on the table beside her. She

picked them up. 'They are checking my phone records,' she said. 'I was not able to give them exact times for the call. I have been going over these myself to see if I can remember anything more, anything of the conversation that might help.' She hesitated. 'Mr Denbigh, would you look at this and tell me the times – the print is ridiculously small, and my eyes are no longer as good as they should be.'

Jake took the paper, which turned out to be an itemized phone bill. He checked the dates until he found the day that Helen Kovacs had died. On that evening, Sophia Yevanova had called Garrick at seven twenty-five – almost the same time Helen Kovacs had phoned her ex-husband. The call had ended at forty-eight minutes past. Twenty minutes. Jake kept his eyes focused on the paper, not letting his face give anything away. The call had been very short to have had the effect on Garrick that he claimed. He looked at it again while his mind sorted through things to say, and he realized that he'd misread it. The call hadn't ended at seven forty-eight, it had ended at eight forty-eight. They'd talked for over an hour.

Now he understood what Burnley had meant by *an alibi of sorts*. Jake had seen the forensic report – Helen Kovacs had been attacked in the library. At seven thirty, she had been talking to her ex-husband. She'd told him that she was going to be home by nine. She must have planned to leave the house by eight thirty. Which meant that she was probably attacked between seven thirty when she phoned her husband, and eight thirty – and all that time, Garrick was on the phone, talking to Miss Yevanova.

Jake had seen the house plan in the papers Cass had given him. There were two phones in the house. One in the hallway at the front, and an extension in the small room at the side where Nick Garrick apparently had his accommodation. The library was at the other side of the house, at the back. It didn't clear Garrick – far from it – but it confirmed the story that he'd told. To date, he hadn't been caught in a lie, and Jake found that oddly convincing.

He looked across at her, letting his new knowledge show on his face. 'This is good,' he said. 'It isn't proof, but it shows that Nick was talking to you around the most likely time that Helen Kovacs was killed.'

She nodded. 'This is what I suspected. But a witness on the other end of a phone is no witness, really. I wasn't there. I believe that this woman brought her own trouble with her and Nicholas's involvement was only poor luck and circumstance. But proof . . . is a different matter.'

'It isn't conclusive,' Jake admitted. 'But they know it makes their case against Nick more difficult.'

She was watching the fire. Her eyes were luminous in her white face. 'Thank you.'

'I didn't do much.' The little he had found had not influenced the situation.

She looked at him and smiled. It was a smile he hadn't seen before, a smile that lit up her face and gave him a glimpse of the girl she had been. 'You have put my mind at rest,' she said. 'And that is worth thanks. Now, I think it is – what is the phrase they use? – *pay-back time*.' She nodded. 'I like that. Pay-back time. I made a bargain. I promised you I would tell you of Kurapaty.'

It was an hour later when Jake left her. She had talked almost continually, pausing only to swallow a mouthful of the water from the glass that stood on the table beside her. Her voice had been dry and unemotional as she had told him the story of her life in Zialony Luh, in the shade of the Kurapaty Forest. He could still hear her voice in his head as he made his farewells. 'I'll come and see you as soon as I get back,' he said.

She looked tired, and Mrs Barker was hovering, so he took his leave and let himself out of the front door. There was no sign of Yevanov, and his BMW was no longer parked in the drive. It was almost noon, and the sun was as high as it would get. The cloudless sky was a deep, clear blue. He walked round the side of the house, and found himself on the lawns where he had watched Nick Garrick the day before.

As he expected, Garrick was there, working in the garden. He looked up as Jake approached, and paused with the spade poised in his hand. He was wearing jeans, and the sleeves of his shirt were rolled up. He looked hot, even though the afternoon was cold. The flush of exertion didn't hide the shadows under his eyes.

'How are you?' Jake said.

Garrick dug the spade into the soil and straightened himself up. 'I'm okay.' His face was wary.

'Looks like they're keeping you busy.'

'I don't like being inside. I need to do things. Anyway, it's best if I keep out of the way. I'm not a hundred per cent welcome here.'

'Professor Yevanov?'

Garrick didn't say anything, but his nod was eloquent.

Jake could remember Yevanov's face as he'd watched Garrick working in the garden. 'What's he got against you?'

Garrick turned a clod of earth over with his shoe. 'He's worried about Miss Yevanova, I suppose.'

Jake let his scepticism show on his face. Yevanov's attitude had been something other than concern.

Garrick looked across at him, and said slowly. 'Yeah, okay. It's more than that. He's never liked me. He thinks I'm like my father.' He shook his head in frustration, and pushed his hair back out of his eyes. 'But he's never been like this before. Everywhere I go, my fucking father . . . That's why I changed my name, but when people find out, they look at me, and I can see what they're thinking . . .'

It seemed there had been little love lost between Garrick-Smith and his son. 'When did you change your name?'

185

'It was after the accident. I wish I'd done it before, so he'd have known. But he'd just have taken it out on Mum.'

Garrick had given Jake only the barest account of the accident that had killed his parents. 'You were driving?' he said.

Garrick looked at him, the defensiveness returning. 'Yeah. So?'

'So what happened?'

Garrick lifted the spade and jammed it deep into the soil. 'They got killed. That's what happened.' He turned to face Jake and his voice was edgy. 'I know what you're thinking. It's like the police. There was one of them, he said, "It's never your fault, is it?" They don't get it. Of course it was my fault. I know that. We were late. My father was royally pissed off about it. I knew he'd start having a go at Mum as soon as I left them. I wasn't concentrating.'

Jake shrugged. If Garrick insisted on feeling responsible, it was his choice. 'The car that hit you came across the central reservation, right? So what could you have done, even if you did see it?'

Garrick didn't seem to hear him. 'After . . . everything was so quiet. Just at first. I undid my seat-belt and got out. Then I realized what had happened and I was trying to get the other doors open, to get to them, and my father – he was just sitting there. There was blood all over him. And he looked at me. He had these pale eyes, he just looked at me as if I was . . . He said, "You stupid *fool!*" And then his eyes sort of went dull, and I knew he was dead.'

'Sounds like a nice guy.'

Garrick's face hardened as he remembered who he was speaking to. 'Look, what is this?'

Jake made a swift calculation. He needed Garrick to trust him, or to trust him enough to talk. 'I'm writing a book,' he said. 'About the war.'

'About Miss Yevanova?'

Jake nodded. 'That's part of it.'

'So why do you want to know about my father?'

'Because I don't understand why she would have anything to do with him.' It puzzled Jake, and he hadn't been able to bring himself to ask her. This reluctance was unfamiliar. He was used to asking the most awkward questions of the most difficult people.

Garrick hesitated, then said, 'She didn't. She hardly saw him. They couldn't stand each other. He was scared of her though, or he'd have stopped Mum seeing her.' His face softened. 'Mum was different. She knew Miss Yevanova before she ever met my father. I think Miss Yevanova tried to, you know, protect her.'

As Jake had suspected, Judith Garrick-Smith was Miss Yevanova's connection with the family. 'And she brought you here?'

Garrick shoved his hands deep into his pockets and took a deep breath. 'Yeah. I came here a lot when I was a kid. I think Mum wanted me to get to know her, so she asked Miss Yevanova if I could come and stay in the holidays, and she let me. I think she liked having me around, you know? Dad wasn't happy, but he didn't dare object.'

Jake tried to picture the huge house, the woman and the child – what had he made of it? 'What did you do for fun? This doesn't look like much of a place for kids.'

Garrick looked at him in surprise. 'You're joking.' He waved his arm, the gesture encompassing the wide lawn, the thicket of trees, the dense shrubbery. 'Look at all this. I grew up in a flat. The only bit of green was a scrubby park down the road with a couple of swings. This was like heaven. The first summer I stayed – I was eight – she took me walking up on the moors. I'd never done that before, getting right out away from everything. And when we couldn't go out, she showed me the garden. She showed me the trees that were best for climbing, and we made a rope swing. Up there –' He pointed up to a branch that overhung the lawn. 'I was the kind of kid who liked making things. I liked putting them together and taking them apart. I wanted to know how things worked, and she used to show me. She's always been great with me.' He gave Jake a warning look. He was prepared to defend her if Jake posed any kind of threat.

Jake found himself warming towards Garrick. There was a naivety about him that was attractive but at the same time alarming. He would be vulnerable outside the circle of Miss Yevanova's protection. He needed to grow up, to develop a few more layers of skin, or his way in the world would be hard. Jake could see why Miss Yevanova was ready to champion him, but he wondered if, in the long run, she was doing him any favours. Nick Garrick needed to learn how to fight his own battles.

Jake found that he was searching for words of advice, and reminded himself that he didn't need anyone's dependency. Garrick was not his responsibility. That was not what he was here for. He nodded to show he understood, and waited for Garrick to go on.

Garrick was deep into his reminiscence. 'I remember the summer after we made the rope swing, I wanted to do something else, and we built this pulley, you know, like an aerial runway – she made me do the design, then I built it. And it worked. That was so cool. I'd designed it, I'd built it, and it worked. She was never like, "Be careful, you'll hurt yourself." She was always like, "You can do it." And – it was the same summer – she showed me how to make a shelter in the trees, a real waterproof shelter, not a kid's den. She learned all that kind of stuff in the war.' He looked across at Jake, and made a face, mocking his own enthusiasm. 'I know it wasn't like that, but when I was a kid, when I was nine, ten, she made it sound exciting, she made it into a game, you know, hiding in the forest, blowing up train lines, escaping.'

'You liked hearing about that?' Jake said.

'I thought it was cool. We didn't play *Star Wars*, me and my mates, we played fighting the fascists. My father liked the fighting bit because it was what boys were supposed to do – you know, wars and guns and things. He was scared shitless I was going to grow up gay.' He laughed, but it had a bitter edge. 'He didn't know who we were fighting, of course.'

Sophia Yevanova's quiet propaganda against the philosophy of the father – her tales of wartime courage and the villainy of the Nazis would have protected Nick from the full force of his father's beliefs. 'She's a brave woman,' Jake said.

Garrick nodded. 'She was. She is. She shouldn't have to fight any more.'

But illness was one opponent that courage couldn't always defeat.

Faith was driving too fast as she left Shawbridge, and when she pulled out into the main road, a van she hadn't seen had to swerve, the horn sounding, the driver mouthing an obscenity at her as he shot past. She made herself slow down. Her heart was still pounding. Helen had always said that Daniel had a temper, but she'd never suggested that kind of controlled menace. Faith could remember the way the muscles in his arms had tensed with the implied threat of violence.

When she got back to her house, she took the box out of the boot, the papers crammed in anyhow, and put it on the table in the front room, then she shut the door on it. She couldn't look at the papers now. She was still shaky with reaction. She didn't want to admit it even to herself, but he had frightened her. He had suddenly become a stranger, and she hadn't known what he might be capable of.

Yesterday's paper was folded in the magazine rack. She picked it up and turned the pages. Helen's death was still attracting some interest, though it was no longer on the front page. The police had released Nicholas Garrick-Smith, and their enquiries were 'ongoing'. There was a comment from 'husband Daniel Kovacs, thirty-eight,' expressing hopes that the police would soon track down the 'animal' who had done this to his wife.

Daniel was portrayed as a grieving husband. The estrangement between him and Helen wasn't mentioned. Faith wondered if grief could excuse his behaviour. But he hadn't been acting under the impetus of grief, he had been acting under the impetus of anger, of long pent-up rage. This was the man who had charge of Finn and Hannah, the two children she cared about as much as she had cared about their mother, the children she had promised Helen she would look after.

She could still see Daniel's face, cold with anger. If she felt afraid at the prospect of confronting him again, what did this mean for the children? She had to find a way to talk to them. It didn't help that Finn hadn't wanted to talk to her the day she'd gone round. And he'd whisked Hannah away from her, fast, so that Hannah couldn't talk to Faith either.

She sat very still, her coffee halfway to her mouth. Daniel had never been a suspect in Helen's murder because he had been at home with the children the night she had died. The police had questioned him and were apparently satisfied with that. But who could have corroborated that alibi? Only Finn and Hannah. She pictured Hannah sitting on the carpet in the front room of that dismal house at Longsight, playing with the modelling clay. *She's coming back on Thursday,* Hannah had said. And later: *This is my mummy. And this is her car. And this is the telephone. And this is me . . .* And then Finn had whisked her away.

She could feel a coldness creeping over her as she realized the implications of what she was thinking. Finn loved his father and craved his approval. If Finn had lied to protect him . . . Would Daniel have asked that of his son?

Daniel had loved Helen as long as she was the woman he

190

wanted her to be – the wife, the mother, the woman whose life was her home and her family. But Helen had changed, and Daniel hadn't liked that. Then she had left him and Daniel had tried to punish her by taking away her children.

And her life? Did he hate her that much?

She didn't know what to do. The police had already investigated Daniel. They must think he had a strong alibi because they knew about the rows and the antagonism between him and Helen – she'd talked about it herself when they interviewed her. She could contact the police with her suspicions – but she was the estranged wife's best friend. They would see her as biased. And if they took her concerns seriously? They would go after Daniel by the shortest route available – Finn. She didn't like to think about what it would do to Finn if he was forced to betray his father.

Tell me what to do.

She had whispered it aloud as if she was asking Helen.

But Helen was dead, Faith was barred from the children, and it looked as though she was going to be excluded from the funeral as well. She wanted a memorial to Helen. She wanted to acknowledge Helen's death. Daniel couldn't stop her from attending whatever service he arranged, but Faith couldn't risk provoking any kind of scene – Daniel knew that.

She could have her own memorial. She looked at the clock. It was after three, but there was still enough daylight, just. She grabbed her coat and went into the garden, where she picked up the odd green stone she had found all those years ago. She got into the car and drove east out of Glossop, taking the twisting road across the Pennines, the aptly named Snake Pass. The road climbed up past the dark edges of millstone grit to the high moors. The land was bleak and dead on the tops, with sparse grasses and peat bogs.

As she dropped down the other side, the land became greener, gentler, and soon she was driving past the cold glitter of the first dam. The sun was low in the sky as she turned off along the minor road that skirted the reservoir. Before long, she was driving through trees and the sun, hanging red above the water, flickered through them, dazzling her eyes with flashes of dark and then light.

The trees were denser here. The road forked, one route heading further along the valley, the other heading deeper into the woods, below the turreted walls of the dam. There was a gate across the road with a red sign: PRIVATE ROAD. NO ENTRY EXCEPT FOR ACCESS. The car bumped and lurched over the unmade surface. Then she was on the other side of the water and the trees thinned out.

It was like coming into a different world. The water of the dam was placid beside her, and the low stone walls that must be the remains of the drowned village were warm in the light of the setting sun. She drove slowly now past the isolated cottages, until she came to gateposts, high and massive, guarding a rutted drive. The Old Hall looked dark and forbidding apart from a red post box in the wall that struck a reassuringly mundane note.

This was the place where Helen had died. She pulled in, forcing the car high up on to the verge. The road was narrow. She picked up the stone from the seat beside her, and got out of the car. She walked slowly up the steep drive. When she looked back, she found she was looking down on the roofs of the few stone cottages that had survived the flooding.

What should I do?

Silence.

The house loomed above her. It was high, with tall chimneys and a gabled roof. The guttering sagged and the walls were stained with water. The windows looked back at her, dark and empty. It was a lonelier place to die than the bleak moor she'd envisaged.

She didn't go up to the door. She could see the black-and-yellow police tape flapping on the handles. There was a sense of brooding darkness in the emptiness and the isolation that

192

chilled her. She felt as though it would be dangerous to step any closer. It wasn't physical danger. She wasn't hysterical enough to think that some murderous madman lurked behind the empty windows, waiting for his next victim. It was the danger of contamination, as though, if she got too close, she would take the darkness with her.

She walked back to the gate and crossed the road. The water was opaque steel as the sun sank below the hills. She called up an image of Helen sitting on the rocks above Conies Dale. The breeze was blowing her hair into a tangle of curls that gleamed auburn in the sunlight. She was looking out across the moors, and she was laughing.

Faith held that image in her mind, and threw the stone into the water, sending the reflection of the hills dancing across the surface. She stayed by the wall as she watched the sun set over the dams.

14

The plane climbed through the dull morning light, the blur of speed slowing into clarity as the landscape stretched out in a panorama below. The view faded into a swirl of mist, and they were among the clouds, then they burst through into blue skies and bright sunshine. The buzzer sounded and the cabin crew leapt into action, to keep their fifty charges fed and docile through the short hop from Warsaw to Minsk.

Jake stretched out as far as the seat restriction would allow him, and took stock. The plane was tiny, an elegant dart with swept-back wings. The pilot's voice came over the PA, his English so heavily accented that Jake couldn't tell if he was welcoming them on board or warning them they were about to plummet to earth.

He smiled his thanks at the pretty woman who served him breakfast – a strange cold pancake filled with what tasted like – and possibly even was – sweetened cottage cheese. He ate without paying too much attention, thinking about the visit ahead of him.

He wanted to see the Kurapaty Forest, he wanted to walk the streets of Minsk, trying to find any traces of the old city. He wanted to find the places where Sophia Yevanova would have walked as a young girl. He wondered if he could find the place where the NKVD building would have stood, the building that she had hurried past, her coat clutched around her against the cold, the mist rising from the grating into the frosted air.

He wanted to spend time browsing the archive material that Adam Zuygev had promised to find for him: Sophia Yevanova's past, the stories of her family. He wanted to visit Zialony Luh, the village where her father had sent her, where she and her cousin had listened to the sound of gunshots in the night.

He wanted to find out what had happened to Raina. Sophia Yevanova had evaded his questions about her cousin. Had Raina survived the war? Or had she, like half the population of Minsk, died? And those who survived felt the guilt. He'd seen enough of this in his research with the refugees. The survivors felt guilty for the mere fact of their survival. He wondered if the perpetrators felt any guilt, or if they had been too busy trying to save themselves, and then trying to justify what they had done.

And he wanted to find out about Marek Lange, find out what he had been doing in Minsk, standing there so proudly in the uniform of his country.

He plugged his laptop into the socket by his seat, and got out his cassette recorder. He could use the down time of the flight to transcribe yesterday's interview with Sophia Yevanova. The stories she told him were of a past over sixty years old. But he couldn't escape the feeling that they were closer than that, just outside the range of his vision or concealed in an unperceived pattern that might become suddenly, horribly, visible. Sophia Yevanova had asked him the question herself: *Where is the past? Where does it go?*

Wasn't that what he was going to Minsk to find out? He put on his headphones and pressed 'play'. As he flew over the plains of central Europe, Sophia Yevanova's voice carried him to the east, to the Kurapaty Forest:

195

It was towards the end of the winter, I remember, when Raina and I, we went into the forest. We were hungry and we were searching for food. It was cold, and the sun was low. We could hear the shooting, but we were used to it. We heard it so often, it was one of the sounds of the forest. It was getting dark so we turned for home, and then we realized that the shooting had stopped. You know how it is with sound. Sometimes you don't notice it until it stops. And that made us afraid.

Then we heard something else. It was strange, like crying, but muffled and weak. We searched, and we found him. He was a boy, no older than we were, leaning back against a tree. He had been shot and there was blood all over him, soaked into his shirt, and he was crying.

We went over to him – we were looking all the time for the soldiers. And I took his hand and he gripped mine tightly. And his eyes opened. But then we heard a truck. Raina grabbed my arm and pulled me away. He tried to hold on to me but he was too weak. She pulled me behind the bushes, and they came, the men, the NKVD men. They saw the boy, and they dragged him away by his feet. They threw him into the back of the truck and drove off . . .

Jake pressed 'pause' and let the images settle in his mind: the wounded boy, the soldiers with their casual brutality, and the two children hiding among the trees, watching, terrified. After Sophia had spoken, she had sat in silence, and hadn't objected when he poured her a glass of water from the jug that stood on the table beside her chair. She had drunk it almost as if she was no longer aware of his presence, then she had sat up and, without any comment, recommenced her story.

They tried to hide what they were doing. They put fences around the killing places, but the children – particularly the boys – cannot be kept away by such barriers. The children saw, and they told what they saw. The soldiers dug the pits in the early part of the day, and then the trucks came. All the time, we heard them. And the men shouting, dogs barking, and sometimes there would be screams that faded away to silence.

They lined them up in front of the grave pits, and they shot them through the head, from the side, so the bullet went through two people. Even with death, with killing, they were economical. And the ones who had been shot fell into the pit, this is what the boys said. Then when they had shot one batch, they threw earth into the pit, made it level and brought out the next to die. On and on. The boys said that the ground was stained with blood.

You must understand that, for some of us, the fascists came as liberators, at first.

Jake switched off the tape and leaned back in his seat. He was too cramped to stretch out fully, and his back was beginning to ache. He kept his mind on his plans for the book to distract him from the discomfort. He needed a starting place, and he needed to decide where it should end. He knew his audience – no matter how terrible the story he had to tell, he had to end on a note of optimism, of a better future to come.

Belarus was a place of despair, a country whose ghosts reached out from the shadows of a past it could not forget. For the people of Belarus, 1945 hadn't brought the liberation that Western Europe had enjoyed. They had been caught in the coils of an oppressive regime before the Nazi invasion, and had been returned to that regime at the end of the war. Prosperity had come eventually, flowered briefly, and then

197

the country had sunk again under the burden of Chernobyl, dictatorship and poverty.

His optimism had to focus not on a time or a place, but on a person. He could end at the point when Sophia Yevanova knew she was safe in England with her son, and though the young partisan who had fathered her child had not survived the war, at least his son lived. But for those who had been left behind, what had it all been for?

His audience didn't need to have that message thrust at them. From their point of view, Sophia's arrival and the birth of her son would mark the beginning of a new hope. That was the place to end his book. And the beginning? He would start in the Kurapaty Forest, today, with the memorial under the trees, and the crosses, disappearing into the forest shade.

He felt the slight vibration as the engine note changed. The past vanished, and he was back in his cramped seat. He gazed out of the window as the plane dropped through the cloud layer that thinned to a wispy mist, and the landscape appeared beneath him. Forest. Vast tracts of forest, marshland, rivers; a land that was flat as far as his eyes could see, covered with a mosaic of trees and wasteland, crisscrossed with rivers. Here and there, he could see small villages. Zialony Luh must have been just such a one. He could see roads, but they were mostly empty, and a railway – he watched a train apparently motionless on the line, falling away as the plane floated ahead and left it far behind.

The landscape tilted and filled Jake's window as the plane banked and turned. They were coming down, lower and lower, and he could see no sign of the city, no buildings, no roads. Lower and lower, and they were skimming the tree-tops. The sense of speed returned. Then the runway markers were blurring past underneath him as the plane touched down. The engines howled, reversing their thrust and Jake felt the deceleration push him out of his seat. Then they were taxiing to a halt at the terminal.

He had arrived. He was in Belarus, the country that had lost a quarter of its population in the last war, the country where Sophia Yevanova had been born.

But it wasn't her words that came into his mind. It was the words of a fairy tale he had seen just a few days before: *Once upon a time, deep in the dark forest where the bears roamed and the wolves hunted, there lived an evil witch . . .'*

He was in the country of Kurapaty.

On Sunday night, Faith had dreamed she was trying to escape through some kind of maze, and something dark and dangerous was close on her heels. It was as if the image of the Old Hall had stayed in her mind and become mixed up with the scene at Daniel's. When her alarm went off on Monday morning, she felt leaden-eyed with fatigue.

Everything looked dull in the grey daylight. She went downstairs and switched on the coffee machine. She was out of milk. She hadn't shopped at all at the weekend. She closed the fridge door wearily. Suddenly she was crying, the tears running down her face as she stood there in the middle of the empty kitchen. Helen was dead.

Then she changed her damp shirt, reapplied her make-up to disguise the reddening of her eyes, and set off for work. The image of the opaque water in the dam stayed in her mind as she drove, the way it had glittered as the ripples from the stone caught the light of the setting sun. That had been yesterday. Now she had to think about today.

When she got to the Centre, she dumped her bag and went downstairs to talk to the technicians. She wanted some add-ons for her computer. When she got to the basement, the room was empty apart from her post-grad student, Gregory Fellows, who was sitting at one of the work stations. He was wearing headphones and his eyes were closed. His body was moving in time to a rhythm only he could hear as he adjusted it on the keyboard. As she came in, he whispered, '*Yeah.*'

Then his eyes opened and he saw her. He took off the headphones. 'Faith,' he said. He sounded a bit uncertain.

'Morning, Gregory. Got everything sorted for your seminar?' She forgave herself a touch of schadenfreude when he looked guilty.

'It was just . . .' He shrugged. 'I'm writing something for a friend.' His face, normally cheerful, was closed and almost sullen. He pushed the heavy mop of fair hair out of his eyes and started to collect his things together. 'I'm going to start work on it now,' he said.

'Morning, Faith.' The technician came in carrying a cup of coffee. 'What can I do you for?' Faith explained quickly what she wanted, and he made some notes. 'I can get that for you,' he said.

She had an idea. 'While I'm here . . .' She explained about the paper she'd been looking for on Helen's disk. 'She must have printed it off and deleted it. I wondered if she left any back-ups with you?' It was an outside chance.

He shook his head. 'Sorry. There's never any need. The system backs up every night, so people don't bother.'

'Okay. I just thought I'd ask.'

'Hang on, though.' He went into the office, and came back a minute later carrying a CD. He looked triumphant. 'I'd forgotten. The morning it . . . you know . . . happened. I knew they were going to take her stuff, so I copied it off the tapes. As it turned out, the police left a copy, so . . . Anyway, the one I made is still here.'

He looked so pleased with himself that Faith didn't have the heart to tell him that she'd already got this on the disk that Trish had given her. 'Thanks,' she said.

Gregory was on his way out. He hesitated then waited as Faith came towards him. 'Could I have a word?'

She hoped it wasn't about the seminar. 'What is it, Gregory?'

'You were a friend of Helen's, weren't you?'

That was unexpected. 'Yes. I was at school with her.'

'I'm sorry. It's just – some of us, we wanted to go to the funeral, only we don't know . . .'

She looked at him. It was easy not to take Gregory seriously. He was fair-haired, well built and handsome, with a casual and laid-back attitude to life that was appealing, if infuriating. She reminded herself that, for all his faults, he was an intelligent, and probably a sensitive young man. 'I think the family want it to be just them. I don't think I'll be going either.'

He started to say something, then changed his mind. He gave her a half-smile and turned away towards the stairs. 'I'll see you,' he said, and was gone.

Back in her room, she looked at the disk the technician had given her, spinning it between her fingers as she thought. This disk would be the same as the one she already had. But optimistic superstition made her put it into the drive and open it.

And there it was. The first folder was labelled 'Working Files'. This was how Helen always labelled her current work. She stared at it in incomprehension, then checked the stored data. The files had last been worked on the day Helen died. So why hadn't they been on the disk that the police gave to Trish?

This disk was a copy of whatever had been on Helen's computer the evening she died . . . No, the police came to the Centre the following day, two days after Helen's death. The system would have backed up, and then, as there had been no activity on Helen's terminal the following day, it would have deleted everything and backed up again. The technician had taken this copy the morning the police came and collected Helen's things – so this was the copy the police had. The disk that Trish had given her was the one that was different.

As she rubbed her eyes, trying to make sense of it, she saw Trish holding the disk out to her with that odd smile. Trish

201

had not liked Helen. She had seemed determined to cause Helen trouble at every opportunity. She didn't pass on messages that hadn't come through the correct channels, she made sure that Antoni Yevanov knew about late arrivals and non-attendances. It sounded petty – it was petty – but it also had the potential to cause damage.

And now, Antoni Yevanov wanted Helen's paper to go to Bonn. Would Trish's dislike of her extend to making sure that it didn't, now Helen was dead? Faith ran her fingers through her hair. She didn't like what she was thinking.

She decided she'd better see what it was she actually had. She opened the folder. Helen's draft was there, just as it should have been: 'Women and Totalitarianism – A Liberation Denied'. Helen's draft. Someone had deleted the file from the disk the police had made.

There was a second file, labelled 'Document'. She opened it, wondering if this was also relevant to the Bonn paper. It should be – there was nothing else Helen had been working on, apart from her teaching. It contained a paper that Helen had probably downloaded from the internet: 'Lithuanian Responses to Nazi Occupation'. Now she understood. After Daniel had destroyed the papers she'd found in his parents' attic, Helen must have been looking for her children's past, wanting to find out what kind of background, what kind of legacy her children's great-grandparents had left them. Curious, Faith started to read.

A Lithuanian Schutzmannschaft Battalion (later known as the 12th) was detailed from Kaunsas in October 1941. The arrival of the Lithuanian battalion coincided with a murderous wave of killings in the area in October 1941 . . . She frowned, puzzled. If Helen had been looking for her children's heritage, this surely wasn't anything she would want them to have. She went on reading. It wasn't an academic paper, it was a series of eye-witness accounts. *Klava and Nura were the first to die . . . From Ostrov, a procession of soldiers*

202

went to the next village. The executioners stopped at a barn and put up two nooses . . . Nadehzhda was almost unconscious before she was hanged . . . She didn't want to read this. Her eyes skimmed down the page: *. . . ordered a fourteen-year-old girl to be hanged. They had the man ask the child in her own language if she understood that she was going to be hanged. She said she understood it . . . most being simply buried alive, the bloodstained earth above them heaving for hours after the event.*

Faith closed the file and stared at the blank screen. This wasn't for the children. What had Helen been doing? Where had all this stuff come from? The images conjured up by the words resonated in her mind. She should know the figures, she'd seen them often enough. They paraded in graphs and charts through her mind: *population displacement, demographic change, industrial production index, patterns of refugee dispersal, political blocs, economic blocs.* And another set of figures: five million dead in Poland, seven million dead in the USSR . . .

It was as if the whole of Europe had been participants in some vast, deadly game, and when the music stopped, half the chairs were empty. Half the players had gone.

Minsk was enjoying an unseasonable spring. Jake sat in the window of his room watching the light over the parkland as he made his phone calls. Adam was pleased to hear from him. 'You did not get arrested!' he said. Jake wasn't sure if this was a joke or not. They arranged to meet in a café on the main street, Praspekt Francyska Skaryny. 'The Pechki-Lavochki,' Adam said. 'Walk to the end of Masherova and up the hill on Lenina. It's near the metro, on the other side of the street from the McDonald's. I am the small man with the grey hair and beard.'

Jake described himself as tall, with brown hair. 'I'll be wearing a black leather jacket,' he said.

He let himself out of his room, aware of the scrutiny of a woman who peered at him from a cubbyhole along the corridor. A cleaner? The carpet was worn and the paint chipped. The elevator lobby was dark and smelled of cigarettes, and the lift clanked and rattled its way to the ground floor. He was amused by the way the building transformed as he came out into the entrance lobby – high-ceilinged luxury, with marble floors, plush settees and uniformed staff. He was beginning to think that he might enjoy Minsk. He stepped out of the hotel to take his first look at the city.

Against all his expectations, he found it beautiful. It was a clear, bright day, and he was greeted by wide streets, bare trees and parkland, and the glitter of water from the river that wound through the city. The skies were blue. But despite the low volume of traffic, the air smelled tainted.

The streets were busy. He wove through the crowds, observing the people who were strolling along the boulevard enjoying the warmth. The young women were lovely. All of them. He watched a group walking ahead of him, stylishly dressed in minute skirts or tight trousers with restrained flares. If this was Belarusian womanhood, then no wonder Sophia Yevanova was so beautiful. And he thought he saw, in the high cheekbones and the tilt of the eyes, an echo of Faith Lange. In the entrance to an underpass, a woman sold flowers, surrounded by shoeless children. There were a few old women wrapped in shawls, one, outside a church, was holding a decorated prayer card and, as far as Jake could tell, offering prayers for money. He gave her a five-hundred rouble note. He probably needed a blessing.

He listened to the voices around him, picking up the rhythm of the Russian, aware of how inadequate his own command of the language was. The street signs and the buses and the minimal advertising were all written in Cyrillic. He had never

204

properly mastered the written language and he felt like a semi-literate as he had to stop and concentrate, carefully spelling out each sign.

According to his map, Praspekt Francyska Skaryny linked five of the main squares of the city. It was a wide, elegant street with buildings that looked as if they dated back to earlier centuries. Jake felt a lift of optimism – maybe the reports were wrong, and substantial parts of Sophia's city remained – until he looked more closely and saw the telltale signs of pastiche.

Following Adam's instructions, he crossed the street and found a series of cafés – an authentic-looking pizza establishment that boasted a wood-burning stove, a Spanish restaurant, and the Russian café that Adam had proposed as their meeting place.

He pushed open the door, and was greeted by a waiter in a red check waistcoat. The young man gave Jake the first smile he'd received that day. He had marked the Belarusians as dour – and they had probably marked him as a grinning fool. He gestured to the youth to wait and looked round quickly until he saw a man with grey hair and a beard watching him expressionlessly from a table in the back of the room.

'There is my friend,' he said in his halting Russian, thankful that Adam's English, judging by their phone call, was good. He'd already found that there were few English speakers in Minsk.

The grey-haired man had risen to greet him. Jake went across. 'I'm Jake Denbigh,' he said.

'Adam Zuygev,' the man said. Then he smiled. 'You wear the biker's jacket.'

He had a cup of coffee in front of him, and ordered coffee for Jake. 'This is our first meeting. We need vodka.' He summoned the waiter again.

Jake didn't want to drink this early in the day, but he didn't demur. He let the waiter put a glass in front of him and fill it with clear, pungent liquid.

Adam raised his glass and said, 'Cheers.'

Jake grinned and raised his in response. 'Cheers,' he said, and when Adam downed the vodka in one swallow, he did the same. He felt the liquid burn its way down his throat, and then felt the sudden lift as the alcohol entered his system.

To his relief, the other man didn't order a refill. Instead, he pulled some papers out of his briefcase, and looked ready for business. He indicated their glasses. 'Later,' he said.

'Later,' Jake agreed. He didn't mind getting wrecked in a good cause.

And Adam had worked hard for him. Jake had asked for all the information he could find about Sophia Yevanova and her family, about Kurapaty, about the perpetrators and about the victims. And about the Nazi occupation. Miss Yevanova might not want to talk about it, but Jake wanted to see what records were left.

'I did not find all you wanted,' Adam said, 'but the archive . . .' he pronounced it *archeev* '. . . committee at Hrodna have sent me these –' He laid out photocopies of what looked like legal documents and certificates.

Jake looked at them. The entries were handwritten in fine italic that was hard for him to read. Adam, watching him, smiled. 'I have translated,' he said. 'See? Here –' he showed Jake a certificate – 'is the birth of your lady Sophia Yevanova. And here, her cousin, Raina Yevanova. Now, we do not have public records of Sophia after 1945, but you may be sure that the KGB will have known where she went.'

Jake knew that Sophia Yevanova, as a post-war refugee and prisoner of the Nazis, would have faced re-education in a gulag had she returned home. 'Her parents?' he said. She had never said anything about what had happened to them. He wondered if they had known that their daughter had survived, and that they had a grandson.

206

Adam spread his hands. 'Who knows? There are no records of them from before the invasion. They sent their child away – they may have been arrested, sent for re-education. Or . . .' Or they might lie in the mass graves under the trees of the Kurapaty Forest. 'So many records were destroyed.'

Jake thought about the way that Sophia Yevanova's face settled into a blank mask when she talked about her past. If her parents had been murdered because of their attempts to protect her, then she would have carried that burden for the rest of her life. It might also explain her fierce loyalty to the child of her friend. She was making restitution for a crime that had not been her responsibility.

'And Raina?' he said.

'Ah, here I have information,' Adam said. He grimaced. 'It is not a good story. Raina Yevanova was found guilty of collaborating with the fascist invaders and was sent to a gulag after the war, where she died in . . .' He turned over the paper. 'In 1946. But there was something I found . . .' He was looking through the pile of material in front of him. 'I have it here,' he said. 'Yes. I thought you would like to see . . .' He pushed a photograph across the table to Jake.

It was faded picture of two girls dressed in white with lacy veils over their hair. There was a handwritten inscription and Jake practised his growing facility with Cyrillic by reading it. It was easier when you knew what it said: R. Yevanova, S. Yevanova. The girls looked as though they were dressed for some kind of religious ceremony. He recognized Sophia at once – the perfection of the bone structure had been apparent even in childhood. She was dark-eyed, delicate, with long hair hanging round her shoulders. Raina was bigger and plumper, a pretty child with fair hair in braids and round eyes in a round face.

They looked so young, maybe just in their teens. The photo must have been taken around the time Sophia went to live in Zialony Luh, in Kurapaty. And just a few years later, Sophia had been a pregnant refugee, and Raina was struggling to survive in the nightmare of the Soviet camps.

'You feel pity for her?' Adam said.

Jake nodded. He didn't think he would have been brave at that age.

Adam was silent for a while. 'I was born after the war,' he said. 'But my parents lived through it. They are dead now, both of them. But they told me about the collaborators, the people who turned on their own countrymen. The children were brave, and the Nazis, they ordered them to be hanged on the streets. It was their policy, part of the terror they wanted to create. There was a proclamation that was enforced from the start: "The youth of the perpetrators will not protect them from the full payment of the death penalty." In 1941, they executed – they murdered – sixteen and seventeen year olds. And sometimes it was our people who carried out those orders. Go to the Museum of the Great Patriotic War, then you will understand. And Raina Yevanova . . .' He met Jake's gaze. 'Some of those who were sent to the gulags were not true collaborators. Many did no more than take employment with the Nazis. Some of those who had been imprisoned were seen as tainted and sent to the gulags as well. But Raina Yevanova – she did more than collaborate. She betrayed her own people. It was her information that led to the arrest of Sophia. She was lucky to live.'

After all these years, collaboration with the Nazis was still the unforgivable crime. Jake wondered what kind of history could underlie such bitterness and such an inability to forget, or to forgive.

Raina had betrayed Sophia. He thought about Sophia's story of Raina drawing her away from the window and the sounds of the forest, of Raina making her leave the wounded boy as the truck full of soldiers came into view. He thought about what Raina had seen and what she had experienced. Sophia had known: *You must understand that, for some of us, the fascists came as liberators, at first.*

208

He shook his head. The story of human evil had been told so often it had become almost banal. It was not the fair-haired child in the picture under his hands who had been evil, but the system that had made her so. Sophia Yevanova had not condemned her, and he couldn't find it in himself to do so either.

He remembered his plan to ask Adam about Marek Lange – to see what the archives might reveal about that family. He hadn't forgotten his intention to try to pin down Lange's origins, and this looked like a good starting point. But first of all, he wanted to find out exactly what Lange had been doing in Minsk. He took out the photograph of the young man in uniform and showed it to Adam, who looked at it with raised eyebrows. 'Interesting,' he said.

'I know who it is,' Jake said, 'but I don't know what it is. I was told it was taken in Minsk, but I don't know if it's possible to tell.'

'You English should learn your languages better,' Adam said. 'The picture tells you, almost. Yes, this was taken in Minsk. I have seen pictures of this building before. Look at the writing on the door – it tells you all you need to know.'

Jake took the photograph back and looked more closely. The initials HK were all he could see, and, yes, something that could be a B. He shook his head to indicate to Adam that he was no wiser.

Adam laughed quietly. 'The sign – it tells you that this building is the headquarters of the People's Commissariat of Internal Affairs.'

He looked at Jake as though he expected him to understand the significance of what he had said. Jake shrugged. 'I don't get it,' he said.

'This is a soldier of the Commissariat, wearing their uniform,' Adam said. 'And the sign –' He wrote the symbols down and pushed the paper across to Jake: НКВД.

Cyrillic. Of course! Shit, it was obvious . . .

He thought about Marek Lange looking out of the window, and heard his voice: *It is wrong. I know!* He remembered Faith, her head bent over the photograph, her face intent. *He brought me up. He's more like my father.* And he remembered Sophia Yevanova sitting upright in her chair, her eyes staring into the past as she talked about the mist rising from the ground one icy winter night, the breath of prisoners crammed into the cellars awaiting their deaths.

And the strange symbols spelled out their message as he looked at them, under Adam's attentive gaze.

NKVD.

At the time the photograph was taken, Marek Lange had been in Minsk, as a soldier of the NKVD.

15

Faith spent the morning clearing the backlog of work from her desk. She rearranged all her meetings, organized the new schedule for the post-graduate seminars, and arranged cover for Helen's teaching. That was a task she had dreaded, but in the end, it was like everything else, routine. The wheels of working life had slotted back into the groove. After lunch, she phoned to arrange an appointment with Antoni Yevanov.

'He's in meetings all afternoon,' Trish said.

'Tomorrow, then. It's important. It's about the paper for Bonn.'

'Are you having problems?'

Faith didn't want to discuss it. 'I need to talk to Professor Yevanov.'

Trish promised to try and fit her in, and Faith put the phone down. She leaned back in her chair and massaged the back of her neck. Now she had a moment of quiet, she could no longer block out the thing she had been working to avoid: Daniel's face, cold with anger as he told her to get out of the house and stay away from the children. It wasn't the anger that had disturbed her – it was the intent she had seen in his eyes when he gripped her arm. He was capable of violence.

But even after the events of the day before, she found it

hard to believe that Daniel Kovacs, the man she had known for over a decade, was capable of brutal, calculated murder. She needed to talk to Finn, to establish a line of contact.

And she'd thought of a way she could reach him. She checked the time. It was just after three. She saved Helen's files on to a disk and put it into her bag. She was about to switch her computer off, then – telling herself she was being paranoid – she changed the password giving access to her data. She packed her things together and headed for the car park.

Finn's school was on the other side of the town, on the Huddersfield Road. She'd timed her arrival well. As she approached it, she began to see groups of teenagers coming out of the gates, girls with their skirts hiked up to a fashionable length, their sleeves casually pushed back, their shirts open at the neck. They wore their uniform with cool aplomb, unlike the boys, who mostly looked young and scruffy.

Faith drove slowly past the groups ambling along the pavement. She pulled in further down the road where she could keep an eye on the gate. It was hard to see through the throngs of children who now came pouring out, reminding her of the crowds in the city centre on Saturday night. They pushed, shouted, chased, occasionally shoving past her car, ignoring the adult usurper in their domain. She stayed where she was, watching. A couple of times, she thought she saw Finn, but it was always another dark-haired boy. She was beginning to think that she must have missed him, when she saw him coming out of the newsagents on the other side of the road.

He was with a group of boys who clustered together on the grass verge. He had his father's build, a shorter, stocky figure, standing slightly apart from his friends. His arms were wrapped round his chest, and he was staring into the distance, a worried frown creasing his face. She wound down the window and called to him. 'Finn?'

He looked round, puzzled. He didn't see her until one of

212

his companions nudged him and pointed at her. He started to smile in recognition, then chewed his lip and hesitated. She got out of the car and he came slowly towards her. 'Hi,' he said. He looked round for his friends who were melting away into the background. 'What d'you want?' He sounded a bit wary, but she could detect no hostility in his voice. Daniel obviously hadn't said anything to him about the events of the day before.

'I was just passing and I saw you,' she said.

He pulled a packet of sweets out of his pocket and held it out to her. 'Want one?'

Faith inspected the contents with their jumble of pinks, yellows and purples, almost fluorescent in their brightness. 'No thanks. I don't want to start glowing in the dark. What are they?'

He pushed the bag into his pocket. He was starting to smile now. 'Okay, I'll have something green, if you're buying.'

She raised an eyebrow. 'Exactly how stupid do you think I am?'

His grin widened, and he looked like the Finn she knew. 'That's what I'm trying to find out.'

She feigned a swipe at him with her bag, and he ducked, laughing. For a moment, it was like it always used to be. 'How's it going?' she said.

He came and stood beside her, leaning against the car. His face was serious again. 'I dunno. It's just . . . you know.'

'I don't think I do.' She watched the other children drifting away down the road outside the school playground, shouting, pushing, fighting. 'My mum hasn't died.'

'What about your dad?'

She shook her head. 'I don't know. I've never met him.'

'Wow.' He thought about this. 'That's tough.'

'Not really. I never knew him, so I don't miss him. It's my granddad I'd miss.'

'Yeah? I wouldn't miss mine.' He gave her a quick glance.

213

His eyes were nearly level with hers. 'Faith . . .' he began, then stopped.

'What?' she said.

He shook his head. 'Nothing.'

She waited, but he stayed quiet. 'Listen, Finn, if there's anything you need to talk about, you can talk to me, you know that, don't you?'

'I know.' He was looking at the ground, pushing at the grass with his shoe. He looked so troubled that she wanted to press him, to try to persuade him to tell her what it was that was worrying him. She wanted to tell him that she would keep it to herself, that anything he told her would be just between the two of them. But suppose he told her that his father had left the house the night his mother died . . . she couldn't make that promise.

'If I want . . .' he began. 'Can I have your number? Your mobile? I haven't got that.'

'Of course.' She got out her purse and gave him her card with all her numbers on. 'Just call me if you need anything.'

He took it and studied it. 'Does this mean you won't be coming round any more?'

She wondered how to answer that. 'I will. Of course I will. But I think your dad needs a bit of time.'

'He's pissed off with you, isn't he?'

'Yes. He is.'

'Why?'

'Lots of things, Finn. I think it's because he was angry with your mum, and I was her friend . . .'

He nodded as if this made sense. 'She phoned,' he said abruptly.

She . . . 'Your mum?' Faith could feel her heart beating faster.

'Yeah.' He glanced at her, then looked down at the ground. 'They argued. They always . . . I wanted to ask Dad why they always had to fight, but one of his mates came round so I

214

couldn't.' He shrugged angrily. 'I could have talked to her,' he said. 'But I didn't.'

Guilt. He felt guilty because he hadn't talked to his mother and it had been his last chance. He was watching her with an oddly speculative gaze, as if he was trying to gauge her reaction to his words. 'You weren't to know,' she said. 'How could you?'

'Yeah.' The boy looked and sounded so like his father that it unnerved her. He glanced towards his friends, who were lurking protectively in the background. He wanted to go back to them.

'How's Hannah?' she said. 'Is she okay?'

He didn't meet her eye. 'She's all right.'

'Tell her I'll come and see her as soon as I can.'

'Yeah. Okay. I've got to go.'

She touched his arm briefly. It was all she could do. She couldn't hug him in front of his friends. 'Remember,' she said. 'If you need me . . .'

'I'll remember.'

She watched him as he walked away across the road.

As she drove home, her mind unpicked the conversation with Finn. She had one cause for relief. He hadn't been the only witness to his father's presence in the house that evening. Someone else had been there, some friend of Daniel's who had dropped in for a drink.

But there was still the problem of Hannah. It had disturbed Faith the way the child had insisted that her mother would be back. Could a six-year-old encompass the idea of death? She didn't think that Daniel had the remotest idea of how to deal with this. There seemed to be no way to get to Hannah past her father's vigilance, no way that didn't run the risk of subjecting the children to a display of his anger. Time. Maybe Daniel would relent in time.

When she got home, she made herself a sandwich, and forced herself to think about work, about the project she had so blithely taken on for Antoni Yevanov. She decided to spend the evening sorting out the stuff that she'd collected from Helen's – she'd put it off for too long as it was.

She went through to the front room and started work. A lot of it was simple – Faith soon had the papers in two piles, one, a large one, for disposal and one, much smaller, for checking. It was all old stuff. There was very little that was worth keeping. Her hands felt dry from the dust that seemed to accumulate on old papers.

At the bottom of the last box was a folder. It looked recent – it was clean, and the writing on it wasn't faded. It was labelled, in Helen's handwriting, 'Family'. Faith wiped her hands on her jeans and opened it. At first, she thought there was nothing inside it, but when she lifted the flap, she found a thin sheaf of letters. She looked at the first one:

Dear Ms Kovacs
Thank you for your enquiry. I am pleased that you are
interested in my collection, but I am afraid you will
have to be more specific about what you wish to find.
My archive is very large. It is not catalogued and I can't
allow indiscriminate searches through it.
    If you can give me more information, I will try to
help you.
    Yours truly
    G. Litkin

Gennady Litkin, the man who had put together the Litkin Archive. Faith rubbed her hand across her forehead, frowning. Helen had never mentioned being in correspondence with Litkin. She looked at the next letter.

Dear Ms Kovacs
I have some records from pre-war Lithuania. They may
be of some use to you in a general way, if not in relation

216

to your family. If you can give me a clearer idea of the focus of your research, I will be able to answer your questions more closely.

I have some photographs of Vilnius in 1940, and I have political pamphlets. I also have some personal papers relating to the last war, and other miscellany, if this would be of interest.

Now Faith understood Helen's interest in the Litkin Archive. As she had suspected when she saw the material Helen had collected, she had been trying to find substitutes for the papers that Daniel had burned. She read Litkin's letter again. If he'd been trying to interest Helen in the archive, he couldn't have found a better way . . . *some personal papers* . . . Helen had been obsessed with old papers. She collected memorabilia, the artefacts of the past. She got excited over tea stains on letters, pencilled notes in the margins of books, scribbled diaries of the minutiae of existence. She wouldn't have been able to resist the lure.

Dear Ms Kovacs
You are correct that this is an area that is little researched. This is one of the reasons I began my archive.

I have items I can make available that may give your children information about their cultural background at some time in the future. As to your request to look at the papers, I will need to think about this. I have to be careful about allowing access to my library. Not all researchers are benign.

Faith was frowning as she stared at the letter. Helen, with her work falling seriously behind, had been prepared to spend time negotiating with Litkin for access to papers because they may have had some faint relevance to her children. It didn't make sense. There must have been something else. Helen had talked to Faith about her next project, about hunting round for ideas that would engage her interest and attract funding. The unarchived Litkin collection would have been a good place to start.

There was another letter, dated a few weeks later:

I have papers relating to the period you mention. There is a wartime diary that you may find illuminating, and some linked correspondence. I should perhaps caution you, given your family connections, that not all stories that come from that place and that time are happy ones. Lithuania was invaded first by the USSR before the Nazis drove the communists out, and this led to some unfortunate alliances. But you must judge for yourself.

    In response to your other query, the only materials I have are a set of workers' records from a nineteenth-century mining company. Perhaps we could talk on the telephone about this.

Faith could feel her legs starting to cramp. She stood up and stretched, then took the folder to the table where she could read the rest of the correspondence in comfort. The records from the mining company were Helen's ostensible reason for visiting the archive, and the Lithuanian stuff was – presumably – for Hannah and Finn. Whatever else it was Helen had been looking for, the correspondence ended here. She and Litkin may have continued their discussion by phone, but the next letter was from a firm of solicitors:

Dear Mrs Kovacs
We regret to inform you that access to the papers of the late Gennady Litkin cannot be granted under the conditions you outline, as you did not obtain written authority from Mr Litkin prior to his death. The estate

is currently being wound up, and you will need to get permission from the court-appointed executors.

The letter went on to name them, the first one being, as Faith already knew, Antoni Yevanov. She felt as though she had gone round a large circle and come back to the beginning.

The Beginning

This is the story of the storm in the forest.

The year made patterns. Spring would come, the fruit trees would blossom, the rain would fall and the forest would blur into green. The skies would be blue at the start of the endless summer when the river was warm and the fields were busy and the days were long. And then before Eva realized it, the fields were golden and then they were bare, and winter came again as the world closed down for its long silence.

But now, the patterns were broken. In the winter of 1938, Mama became ill. Eva still went to school, but she looked after Mama and Marek. She prepared the food and cooked it. She watched the stores and mended the clothes, she swept the house and washed the pots. The January snows came and went. Marek brought her a red hair-ribbon for her birthday. 'Because you are pretty, little one.'

She was thirteen. She tied the ribbon in a butterfly bow at the side of her head and wrapped Mama's lace shawl round her shoulders. She tilted the dresser mirror, trying to see her reflection. Her hair curled round her face. Under the draping lace, her shoulders looked white and slender, and her neck arched above.

She stepped back, and the woman in the glass became a child in a heavy skirt and boots with grubby hands, an incongruous shawl draped round her. She let it slip off, holding it as if she was going to drop it on the floor, then she folded it carefully, burying her face in its softness, breathing in the scent of lavender.

Times were hard. The police had come for Papa, and had taken him away. And there was fear throughout the village. Across the border, far away in the west, something dreadful was coming, and Eva woke in the night sometimes, with the memory of stealthy feet in their relentless pursuit echoing through her dreams. Marek's face was grim when he and the men from the village talked, their differences forgotten.

He tried to keep his worries secret from her and from Mama. Mama, coughing in the night and flushed and feverish in the day, was unaware, but Eva knew. 'What?' she said to him. 'What?'

'Too much work.' He gave her a ghost of his usual grin. 'Without Papa, it's hard. And we are short of money. Nothing we haven't dealt with before, little one.'

But it was more than that, she knew it.

Marek started talking to Mama about her family. Mama had a sister, Zoya, Eva's aunt, who lived in Minsk. 'Maybe you and Eva should go to Zoya,' he said.

Mama shook her head. 'How can we? And Zoya says that times are hard there, too.'

As the spring became summer, Marek's face grew thinner and more drawn. Eva worked, and slowly, Mama's health improved.

'She must rest,' Marek warned Eva.

'I know.' She was mending a seam that had worn away on one of Marek's shirts. 'Marek?' she said.

'What is it, little one?'

'Is there going to be a war?'

'Why are you asking me?' he said. 'I just . . .'

'Marek. I know what's happening. And Mila . . .' Mila was her friend. 'Mila says she's afraid of what they will do if they come here.'

He sighed. 'Yes. And . . . Eva, it will go badly for people

220

like us, too, like Papa, like me – and maybe for you and Mama. I want you to listen.'

She pulled the thread tight to make the seam strong. Marek was talking to her, telling her things. 'I'm listening,' she said.

'The fascist armies – if it comes from the west it will be the fascists. They hate the Jews – that's why Mila is afraid. And they hate the communists, like us. Papa thought that we should try and cross the border, go to Zoya in Minsk. You'll be safe there, you and Mama.'

'And you? And Papa?'

He laughed, but it didn't sound like his real laugh. It sounded sad. 'I would join the army. And Papa.'

Eva looked across to the chair by the fire where Mama was asleep. 'But Papa's in prison.' She kept her voice low.

'Don't say anything yet, but he may be coming home,' Marek said. 'We've been doing some work. But if not – Eva, I think we will have to go to Minsk. It won't be safe here.'

But the year wore on, and Papa didn't come home.

Then one night in August, Eva was waiting in the house. Mama had caught a bad cold that had left her with a cough she couldn't shake off. She was resting. Eva had collected wood from the shed before the light went and stacked it by the stove. She fed the hens and secured their cages. Marek had gone out hours before. He hadn't said where he was going.

The autumn storms had come early that year. The day had been heavy and oppressive, and now the evening was filled with a sense of waiting. The air was still and breathless. Mama was dozing in her chair. Eva sat by the window, mending some shirts and watching the light fade into the summer night as the moon rose. Black clouds were gathering in the sky, and the air was electric. She could smell the storm coming. Marek was late. It wasn't safe to be out in the forest in the storm.

The clouds rolled in across the moon, and then something

split the night from top to bottom in a dazzle of white light that faded to blackness, and then the thunder crashed. The winds came with a roar. The trees were whipped and tossed, their branches lashing through the air. And the rain came, chilling the warm night like death. And somewhere, in the wildness of the storm, in the deep glades of the forest, something raised its head and tested the air.

Baba Yaga was waiting.

Eva put the lamp in the window to guide Marek home, but the rain fell in sheets through the black night. The thunder roared again. Mama's eyes opened and she murmured, 'Stanislau . . . ?'

'It's all right.' Eva got her shawl and wrapped it round Mama's shoulders. 'It's . . .' She went to the window and peered through the shutters again, aware of Mama stirring behind her.

The rain was a continuous drumming on the roof, and the roar of the wind drowned out any sound. Eva and Mama looked at each other. 'Marek?' Mama said.

'He hasn't come back.' Eva's whisper filled the room in a moment of silence.

Mama stood up. 'Where's my coat?' she said.

'You can't,' Eva said. 'You can't go out there. I'll go. I'll find him.' She was pulling on her boots as she spoke, throwing open the door.

And then the thunder and the lightning came together in the loudest crash of all, the white light coming straight down out of the sky, turning the night into stark day. And in the yard there were two people, huddled together, frozen in the instant before the light went and the blackness returned.

Mama stood quite still, her hand to her throat. Her eyes were huge.

Eva stood in the doorway, and out of the night, the two figures stumbled: Marek, tall and strong, supporting the other man who breathed hard as though he had run a long race.

Papa.

Marek had brought Papa home.

'Stanislau!' Mama said. For a moment, her voice shook, then she was herself again. She brought blankets. 'Marek,' she said. 'You too. You're soaked, both of you. Here, by the stove.' She wouldn't sit down, but pushed them into the warmth. The movement made her cough.

'We have to go,' Marek said. 'Before they find out.' As he talked, Eva realized what he had done. He had arranged with a sympathetic policeman for Papa to leave after his visit to the police headquarters, as though he wasn't already an imprisoned man. 'They are so pressed, they may not realize, they may not even come after him, but I have to get him away.'

'I know some people,' Papa said. 'But wait.' He put his arms round Mama, and round Eva, and hugged them. 'Marek will go with you to Minsk, to Zoya,' he said. 'I'll get there. You mustn't worry.'

Papa was back. Marek had brought him back. Eva wasn't worried.

They were going away. They were going somewhere safe.

16

When Faith arrived at work on Tuesday morning, everything seemed so normal that she thought the events of the previous week must have been a dream. Groups of students assembled in the lobby, talking and laughing, a new display of posters brightened the noticeboards. The receptionists sat behind their glass window, answering phones, working at keyboards, getting on with the routine of the working day. It was as if time had split open and she had fallen through the gap, as if none of it had happened and it was all still to come, Helen's death, the police, Grandpapa's roses, cut to the ground, the opaque waters of the dam shattering into dancing reflections as the stone hit the surface, Finn's voice: *I could have talked to her*. She walked through the lobby towards the lifts, answering the usual morning greetings with a nod and a smile that felt frozen on her face.

When she got to her room, it was just after nine. The first thing she did was to phone Grandpapa. These days, she found herself checking up on him more and more frequently. 'I am well, little one,' he said in answer to her query. 'And you? You sound tired.'

'I am a bit.' She hadn't told him about Helen, and she wasn't going to. 'I'll be all right.'

224

'You are coming tonight?' he said. 'I make you something nice and we have the wine.'

He'd forgotten. 'Tomorrow. We said tomorrow, Wednesday.'

'Tomorrow, then,' he said. 'You are coming?'

'Of course I am, but why don't we make it tonight instead?' She didn't like it that he was losing track of the days. Ever since Jake Denbigh had interviewed him, there had been something odd, something out of kilter.

'No. Tomorrow. As we agree. I make the treat.'

'What's wrong with tonight? It'll be better for me, actually.'

'No, little one. If tomorrow is difficult, then you come next week.'

Game, set and match to Grandpapa, as usual. She sighed with exasperation. 'Tomorrow, then,' she conceded reluctantly. 'Shall I bring some wine?'

'Yes, yes, that is good. Let me see . . .' He fussed for a few minutes about what she should bring. She knew that age had more or less destroyed his palate, but he still enjoyed the ritual. When she rang off, she felt a bit better about him, her sense of unease assuaged by the normality of their conversation.

There was a message on her desk to let her know that Antoni Yevanov could see her at four thirty that afternoon. She thought carefully about what to say to him. She could report good progress on Helen's paper – it was, to all intents and purposes, complete. But she had to tell him about the missing file, and that would be more difficult. She would effectively be accusing someone of tampering with the disk. She had no proof that it had been Trish, and she wasn't going to make that accusation, but it would be there by implication.

Her morning was taken up by one of those meetings where no one seemed to have much to say but used as many words as possible to say it. She could feel the glaze of boredom forming over her eyes as she struggled to pay attention. She doodled rose vines down the side of her notes, and watched the clock as it dragged round to the end of the morning.

The meeting finished at one, and they emerged from the room dazzled and confused like animals emerging from a long hibernation. Faith had to get out. She detached herself briskly from the meeting post-mortem and went out on to the campus. She decided to skip lunch and pay a visit to the nearby art gallery. They had an exhibition of Russian icons that she'd been meaning to see.

The gallery stood in a small garden surrounded by a white wall and railings. The grass was flat and dispirited, as if struggling for life in the pollution from the constant traffic. The gallery itself was light and airy, and the silence that closed round Faith as the doors swung shut behind her was soothing. Art galleries were places that were out of the world, out of time. She could hear the measured footsteps of the other visitors, and the low murmur of voices.

She went straight to the room where the icons were exhibited. The walls glowed with colour, but as she looked more closely, she found their stylized inhumanity chilling. The icons depicted religious scenes, the Crucifixion, the Madonna and Child, the Adoration. From icon after icon, the figure of Christ gazed at her dispassionately from the cross, the Virgin watched with empty eyes, the Christ-child gazed out into the world from an old man's face. The colours had the icy brilliance of jewels.

There was only one other person in this part of the gallery. As she moved round the room, she was aware of a tall man in a dark suit with a trench coat slung round his shoulders, standing in front of a triptych of the Fall. She glanced at him, then looked again. It was Antoni Yevanov. He was absorbed in the painting, his patrician face as cold and distant as the icons themselves.

He didn't look as though he would welcome company, and neither would she. She had seen what she came to see, so she withdrew quietly. When she got back to the Centre, she saw Trish entering the lobby in the company of Gregory Fellows. They were talking animatedly, and Trish looked flushed and pretty. As Faith came nearer, she heard Gregory say, 'I thought you'd like to know.'

'Well, thanks Gregory.' Trish looked up and saw Faith, and the animation died from her eyes. She gave a nod of acknowledgement. Gregory's gaze dropped, and he went towards the basement without acknowledging Faith.

The work had piled up on Faith's desk while she'd been out. By the time she'd worked her way through it, it was time for her meeting with Yevanov. She collected her notes, checked through them quickly and went down to his office. Trish was back at her desk, and the look she gave Faith was cool and impersonal. She picked up the phone to let Yevanov know that Faith was there. 'You can go straight in,' she said.

Yevanov's greeting was brisk. He directed her to a seat and took a folder marked 'Bonn' out of his in-tray. 'There has been a slight change,' he said. 'I have explained the situation to the organizers. They have suggested that you give a paper on your own work in the slot that was allocated for Helen, and present her paper as a poster. That way, it will be included in the proceedings.'

Faith nodded. It made sense and it made her task easier. She told him what progress she'd made, and that she was confident that she could now get the paper finished. 'And I found some letters to Helen from Gennady Litkin,' she said. 'But they didn't give any idea of what she was looking for that night.'

He raised an eyebrow. 'But she was looking for something? Other than data for her paper?'

'I think so.' Faith told him briefly about what she had found.

He sighed. 'Maybe the police have been able to follow it up. It was an ill-fated piece of research. I wish . . .' He shook his head. 'I was surprised when you told me you had found Helen's draft. Trish told me you were having some difficulty.'

'I was, at first.' She'd been wondering about the best way to bring this up, and explained quickly how she had got the copy of Helen's documents.

He was sitting with his chin resting on his hand, his curled finger against his mouth. His face hardened as she spoke, and she realized that he was not a man to antagonize. She remembered the question the young policeman had asked her about Yevanov's relationship with Helen and, looking at him now, she wondered how likely that seemed.

He would have been a hazardous choice for the happy-go-lucky Helen. Faith admired and respected him, but he was a private and complex man. If she were venturing on to the emotional quicksand of a relationship with someone like this, Faith would have retreated, warned off by the danger signals that were clear enough to read. But maybe that would have drawn Helen; she had, after all, chosen a cold and emotionally withdrawn man as a husband and father to her children.

He didn't comment when she had finished. 'I see,' was all he said. Whatever action he had decided to take, he was keeping to himself. 'Is everything else progressing well? Have you given any thought to my suggestion that you might like to visit Moscow next year?' He raised an eyebrow. 'You appreciate Russian icons. You should go.'

He'd seen her at the gallery. She smiled in acknowledgement. 'You didn't look as though you wanted to be disturbed. I'd like to visit Moscow, yes. I thought I might take the opportunity to travel a bit. I don't know Eastern Europe. I'd like to go to Poland. And maybe Belarus.'

His eyebrows arched in surprise. 'Belarus?' he said.

'My grandfather may have been born there. I think he's Polish by treaty rather than by birth.' She had a sudden picture

228

of Jake Denbigh leaning in the doorway as they discussed the changing borders of Belarus.

Yevanov's dark eyes studied her with interest. 'You look as though your blood comes from further east,' he said. 'You look . . .' he hesitated, then said, 'Russian, perhaps.' She had the feeling he had been going to say something else.

'And further west. My grandmother was Irish.'

He looked at her thoughtfully. 'Irish-Russian. That's an interesting mix. And an unusual one, I think.'

By the time she left Yevanov's office, it was after five. She felt tired as she drove home, and was relieved she didn't have to go to Grandpapa's. She decided she'd earned a relaxing evening, so she called in at the deli on her way home and bought some ravioli and salad. That was supper taken care of. When she got in, she dumped her coat and her bags and headed upstairs.

Half an hour later, she was in her dressing gown running a bath. The bathroom was warm and steamy, and the air smelled of lavender. She'd poured herself a glass of wine and was just testing the temperature of the water, when she heard the phone ringing downstairs. She ignored it. Whoever it was could leave a message. She was about to get into the bath when her mobile vibrated in her pocket, almost making her drop her glass into the water. She checked the number. It was Grandpapa.

'Faith,' he said. He sounded puzzled and bewildered. 'You don't come.'

'I . . . ?' She didn't know what he was talking about.

'I make the treat, but you don't come. I don't know . . .' His voice trailed off.

There was a sinking feeling inside her. 'It's only Tuesday, Grandpapa. We talked about it this morning.' Something was wrong. Something was horribly wrong.

'Tuesday.' His voice faded away. 'Yes, yes . . . I just . . . The camellia has the buds, you must see it.'

229

'Of course I will.' The anxiety was sharp inside her.

'So many buds. I . . . I show you . . .'

'Grandpapa. I'm coming. I'm on my way. Hang on.'

'I . . .' His voice faded again.

'I'll be there in half an hour. Sooner. Will you be okay?'

'I show you that Doreen doesn't come. And Faith, I am worried about the locks. What if the burglars . . . ?'

Doreen again – he'd talked about her on Sunday, but Tuesday was one of Doreen's days. She should have been there today. He'd been fine when she'd spoken to him that morning. 'I'm coming,' she said. 'Sit tight. Don't worry.'

She was making her plans as she hung up. She might need to get the emergency doctor out. She definitely needed to stay overnight, and possibly tomorrow night as well. She packed up her laptop and threw a change of clothes into her bag. Books, books, she needed her books. She pulled what she needed off the shelves, and slung the bag – which now wouldn't close – over her shoulder. She dumped it on the passenger seat as she got into the car, struggling one-handed with her seat-belt.

As she drove too fast through the empty streets, one eye on the mirror for patrol cars, her mind was preoccupied by Grandpapa's phone call, the incoherent jumble of words that tried to hide something she had never heard in his voice before: fear.

17

It was dark by the time Faith got to the old house. The wind blew, making the trees sway. The low-hanging leaves brushed against her face. The moon came out, illuminating the ivy-covered walls, the high laurel against the windows, then the clouds covered it again, leaving her in darkness.

The windows were black. There were no lights. The house could have been deserted. She hurried up the drive, fumbling in her bag for her keys. Her fingers were clumsy and for a panicky moment the lock jammed as she tried to force it. She made herself take a deep breath, and turned the key smoothly. The door swung in, then stopped. 'Grandpapa?' She pushed the door again, then realized that it was on the security chain. 'Grandpapa?' she called, rattling the door. 'It's me. Let me in.'

Silence.

She rattled the door again. 'Grandpapa? Grandpapa!' She could hear the edge of panic in her voice. Anything could have happened. She was going to have to break in. She shoved against the door with her shoulder, but it wouldn't give. It was going to take . . . She wrapped her scarf round her hands to protect them, and using her handbag, smashed the centre pane on the front door. The glass shattered. She froze, expecting an instant outcry, but nothing happened. She slipped her hand carefully through the broken glass and felt for the chain. She slid the bolt along until it fell free. The door opened.

She was standing in the hallway, tense, her hand on her phone. And now she was aware of the empty house around her, the sound of the bushes stirring in the wind, the scraping of branches against the windows, like fingers working insistently at the frames. The living room ahead of her was a pool of darkness, Grandpapa's study, the door partly open, was in shadow. The corridor down to the kitchen was a black tunnel. 'Grandpapa?' The house was icy cold.

She could hear the sound of breathing, heavy and quick. There was someone in the passage, in the shadows. She had a vision of Helen lying dead in the abandoned house, surrounded by old papers and the relics of the past. Her hand groped along the wall for the light switch, and the dim illumination from the bulb filled the corridor, lighting up the figure that was standing there.

Her heart lurched, then steadied as the figure resolved itself into Grandpapa. His hair was tangled, his shirt unevenly buttoned, and his stick was grasped in his half-raised hand. 'The light!' he said. Then he seemed to see her. He lowered the stick and looked around him. His face expressed bewilderment, and a dawning fear. She was shocked to see the shiny tracks of tears on his cheeks. He never cried. She had never seen him cry.

'Grandpapa. It's okay. It's me. What's wrong? What happened?' She slipped her coat off and wrapped it round his shoulders. She could feel him trembling.

'The light,' he whispered. 'The light. You must go!'

'It's okay,' she said. 'It's okay, I'm here now.' She was trying to lead him into the front room, somewhere warmer, but his hands were pushing her away.

'No. No. It isn't safe. Listen to me – someone is watching. You must go. You must go!'

'It's okay now,' she said. What was this? 'Whoever it was, they've gone. It's okay, come on.' Talking quietly, she managed to guide him across the hallway into the living room. She got him into his chair, lit the gas fire and tucked a rug round his legs. 'You're frozen,' she said. She felt the radiator. It was cold.

He was huddled in his chair, blinking in confusion. She needed to get him calmed down, and she needed to get him warm. 'I'm going to get you a hot drink,' she said. 'And I'm going to see what's happened to the heating. Will you be okay? I'm not going far.' She looked at him closely, trying to make sure that he knew her, that he knew where he was. He nodded, his eyes moving round the room, checking the shadows.

She waited a second, then went through to the kitchen. The smell hit her as soon as she opened the door.

The sink was full of pans, crockery, cutlery that had been used and then dumped, the food still on the plates or in the pans, crusts of bread floating on the water. It looked as if no one had cleaned up for days. There were open tins on the work surfaces, some empty, some half-full. Spilled food had dripped on to the floor and into the open drawers. The frying pan on the hob contained a burnt mess that looked like eggs and half-cooked potato. He'd been trying to make *draniki*. He'd said he was making her a treat.

She looked round her in silence. She'd been here on Friday – and she remembered how he wouldn't let her into the kitchen, and how easily she'd accepted her exclusion. And she remembered what he'd said to her on the phone, twice now: Doreen doesn't come. She could feel anger starting inside her. He hadn't been confused, he'd been telling her the truth – Doreen hadn't been here for days by the look of things.

But she needed to deal with the here and now. She ignored

the chaos and dug around in the cupboards until she found a clean pan. She looked in the fridge. There was a plate with some half-eaten food pushed on to the shelf. An egg had smashed and trickled, then dried, over the inside. But at least there was some milk She tipped it into the pan – he needed something warm – and looked at the boiler while the milk was heating up. The pilot light was out. She managed to get it lit, and the boiler ignited with a roar.

She took the hot milk through to the living room. The gas fire had warmed the room a bit, and when she put her hand on the radiator, it felt tepid. He took the mug from her and drank slowly. Some colour came back to his grey-tinged skin, and the haunted, bewildered look began to change as he took in his surroundings. 'Faith?' he said uncertainly.

'Yes.' She crouched down in front of him and took his hands. 'What happened? What upset you?'

'What . . . ? I . . .' He was looking round the room as if he had just woken up. His gaze settled on the window. 'It was out there,' he said. 'I think I see . . .' He shook his head.

'What was out there? Was there someone in the garden?' There could well have been someone. It was no secret that an old man lived here on his own. His fear of burglars was hardly irrational.

Slowly, he was returning to normal, becoming the grandfather she knew. 'No one,' he said. His eyes went back to the window, and he shook his head. 'Crazy old man, just . . . crazy old man.' He patted her hand. 'Nothing, little one.'

'There's no way that was nothing. Grandpapa, you're ill. I'm going to call the doctor tomorrow.'

He looked at her over his spectacles: his way of indicating that, as far as he was concerned, the matter was closed. 'Is just . . . dreams. I have the bad dreams.'

Bad dreams. Wartime memories and burglars. But at least he was more himself. She wasn't going to argue with him now about the doctor, that could wait until the morning. The

234

important thing was to get him warm and settled. 'I'll make us something to eat,' she said.

He began to push himself out of his chair. 'No,' he said. 'I do it. The treat – I promise you the treat.'

'I'll see to it,' Faith said. 'You stay here where it's warm.' She didn't want him going through to the chaos of the kitchen.

She worked quickly, not wanting to leave him for too long. She found some bread that wasn't too stale for toast, and some eggs. To cheer him up, she decided to use the silver cutlery. He liked to make small occasions of their time together. She opened the drawer where it was kept, but there was nothing there, not even the felt-lined cutlery tray. Odd. She had a quick look in the other drawers, and the cupboards, but she couldn't find it. She shelved the problem. That was something else to deal with later. The important thing was to get him warmed up and eating.

She put the eggs on to boil and, while they were cooking, she drained the sink and threw out the rotting food that had been floating in the water. She stacked the dishes, emptied a kettle of boiling water over them, and bagged up the rubbish. She'd need to get on to the agency tomorrow, find out what had happened to Doreen.

Grandpapa struggled out of his chair as she brought the tray in, and insisted on helping her set it down on the table. He'd found a bottle of wine – one that was already open – and he'd poured them each a glass. He held his up in a toast. 'Many happy days,' he said, the toast he always used to make. She took a mouthful of wine. It was sour, but he didn't seem to notice. She felt an ache of sadness.

He grew quiet as he ate. He picked at the food on his plate as she talked to him about her work, about the things she'd been doing. He seemed to listen, but she wasn't sure if he understood. Then he told her about his plans for the garden. 'Maybe this year, we get the cherries,' he said. 'The camellia – so many flowers. Red flowers.'

'Like the hair-ribbon you bought me,' she said. She still had it, tucked away in the back of the box where she kept her few bits of jewellery.

After he'd finished, she took the tray back to the kitchen and made him some cocoa. When she took it through, he was sitting in his chair by the window. There was a book open on his lap, but he wasn't reading, he was staring out into the night. The room was dark, and the standard lamp made a pool of light around his chair. She could hear the sound of the wind as it stirred the trees. She remembered his earlier fear and started to pull the curtains closed, but he stopped her. 'I must watch,' he said.

She put the drink on a table beside him. 'Watch what? It's dark out there.'

The wind was rising, and the trees swayed and sighed. He shifted in his chair. His gaze stayed on the window. 'The forest . . .' he said.

Faith looked at him. His eyes were far away. His face was sad. 'So many die. So young . . .'

'Grandpapa . . .'

He looked at her, but it was almost as if he didn't see her, or didn't believe she was really there. 'I think I have left it behind, and all the time . . . It is better if I die, too.'

'Of course it isn't!' she said. 'You mustn't say that!' She pulled the curtains across, shutting off the black space that was the window.

He seemed puzzled, like someone waking up from a dream. 'Faith . . . you are a good girl,' he said. He stood up slowly. 'I go to bed.'

She watched him up the stairs and waited until his bedroom door shut. She found a piece of card and taped it firmly over the broken pane in the door, then went back to the kitchen and started tackling the job of clearing up. It took her almost an hour to get everything straight, then she made herself some coffee and took it through to the front room. The book he'd been reading was on the table. She picked it up. It was open at the story of Baba Yaga. There was a picture of a dense wood, with a path through the trees, and a young girl peering anxiously though the darkness. *Once upon a time, deep in the dark forest where the bears roamed and the wolves hunted, there lived an evil witch . . . Once upon a time . . .*

She turned the page. Baba Yaga's house waited in the darkness, poised on chicken legs, behind the fence hung with the heads of the people she had killed. Baba Yaga's house could stalk its victims, and the witch herself flew through the air in a mortar, rowing with a pestle. Stories for children! Except, according to Antoni Yevanov, these weren't really children's stories. They were some kind of fossil from the days before laws and lore could be written down. In a way, these stories were supposed to tell a truth.

She sat for half an hour, trying to distract herself with the book, trying not to think about the evening, about what it presaged for the future, but the anxieties pressed in as she stared at the page, reading the same lines over and over again: *Once upon a time . . . an evil witch . . . an evil witch . . . an evil witch . . .*

He couldn't stay here on his own. The house was too big and too old. He needed more care than someone like Doreen coming in a few days every week. He needed someone there to watch out for him. He needed company to keep the dreams at bay.

She sat and listened to the sounds of the house, as he must sit and listen, on his own, night after night – to the wind that was stirring the trees in the garden, to the murmurs and whispers of the draughty corridors, and she found herself listening, straining her ears, for the sound of feet, chicken feet, placing themselves with stealthy malignity as they advanced.

Enough. She was being morbid. She needed something to distract her. Then she remembered her last visit here, when she'd found the pile of old newspaper cuttings in his desk drawer. There was an article there that Jake Denbigh had written. His expression had changed when she'd mentioned it, and she wanted to read it again, to see what it was that had wiped the easy smile off his face and left him looking, just for a moment, bleak and haunted.

She walked towards the door of Grandpapa's study, moving quietly, as though she was doing something secret, something illicit. *That is enough, little one*, and the study door clicked shut in front of her. *Once upon a time* . . . She pushed it open. The cold darkness greeted her. She pressed the switch, and a dim light illuminated the room. The roll-top desk was shut, but the lock hadn't caught. She opened it, breathing in the smell of leather and ink, and released the spring that held the secret drawer closed.

It was empty.

The certificates, the cuttings, and the will – they were gone.

That night, Faith dreamed about the roses. They had grown up from the dead ground, the stems curling out in spiky tendrils that wove a barrier against each path she tried to follow, faster and faster. There was something following her, something she had to escape, but now the shoots were coiling round her arms, pinning her legs, round her neck, and she could feel them tightening and felt the panic of her breath about to be cut off. Then she was awake, gasping, covered in sweat that had nothing to do with heat.

She was at Grandpapa's. She had been dreaming, and something had woken her. She sat up and touched her neck where she could still feel the stem pulling tighter. A stem from one of the dead roses, cut down and lying on the grass. Was that what Helen had felt, that last moment of blind, choking panic?

It was freezing. She tried to get warm again, pulling the blankets around her, but the cold air crept in through the gaps, sank through the coverings, made her draw her legs up and curl into a ball in the middle of the mattress.

She needed to pee. She swore and sat up, reaching for her dressing gown. If she had to get up, she might as well make herself a hot drink before she came back to bed, and take a couple of aspirin. Her fatigue from the day before had left her with a dull headache. She looked at the clock. It was just three. She was going to be good for nothing in the morning.

Faith picked up the tumbler she'd filled with water before she came to bed – it was empty and she wanted to refill it – slipped her feet into a pair of mules and went quietly to the door. She didn't want to disturb Grandpapa, who slept lightly these days. 'When you are old,' he had told her once, 'you do not have the time to waste in sleep.'

She didn't turn the light on, but guided herself along the landing using the balustrade. She looked down the stairs into the empty hall. Moonlight shone though the glass, making a space of hard edges and shadows.

And underneath the door to Grandpapa's study was a line of light.

She'd turned all the lights off before she went to bed – he was always insistent on that. Had she forgotten the study light? No, they hadn't been in there. He must be sitting downstairs reading. He did that sometimes when he couldn't sleep. That must be what had woken her. She shivered again and wrapped her dressing gown closer round her.

She went to the bathroom, then went downstairs. If he was sitting up in this cold, she was going to make him a hot drink as well, and switch the heating on. She went to the study, and stood there listening. She was six again, standing outside the heavy wooden door.

The grandfather clock chimed the hour, making her jump. She pressed her hand against her throat, her heart hammering. When she pushed the door, it swung quietly open. The faint smell of books and dust enclosed her. The room was dimly lit by the table lamp that stood on the bureau. He was sitting at the open desk, his back towards her. The desk was strewn with papers. He seemed unaware of her presence.

'Grandpapa?' she said. She pressed the light switch and the overhead light came on. 'Grandpapa? What are you doing?' She came further into the room.

He was still, so still.

'Grandpapa?' And she was beside him now, her fingers touching his hand, which was as cold as ice, her eyes looking into his, which were blank and empty. His jaw hung slack.

'Grandpapa –' The tumbler dropped from her hand and smashed on the corner of the desk, showering him with shards of broken glass. *Oh, God!*

She tried to brush the pieces off him with her bare hands and the sharp edges cut into her fingers, and now her hands were bleeding, staining the fabric of his dressing gown. And he was cold and there didn't seem to be any way to make him warm.

'I'm sorry,' she said. 'I'm so sorry. Grandpapa? I'm sorry. I'm sorry.'

The Soldier

This is the story of a parting.

For the first time in her life, Eva had ridden on the train. It had stood by the platform, the smoke pouring from its funnel, catching in their throats and eyes. Steam leaked from around the wheels, the engine hissing as it tried to contain its power. There was a smell, like the faint smell of the line when the trains had passed, but this was alien and strong, and it said the train was here, and alive. Eva could feel its heart beating.

Marek lifted Eva, and then Mama, into the carriage. It was bare except for the wooden benches and the stove in the middle. He threw their bags aboard, and climbed in after them.

The track lay ahead of them, vanishing into a distance that was flat as far as the eye could see, marsh and waste and forests. The whistle sounded, and slowly, the train began to move. It was taking Eva away from the forest forever.

The city was noisy and crowded and dirty. Everywhere she looked, there were people, the streets were packed with cars, buses, horses and carts, all hustling and barging to find their way through. And there were soldiers. Everywhere, there were men in uniform. The war had come. Not long after they left, under the blue sky of summer, the Soviet army had swept through the forest and engulfed the village they had left.

Papa had stayed behind. He had been made a local commissioner, and he had to organize the village after the Soviets came. But now there was more unease, talk of trouble on the borders, and he'd come to Minsk to see them, before he left to go to war. Marek and Papa were leaving to join the troops on the border. Eva and Mama were to stay behind, crammed into the rooms that Zoya shared with her family. Papa held Mama close for a long time. 'I'm coming back, Katya.' His pet name for her.

Marek walked with Eva through the town the day before they left. They stopped outside the iron gates of the distillery, one of the first landmarks of the city that Eva had begun to recognize. The gates were wrought iron with a high, ornate arch where a stylized bear danced. Marek spoke to her seriously, he didn't tease her or tug the ribbon she wore in her hair, the red ribbon he'd given her a long time ago. 'I don't know what will happen, little one,' he said. 'I'll write to you, and I'll send you messages – people will be coming to Minsk all the time – you'll know what we're doing, and we'll know about you.'

'I want you to stay,' Eva said.

Marek's face was sad. 'I know,' he said. 'But we have to leave. You'll be safe here.'

And the next day, Eva went to the train station with them

241

where hundreds of soldiers milled on the platform waiting for the trains that were taking them away from their families, their friends and their homes. Papa kissed her on the forehead and said, 'Look after your mother, Eva.' His eyes were wet as he turned away to board the train. Marek looked tall and handsome in his uniform. He hugged her. 'Remember,' he said.

'I will. Take this –' She gave him a photograph, one that he had taken after they had arrived in the city.

He looked at it, then tucked it away in his pocket.

She waited until the train pulled away. She tried to see them among the crowds of men packed into the carriages, but they were gone. And then she had to walk back through the narrow streets to the tiny apartment that seemed somehow empty now that Papa and Marek were no longer there.

In the apartment below, there was an old woman and her son who had been an officer in the Red Army, but who had lost his leg. He had an artificial one that made him walk with a lurch and the false leg hit the ground with a metallic thump. He spent his days on the landings or in the doorways, watching people as they went past. He used to call out to Eva when he saw her on the stairs. 'Hello, pretty one.'

'Petr Dyakin. He's a troublemaker, that one,' Zoya warned.

His eyes used to follow Eva as she went out to school, as she ran her errands for Mama and Aunt Zoya, as she hung the wet washing out in the courtyard at the back of the building. She didn't like the way he looked at her, but she used to return his greeting politely: 'Comrade.'

One evening shortly before Christmas, Eva came home later than usual. The winter was closing in, the glass had dropped and dropped and the streets were shiny with ice. She was late because she had found some wood in the road that must have fallen from a cart. Collecting such things was illegal, but everyone did it. They needed to keep warm. She looked round quickly, but the street was empty and there was no sign of

242

a patrol. She picked up as much as she could to take back to the apartment for the stove. It was cold, and Mama's cough was getting worse.

She turned into the dark entrance of the apartment block and started up the stairs. The air felt dank, and the stairwell smelled of mould. There were no lights, and she hurried, keen to get to the apartment.

The voice came out of the shadows on the second landing. 'Hello, pretty one.'

Eva jumped, and dropped one of the pieces of wood. She knelt down quickly to pick it up. 'Comrade,' she murmured.

'Now then.' She could hear the *thump* of his artificial leg as he moved towards her. 'What's all this, pretty one?'

She stood up slowly. In the half-light, she could see the glint of his teeth through his moustache. He had a bottle in his hand and she could smell the waft of spirits on his breath.

'Nothing,' she said. 'I must go now.'

He ignored her, and leaned down to pick up the wood she had dropped. He was standing so she couldn't get past him. 'What's all this?' he said again. 'Taking wood, pretty one? You know what happens to people who steal.'

Eva knew. They arrested people for less, and those people disappeared, unless they had enough money to buy their way home again. 'I bought it,' she said, trying to tuck the rest under her coat.

He grinned at her. 'Black market? Don't worry. I won't tell.' He tapped the side of his nose. 'Have a drink.' He held up the bottle he was holding. It was half-full, and she could see the picture of the dancing bear on the label. 'With a friend,' he said.

'No. I must get home.'

'We're friends, aren't we?' he said. 'I promised not to tell about this. I never tell on my friends.' His face looked hot and his eyes were bright.

'Yes,' she said again. 'But Mama . . .'

243

'Mama.' His voice held a jeering note now. He stepped towards her, still holding the bottle. He was pushing her back towards the wall. He held the bottle up to her mouth. 'Drink!' he said.

'No.' Eva turned her face and pushed the bottle away. He tried to bring it up to her mouth again, and she struggled, catching his arm with her elbow. He lurched back, and she heard the smash of breaking glass as the bottle fell on to the concrete floor. Vodka fumes filled the landing.

Eva froze, her eyes meeting his. She could see the fury there, and she turned and ran up the stairs to the apartment. She lay awake all night, waiting for the knock on the door.

The next day, Petr Dyakin wasn't to be seen, but the day after, he was back, standing in his doorway. He smiled as usual, but his smile was cold and speculative. 'Hello, pretty one,' he said.

Eva dropped her eyes and hurried past without answering.

18

Faith watched helplessly as the paramedics wrapped a blanket around Grandpapa and strapped him carefully on to the stretcher. 'It's okay, Marek,' the older one said. 'We'll get you sorted.' She felt useless. She hadn't known what to do. When she'd found him she'd thought he was dead, then she'd felt the pulse in his wrist, faint but steady, and had run to the phone to summon help. She'd tried to warm him, she'd put a blanket round his shoulders, rubbed his hands, talking to him all the time – nonsense about the garden, about what they were going to do, but what she was really saying was: *Don't go. Not yet. Not like this.*

When the paramedics arrived, her first feeling was relief as she watched them put a drip in his arm, administer oxygen. They were in time. He was going to be all right.

But he wasn't. The treatment would only give him a few hours, a few days, a few weeks. No more than that. All they were going to do was to prolong his death.

'We'll see to him now, love,' one of the men said. 'We'll take care of him.'

'I'm coming with you.' He wasn't going to leave this house alone.

They manoeuvred the stretcher down the steps and into

the ambulance. The door slammed shut, and it pulled away down the drive. She wondered if he would ever come back here. The night was fading into the pale morning light as she followed in the car. The roads were almost empty, but once or twice they met traffic and the blue lights flashed and the wail of the siren echoed in the air.

The hospital was close to the university. When they arrived, she held Grandpapa's hand – cold and unresponsive – as the paramedics wheeled the stretcher through the hospital door. They took him and left Faith to answer the questions of the admissions clerk: Age? *Eighty-six*. Date of birth? *September 1918*. Grandpapa had never celebrated his birthday. Religion? *None*. She answered the litany of questions shifting from foot to foot with impatience. She wanted to be with him. She was scared he would slip away while she was here filling out forms, that he would die on his own.

Next of kin? Oh Christ. Katya. She had to let Katya know.

Once the forms were complete, she was left sitting in the waiting room of the Accident and Emergency department. Her eyes felt hot and dry, and the harsh light seemed to bounce off the walls and burn into her head. The plastic covers on the benches stuck to her. It was five o'clock in the morning, and only a few people were scattered here and there around the large waiting space. A TV – the screen too small to be seen from where Faith was sitting – crackled some kind of news at her.

She heard footsteps and voices. A group of people went past, not looking at the benches where the last few casualties of the night waited. They may have been medical staff coming off duty, or relatives at the end of a night's vigil. She didn't know and she didn't care. A heavy *clunk* made her jump. It was the vending machine dispensing a canned drink.

'Miss Lange?' Faith turned round. One of the nurses was signalling to her.

'You can come and sit with your granddad now. We've

246

made him comfortable.' She led Faith through a door to a room full of curtained cubicles. Grandpapa was lying on a trolley. He was wearing some kind of hospital gown, faded, incongruously patterned with flowers. The tubes from the drip ran from his arm, and he was attached to a heart monitor which beeped with reassuring regularity.

'What's happening to him?' she said to the nurse.

'The doctor needs to see him.' She hesitated. 'We don't know for sure yet, but it looks like he may have had a stroke. How old is he?'

'Eighty-six.'

She nodded and checked the drip. 'The doctor will be in soon.'

'Grandpapa?' Faith said. 'It's all right. You're going to be okay.'

He lay still, his eyes half open, his jaw sagging.

'Grandpapa?' she said again. She couldn't keep her voice steady. 'Can he hear me?'

'Of course he can.' The nurse's voice was kind. 'Talking to him is the best thing you can do just now. Is there anyone we can contact?'

Faith shook her head, then remembered. 'I haven't managed to contact my mother,' she said. The nurse took the details and left her. Faith sat on the hard plastic chair, but that made the trolley too high for her to see him properly, so she stood up and took his hand. It felt limp and lifeless. 'Grandpapa?' she said. 'It's me. It's Faith.'

There was no response.

She looked down at him, at the grey face and dull, half-open eyes, his body, under the blanket looking oddly diminished. He seemed out of place in this high-tech environment, frail and damaged beyond repair among the shiny machines and crisp white sheets. What had happened last night? Something had woken him in the small hours of the morning, something that had taken him to his desk, to wherever he had stowed away those papers, made him take them out and read them. What was it that had sent him there, and what had he seen? Was it something in the cuttings that had triggered the fatal moment of stress?

'Miss Lange?' She looked up. A young man in a white coat was standing behind her. He looked as tired as she felt. 'Your grandfather, Mr Lange . . . he's had an interference with the blood supply to his brain.'

'A stroke?'

He nodded. 'It's a bit early to say how extensive the damage will be. It looks as if he may have had some minor episodes in the past . . . Have you noticed any changes in him recently?'

'He's been a bit forgetful,' she said.

He nodded again, as if that was what he had expected, and said that they were going to admit Grandpapa as soon as a bed became available.

'And . . . ?'

His eyes drifted away from hers. 'The degree of recovery from an episode as severe as this is hard to assess,' he said. 'It's a matter of time. His system is in shock. We'll be able to get a better idea in a couple of days.'

'But . . . aren't there drugs or something – to stop the damage?'

'We've given him what we can,' he said. 'Your grandfather's very frail. We don't want to subject him to too much stress. We want to observe him for a while. You found him, didn't you?'

. . . in the dark of the morning hours and the silent house. 'Yes.'

'Did he fall?'

She shook her head. 'He was at his desk. He'd just . . .' she demonstrated '. . . sort of slumped down in his chair.'

He nodded, frowning slightly.

'Is there something wrong?'

He shook his head. 'No, I just thought he might have fallen.

248

There are some bruises on his face . . . He might have knocked himself against the desk. It doesn't matter.' His pager went and he smiled a weary apology at Faith. 'There should be a bed available soon and we'll take him up to the ward.' He hurried away.

Jake had breakfast in his room. He'd bought himself some fruit from one of the pavement kiosks, and some spiced meat from the supermarket the day before. One experience of the hotel breakfast had been enough. He watched CNN while he ate, then spread his research notes over the desk in his room and began to chart the progress he'd made.

He'd got the background he needed on Sophia Yevanova. Now he wanted some kind of access to the destroyed city, the city of her youth. His mission for the day was one of the museums, Minsk's renowned Museum of the Great Patriotic War. It was the place, according to Adam, where he might best see the city that Sophia Yevanova had known, the city as she had last seen it before she fled her native country.

Minsk seemed to be going out of its way to welcome him with sunlight and blue skies. He strolled through the centre, watching the street cleaners with their besoms, and the pavement stalls setting up for the day. The museum was housed in a concrete block opposite the Palace of the Republic in Oktiabrskaya – October Square. There was huge neon lettering protruding above its roof – something about the heroic deeds of the people living throughout the centuries, as far as Jake's imperfect translation could tell. The entrance was a small door to one side of the building. It didn't look welcoming. It opened on to a large vestibule with stairs at each side leading to a gallery, and a stairway down to his left. He hesitated, expecting an official in a large hat to arrive and eject him.

There was a small booth to one side of the vestibule which he hadn't noticed at first. He approached it and crouched slightly at a low glass window where a woman peered back at him. He held up one finger, and she said something that he couldn't catch. He offered her a note; she took it and shoved some pieces of paper at him along with a ticket. The paper proved to be low-denomination notes – worth less than a penny – but he had his admission.

Adam had told him to go to the downstairs galleries. 'If you want to understand Minsk, if you want to understand modern Belarus, then that is what you must see,' he had said. These were the rooms devoted to the occupation of Minsk – he knew better than to expect any disclosures about Stalinist atrocities here, but he would get enough material about the fascist occupation, probably more than he wanted.

He went down the stairs and found himself in an ante-room, walking between glass-topped display cabinets, and framed maps and treaties on the wall. The light was dim and the colours were dark and faded. An unsmiling woman took his ticket. He pushed through the dusty curtain, and stepped into the past.

Old photographs, rummaged from the backs of drawers, arte-facts, meaningless in themselves – identity cards, buttons, frag-ments of clothing. The display cases were labelled, but Jake barely needed to read them to understand the contents: here are the remains of our people. There were photographs of weary soldiers and starving civilians, the ruined city – and the dead.

And then the occupation: Jake looked at the pictures – soldiers in uniform with Nazi insignia, in cars, on motor-bikes, on foot. A placard on a fence: *Der Ruße muß sterben damit wir leben*. 'The Russian must die that we might live.' A woman wept over her dead son; two children, toddlers, crouched in the dirt. The face of one bore an expression of blank bewilderment at what its world had become, the other cried with the open-mouthed despair of a child who couldn't understand why there was no one to comfort her. Soldiers lounged against a fence, workers taking a well-earned rest in front of a farmhouse where an old couple had been hanged from the roof beam. The woman's feet dangled below her heavy skirts, neatly stockinged and shod.

And there were the pictures of children's bodies, laid out in rows – neat and meticulous, silent and dead. The order of insanity, for the fascists now were here.

He felt a reluctance to move on. He had seen enough, and he knew there was more. The drapes that curtained off the rooms carried the dry smell of age. The photographs were faded, with none of the bright polish of restoration that could allow him to distance himself. He stepped through into the next gallery.

And here, the rubble of old Minsk surrounded him, rubble through which people picked their way in rags. Men marched in uniform battalions, their officers smart and glittering with the gilt of victory. All around him, the bodies of the dead hung from lampposts, from trees, from high gates, anything that would serve as a makeshift gallows.

A group of uniformed men marched three prisoners a young boy, a girl and a man – through the streets. There was a placard round the girl's neck, crudely lettered in Cyrillic and in Latin script: *Wir sind Partisanen und haben auf deutsche Soldaten geschossen.* МЫ ПАРТИЗАНЫ СТРЕЛЯ-ВЩИЕ ПО ГЕРМАНСКИМ ВОЙСКАМ. 'We are partisans and we have shot at German soldiers.'

Men in uniform crowded round, interested spectators. Now they were at a building that looked faintly industrial. An officer in a peaked cap was placing a noose round the neck of the girl, his face calm and intent. The soldiers watched.

And now she was hanging, her face distorted in agony, and now she was dead, and the officer was placing a noose on the boy whose mouth stretched in a mute plea and whose wrists strained against the bindings, and now the man who had watched the death of the others was noosed. His face was a mask of terror. And then they were dead, left hanging from the gateway.

Jake stood for a while, trying to decipher the words on the card by this cabinet. The 'episode' had occurred on 26 October 1941, just three months after the fascist invasion.

A sentry box stood empty at the far side of the room, except for a pair of soldier's boots that symbolized the guard who would have stood there. To the right, there was a wire fence hung with photographs of people, like trophy heads – men, women, children. Behind the fence was a gallows. Beneath the gallows was a box of earth that contained fragments of bone.

The gallows was . . . he took out his dictionary as he tried to transliterate and translate. It was the original taken from a camp – a death camp – that had been established at a village on the outskirts of Minsk. He didn't know there had been one so far east. He read the inscription carefully. He wanted to know about the camp, its name and when it was established. The photographs hanging on the wire fence were just a few, a very few, of the people who had died there. He looked into their faces trying to commit them to memory.

The camp had been established in May 1942 and torched by the fleeing Nazis in June 1944, as the Red Army advanced. It had been the third largest death camp in Europe, and of its victims, less than twenty had survived. But its name?

He found it in the confusing script, and began the task of transliteration. He was getting quicker. МАГИ ТРОСТЄНЄ . . .

M . . . a . . . l . . . y . . .

He'd hoped for some revelation, some recognition, but it meant nothing to him.

Just another Belarusian village.

Maly Trostenets.

The Firebirds

This is the story of how war came to the city.

The attack came without warning. There had been the

chaos of the invasion days before as the Nazi troops poured over the border. There was nowhere for the Red Army to stand. They fought and fell back, fought and fell back. Brest fell, Lvov fell, Baranoviche was overrun as the fascist army advanced. The planes came out of an empty sky on a clear June morning. In the streets, people were running, mothers looking for their children, children screaming in terror as they fled to find some kind of shelter, any kind of shelter.

Eva, huddled in the basement with Mama and Zoya, listened to the heavy engines in the sky, the *thump, thump* like giant footsteps marching across the city towards them. And the ground shook and the air ignited. Wave after wave of planes flew over unopposed.

Minsk was burning, and the flames made the air dance as the smoke blackened the summer sky. Wave followed wave, and for hour after hour the planes pounded the city to rubble.

For Eva and her mother, life became animal, hiding in dark places, in the cavities and crevasses that the predator couldn't find. There was no food, no water, no light. And there was no escape. They were too late. For endless days and nights, they hid in the basement, slipping out in the rare breaks in the bombardment to try and find food and water. The Red Army fought and died in the streets of Minsk. Eva knew that, somewhere out there, Papa and Marek were fighting, and maybe they were dying too.

Ten days after the invasion had begun, the fascists entered Minsk. Their planes flew ahead of them. The tanks pushed the rubble aside and the battalions followed. They swept through the city and took everything of value they could find. They killed the hens that were laying and slaughtered the pigs that were to provide the food for autumn. Behind them, the countryside was plundered, the farmers left destitute or dead. The soldiers marched, singing and laughing, their feet lifting and stepping, lifting and stepping as they moved through the forest of rubble that their bombs and their guns had left behind. The Red Army had been beaten back, and the people of Minsk were left to face the occupying forces undefended.

The invasion became a war of annihilation. Following in the tracks of the army came the Secret Field Police, the *Schutzmannschaft,* whose notoriety ran ahead of them as swathes of the dead trailed in their wake.

Eva picked her way around the fallen buildings, watching as the other survivors crept out of the basements and cellars, or the caves in the rubble where they had been hiding, their faces dazed, trying to make sense of the changed world that surrounded them. The smell of burning hung in the air, and the stench of death. For a moment Eva was a child again, edging cautiously along a new path among the trees, hunger gnawing at her, . . . *as her feet pressed into the ground, she could smell the damp earth and the leaf mould. And she could smell something else, faint on the breeze that stirred the branches and made the shadows dance on the forest floor . . .*

But for those who were alive, hiding was no longer possible. The city had to be restored, work had to be done. They needed water, they needed food, they needed warmth and they needed shelter before the winter came again. Eva watched and waited day after day for news of Marek or of Papa, but none came.

The nightmare began – deportation to slave labour camps, looting, rape, murder and starvation. The partisans fled to the forests and began their long resistance. In response, the occupying forces proclaimed their intentions: *Die Juendlikkeit der Täter schutzt in Keinem Falle sebst vor Vollstreckung des Todesurteils.* 'The youth of the perpetrators will not protect them from the penalty of death.'

And they carried out their proclamation.

The fascists had many methods of execution, but in Minsk, public hanging was the preferred way, as it made the most potent of examples, and provided a salutary lesson. If the fascists would hang a teenage girl, then they would hang anybody.

The hangings were brutal. The victims were hanged separately, so those who died last would know what was to come. They were not hooded or blindfolded. The gallows were crude. The victims were given no drop, and the noose was made of thin twine in a simple slip knot. Death was slow.

The first public hanging took place in October. Three people, Kiril Trous, a veteran from the last war, Masha Bruskina, a seventeen-year-old girl, and Volodia Shcherbatsevich, a sixteen-year-old boy were hanged in front of the gates of a local factory. The Nazis slung a crude sign around the girl's neck: 'We are partisans and we have shot at German soldiers.' They hanged them one at a time.

Afterwards, the silence of terror fell on the city. Eva learned which streets to use to avoid the marching killers, learned to avert her eyes from the trees and lampposts where the dead were left. She listened for news of the fighting that was moving closer and closer to Moscow.

One day, as she came back to the apartment block, a woman in an old black coat pushed brusquely past her. Eva stumbled, and the woman grabbed her arm to steady her, then she strode off without a backward glance. Eva watched her go.

As the woman's hand had touched hers, she had slipped something between Eva's fingers, a piece of paper. Eva kept her hand tightly closed and shoved it deep into her coat pocket. As she went through the entrance, she saw Petr Dyakin watching her. The men and boys had been taken by the Nazis, but Dyakin remained – maybe his leg made him useless for work. He looked thinner and shabbier, but he still gave Eva that speculative smile, still greeted her with, 'Hello, pretty one.' Today he said, 'What are you up to now, pretty one?' His eyes glittered.

Eva responded with a wordless murmur and hurried past.

She was aware of his eyes on her as she went up the stairs. She stopped in the doorway of her own apartment, calling a greeting to Mama, and took the paper out of her pocket. It was folded small, but her heart began to beat faster as she recognized the handwriting. *Marek!*

The note was brief. *I am well. I have had news of you. Keep brave. I don't know what has happened to Papa. We are fighting back.* The resistance. Marek was with the partisans, and he wasn't far away. The surge of gladness she felt retreated at the thought of the danger he was in.

That night, she was suddenly awake in the darkness. She listened for what had woken her – but everything was silent. Then the wind rattled the window, and a deep fear began inside her.

Somewhere far away, there was the soft movement of a chicken foot on the ground, the sound of something testing the wind as it raised its head in gleeful realization.

19

It was well into the morning before Faith left the hospital. She felt oddly detached from the day around her. While she had waited by Grandpapa's bed, she had wanted nothing more than to sleep. In the close, oppressive atmosphere of the hospital, her eyes had kept closing, and she had drifted in and out of the twilight world of semi-sleep, where he was saying to her: *That is enough, little one.*

I need to know, she said, then she jerked back into the small admissions ward in the Accident and Emergency department, and Grandpapa lay on the bed, his breathing stertorous, his eyes half-closed and empty.

She stayed until they moved him to the intensive care ward.

'We'll take care of him,' the charge nurse told her. 'You get some rest.' They'd contacted Katya. She was on her way.

'You'll call me if . . . ?'

'Don't worry,' he reassured her.

The house was cold and silent, as she had left it. Moving slowly, she went upstairs to his room. She packed a bag with toilet things, clean pyjamas, the book that lay on his bedside table. It felt wrong to be hunting through his private things, looking for what he might need. She opened the wardrobe, looking for some clean clothes.

His clothes. What had happened to . . . The metal hangers chimed as they swung together. There was nothing there apart from his tweed jacket, a waistcoat, a shirt and couple of pairs of trousers. He used to have suits, shirts, jackets . . . She could picture him on his way out of the house, wearing the black suit that meant he was going to a meeting, or the jacket and trousers that meant a site visit, carrying the battered attaché case he never would replace.

And the heavy knitted sweaters he'd favoured in his retirement . . . She began pulling open drawers. They were empty apart from some socks, some underwear, a shapeless old jersey that he'd had for years and used for gardening.

Now she remembered the missing silver from the night before. What else would she find gone if she searched the house? Burglars. He'd talked about burglars and she'd dismissed it as confusion and bad dreams. But what kind of burglar stole old clothes? What kind of burglar broke in to steal the silver and left no trace?

She couldn't think about it now. Tomorrow. She'd start dealing with it tomorrow. There was something she needed to do now, and she had been putting it off. She went down the stairs to the study, hesitating at the door, reluctant to cross that threshold, afraid she would see him slumped and helpless in his chair, his eyes staring sightlessly ahead. The desk was still open, the cuttings lying face up stained with water from the tumbler that she had dropped. The shattered glass still lay on the floor.

She sat down slowly, trying to feel some awareness of what had happened just a few hours before, but the room felt dead around her. She started to look at the cuttings, knowing what she was going to see:

WAR CRIME SUSPECT DIES AGED EIGHTY-FIVE.
ROW OVER 'NAZI' ARREST.

AUSTRALIA'S SHAME
EXTRADITION CASE FAILS
THE LAST VICTIMS: VIGILANTE JUSTICE AND WAR CRIMES.

Why had he kept these? Why were these stories so important to him, and why had he come down in the night to read them? He had been afraid, she remembered that. He had told her someone was watching.

Belarus. Jake had been convinced that Grandpapa came from Belarus, or had been in Belarus during the war. Maybe he was right. These men had been platoon commanders in some kind of police force whose brutality had startled even the German occupiers. They must have been figures of terror to the population. Had Grandpapa seen them, known of them, seen what they had done? Had he made his escape with men like this in pursuit? After all these years, had the stories that now lay in front of her brought it back, turned them into the creatures of nightmare that hunted him in his dreams?

Had he woken in the night to the sound of marching feet, and gone downstairs to make sure, again, that they were dead or far away, and he was safe? Because they were far away. They had lived lives of prosperity and even renown. And her grandfather? He had had prosperity too, but he lived his adult life in the shadows of his wartime memories, and now they had come back to destroy him.

Her broken night was catching up with her. There were things she needed to do, urgent things, but her mind fuzzed into incoherence. She was too tired to drive. She'd just rest for a few minutes, get her second wind. She went into the front room and sat in Grandpapa's big armchair. The familiar smell of tweed and pipe tobacco enveloped her. She let her head fall back and her eyes close. Then she was drifting in a dark place, and she could hear his voice saying, *The light! You must go . . .*

And the light was flickering through the trees, dark and then light, dark and then light; and then she was asleep.

Jake had two more days in Minsk, and before he left, he wanted to see the Kurapaty Forest. He found out there was a bus that would take him to the memorial. His enquiry at the Belintourist office provoked no surprise, no curiosity. He had half expected a secretiveness about this aspect of the country's past, but a memorial had been erected to the victims some years ago.

In the end, though, he decided to take a taxi. He wanted to hear the views of local people on the history of the massacres, and he was willing to bet that Belarusian taxi drivers – like the breed the world over – would have opinions, and would express them.

He got a taxi at the hotel. The young man who was to drive him appeared friendly, but also seemed happy enough with silence. Jake tried his halting Russian, and after a couple of attempts, managed to get the young man talking. His name was Karel. He told Jake he made a fair living – by local standards – working as a driver. Most of his customers were foreign visitors.

'You get many?' Jake was surprised.

They were mostly businessmen, Karel explained. There was still trade between Russia and Belarus, there were still some western businesses operating in the country.

They were away from the built-up area now, driving along a two-lane highway through stretches of forest, until Karel pulled the car over and drew to a halt. 'This way,' he said, as he held the door open for Jake.

Jake followed him down a steep path. The trees around him were pine and birch. The forest opened into a grove, and Karel halted. Jake came to stand beside him. It was silent apart from the sound of birdsong. In front of him stood a cross, a Russian Orthodox cross. He looked at the engraving, trying to decipher what it said. *In memory of the victims of* . . . he couldn't understand the next bit – the killings? The cruelties? But the dates were there: *1937–1941*. The breeze blew, wafting the scent of pine through the air, and the shadows danced on the forest floor. He could see through the trees where the ground had sunk, could see the shadows of pits that were overgrown with scrub and brambles. And in the shadows he could see the crosses vanishing among the trees, the crosses of Kurapaty.

Sophia Yevanova had crept through trees like these. A young boy had escaped the killing fields to touch her hand before he was dragged away to his death. Jake shivered, and looked at Karel, who was leaning against a tree, lighting a cigarette. A thin drizzle began to fall. 'My grandfather,' Karel was looking up at the trees as he spoke, 'he came here after the war. He said that it was all dug up and abandoned, left to the tall grasses that are the first to come back. And the toadstools. Red toadstools, and pink mushrooms on long stalks. The people said it was from the blood.' He gave a shrug, implying that Jake could believe that story or not, as he chose.

'Are there people still alive,' he said, 'who remember?'

Karel made the same shrugging movement. 'Maybe a few,' he said. 'Who knows?'

'Can I get to Zialony Luh?' He hadn't been able to find the village on the map, but maybe, just maybe there would be people there who remembered the Yevanov family.

Karel shook his head. 'It was demolished,' he said. 'More than twenty years ago.'

Jake got out his camera and took photographs, feeling like a tourist, like an atrocity groupie, the kind of person who would enjoy the vicarious grief of places such as this. He wondered if the Belarusians of the time had had that same sense of inevitability that he sensed in Karel, a belief derived from knowledge that the world was an unstable place, and the powerless would provide endless fodder for the massacres of the powerful under whatever ideology they proclaimed, whatever flag they happened to fly.

As the fascists began their deadly game, the people of Belarus had reeled under the repression that was killing thousands upon thousands of their countrymen. The clouds of the invasion darkened in the skies unnoticed. How could the people have foreseen the storm that was coming?

You must understand that, for some of us, the fascists came as liberators, at first.

Faith surfaced from a dream of needing to be somewhere urgently but being endlessly prevented or distracted. Her head was twisted at an awkward angle, her arms and legs were stiff and aching. For a moment, she thought she was at home and reached out for her bedside light. Her hand brushed against an unfamiliar shape and she sat up, confused. She was in a chair. She had fallen asleep in Grandpapa's chair. The rug she'd wrapped around herself had slipped off, but the room felt warm. She sat up, rubbing her eyes. The gas fire was lit.

Grandpapa must have come back and . . . The events of the night before flooded into her mind. She needed to take his stuff to the hospital. She needed to phone . . . The thoughts swirled round in confusion, then she became aware of someone moving around, close by. Someone had lit the gas fire. There was someone else in the house.

Doreen? She stood up slowly. 'Doreen?' she said. Whoever it was, was in the study. She crossed the hallway and pushed the study door open, her greeting freezing in her throat before the words came out.

A woman was sitting at the desk, sorting through a pile of papers. She must have been there a while, because there were stacks of papers on the adjacent tables, boxes on the floor, and the drawers and cupboards were all standing open and empty. The woman turned round: it was Katya.

'Faith,' Katya said. She stood up and came across. The two women embraced awkwardly. 'How are you? You look exhausted. I thought I'd better let you sleep.' Despite the disorder around her, she looked her usual immaculate self, model-thin, her dark hair pulled back from her face, her make-up impeccable, her grey suit a masterpiece of understated elegance.

'What time is it?' Faith said slowly.

'It's just after five. I phoned the hospital.' Katya's voice was quick and brittle, as though talking would stave off something else, something she was trying to avoid . . .

'How is he?' Her mother's manner unnerved her.

'They said there was no change.'

Faith breathed again. Silence fell as the two women looked at each other. 'What are you doing?' Faith said.

'I'm going through Marek's papers. There's cupboards full of stuff that hasn't been touched for decades by the looks of things. This room is filthy. Does it ever get cleaned?'

'Why are you going through his papers?' The empty cupboards, the boxes suddenly exposed to the light looked naked.

'Because I found these –' Katya pointed to a pile of envelopes on the table. 'They were all stuffed into this bottom drawer here.'

Faith looked at her mother, then began to sift through them.

There were unopened letters going back weeks, months – junk mail: *Mark Lange – Winner. Your guaranteed prize certificate is enclosed!*; Christmas cards; letters from the bank: *Private and Confidential*; letters . . . She opened one. It was from the agency that supplied Doreen: *overdue account . . .* And another that was the same: *overdue account*. It looked as if they hadn't been paid for weeks. That would explain Doreen's absence.

She unfolded one of the bank statements. It was from three months ago, and showed that Grandpapa had an overdraft of £8,000. There were several letters dated after that statement threatening sanctions. No wonder the agency bill hadn't been paid . . .

'It's a mess,' Katya said. 'God knows what else I'm going to find.' She wiped the dust off her hands with a tissue and looked round the study with its dim light and dark furniture. 'When I was a child, I always thought this room was the place where he kept his secrets. He was always in here, night after night. I never used to see him. Even before my mother left . . .'

That is enough, little one. Faith could see the study door closing inexorably, leaving her outside. His secrets. The things he had seen, the things he knew, the things that made him cry out at the light. The open cupboards, the papers piled up on the table were a violation of his long-guarded privacy. 'This stuff is old,' she said, running her fingers through the dust that lay on the tops of the boxes. 'There's no need to go through all of these.'

'Maybe not, but I intend doing just that until I find the deeds to the house and his share certificates.'

'His solicitor will have them. Or the bank. There's no need for all this.'

'He kept everything here,' Katya said.

Faith ran her fingers through her hair. 'Okay. I'll give you a hand. But once we find those, then we leave it, okay?'

Katya started to say something, then she sighed angrily. 'It depends on what we find,' she said. 'That pile on the left is the stuff I've sorted. It's all finance and insurance. All the rest needs going through.'

Faith started turning over the jumble of papers on the table. 'Is there anything about his family?'

'What would there be? He got out in the clothes he was wearing.'

264

'Do you know what happened to them?' To Stanislau and Kristina. And to Eva.

'Don't ask me. He's never talked about it to me.'

Faith moved from box to box, giving the contents of each a quick glance. It was going to take weeks to go through it all thoroughly. Most of what she could see seemed to relate to Grandpapa's work. Records of his business, none of his family, like the photographs he had burned.

Slipped down the side of one box was a thin book of grey card, tied with a ribbon. It had faded lettering on the cover. *Wedding*. She'd never seen it before. She picked it up and turned the pages slowly. She recognized Grandpapa at once. The fair-haired young man from the photograph looked back at her, only this time the suppressed smile was gone. His face was expressionless. This was the grandfather she knew – age had taken away the upright bearing, but the cold severity of his face had changed very little over the years.

The bride was wearing a dress with a calf-length skirt and a hat that was wreathed with flowers. She was small and pretty with dark curls that hung round her shoulders, and in all the photographs her smile shone out. She smiled at the camera, she smiled up at her new husband. Her face glowed with happiness.

Faith became aware that Katya was looking over her shoulder. 'I never knew he'd kept this,' she said. 'He told me she'd taken it, that it was lost. I thought I'd taken all the photographs of her that there were.'

Faith turned the pages. The only other people in the photographs were a middle-aged couple. 'Are they my great-grand-parents?' she said.

'No. They didn't come to the wedding. It was a registry office – they didn't recognize it. As far as they were concerned, she was condemning herself to a state of mortal sin. They were staunch Roman Catholics.'

'Was she Catholic too?'

Katya nodded. 'She went against the church to marry him – they were Irish Catholics. You didn't rebel lightly against that system, not in those days. She must have really loved him.'

Faith looked at the picture again. Her grandmother, Deirdre O'Halloran. She looked glad, looked like a woman who had made a choice she was happy with, but Grandpapa looked . . . nothing.

'Why did they split up?' It was only a few short years after this picture was taken that the couple had separated.

Katya's fingers touched the photograph of her mother's face. 'It was so long ago. Every time I think of her, I see her on her own. I can remember the evenings – my mother would be sitting in there with her books and her sewing, and he would be in here, working, night after night. She was always alone. She must have been lonely. I know she wanted more children, but I don't think he did.' She shrugged. 'He didn't have time for the one he'd got.' She'd evaded the question.

'She looks like you,' Faith said.

'Oh, she's much prettier than I ever was.' Katya's voice was brisk.

The awkward conversation died to silence. Faith looked at the clock on the wall that was measuring out the time in slow ticks. It was after six, and the night was dark outside the windows. She thought about Grandpapa sitting in the front room, staring into the pitch black of the garden.

'I'd better get back to the hospital,' Faith said. 'I want to sit with him for a while. Are you coming?'

Katya looked at the chaos around them. 'I'll keep going with this lot for a while.'

'Okay. Where are you staying? Why don't you come to my place? I've got a spare room.'

'There's no need. I've booked myself into the Malmaison. It's closer. I'll come straight here first thing in the morning. You come along when you can.' Katya's voice was brisk.

'I've got a meeting at ten thirty. Why don't you come to the hospital? I'll go there straight after – around twelve.'

Katya studied her fingers, scratching a speck of dirt from her fingernail. 'I'll have to deal with all of this –' she said, gesturing round the room. 'I haven't got much time. I've got to go back tomorrow night. I have to get back to work.'

Faith shook her head. 'So when are you going to visit him?'

'They told me that he wasn't conscious.' Katya wouldn't meet her eye. 'Someone has to sort this mess out. There's no point in sitting beside his bed when he won't even know I'm there.'

'Of course he'll know,' Faith said. 'He needs people sitting with him, talking to him . . . Katya, you have to see him. He's your *father,* for Christ's sake.'

Her mother's voice was suddenly cold. 'He was never a father to me. He came and took me from my grandparents after my mother died, and sent me away to school. I was only seven, I didn't understand what had happened, and he sent me away. He never came to see me. And when I did come home, he shipped me off to nannies and holiday schemes. *I* needed *him,* but he didn't care. He kept me fed and he kept clothes on my back and that was it. And when you were born – I was only sixteen – suddenly he was the perfect grandfather. But he's never been a father to me.'

Faith's mind went back to her own childhood. Katya had left her when she was small, had gone in search of her own life. The words *And what kind of mother were you?* stopped against her tongue.

But it wasn't that simple. People learned good parenting from their own parents, and Grandpapa, for whatever reason, had not been a good father to his own child. Something had happened to him that left him unable to care. Katya had never been a mother to Faith because no one had shown her how.

The two women faced each other in inarticulate silence, then Katya turned away. 'You're the one he wants to see. I'll be much more useful here.'

20

Jake was due to leave Minsk early on Friday. He spent Thursday collecting material for the article he'd been commissioned to write, the one that was, in theory, going to cover the costs of his trip. He went into the city and took pictures – the war monuments, the slender obelisk that celebrated the achievements of the Belarusians, the eternal flame, the strange dancing figures that lined the sidewalk along Masherova. He took pictures along the Svisloc, showing the walkways and the parkland, the fairground, the trees.

And, with truth in mind, he took pictures of the battered trams and buses, the cracked pavements, the ragged old men and women who swept those pavements with besoms, the beggars and their barefooted children.

That evening, he had dinner with Adam at the Russian restaurant on Skaryny where they'd first met. 'So, how have your researches gone?' Adam said, stirring sugar into his coffee. 'It's been a short visit. Have you found everything you need?'

Jake shook his head. 'I could stay here for a month,' he said. 'But I've got what I need for now. I'll come back for the rest.' To his surprise, he realized that he wanted to.

'You know I will help you.' Adam looked out of the

window. 'We're forgotten here. We need the world to remember us, and we need to find our way out into it.'

'I don't think my book will do that,' Jake said. 'It's all in the past.'

Adam shrugged. 'I think we live in the past,' he said. His gesture encompassed the city with its monuments and memorials. 'No matter. I think I may have found your family,' he said suddenly.

'My . . . you mean the Lange family.'

Adam nodded. 'There is a record of a Stanislau Lange who was an officer in one of the local militias after the Soviet invasion of eastern Poland. As far as I can tell, he operated on the Polish border of that time, around Baranoviche. And then the family moved to Minsk, in 1941. That fits in with your own research, no?'

It seemed that the Lange men, at least, had a record of collaboration with the Soviets.

Adam was looking at him. 'You are finding this unpalatable?' he said. 'You are reading it with the wrong eyes. Byelorussia had been split in two. The Poles were not kind to the Belarusians whose territory they were given. This man – maybe he was a patriot. He may have felt that his loyalty belonged to the Soviets rather than the Poles.'

'Okay.' Adam had a point. The twenty-twenty hindsight of his 21st-century perspective was perhaps not the most useful here. 'When can you let me know?'

'The bureaucracy here is slow,' Adam said. 'I have to get permission to access the archives, and then I have to get permission to take copies – I can't say.'

'Can you fax documents through?'

Adam smiled. 'We are not entirely stuck in the past. Yes, I can fax, if I have permission to copy the material.' He called the waiter over. 'We need vodka,' he said. 'This is a farewell. Did you visit the museum?'

Jake nodded. 'It was . . .' He couldn't find the words. 'What happened to them?' he said. 'To the people who did that?' In his mind, he could still see the face of the officer placing a noose round the neck of a child, the obscene concentration in his expression. 'The killing, the death camp . . . Maly Trostenets?'

'Some were taken by the Red Army. Some got away. The man who commanded one unit of the Security Police in Minsk fled to the west. Karlis Ozols was his name. He was an excellent chess player – he became the Australian chess champion.' Adam raised an eyebrow. 'God has a sense of humour. Another, a platoon commander in the *Schutzmannschaft*, Antonas Gecevicius, changed his name to Gecas and escaped to Britain. He was still there not so many years ago.'

Jake nodded. It wasn't over. Those pictures, frozen in time, were living memories for the people who had done it.

They spent the rest of the evening talking about the legacies of the war.

When Jake got back to his room, he wasn't tired. He was adept at living out of a briefcase and had done what packing he needed to do. He switched on his laptop and started putting his article together. He found himself falling into the house style of the magazine easily enough, the cool cynicism that was appropriate for monuments to The People and the glories of The State. He could throw the article together in a couple of hours.

But the monuments were all that was left.

The dead had their graves and the living tried to forget.

Faith left work at lunchtime to go to the hospital. Grandpapa had been moved from intensive care on to a ward that consisted of a long corridor with four-bed units opening off it. It didn't have the sense of subdued urgency she'd felt in the ITU. She tried to tell herself that this move must mean he was improving, but the ward was full of old people. Some, like Grandpapa, were comatose, others wandered vaguely, apparently lost in a world that only they could see. It felt like a place where people were taken to die.

She sat down beside his bed and took his hand. 'It's me. It's Faith,' she said. Her voice sounded loud against the background noise of the hospital. It was a place where no one spoke, apart from the interminable television at the far end of the room. He wasn't lying in that deathly stillness any more. Instead, he shifted restlessly on the bed, his lips moving in an urgent monologue that was impossible to decipher.

'What's wrong? Is he in pain?' Faith asked one of the nurses.

The nurse shook her head. 'There's something worrying him,' she said. 'He won't settle.' She raised her voice. 'Are you all right, Marek? You've got a visitor.' She watched him for a minute, then straightened up. 'He needs to rest.'

Faith leaned over the bed. 'Grandpapa,' she said. 'I'm here. What is it?'

His eyes focused on her: '. . . the light . . . you must . . .' His voice was slurred and tailed away into incoherent mumbling, but his hand reached out towards her, urgently.

'Does he know I'm here?' she asked.

The nurse straightened the sheet. 'Yes, he's probably very aware, but he can't communicate. Talk to him. Let him know you're trying to understand.'

Faith watched him as his head turned on the pillow and his eyes sought something he couldn't find. She took his hands and tried to keep them still, but he pushed her away. After a while, he sank into an exhausted sleep.

Faith sat and watched his face. On Tuesday, before he collapsed, he'd been frightened of something. What was it he'd said when she found him in the dark hallway? *The light . . .* The light had disturbed him, and later, he'd kept watch on the garden. *I think I have left it behind, and all the time . . . It is better if I die, too.*

'He looks so small . . .'

Faith jumped. Katya was standing behind her, looking down at the bed. She leaned over and brushed her lips against her father's cheek. 'It's Katya, Papa,' she said. 'I'm sorry you're ill.' She looked at him for a moment longer, as if she was expecting some kind of answer, then she straightened up. 'I wanted to see you before I go back,' she said. 'You weren't answering your phone.'

'I've been busy,' Faith said evasively. She hadn't answered the phone because she didn't know what to say to her mother.

'How is he?' Katya was studying her father, her expression unreadable.

'There's something . . .' Faith told her about his restless urgency, his inability to rest. 'Something's worrying him.' Worrying him to death.

Katya frowned. 'We need to talk.' She held up her hand. 'Not things we can talk about here,' she said. 'I'll meet you in that café place across the road. Don't be too long.' Her heels tapped briskly as she left the room.

Faith lingered by Grandpapa's bed. She needed to talk to Katya, and she had a meeting in an hour, but she was reluctant to go. 'I don't want to leave him,' she said to the nurse. 'What if . . . ?'

'He's stable,' the nurse said. 'We'll call you if there's any change.'

She made sure, again, that they had the number of her phone. 'Don't worry,' the nurse said. 'We'll call you.' But Faith couldn't shake off the idea that in the chaos of the busy ward, the needs of an old man might easily be forgotten.

By the time she got to the café, Katya was sitting at a table, an empty cup in front of her. 'Coffee?' she said as Faith came across.

Faith pulled out a chair and sat down. Katya ordered more coffee and busied herself with rearranging the table. By unspoken agreement, their last conversation wasn't mentioned.

273

'I wanted to see you because I've got to go back today,' Katya said. She met Faith's gaze and shifted defensively. 'I have to. They want me back at my desk tomorrow morning. I've been going through Marek's papers, and there are some things I need to tell you.' Faith listened in silence as her mother explained what she had found. Grandpapa's financial affairs were in a mess. 'As far as I can tell, he's been living off his state pension. He's got a massive overdraft. I'm trying to sort it out. But it's worse than that. He took out a mortgage on the house. He hasn't been paying that, either. I think it might have to be sold.'

Faith rubbed her hand across her forehead as she tried to take in what her mother was telling her. 'He won't want to leave the house.' He would hate that and would resist it to his last breath. 'I don't understand what's happened to his money.'

'Neither do I.' The coffee arrived. Katya picked up her cup – she always took coffee black – and sipped. She pulled a face and put the cup down. 'It's impossible to get decent coffee in this country.' Her voice was brisk and businesslike as she went on. 'One of us will have to get power of attorney – I'm not sure how it works if Marek is too ill to give consent. We have to move fast. He's going to need to go somewhere when he comes out of hospital and I don't know where else the money for that can come from.'

Katya was right. He couldn't live alone again, but Faith couldn't imagine him living in a care home, taken away from his garden, his solitude destroyed. If he survived the stroke, that alone would kill him. She prevaricated. 'Let's wait and see what happens.'

Katya studied the surface of the table, tracing the grain of the wood with a manicured finger. 'There's something else I need to talk to you about. I've been thinking about this a lot recently. There are papers at the house – you'll need to go through them before it's sold. I'm . . .' She seemed uncharacteristically reluctant to go on. 'I'm worried about what you might find.'

Faith looked at her blankly. 'What do you mean?'

'Why do you think he never talks about his family, or about the war?'

Because he wants to forget was on the edge of Faith's tongue, but he had not forgotten and he had not wanted to forget. Someone who wanted to forget would not have collected – and kept – all those cuttings.

'There's all the mystery about his past – he doesn't want us to be able to check back.' She didn't look at Faith, but gave her attention to stirring her coffee. 'There's something he doesn't want anyone to know. And I think that if he's kept it secret all this time, then it's better if it stays a secret.' Katya paused as if she was trying to choose her words. 'I know where some of the money went. He's given a fortune to the Red Cross over the years, and to charities in the old Iron Curtain countries, for reconstruction and education and all that sort of stuff.'

'What kind of secret?' Faith's lips felt stiff, as though she didn't want to speak.

'Do I have to spell it out? Something in the war. People did dreadful things then, it was . . . just the way it was. And then they went as far away as they could and tried to forget about it.'

A whole series of random bits and pieces that had been cluttering Faith's mind, apparently unrelated, now fell into place. It was like seeing a picture in a series of formless blobs, and once she had seen it, she couldn't believe that she hadn't seen it before. It would explain Grandpapa's unhappiness, and his guilt. It would explain why Jake Denbigh, a man with an avowed interest in war crimes, had appeared on the scene, asking questions. It would explain his restless search as he lay ill. She thought about the names in the cuttings on his desk – Karlis Ozols, Antonas Gecas.

'How long have you believed this?' she said. Her voice, cool and steady, surprised her.

'Always,' Katya said. 'As long as I can remember. My grandparents told me when they thought I was old enough.'

'How would they have known?' They hardly knew him. They hadn't come to the wedding. They were horrified by their daughter's choice.

'My mother must have told them.'

'But she didn't tell you?'

Katya shook her head. 'I was far too young. But she must have found out. Maybe he told her. It explains why she left him – she found out.'

'There's no mystery about that. The marriage wasn't working,' Faith remembered the bleak picture that Katya had painted, the laughing Irish woman from the photograph sitting alone night after night in that empty house, her husband shut away in his study.

Katya shook her head. 'You don't understand about Catholics,' she said. 'Or not that kind of Catholicism. She was brought up in one of the most fundamentalist traditions there was. It was a tradition that told her she was risking eternal damnation by living with a man she hadn't truly married. She loved him enough to do that. Only a Catholic marriage service would have counted in the eyes of her Church. I think she must have hoped to bring him round to the idea eventually. But having made her decision it would have been more sinful for her to go rather than stay. So what did she find out that drove her away?'

'And you've never talked to him about it?'

Katya gave her a cool look. 'Would you?'

'Yes. Of course. I would have asked him. Why didn't you tell me before?'

'I made you see him as a father – I left you with him. When was I supposed to tell you? When you were a child? When you were in your teens and going through that "You've

276

stolen my identity" phase? There seemed no reason why it would come to light, so why should you ever have to know? Whatever he did, it was nothing to do with you.'

Faith thought about the cuttings she'd read, about the eye-witness accounts she'd found among Helen's documents, about the records she'd seen. She thought of the public hangings, the mass killings, women and children shot in cold blood, people driven into buildings that were then set alight, women raped, children starved, beaten and tortured.

And she thought of the man she had known all her life, the man who brought her up, who told her stories, who supported her, the man who understood the cycle of the seasons, the man who loved roses. He was a flawed man, she knew that. He had been a ruthless businessman, an implacable opponent, an inadequate father and husband, but she still couldn't find any space in that picture for a man who would murder and rape.

'I think you're wrong,' she said.

Katya sighed. 'I know you don't want to believe it. I wouldn't have said anything if I hadn't thought you might find out anyway. Well, I've told you now. The rest is up to you.' She offered Faith a cigarette.

Faith shook her head. 'If we're finally sharing secrets, maybe it's time for you to tell me who my father was.'

Katya froze, then said, 'I don't see that there's any point, not now. I want some more coffee.' She looked round for the waiter. 'What does it matter?'

'I won't know until you tell me,' Faith said. They were a family with too many secrets, Grandpapa with the war he would never discuss, Katya with the lover she had never named. Faith wasn't letting her off the hook this time. There was a tense silence as each one waited for the other to speak.

'All right, I'll tell you.' The words seemed to be jerked out of Katya in an angry rush. 'It was when I was at school. We used to go out in the evenings, some of us. We weren't supposed to, but we did. We weren't supposed to go anywhere near boys, or drink, or anything like that. Anyway, there was a student party. I met him there. His name was Mike. I drank too much, and it all got out of hand. A few weeks later, I realized I was pregnant. I didn't know how to get in touch with him – I didn't even know his surname. I had to leave school, of course, and come home. I thought Marek would be angry, but he just dealt with it the way he dealt with everything.' Katya's jaw snapped shut. Maybe she had hoped her father would be angry, that he would care enough to be angry.

Faith looked across the table at her mother. She was dressed casually in grey trousers and a cream jersey. The trousers were beautifully tailored and the jersey was flawless cashmere. Her face was lightly but perfectly made up. She was thin to the point of emaciation. She always watched her diet like a hawk. From Faith's earliest memory of her, Katya had been the epitome of control. Out of all her imaginings, the story Katya had told her was the last thing she had expected.

She understood, now, why her mother had never told her. The sixteen-year-old Faith, the Faith who wanted to know, the Faith who had invented the debonair and dashing dream-father would have made her mother pay for that bit of honesty. Now she had to come to terms with the fact that her father was a student who had had casual sex with a drunken schoolgirl and had never bothered to find out if there had been any consequences.

She helped herself to one of Katya's cigarettes and inhaled deeply, holding the smoke in her lungs until she felt the slight dizziness of the nicotine hit. 'Thank you for telling me,' she said into her mother's silence.

'I didn't want . . .' Katya began.

A man came through the door and looked round. 'Taxi for Lange,' he announced.

For a moment, Katya looked guilty. 'I do have to go. My train . . .'

Faith nodded. 'I know.' She realized now that there would never be any reconciliation between father and daughter.

Hesitantly, Katya touched Faith's arm. 'Look after yourself.'

'Of course. You too.'

Faith watched her mother's taxi drive away. She could feel a sense of pity for her mother that she had never felt before. Katya had grown up with a father who was unable to show that he loved her. And she had grown up believing that her father's past carried a monstrous secret.

Now Faith had to decide what she was going to do. Something was haunting her grandfather. Something that made him collect old newspaper cuttings, something that made him give all his money away, something that wouldn't let him rest, perhaps something that wouldn't let him die. She needed to help him find a resolution.

The Return

This is the story of a promise.

Minsk approached its second winter under the grip of the fascist occupiers. The Nazi advance pressed towards the east. Moscow would fall, was the whisper on the streets. Stalingrad had fallen. And then the advance slowed and stopped. But deep in occupied territory, Minsk was enslaved.

It was December. The damaged city had carried on as the occupiers tried to subdue it. The executions, the deportations, the reprisal killings were just parts of the battle to survive. Zoya had been deported to work in Germany. Eva took work as a nurse at the local hospital, and had been allowed to stay.

Everyone was hungry. Even the soldiers now shared the democracy of hunger. Only the officers looked sleek, but their eyes were haunted too, as the stories began to trickle through of what was happening at the front. The tide of the war was about to turn.

Eva worked. She was quiet, she scrubbed floors, she washed bloodstained bandages and soiled sheets. She washed the bedpans and cleaned the latrines. This was the work she was good for. And because she was quiet and inconspicuous, the orderlies used to take pity on her and trade food from the hospital kitchen for tobacco or the cheap vodka that was easy enough for anyone to get. Eva was glad enough for the eggs and the milk that came her way. Mama was ill and getting sicker. She coughed in the night, and tried to hide the blood on her handkerchiefs from Eva, and Eva pretended not to see.

She screwed up her courage and spoke to one of the doctors. He was a distant, busy man, but she had observed that he wasn't unkind. He listened as Eva told him about Mama's sickness. He shook his head. 'There's nothing to be done,' he said. 'Not here. Not now.'

If Mama was her despair, Marek was her secret hope. Since the first note, she had heard from him twice. He was still alive, still fighting. *It's hard but we are hurting them*, he said in his second note. *Don't give up*. Eva, who went silently through the streets from the hospital to the apartment, from the apartment around the city in the endless search for food, began to carry notes herself, spreading the network of resistance throughout the city. If she was caught, they would kill her, but the small, trudging figure attracted no attention from the patrols. Eva had learned about invisibility in the forest and she passed through the occupied streets, a shadow among shadows.

The new year was about to begin. A child running past her on the frozen street held out his hand to her and they skated together briefly over a patch of ice, then the child ran on.

This was the third note from Marek, but this time, it was different.

It isn't safe for you in the city any more. I will be at the gate with the bear on Thursday evening at six. Meet me there and I will tell you what to do.

Marek was coming into the city. Marek was going to risk the patrols and the informers, because he thought she was in danger. She wanted to tell him to stay away, but she had no way of contacting him. *It isn't safe for you in the city any more.* It wasn't safe for anyone, anywhere. She wasn't safe, Mama wasn't safe, Papa had gone, and Marek lived with danger every day.

Don't come. Don't come. She projected the message, but at the same time the thought of seeing her brother again filled her with a sense of lightness, as though Marek's presence would make everything come right.

21

Jake's plane got in at ten in the morning. It was raining as he drove back up the motorway. The traffic was heavy and he got stuck behind a line of cars, the wheels of the heavy lorries spraying dirty water across his windscreen. It made him think of the country he'd just left with its landscape of empty roads, flat marshlands and dense forest.

It was after two when he got into Manchester. He hesitated. He felt tired and travel stained, and he'd planned to go straight home, but instead he found himself taking the road that led to the Yevanov house. He couldn't forget what Miss Yevanova had said to him when she agreed to tell him about the Kurapaty Forest: *I may be ashes next time we meet.*

And when he saw her, he was shocked at her deterioration in the few days that he had been away. The skin of her face looked more tightly drawn, the shadows under her eyes were darker and he noticed a tremor in the hand she extended to him.

'Mr Denbigh, how quickly you have returned. It's good of you to call,' she said. Her voice was almost a whisper. She went through with the ritual summoning of tea, but this time Mrs Barker served, checking Jake's preferences with a swift glance and raised eyebrow, placing Miss Yevanova's cup so that she could lift it with the smallest amount of movement. The nurse then withdrew discretely. Miss Yevanova had distanced herself from the whole process.

Jake wanted to say something to indicate his concern, but he knew that the only way she could bear to deal with her increasing debility was to ignore it. 'I just got back,' he said. 'I wanted to tell you about it.'

She smiled. That had pleased her. He studied the icon on the wall behind her. It was a jewel lifted from its setting – a bit like Sophia Yevanova herself.

She was watching him and he nodded in the direction of the painting. 'I've seen where it came from now,' he told her.

She looked at him and shook her head. 'Minsk is dead,' she said. 'They built a memento mori on its corpse.' She lifted her cup with some difficulty. He kept his eyes on the icon until she had negotiated it back on to the table. 'And where else did you go?' she said. 'The forests and the Pripyet Marshes can be very beautiful – or they were when I was a child. Now, who knows?'

'I believe they still are,' he said, 'but I didn't have enough time. I went to Kurapaty.'

'You know, of course, the Kurapaty Forest that stands now is not the forest that was there before the war?' she said. 'It was cut down. They replanted it – but the trees must be mature by now.'

He hadn't realized that. He hadn't thought about it.

'And the village, Zialony Luh?' He could hear a slight tremor in her voice. She was trying to keep this conversation light and casual, but she was finding it hard.

'It's gone,' he said. 'There's nothing there.'

She picked up the embroidery that was stretched on the hoop beside her, again carefully placed for easy reach. He watched her as she ran her fingers across the design, almost as if she were having trouble seeing it. 'And in Kurapaty? Was there anything there?' she asked.

'In the forest? There's a memorial, and crosses under the trees. I could see the places where the ground had sunk, the places where the burial pits had been.' He described his drive from the city, the walk through the trees with the taxi driver. He told her about the rows of crosses disappearing into the shadows. There was no point in trying to soften it. He had seen only the distant aftermath. She had been there.

She pushed her needle through the fabric. She seemed more herself now, the concentration on her work calming her. He could see that the tremor in her hands had lessened. 'Since we last talked, I have been thinking about it,' she admitted. 'I sometimes think it must still be there, still waiting. I think that somewhere those trucks are still running through the night, those sounds still echoing in the trees. Sometimes in the night, I am afraid I will open my eyes and find myself back there.' Her dark eyes fixed on his face. 'Where is the past, Mr Denbigh? How can things like that ever be ended?'

He didn't know what to say. He thought about the frozen moments he had seen in the museum: the crying child, the grieving mother, the girl hanging in her eternal agony. Were those moments truly finished, or did they still exist somewhere in the place where the past had gone? 'I don't know,' he said. 'I just know we can't get back to it.'

She kept her eyes on him, as if she was expecting him to say more, then she sighed. 'What else did you see?'

He told her about the museum. 'There were photographs of the occupation,' he said. 'They were . . . bad. But I don't need to tell you that. And there were artefacts from the death camp at Maly Trostenets – photos of some of the victims, the gallows. I'd never heard of it before – I don't think many people have. I'd like to write something about that.'

He looked across at her. She was sitting very still and her face was a white triangle above her dark shawl. 'Of course.' Her voice was little more than a whisper and her breathing was laboured.

She needed help. He was at her side at once. 'Let me . . .' She raised her hand in refusal as the door opened, and Mrs Barker came in.

'The professor is home,' she said to Miss Yevanova. Her voice was calm, but she spoke quickly. 'He will come and see you in a few minutes.' She caught Jake's eye, and gestured with her head that it was time for him to leave.

He stepped back. 'I'll tell you the rest next time,' he said, trying to keep up her pretence that all was well, trying not to make it sound as though he were saying goodbye.

She didn't reply, and he left the room quickly, leaving Mrs Barker to see to her. As he closed the door behind him, he became aware of Antoni Yevanov watching him from the doorway of another room.

'You're back, Mr Denbigh.' Yevanov didn't make this sound like a matter for celebration.

'Miss Yevanova seems tired,' Jake said. Yevanov's first comment didn't seem to warrant any kind of response.

The other man came across the hall towards Jake. His face was cold. 'I am sure that in some way my mother feels obligated towards you . . .' He held up his hand as Jake was about to speak. 'Please, I have no interest in the details. Whatever that obligation is, you must consider it discharged. I would prefer it if you didn't visit her again.'

And Jake had no option but to leave.

Faith decided she would stay at her grandfather's for the next couple of days. She could finish off the work Katya had started. There were still crucial documents missing among the

285

mountains of paper he had accumulated over the years – the deeds of the house, his share certificates, anything that might be converted into money to pay for the care he would need.

She went home to pack a bag, and stocked up at the supermarket. She didn't know how long this was going to take. It was after eight by the time she pulled into the drive. The house looked as if the life had gone out of it and now it was starting to decay. In the moonlight, she could see the ivy growing over the windows, the peeling paint and the water stains where a fall pipe had come away.

She let herself in through the front door, feeling the cold close round her. She switched on the heating and turned the thermostat up full blast. She went through to the kitchen and cleaned out the fridge before putting away her shopping. Warmth began to leak into the air as she worked, accompanied by the roar and clank of the boiler. She could remember this kitchen from her childhood. The red lino was still the same, and the wooden cupboards, but in her memory it was warm and bright, and it smelled of herbs and of cooking as Grandpapa worked. She blinked, and she was back in the empty, dimly lit room.

She scooped up all the stuff she had discarded from the fridge and bagged it. She unlocked the kitchen door and dumped the rubbish in the bin. As she came back in, her phone rang, vibrating on the hard surface of the table. Her first thought was that the hospital was calling, and she took a deep breath before she answered. 'Hello?'

'Faith. It's me.'

It was Helen's voice. The phone almost slipped from her fingers, then she realized the voice had the reedy timbre of male adolescence. It was Finn.

'Finn! Are you okay? Is everything all right?'

'Yeah. I just . . . I wanted . . .' She heard him breathing, then the words came in a rush. 'I called you at home and you didn't answer.'

'I'm at my grandfather's – what's wrong, Finn?' There had to be something wrong if he was calling.

'The police came round to see Dad.'

'The police? What did they want?'

'I listened,' Finn said. 'Outside the door. They didn't want to tell me, but I've got a right to know. She was my mum. They came to tell him that it wasn't that caretaker guy that . . . you know . . . hurt her. *Killed* her. They told Dad. I heard them.' Finn sounded distressed. He had been directing his hate and anger towards this man, and now he didn't have anyone to blame.

'How do they know?'

'They found her watch, mum's watch. It was broken – it got smashed up when he . . . when . . . It got broken. They had to do some tests, but now they know what time it said. So they know when it happened.'

Helen's watch. The mysterious new watch with the delicate silver band. And it had recorded the time that Helen had died.

She didn't ask, but Finn told her anyway. 'They said eight fifteen. It happened at eight fifteen.'

Her mind flew back to that evening, trying to remember what she had been doing, but she had no recollection. Finn must have been thinking the same thing. 'I was reading Hannah a story,' he said. 'She wouldn't go to sleep because of her party, so I was reading her a story.'

'I'm sorry, Finn,' she said. There wasn't anything else to say.

'Who do you think they'll look for? Now? They'll start looking again, won't they?'

'Yes. Of course. They'll find the person who did it, Finn, I'm sure they will.' She could hear the hollow note in her voice as she spoke.

When he spoke again, his voice was tentative. 'Do you think . . . if someone . . .' He fell silent.

'What, Finn? What is it?'

He spoke quickly. 'Nothing. I've got to go.' She could hear sounds, voices in the background, then he rang off, and she was left staring at the silent phone.

Helen had died at eight fifteen. For some reason, that put Nicholas Garrick in the clear. Helen's watch – the expensive new watch – had been broken, had been *smashed-up*, Finn had said. She had a sudden picture of a heavy boot stamping on the watch, powered by a jealous rage.

Her mind was filling with images of things she didn't want to see, and there was something nagging at her, something Finn had said that had alarmed her, but she couldn't pin it down. He'd said . . . She suddenly remembered the day they'd talked outside the school gates. Finn had said something about a visitor, about Daniel having a visitor the night Helen had died, and he'd watched her with an odd expression. His face had been speculative, almost sly. She'd said: *Exactly how stupid do you think I am?* And he'd said: *That's what I'm trying to find out.*

And . . . now she remembered what it was that had worried her. Finn had said: *I was reading Hannah a story.* Finn didn't read to Hannah – he always refused if Helen asked him, always refused if Hannah nagged. He thought Hannah's books were *lame* and *girly* and *spaz*. But if he'd been left alone with his little sister who wouldn't sleep, then maybe he'd had no choice. And then Helen had phoned, and the children had listened to her voice on the machine, but they couldn't answer because Helen was not to know that their father had gone out and left them alone. Hannah had tried to tell her – and Finn had taken her away.

She knew, suddenly, that when he had told her there had been another witness to Daniel's presence in the house that evening, Finn had lied. But the police must have had the same story. They would have talked to whoever it was Daniel claimed had been there. And the fact that Daniel had phoned

Helen back in response to her message didn't mean he'd been in the house. Finn could easily have contacted his father.

The phone rang again, it's sudden vibration unnerving her. She grabbed for it, almost dropping it as she picked it up and answered it before she thought to see who was calling. 'Yes? Hello?'

It clicked off to silence.

She checked the number. It was Daniel's phone. She knew what had happened. Daniel had come in and seen Finn talking on the phone. He'd checked by the simplest expedient who his son had called, and she'd answered.

Jake drove straight home. He wondered what had happened since he last saw Sophia Yevanova to make her son issue his ban. He wondered where Nick Garrick was, and what had happened on the case while he'd been away. Thinking about this, he stopped and picked up a local paper.

The flat was empty and unwelcoming as he let himself in. The letters waiting for him were all in buff envelopes. For the first time in his life, he felt lonely coming back from a trip. He wondered what it would be like to have someone waiting, someone whose face would light up because he had walked through the door. *For Christ's sake*, he told himself exasperatedly, *if you want that, get a dog*.

He picked up the phone and checked his messages. There were several *When are you back?* queries from his editor – who knew perfectly well. Their relationship was still edgy from the Juris Ziverts incident. He wanted Jake's next column e-mailed through by nine the next morning. There was also a message from Cass, who'd called not long before he'd got in. *Are you there? I know you're home today. Listen, developments. Give me a ring*.

He lit a cigarette and poured himself a glass of whisky, then dialled Cass's number. 'Cass? It's Jake.'

'Oh. You're back then.'

'No, I'm in Turkmenistan . . .'

'*Really*? Oh . . . For God's sake, Jake, spare me the wit. Did you get my message?'

'Developments. Sounds interesting.'

'Well . . .' she said, drawing it out, 'It'll probably be in the papers, but *I* know the details.'

'The Kovacs murder? Nick Garrick?'

'Garrick-Smith,' Cass said. 'And there's ne-ews.' She drew it out on a teasing note.

She was making the most of it. News about Garrick – Miss Yevanova hadn't said anything. He waited, knowing that any sign of impatience would just make her worse.

'Don't you want to know?' Cass said.

'Do you want to tell me? Or shall I just check the paper? I've got it here –' He rustled it encouragingly.

'Oh, all right. Garrick's out,' she said.

He was disappointed. 'Is that all? He was out before I went away.'

'No,' she said impatiently. 'I mean, he's out of the picture. He's in the clear.'

That was news. 'Why?'

'I don't know. They've managed to get a fix on the time of death.'

If that was the case, then the phone call that Sophia Yevanova had made would be crucial. He made a quick note – he wanted to check this with Burnley. 'So who's in the picture now?'

Cass was revving up to play games with the information again. He put his hand over the phone, but not in time to stop his sigh of impatience reaching her.

'What's wrong with you? You sound as if your pet goldfish died.'

He needed to explain his lack of response. 'I'm tired, that's all.'

'Well, you flew with Polish airlines,' she said. 'It's a bit third world, isn't it?'

'There was nothing wrong with it.' He couldn't keep the irritation out of his voice. What was the matter with him? Why couldn't he make a joke of it, tell her about the pilot's accent, the pretty hostesses, anything to get the talk flowing? 'I'm just tired,' he said again. 'I've been up since six this morning.'

'Okay,' she said. Her voice was suddenly cool. 'They're checking up on the husband again – apparently he was threatening to take Kovacs to court over custody of the kids – but he's got an alibi. He was at home. Kovacs spoke to him after seven thirty, and he had someone with him from about eight thirty. No way he could get there and back in the time. They think there was a boyfriend, but they haven't managed to track him down. The professor is a prime suspect there. He denies it, the secretary denies it . . .'

'Oh well, *that's* conclusive.' Jake was suddenly alert.

'It probably is,' Cass said. 'Secretaries usually know. But he's got an alibi as well – he was at home looking after his sick mum. Bless! Mick Burnley – he thinks they got it right first time.'

'Garrick?' His mind was working quickly. If the time of death coincided with the phone call, then no matter what Burnley's not inconsiderable gut told him, Nick Garrick was in the clear.

He let his mind go back to the afternoon in Sophia Yevanova's garden, Nick Garrick leaning on the spade he had dug into the earth, talking about the way she had taken care of him when he was a child. Garrick had looked as though he'd be more at home on the rugby pitch, or on the rock faces of Derbyshire than caught up in the dark coils of a past that had nothing to do with him. Jake realized he was relieved that he no longer had to watch Garrick with suspicion.

And the suspicions about Antoni Yevanov? Something told him that if Yevanov was involved in anything criminal, he would have covered his tracks far more effectively than had Helen Kovacs' killer.

'So what are you doing tonight?' Cass was saying. 'We could celebrate your return.'

'Cass, I can't. I've got too much to do.'

'Since when did you become such a fucking workaholic?'

'Since always. It's what I want to do, Cass.'

'Rather than see me?'

He didn't say anything.

'Okay,' she said. Her voice was bright and brittle. 'Fuck you then. Just . . .'

He thought she was crying. 'Cass . . .' But she'd hung up. He reached to phone her back, then decided there was no point. He couldn't say anything she wanted to hear, and he didn't have the energy for a row. She was hurt, but maybe it was better now than later. He'd let it drift for too long.

He was just . . . The faded black and white of old images floated at the back of his mind: rubble and dead babies and the anguished face of the girl choking her life away on the end of a rope . . . *Shit!* He pressed the button on the TV remote, then turned if off again just as quickly as the imbecile babble of a quiz-show presenter filled the air.

He unpacked his bag and shoved the dirty clothes into the washer. His eyes felt sore and gritty. He looked out of the window. The London rain had followed him up the motorway. The pavements shone in the dull afternoon light. He'd try and make contact with Miss Yevanova tomorrow, choose a time when Yevanov was likely to be out of the way. He'd accept his dismissal if he heard it from her, but not before.

There was something else he needed to do, and he felt a heavy reluctance. He needed to talk to Marek Lange again.

NKVD. He hadn't expected that. If he closed his eyes, he could see the burial pits vanishing into the shadows under the trees. Lange had survived the war. He had been in Minsk before the Nazi invasion – Minsk had been attacked and overrun in days. A soldier trapped in Minsk would not have had a long life expectancy, but somehow Lange had lived through it, and escaped.

In Minsk, in those days, there had been another way of surviving. What was it that Lange had said? *I should know. I did know. It is wrong.* Wrong. What was *wrong*? Kurapaty or collaboration? Or both?

He'd liked Lange when he'd interviewed him. He'd enjoyed the old man's curmudgeonly independence and his sharp mind. And he knew that he could be on the edge of something with Faith Lange, something that could be valuable, something that could be worth having. But if Lange was implicated – either in Kurapaty, or in the Nazi atrocities on the streets of Minsk – Jake wouldn't shield him. He couldn't. He thought about the crosses under the trees of Kurapaty, the sunken earth marking the death pits, the dying girl on the end of the rope. There was nothing morally ambiguous about exposing a war criminal.

He felt more tired than he could remember.

He picked up the newspaper and checked through it, looking for any references to the Kovacs story. It had been relegated to the inside pages. The police were 'no closer' to making an arrest. Nothing new there, then.

He almost missed it. It was a small paragraph tucked away at the bottom of the page: *Local businessman and philanthropist Marek Lange was admitted to hospital earlier this week after collapsing at home. Doctors said that his condition was 'causing concern'.*

Lange. But it had been Sophia Yevanova who had joked about dying, who had said, *I may be ashes next time we meet.* Without stopping to think, he found Faith's home number in his diary and called her, but her phone rang and rang unanswered.

The call had left Faith nervous and edgy. She didn't know what to think. The man they thought had killed Helen was innocent. Finn was telling lies. She knew that the children had been alone that evening. Which meant . . . Even now, even after the events of the past few days, she found it hard to accept that Daniel, a man she'd known for twelve years, could have killed Helen, could have coldly and deliberately strangled his wife.

She couldn't settle. She found herself wandering through the house trying to distract herself by making mental notes of everything that needed doing before Grandpapa could come back, as if this might make his return a possibility. She switched the lights on as she went, trying to counteract the loneliness of the house, but the lights were dim and cast shadows as she moved. The rooms were silent and unused.

She shivered. The wind was picking up and the house seemed to be getting colder. She could hear the trees swaying, and remembered her childhood fantasy that the house was in the middle of a forest. As she listened, she realized that the noise of the boiler had stopped. It had shut down. She sighed, and went through to the kitchen to see if she could start it up again.

The wind rattled the kitchen door, and she heard the sound of something falling over and tumbling across the yard outside. She yanked the cover off the boiler, and saw that the pilot light was out. She relit it, after a struggle. Thank God for the gas fire in the front room, antique though it was. Grandpapa had coped with the cold by shutting the house up, room by room.

And now it seemed alive with sounds, the wind that sighed in the night, the susurration of the trees. It was starting to rain. The twigs scraped and clawed, and the raindrops rattled against the panes. She could hear an owl calling, and the high-pitched bark of a fox. The hunters were out in the night.

The wind gusted, making the doors rattle, and she heard the crunch of gravel in the drive. A car. Someone had driven through the gate. At first, she thought it might be Katya, relented and returned, but Katya had left on the train. Then the door bell sounded, ringing in the back of the house, in the kitchen. She had no idea who could be calling at the old house so late. The bell sounded again. She went to the door, making sure it was locked and on the chain. 'Who's there?' she said.

'Daniel Kovacs.' He must have pressed the bell again because it shrilled with a long peal. 'Are you going to open this door?'

Now the cold was inside her. She could still see his face as he'd advanced on her in the house, his eyes cold with menace and the muscles in his arms bunched. 'I don't want to talk to you, Daniel,' she said. 'Go home.'

The door rattled as he shook it, but the lock held. She could see the piece of cardboard she'd taped over the broken pane a few evenings ago. She hadn't had time to get it fixed. The porch was dark. He might not notice it. 'Please,' she said. 'Go.' The fear was like a lump of ice in her stomach, but her voice was steady.

He didn't answer, but hit the door once, hard. She held her breath, listening. She'd left her mobile on the kitchen table, but there was the phone in the hallway. She could hear the crunch of his feet on the gravel as he moved away. He was going. The footsteps faded down the drive. She had a sudden conviction that when he had told her there had been another witness to Daniel's presence in the house the evening Helen died, Finn had been lying. But the police must have had the same story. They would have talked to whoever it was Daniel claimed had been there.

There was something nagging at her, something she'd forgotten.

She straightened up, still listening. Silence.

The car.

She hadn't heard the car drive away.

And then something cold touched her spine and she was running towards the back of the house, towards the kitchen. She could picture it in her mind. She'd opened the kitchen door to put out the rubbish. She could see herself coming back through the door, distracted by a ringing phone, carelessly pushing it closed with her foot.

And he was there, the door wide open behind him, standing at the other side of the kitchen table, his face that mask of cold menace she remembered too well. She grabbed at her phone which was lying on the table, but he knocked it away. It skittered across the wooden surface and dropped off. 'You should keep your fucking doors locked,' he said.

Helen had been strangled and her watch had been smashed as a foot had stamped down on it. She could feel her breath coming in uneven gasps. She couldn't speak. Think. She had to think. She couldn't get back to the phone in the hall – he was too close. Her mobile. She hadn't heard it hit the floor. It must have landed on the chair. She began to back away towards the table.

He looked at her, working his jaw as if to loosen it. 'You don't listen, do you? I told you to stay away from my kids.'

She could feel the edge of the table against her thigh. She moved away from him, putting the table between them, trying not to look down to where her phone had landed. Did he realize that she knew, that she had worked it out? Something caught against the back of her legs, knocking her off balance. The chair. The chair where her phone must have landed. She grabbed the table for support, her hand reaching down. She felt across the seat of the chair. Her fingers brushed against the phone, knocking it sideways. *Christ!*

296

He was moving closer, using his bulk to intimidate her. 'I told you to keep away from them. You know what it means?' he said. 'Did they teach you that at your fancy-pants university?' He thrust his face towards her. '*Keep away from my kids!*'

Her fingers closed round the phone.

'Is this the old man's place? It stinks in here. Is that how you live, people like you? Stink and dirt and mess?' He was looking at her in contempt.

She felt across the keypad and was punching in the emergency number as she backed away from him. She could feel the warmth coming off him and smell the sweat of tension. 'You don't know what you're doing! You haven't got a clue . . .'

She held the phone up now that she could hear a voice speaking. 'Police!' she said, giving Grandpapa's address before the operator could connect her. 'Quickly!'

His face flushed with rage and he reached towards her, but the table kept him away. She pressed herself further back. 'Police,' the phone said in her ear.

She gave the address again. 'He's broken in. Daniel Kovacs. He's broken in. Please! Hurry!'

Then she felt the wall against her back. She'd retreated as far as she could, and now she was trapped in the corner. Daniel hesitated, moved towards her, then backed off, suddenly indecisive. He pointed his finger at her. 'Cunt!' he said. His voice was low and tight. 'You stupid cunt! Just stay away from my kids or you'll be sorry.'

And then he walked out, not hurrying, apparently unconcerned that the police would be on their way. She stayed frozen in place, then she was across the room to the door, turning the key and pulling the bolts across, trying to control the shaking that was threatening to make hers legs collapse. She heard the thump of a van door, the crunch of the gravel, but it was a long time before she could make herself go to the window. When she did, the drive was empty. He'd gone.

Then she sat down to wait for the police. She'd left it for too long. She had to tell them about Daniel.

22

Jake was finding it hard to concentrate. He was trying to get his article finished so he could e-mail it for the deadline, but his mind kept circling around Minsk, Marek Lange, Lange's illness, Nick Garrick, Sophia Yevanova. He thought about the scene in the hallway of the Yevanov house, Antoni Yevanov's voice, cold and distant, saying, *Whatever that obligation is, you must consider it discharged. I would prefer it if you didn't visit her again.*

And Jake had left. He'd hated giving in to Yevanov without argument, but he'd had no choice. He knew it was the battle he'd lost, not the war, but it still rankled. He was worried about Miss Yevanova as well. For the first time, he had thought of her as frail – a word that she would hate and that seemed almost obscene in connection with her.

He read back what he'd written and pressed the 'delete key' in frustration. He lit a cigarette and stared blankly at the screen in front of him. He'd had an idea. He picked up his phone and checked the numbers. He didn't have one for Nick Garrick. He remembered Garrick saying he'd cancelled his contract when he couldn't pay the bills. He keyed in the number of the Yevanov house, his mind working quickly as he heard the phone ringing.

He was lucky. Mrs Barker answered so there was no need for subterfuge. 'It's Jake Denbigh,' he said. 'I'm sorry to call so late . . .' It was only eight, but he suspected that the household – Mrs Barker and Miss Yevanova at least – retired early.

'Mr Denbigh.' Mrs Barker sounded puzzled, but there was no hostility in her voice. Antoni Yevanov must not have said anything to her, or not yet. 'Is something wrong?'

'No, not at all. I was a bit worried about Miss Yevanova. How is she?'

'She's had a bad couple of days,' Mrs Barker said. 'She was better this evening.'

'That's good. Listen, I need to talk to Nicholas Garrick. Is he there?'

There was a moment's silence. 'Nicholas? I believe he's in his room. Why do you want . . . ?'

Jake didn't respond, and when she spoke again, she sounded flustered. 'Of course. I'll go and get him.'

Jake heard the clatter of the phone being put down, and the sound of footsteps. There was a murmur of voices, and then silence.

'Yeah?' Garrick's voice took Jake by surprise. There was an echo that told him Garrick was speaking on an extension.

'It's Jake Denbigh,' he said.

'Mrs Barker told me. What do you want?'

Good question, but not one he could answer. He was following his instincts, and something told him that a conversation with Garrick might be useful. Jake didn't want to talk on an open line. He could picture the phone in the hallway, the receiver lying on the table, and someone – Antoni Yevanov? – standing beside it, watchful and silent.

'There's something you can help me with – for the book, you know?'

'What –' Garrick stopped abruptly, apparently struck by the same thought that Jake had. 'Okay,' he said. 'When?'

'Tonight. If you're free.'

'Yeah, right. What would I be doing?' But Garrick sounded friendlier. He vetoed Jake's suggestion that he pick him up, and arranged to meet him at the pub close to Jake's flat. 'I know it. I'll be there. Nine, okay?' He hung up.

Now that he'd done something, Jake found that he was no longer distracted. He put everything else out of his mind and concentrated on putting the finishing touches to his article. Three-quarters of an hour later, he e-mailed it, then he grabbed his jacket and headed for the door. He knew what he wanted from Garrick now. He wanted an insider's view of Antoni Yevanov.

The pub was fairly quiet. He waited at the bar, watching out for Garrick. It was ten past the hour before he arrived, standing in the doorway and looking round cautiously as if he wasn't sure that he should be there. He saw Jake and came over. 'Drink?' Jake said.

Garrick shook his head. 'I'll get my own.' Then, as if aware this sounded a bit abrupt, he added, 'I can't afford to buy rounds.'

'Okay.' Jake stood back and waited as Nick ordered a bottle of lager. The girl who was serving behind the bar was pretty, wearing a tight T-shirt and low-cut jeans. Jake could see the flash of the ring piercing her navel. She seemed interested in Garrick, throwing a comment at him, laughing, prolonging the transaction to see if he wanted to chat, but Garrick was oblivious, digging his cash out of his pocket, nodding vaguely to something she said as he counted it out. She shrugged and went to the till.

'Okay,' Garrick said, once they'd found a table. 'What did you want to ask me?'

'You know that I'm writing a book about the war, about Sophia Yevanova's story, right?' He checked Garrick with a quick glance. Garrick nodded. 'I need to know a bit more about Antoni Yevanov.' Jake wasn't sure what he'd done to antagonize the man, but the hostility between them had been instant and mutual. *Know your enemy* seemed to be a good starting point. 'I know about his work, I know about his political stuff, but that's all I know. He keeps everything else under wraps.'

Garrick looked confused, as if he hadn't expected Jake to ask this. 'I thought . . . Don't you want to ask me about the library? About what happened?'

Jake shrugged. 'It's nothing to do with me.'

'I thought you were doing a story – you know, evil father, killer son. I thought that was why you were asking all those questions.'

Journalists and sewer rats occupied the same ecological niche in a lot of people's minds, Jake knew that, but Garrick's quick assumption still annoyed him. 'You were a news item for a couple of days. It's over – as far as you're concerned. They've moved on.'

Garrick's first response was anger. 'If you'd had all the . . .' He stopped abruptly and picked up his drink. 'Right. Sorry. Sometimes I forget he isn't around any more.' He ran his hand over his face. 'I don't know about Yevanov. I don't think I can tell you anything you don't know. He didn't visit much when I was there.'

'What about now? Why did he come here?' The Manchester appointment might be prestigious within the academic world, but Yevanov operated on a wider stage.

'I don't know. When I came out of hospital after the accident, he'd come back. Miss Yevanova's been a lot sicker this past year or so – he *said* he wanted to look after her.'

Altruism. Sophia Yevanova was close to her son. *The only thing of value . . .* Maybe that closeness was reciprocated, or enough to bring Yevanov to Manchester for the few years his mother had left, but Jake wasn't convinced.

He remembered the rumours about Yevanov and Helen Kovacs. Could it have been this woman who had brought Yevanov to a place on the outer edges of the European Union?

302

But he couldn't picture Yevanov acting under the impulse of his emotions. And anyway, a mother of two, struggling at the beginnings of her career seemed an unlikely candidate. What would she have had to attract a man like Yevanov? He had seen photographs of Yevanov's ex-wife, a French diplomat who was startlingly talented and startlingly beautiful. The marriage had ended in divorce about five years ago. Maybe the clash of egos had been too much. 'Did you ever meet his wife?'

'She wouldn't have come here.'

So much for inside information. Jake felt frustrated. He knew that Garrick could tell him stuff he wanted to know, but pushing the questions tonight would just make him hostile and suspicious. He leaned back in his chair and offered Garrick a cigarette.

Garrick shook his head. 'Those things'll kill you, man.'

Jake grinned, 'I'm holding out for the jealous husband on my eightieth birthday.'

Garrick's face twitched in a quick, reluctant smile. He was nursing the bottle of lager he'd bought, lifting it to his mouth and putting it down undrunk.

'Look, let me get you another. Call it payment for information.'

Garrick hesitated, then nodded. 'Okay.'

When Jake came back from the bar, Garrick nodded his thanks, but didn't say anything. Jake sat back and let the silence develop. After a while, Garrick spoke suddenly, as if what he had been thinking about had burst to the surface. 'I don't know what to do next. I can't stay there. And I've got to go back to uni in September.'

Jake had forgotten that Garrick was halfway through a degree. 'What subject?'

'Politics.' He didn't sound enthusiastic.

It seemed an unlikely subject for Garrick. Jake would have expected something more physical, something practical – engineering, sports studies, something like that. 'Why?'

303

'I always thought about going into politics. I thought, if I was there, I could do something about people like my father. Miss Yevanova thought it was a good idea.'

Jake couldn't imagine a less likely contender for the political world than Nick Garrick. 'Seriously? Is that what you want to do?'

'I thought I did, but . . . It's all stuff written by dead people and it's not much about *doing* anything. I mean, like you're Joe Blow for Scumborough East, and you sit in Parliament for fifty years and then you die. Who cares?'

Jake was amused by this quick – and to a certain extent accurate – summing up of parliamentary democracy. 'So what are you going to do?'

Garrick frowned. 'I don't know. I've got to finish the course.'

'Why? You don't have to. Switch courses, if that's not what you want to do.'

'I just . . .' Garrick fiddled with a beer mat, then looked at Jake. 'I want people to know. I want to stand up somewhere where they'll listen, and say "I am not my father".'

Jake could remember the egotism of his early twenties when he knew that the whole world was waiting in breathless anticipation to see what Jake Denbigh was going to do next, and he remembered the slow and painful dawning of the truth. 'You know something?' he said. 'No one cares.'

Garrick looked at him blankly. '*I* care.'

'So stand in front of the bathroom mirror and say it.'

'Yevanov cares. And my father did. He never knew what I thought, not really.'

Jake suppressed his exasperation. He could understand Garrick's predicament. He'd grown up with a cold and didactic father and a loving, but rather ineffectual, mother. His opinions had been formed more from rebellion than conviction. 'Yevanov doesn't give a toss. He just doesn't like you. It happens. And your father's dead.'

Garrick's face flushed. 'So I just . . . get on with it? Pretend it never happened?'

He would be angry with his father for the rest of his life. With reason. And there was probably a lot of anger towards his mother that he wasn't prepared to admit. Jake told himself to stop playing amateur psychiatrist. 'All I'm saying is, don't let all of that push you into something you don't want to do.'

Garrick was carefully peeling the beer mat in two. 'Thing is, I don't know what I do want to do.'

'You're – what? – twenty-two? Why do you have to make a decision now? There's a whole world out there. Take a year out. Give yourself a bit of time to think.'

Garrick looked thoughtful. 'I've never really been anywhere. I could get some cash together . . . I want to walk the Appalachian trail.' He crushed the beer mat and dropped it in the ashtray. 'You can do it in six months, easy. I could . . .' He looked into the distance, calculating.

For the rest of the evening, Jake let Garrick lead the talk. He listened to accounts of walking coastal paths, of the Pennine Way, of walks that Garrick had never done but heard about, of the particular demands of the challenging route up the spine of the USA.

It was almost ten thirty when they left the pub. The sky was clear. 'They say . . .' Garrick was looking up at the sky '. . . that out in the wilds, the stars . . . You never see them here, not even in the countryside. There's too much light. They say that the universe is expanding and everything is moving apart so fast that, in the end, there'll be no light from the stars at all. We'll just be on our own.'

Jake looked up at the night sky. There was something chilling about the prospect.

'You live near here, don't you?' Garrick said.

'Over there.' Jake indicated the apartment block.

'I don't know how you stand it. I can't stand being closed

305

in. I want to live somewhere open – where you can go for miles and not see a building or a road or anything.'

Jake grinned. 'You'd make a lousy politician then.'

'Right. Dead right. Look, thanks for the advice. I'm sorry if I thought . . . I got you wrong. Thanks.'

Jake watched as Garrick walked away towards the main road. He wondered if anything would come of their talk. He remembered, uneasily, a saying he'd heard about advice. If you gave someone advice and they took it, you were then responsible for the outcome. He shrugged the feeling off and walked back to his flat, the cobbles uneven under his feet. He found his mind going back to the things he'd been thinking about earlier, to Minsk, to Marek Lange, to Faith . . .

After the police had left, Faith went round the house obsessively checking the windows and doors. She no longer felt safe. She thought about going home, but she would have felt no safer there. Daniel knew how to find her and the two officers who had answered her call had not reassured her.

They'd seemed professional enough, but their questions had been oddly off-key, their responses more designed to sooth than to promise any action. 'So he didn't break in?' the older one said.

'Only because I'd forgotten to lock the back door.' They seemed to think this was important, and she couldn't get the violence of Daniel's entry into the house across to them.

'Don't worry,' he said. 'We'll have a word. He won't bother you again.' His avuncular manner grated on her nerves.

They promised to pass on what she had told them about Daniel's alibi the night of Helen's death, but she didn't feel reassured. She found herself jumping at every noise, lying awake through the night, listening intently as the old house creaked and settled around her.

Next morning, she felt better. Sleep had given her perspective. She had reported Daniel's behaviour, she had passed on her suspicions to the police. It was no longer her responsibility, and if the men who'd called round in the night hadn't seen the importance of what she'd told them, the people investigating Helen's death would. She felt lighter, as if she had been carrying something heavy, and now at last she was able to put it down.

When she phoned the hospital, the nurse she spoke to told her that Grandpapa was improving. 'He's a tough old bird,' she told Faith cheerfully.

Faith asked the nurse to tell him that she would visit later and she hung up feeling more hopeful. Maybe he would be able to communicate with her when she saw him. She told herself not to be too optimistic – whatever happened, his health would be poor for what time he had left.

The sun was shining, and she wanted some fresh air, so she walked down the road to the village where shops clustered round a small green, and picked up a paper and some croissants for breakfast. The woman behind the counter smiled at her as she put the pastries into a bag. 'How's your grandfather? We were so sorry to hear he'd been taken ill. He often used to come in here of a morning.'

'He's a bit better, thanks.' Faith was touched by this evidence of concern.

When she got back, she heated up a croissant and made some coffee. She started flicking through the paper, and then stopped as her attention was caught by a headline: MANCHESTER CLUB KING ACCUSED. There was a photograph of a prosperous-looking man leaving a building – a police station? But it was the man's name that had caught her eye: Terence Lomas. This must be the man that Daniel worked for, the man Helen had, accurately, it seemed, described as a crook. Lomas had been arrested for his involvement in a gang shooting just over a week before.

She rubbed her forehead, trying to remember. Lomas had phoned Daniel the day she'd gone to Longsight. She could

307

remember Finn picking up the phone and calling through to his father, *It's Uncle Terry.* Then Daniel had rushed her out of the house. And now Lomas was involved in some kind of gang war . . . She thought about Finn and Hannah, close to this man, and close to a father who . . . Daniel's face, cold and threatening, was suddenly in her mind.

There was nothing she could do, not now, not straight away. She told herself that Daniel loved the children – Helen had never complained about him as a father. Whatever Daniel was, whatever he had done, Finn and Hannah were safe for the time being. The police knew about his alibi. She had to be patient. She had to wait.

Her coffee tasted suddenly bitter. She left it and went across to the table where she had set out all of Grandpapa's papers. Work would distract her. And as she began to go through the boxes, gradually her anxiety retreated.

She was interrupted by the doorbell. She felt a moment of déjà vu, then shook it off as she went to answer it. There was a policewoman on the step. She showed Faith her ID and asked if she could come in. Faith took the woman through to the front room, apologizing for the cold. She'd given up on the old boiler and had put on a couple of extra jerseys.

'Don't worry about it,' the woman said, refusing Faith's offer of coffee. She waited until Faith was sitting down, then took the chair opposite her. 'I've come about the incident last night,' she said. 'We spoke to Mr Kovacs. He's sorry he alarmed you. He was upset, and he says it won't happen again.'

Faith shook her head. The response seemed ludicrously inadequate. And now there was this Lomas thing. 'I don't think he's enough in control to make those promises. That wasn't the first time he's threatened me. I'm worried about the children.'

'Miss Lange,' the woman said, her face serious, 'are you

aware that Mr Kovacs has already made a complaint against you, before last night's incident?'

Shock silenced Faith. It was a moment before she could speak. 'Against me?'

'Yes. He said that you have been harassing him and his children since his wife's death.' She paused to make sure Faith had taken this in, then went on, 'He says that you came to his house twice – he had to ask you to leave, the second time. He says that you waited for his son outside school, and he believes you might have been to his daughter's school as well. He says that you encouraged his son to contact you against his clear and express wishes. It was that last incident that made him come round here last night. He says that he didn't break in, you admitted him, and that you only made the emergency call when he wouldn't do as you asked. He agrees that he shouldn't have come here, and says he won't do it again.'

'That's . . .' She felt as if the breath had been punched out of her body.

'The officers who called last night said that you made claims against him relating to the death of his wife. I don't know what the problem is between you and Mr Kovacs, but I think it's important that you realize he has been thoroughly investigated, and he is not under suspicion. If you'll take a friendly warning, Miss Lange, you won't repeat those accusations.'

'This just isn't true. I –'

'Do you deny going to the house? Or the school?'

'No, of course not. But I was invited. I didn't just –'

'To the school?'

Faith shook her head. 'No, not to the school.'

The woman stood up. 'Mr Kovacs has no intention of taking this any further at present. He understands that you are upset about his wife's death, and your grandfather's illness. He has given his assurance that he will stay away from you.

I want your assurance that you will stay completely away from him and from his children. You're obviously under a lot of strain. I suggest that you do as Mr Kovacs asks.'

When the woman had gone, Faith sat at the window staring out into the garden. The stumps of the roses looked dead in the ground, and the trees were bare. Daniel had been clever. He had connections she knew nothing about. He had used his son. He had distorted the truth to make the police see her as hysterical and manipulative. All she had were beliefs and deductions. She was certain that he hadn't been in the house the night Helen had died, but she couldn't prove it, not unless Finn agreed to say what had really happened – and he wasn't going to.

She abandoned the piles of papers and packed her bag. She'd decided to go home after visiting the hospital. She no longer felt worried that Daniel might come back – he seemed to have found a more effective way than threats of silencing her. At the bottom of her bag, she found the piece of paper with her attempts to sort out the cryptic and incomplete notes that Helen had left: *Ma_y _ro_ _ene_ _.*

Ma_y, Maay, Maby, Macy, Mady.
choiceness, shortness
browbands, croplands
thousands
many thousands

She looked at it, then discarded it on the table. It meant nothing, and she had to go.

The hospital ward smelled of urine and disinfectant. The light reflected off the floor and walls, and the beds looked disordered and cluttered. The nursing staff had reported an improvement in Grandpapa's condition, and he seemed more alert, but he was also more restless and distressed. His eyes were open, wandering round the room as if he were looking for something. She sat beside him and took his hand, but he didn't seem aware of her. Once or twice his eyes focused on her and she thought she saw a moment of recognition, but it faded into confusion as his search started again.

And all the time he was muttering urgently. Sometimes his slurring words were comprehensible: *light, the light* . . . *watching* . . . *go* . . . She recognized them from when she had found him in the dark hallway. Sometimes they seemed to be nothing more than meaningless rambling, where she thought, sometimes, she could hear words, but they made no sense: *predatel* . . . *soldat* . . .

Faith sat beside the bed and talked to him. She told him some of what she had been doing, she told him about her visit to the art gallery, she told him that Katya had visited, and that she sent her love. Nothing seemed to break through the intensity of his need.

'He has to rest,' the nurse told her. 'He's wearing himself out.'

'Can't you give him something?'

The nurse shook her head. 'We've given him everything we can. Do you know what it is that's worrying him?'

'No. I've no idea.' But she had. She could still hear Katya's voice. *Marek* . . . *may have had to make some hard choices.*

'You look exhausted,' the nurse said. 'Go home and get some sleep. You won't help him by making yourself ill as well.'

Faith managed a smile. 'I'll do that. thanks. You'll call me if . . .'

'Don't worry.'

The idea of sleep was compelling. Her eyes felt gritty from fatigue. But time was passing by. She could feel it slipping away faster and faster. Instead of going home, she turned the car round and headed back to Grandpapa's. She'd had an idea. In her hunt through his papers, she'd been looking in the wrong places. He wouldn't have kept his secrets among the papers in the cupboards where anyone – she, Katya on her rare visits, Doreen – could see them. Anything private he kept locked in his desk, or in the secret drawer for added security.

When she got back to the house, she went straight to the study, and to his desk. But Katya had already been there. The desk looked like a picked-over corpse. The drawers hung half-open and all the pigeonholes had been cleared. She wondered if her mother had checked the secret drawer. It was easy to miss with a cursory glance. She pressed the spring to release it and slipped it out. It was empty. Katya had been thorough. Faith looked at it, remembering how it had been stuffed full to overflowing the day when she had first seen the newspaper cuttings. Something could easily have . . . She pulled it out completely, and slipped her hand into the space where it had been.

There was something caught at the back. Carefully, she freed it and pulled it out. It was an envelope, tattered and old. She stood there with it in her hand, a feeling of reluctance making her hesitate. Once she opened it, she would know what was in it.

It was probably nothing – more cuttings, something to do with the business – but if it was something else . . . And then she knew that she wasn't as convinced as she had claimed that Katya's beliefs were groundless. People had committed extraordinary acts of heroism and of barbarism in those times. Her grandfather's humanity, the thing that made her deny the possibility of his involvement, would have left exactly the gnawing, destructive guilt she was seeing.

She opened it and slipped out a sheet of paper with writing on one side – a letter – and a small wallet. Tucked into one pocket of the wallet, she found a photograph, a black-and-white one, like the two Jake had returned to her. It looked like a pair to the one of Grandpapa in uniform. It was the same size and had the same deckle edge. It showed a girl,

312

fine-boned and slender, gazing unsmiling at the camera. Faith looked at the pale face, the dark hair and wide, dark eyes, and felt a nagging sense of familiarity. She knew who it was, or thought she did, but that didn't account for her feeling that she had seen this girl before.

She turned the picture over. There was something written on the back in a faded scrawl of ink: *Эва, 1941*. She stared at it without comprehension, then she realized what it said: Eva, 1941. It was a photograph of her great-aunt taken on the eve of Barbarossa, the Nazi invasion of the Soviet Union. Eva. She had found Eva. She felt as though she had one part of the puzzle in her hand.

She looked at the letter and the wallet, suddenly reluctant to go any further. He had hidden this in the secret drawer. He had burned a whole box of photographs in an attempt to get rid of the ones that Jake Denbigh had taken away with him. Maybe this picture of Eva was one that he thought might be there. She didn't know if she had the right to look. She didn't even know if she wanted to.

She was still hesitating when the phone rang. It was the landline. The hospital would call her on her mobile. She went through to the hall and picked it up. 'Yes?'

'Faith? It's Jake Denbigh.'

She'd forgotten about Jake Denbigh. It seemed no time since she'd last seen him, a glimpse in her rear-view mirror, standing in the car park watching her as she drove away. 'Jake,' she said. 'You're back.'

'I got back yesterday. I saw something in the paper about your grandfather. How is he?'

'He's holding on, but there's a long way to go.'

'I'm sorry.' There was a moment of silence, then he said. 'You don't sound too great yourself.'

'I'm okay. I'm just tired.' The emptiness lay like a pool of silence around her.

'I know what it's like. When my father was ill – it's a few

313

years ago now – I gave up trying to sleep. I used sit up until three in the morning smoking too much and wondering if there was any news.'

She thought about the night before when she'd lain awake listening out for the phone as the house creaked and whispered around her. 'What happened? To your father?'

'Oh, he pulled through. Look, is there anything I can do?'

'No. Thanks. I've got everything I need. You could count sheep for me if you want,' she said.

'Sheep? I can do that. Anything else?' There was a brief pause. 'Would you like some company?'

His offer took her unawares. It was too late to go home – she was too tired to drive safely – and the thought of another solitary evening in the empty house lay in front of her like a steep hill she wasn't sure she could climb. So what if he had an agenda – at the moment, she didn't care. 'Company would be good.'

'I'll be with you in half an hour. Shall I bring some wine?'

Wine would be the best insomnia cure, or the best one she was prepared to try tonight. After he'd rung off, she felt better. She went to check herself in the old mirror that hung over the fire. Her reflection, in its brown depths, looked pale and far away. She could see the shadows under her eyes from lack of sleep. Her clothes were dusty from the hours she'd spent looking through the piles of old papers. She twisted her hair up on top of her head, then let it fall down on to her shoulders again.

She went up to her room and had a quick wash. She didn't have much with her, but she changed into a clean pair of trousers, and pulled on the soft white sweater that Katya had given her last Christmas. She brushed her hair back from her face, then let it fall forward again. Her reflection gazed back at her, giving her a tantalizing moment of déjà vu.

She was straightening up the front room when the doorbell rang.

*   *   *

The Lange house looked dark and forbidding as Jake walked up the drive. There was a glimmer of light behind the curtains of one window, but otherwise the place looked deserted, a gothic pile against the evening sky. He pressed the doorbell and waited, remembering his fantasies about fairy-tale princesses and wicked witches the first time he had waited here.

This time, the princess was in. It was Faith who opened the door. She was wearing jeans and a heavy white sweater against the cold. Her hair was loose and her face was devoid of make-up. She looked younger and more vulnerable than he remembered. 'Come in,' she said.

It was almost as cold inside the house as it was out. 'It's a bit better through here,' she said, taking him into the room where he and Lange had sat the week before. The curtains were pulled across the window, and the room was lit by a dim overhead bulb. Shadows lurked in the corners. A gas fire was burning, leaking some warmth into the room, and a one-bar electric fire was plugged in by the table where she had obviously been working.

'The boiler's broken down,' she explained. 'I've been dragging this thing round the house with me.' She gestured towards the electric fire. It was an antiquated heater with an element that glowed red-hot in places and was dull in others. The cord was frayed. She saw him looking and made a shrugging face. 'I'm going shopping tomorrow. It was the best I could do for now.'

He dreaded to think what the wiring might be like. 'Let me have a look at that boiler.' She gave him a look of such surprise, it made him laugh. 'What?'

She shook her head. 'You don't seem like the kind of person who fixes central heating, that's all. Okay, it's through here.'

She led him through to the back of the house, to a cold, bare kitchen. The boiler was ancient, backed into a corner. He took off the front.

'Here.' She crouched beside him and held a torch while he peered into the innards. He checked the burners and the pilot light. The whole system was clogged up with dirt. It looked as if it hadn't had any serious maintenance done for years. He cleaned the pilot light and, on his second attempt, managed to get it working. He sent up a silent prayer to any deity that might be listening and pressed the 'on' switch. The burners ignited with a roar.

He stood up, brushing the dust off his trousers. 'Done.'

'Okay, now I'm impressed,' she said, giving him a towel so he could wash his hands. 'You're a man of many talents. Thank you.'

'I've lived in some dodgy flats in my time – boiler maintenance is a survival skill. But if you're staying here, you need to get it fixed. Your grandfather's lucky it didn't poison him.'

'I know. It isn't just the heating – it's the whole house. He's been letting it fall apart and I just didn't see it.' She bit her lip, then changed the subject quickly. 'You've got some oil or something on your shirt. Here, let me.' She dabbed at it carefully with a piece of kitchen paper, her face intent on what she was doing. Her hair brushed against his face. It smelled faintly of lavender. 'There. That's better. It should be okay when you've washed it.'

'Thanks,' he said. They looked at each other, and the silence lengthened. Finally he said, 'I brought some wine. Let's celebrate fixing the boiler with a drink.'

Her face relaxed into a smile. 'That's the best thing anyone's said to me today.'

She took some long-stemmed glasses out of a cupboard and they went back to the other room. There was a low table in front of the settee which had been pulled closer to the gas fire. He poured some wine and touched his glass to hers. He could feel the heat of the fire on his face, and the chill of the house behind him. 'Here's to . . . keeping warm in winter.'

'Okay,' she said. 'I can drink to that.'

He took the opportunity to study her. He was reminded again of Sophia Yevanova as he noted the delicate line of her jaw, the high cheekbones, the fair skin. She looked pale and heavy-eyed. She must have had a rough few days 'What's happening with your grandfather?'

'He's improving.' She didn't look at him, and seemed to be hunting round for a subject. He waited. 'You said your father had been ill. What happened?'

'What's to tell? He was one of these city types, a high flier. He had a heart attack – out of the blue, my mother said, but it turned out after that he'd been having chest pains for months. Only wimps get ill, so he ignored them.'

Jake had been in Tanzania. The Rwanda story had just broken, and he'd known that if he could cross the border and get some eye-witness reports back to the UK, he would make his name as a political writer. His mother's message had reached him just before he was due to make the crossing, after which he would be incommunicado. He'd made the decision and gone.

He'd spent the next few weeks seeing things he hoped never to see again. He could still remember it – the country that was so beautiful; the obscenity of the killings; the smell of death that pervaded the air around them; the danger, and the long nights when no one could sleep. They used to sit up until dawn with cigarettes and beer, chatting, joking, passing the time, trying to shut out the reality of what had happened around them, of what they had witnessed. And all the time, at the back of his mind, he'd had the image of his father, dying.

'But he was okay?'

'He was fine. He still is, except it made him decide that his life had been wasted. He got religion, and he's spent the last ten years trying to decide which god to invest in. He's looking for the best return on his belief.'

She laughed. 'Oh, come on.'

317

'No,' he said, 'It's true. Once an investment banker, always an investment banker.'

'I can't see my grandfather getting religious.' Her glass was almost empty. He topped it up. 'How was your trip?'

She'd neatly sidestepped the topic of her grandfather again. He didn't mind; there was plenty of time. He leaned against the back of the settee – it was old, but it was deep and comfortable – and thought about what to say. He wanted to keep away from Minsk for the moment, he had it marked down as dangerous territory, so he told her about the journey instead. He talked about the flight, about the flight attendants and the pilot's accent. 'He kept coming on the public address system. He was speaking English, and he was probably telling us something crucial, but I couldn't understand a word.' He told her about the slightly unnerving moment on the way back when they had to make an unscheduled landing in Posnam because the fuel they had taken on in Minsk was too sub-standard for the flight.

'What about Belarus? How much of it did you see?'

'I stayed in Minsk. The trains seem to be good, but it's a big country – I didn't have time to travel any further.'

'You could have flown.'

He shook his head. 'Not unless I had to. Belavia is one of the worst airlines in the world. It's a real Sellotape and glue-stick operation. Rumour is that they censor out all the news about the crashes. I was terrified I might have to take an internal flight. Intrepid journalist, see?' The room was staring to warm up. 'You don't want to hear my travel stories.'

'I do. I like hearing about places I've never been.' But it was more than that. She was asking questions. Since they last talked, she'd developed an interest in Belarus.

He watched her reactions as he told her about the hotel, about the army of formidable women who sat in cubbyholes on each floor, smoking and talking, and presumably cleaning the guests' rooms once in a while. 'Every time I opened my door, this head came popping out to check up on me. I didn't know if I ought to start getting paranoid and check my room for microphones, or if they were just keen on their work. Whatever that was.'

'Tell me what the people were like,' she said.

'They were okay,' he said. 'They didn't smile much, but they were friendly. Except for the police. It's a beautiful country in a strange way. It's very flat – all marshes and forests.'

'My grandfather grew up in the forest, a pine and birch forest. He said that the birch trees were like candles in the shadows.'

'That was what the Belarusian forest was like,' he said. Candles in the shadows and death pits in the deep glades.

She was quiet for a minute as she thought about this, then she said, 'I think he must have come from the Belarusian side of the border. I've been looking up the treaty and checking the maps. They gave the east part of Belarus to Poland around the time he was born, and then the Soviets took it back. Troubled times.' She looked at the wine in her glass, distracted again.

'What is it?' he said.

'Nothing.' The light caught on the facets of the crystal, reflecting on to her face.

'If you want to talk about it, I'm not going anywhere,' he said.

'I want to show you something.' She stood up and went across to the table. She came back with a small piece of paper in her hand. 'Look,' she said, holding it out to him.

It was a photograph, another black-and-white one, the same dimensions as the one of Lange in his uniform. He looked at it. It was a picture of Faith, a younger Faith wearing . . . He realized it couldn't be her. The photograph was far too old.

'That's Eva,' she said. 'My grandfather's sister.'

'She looks like you. She looks a lot like you.'

She took the photograph back and studied it again, nodding slowly. 'He never talks about the war, I told you that. But after that day you came, he – it seemed to start something. He had a load of cuttings about the Nuremburg trials, about the people who got away, the ones who escaped to the west and got rich and lived happy lives. He was reading them the night he had the stroke.'

He didn't know what to say. This was what he'd been waiting to hear, but now the moment had come, he didn't want to pursue it. Instead, he steered the conversation away. 'Did you know he was ill?'

'I knew there was something wrong.' She told him about a phone call she'd had, her grandfather's confusion and his apparent but unspecified fear.

'And he just collapsed?'

'I don't know. I found him when I came down in the night. He was just sitting at his desk . . .' She frowned. 'The doctor thought he might have fallen – there was a bruise on his face, but he was just, you know, slumped in his chair . . .' She stopped abruptly.

Jake touched her hand. 'But he's improving?'

'He won't settle. Something's worrying him, but he can't tell me what it is. They say if he won't rest, he won't recover.'

'I'm sorry,' he said.

'It's so strange,' she said. 'There's nothing left. All his things – they've gone. I think he must have sold them, or given them away. He's got no money, nothing.'

Jake reached out and brushed the hair back from her face so he could see it more clearly. 'Faith?' he said.

She turned towards him, and he ran his fingers down her cheek, tracing the outline of her mouth, and the line of her throat.

When he kissed her, her mouth was soft. Her lips parted under his and he pulled her closer, slipping his hands under the soft wool of her jersey. Her skin was smooth and felt warm under his fingers. He could taste the wine on her tongue, and smell the fragrance of her hair. He stopped thinking about why he was there. He moved back on the settee, easing her on top of him, letting his hands find the inside of her arms, the smoothness of her back, the soft hairs at the nape of her neck. He could feel her relaxing into him with each touch, and time drifted away.

The ringing of a phone jerked him back to the present. She reached for it, pulling herself away from him, her sudden urgency making her fingers clumsy. She checked the number, and the alarm faded from her face. 'I thought it might be the hospital,' she said, putting it down without answering it. She looked at him, then her eyes dropped and she reached for her jersey that had fallen on to the floor, smoothing it out slowly. 'Maybe this isn't such a good idea,' she said.

The break had given him time to think as well. He'd been stupid, he'd let himself get carried away. The moment had taken them both and, if the phone hadn't rung, he knew where the evening would have ended. He was here as part of his investigation into her grandfather, and if what he suspected were true, he was going to expose Lange. He was, irretrievably, the enemy. 'I'm sorry,' he said.

'Don't be. It's me. I'm just not . . . Things are in chaos right now.'

'I know,' he said. He smiled at her. 'I can still be sorry, right?'

'Me too.' She smiled back at him as she slipped the jersey over her head and pulled the arms straight.

He spoke quickly before caution could stop him. 'There's something I have to tell you.' In his mind, he could see the face of the girl choking to death on the end of the rope, watched by the curious eyes of the soldiers. It made it easier to go on. 'I found something out when I was in Minsk. About your grandfather. It might have something to do with what's

321

upsetting him now, but I don't think it's what you want to hear.'

She was suddenly still. 'Go on.'

'You remember that photo I gave you, the one I found in my notebook?'

She nodded, but didn't say anything. He found it hard to meet her gaze.

'He told me it was taken in Minsk. I got a copy of it and took it with me. I wanted to see if I could track it down.'

She didn't say anything. Her face was impossible to read.

'It was taken outside the old NKVD building. And the uniform he's wearing – it's their uniform. Faith, your grandfather was a member of the NKVD.'

She rested her forehead on her hand as she absorbed what he'd told her.

'The NKVD – they helped to carry out one of the worst massacres of the last century – and one of the places they did it was close to Minsk, in the years up to the Nazi invasion. That was one of the things I went to research, that massacre. I didn't expect to find your grandfather there. I had no idea. But he was. Thousands upon thousands of innocent people were shot and some of them were buried alive. I've seen the memorials. I've seen the death pits.'

'And he was involved? You *know* that he was involved?'

He shook his head. 'I don't know anything yet.'

'Then maybe you should wait until you do.'

He sighed. In every way but one, she was right. Part of him was cursing the way he'd put her on her guard, but he'd made the choice deliberately. 'I wanted to warn you what might be coming.'

Her hands tugged nervously at the sleeves of her sweater, pulling them down over her wrists. 'Is this why you interviewed him in the first place? Is this why you came here tonight?'

'I interviewed him for the reason I said. I was doing some

322

articles on refugees. But I had to research his background, and that's when I began to wonder. It was obvious he was hiding something, and then I picked up on the Minsk connection. So that's why I wanted to see him again. Tonight, I wanted to see you.'

She looked sceptical, but she didn't comment. She was holding the photograph of Eva, and when she spoke, she kept her eyes fixed on it. 'That photograph – I think it must have been taken around the same time as this one. They look as though they come from the same set.' She looked at him to make sure he was following what she was saying, and he remembered that she was an expert in interpreting old documents. 'Photographs were a luxury – there must have been a reason for taking them. They wouldn't have had money for casual snaps. It was 1941 – the invasion was imminent. He would have been about to leave them. It's a picture taken for his family. You've seen it. He was proud of it. He wasn't involved in anything he was ashamed of.'

This was more or less what Adam had implied when he had accused Jake of interpreting what he was seeing with 21st-century hindsight. Jake was impressed by her reasoning. It was possible that Lange had been a young and naïve recruit to the security police – but how long would that naïvety have lasted, under the onslaught of Barbarossa and all that came afterwards? Jake thought about Lange's reticence, his hidden past, the place he had been and the time he had been there. Lange acted like a guilty man, and Jake knew what guilt there was to feel.

It wasn't only the Stalinist massacres. He had listened to Adam's stories of the men, the officers of the law, who had saved themselves by turning on their own people once the Nazis had overrun the country. And Lange was tormented by some kind of remorse. *I should know. I did know. It is wrong.* 'Maybe,' he said. 'I just know that your grandfather lied about his past and he lied about the war. He's trying to hide something.'

'But not that. He brought that picture out of there with him, remember.'

He could feel her breath on his face. He would just have to move his hand an inch to touch her, but it might as well have been a mile.

'What are you going to do? Are you going to write about him?' She looked tired and defeated.

'I'm waiting for more information.'

'And then you'll write about him?'

He nodded. 'Yes. I will.'

She sat staring at the light glinting off the facets of her glass. 'I think you'd better go,' she said.

He stood up. 'I'm sorry.' He wasn't sorry for having told her, he was sorry that the story was there to tell. He picked up his coat which he'd left round the back of a chair. He shook it out, and the movement in the air blew a sheet of paper on to the floor. He picked it up and glanced at it.

Ma_y _ro_ _ene_ _.

Ma_y, Maay, Maby, Macy, Mady.

He felt the electric shock of recognition. 'What's this?'

She took the paper off him and looked at it. 'It's something the police found in Helen's notes,' she said. Her voice was weary. 'I was trying to fill in the gaps. No one knows what it is.'

He knew. The gaps had filled themselves in as soon as he saw it.

Ma_y _ro_ _ene_ _.

Maly Trostenets.

The death camp outside Minsk.

Faith sat in the house, turning the photograph round and round in her hands. Jake had gone. The next time they met, if they ever saw each other again, they would be polite and distant as if tonight had never happened. She could still feel the warmth of his mouth on hers, the pressure of his arms, and she knew – and felt angry with herself for knowing – that she had wanted him to stay, that if he'd kissed her again . . . She had wanted him to stay. They shouldn't have talked, they should just . . . it was a time for a different kind of communication.

Her head was aching. She switched off the gas fire, not trusting it after what Jake had said. She looked at Eva's photograph again, a girl with a delicate beauty, on the brink of adulthood. *She looks like you . . .* His face had been warm when he'd said that.

She had to forget Jake Denbigh. She'd found other things with this photo, a wallet and a letter. She'd put them aside because she was afraid of what she might find. She unfolded the letter and looked at it. She didn't know what she expected, but the letter surprised her. It was dated 1965.

Dear Marek Lange
We cannot consent to what you propose. When our daughter came back to us, it was on the clear condition that she return to the Church and the ways of the Church, and that she raise the child in the Catholic faith.

Now our daughter is dead, we fully intend to carry out the obligations she undertook. We do not think you are a suitable person to do this. We have sent the child to the Sisters of Mercy. They will care for it in their children's home in Cork.

We pray for the soul of our daughter every day, and pray for you in the hope that one day your soul, too, will be brought to God.
Patrick O'Halloran

Her great grandfather. He believed terrible things about his son-in-law. It was as if even addressing him was an occasion of contamination. *Dear Marek Lange . . .* The letter was about Katya, their granddaughter, but it sounded so cold. Maybe they thought that she was tainted by the identity of her father. *The child*. Faith shivered. Whatever bargain Deirdre O'Halloran had made with her parents to be allowed back into the fold, Grandpapa had not been prepared to fulfil it. He had brought Katya back to England – and honoured his dead wife's wishes by sending her to the convent she came to love. No matter what rebellions she may have had when she was younger, Katya's Catholicism was an abiding part of her life.

Faith put the letter on one side. Whatever that story was, there was no one left to tell it. She opened the wallet again. She was looking for something, anything, that would refute the charges that her mother and now Jake had made. There was something else in one of the pockets, a small card. She pulled it out and looked at it. It was a membership card that told her in 1959 Grandpapa had been a member of the Communist Party of Great Britain.

He hadn't repudiated Stalin. For the first time, she found herself wondering if Jake, if Katya, could be right.

The Meeting

This is the story of a betrayal.

The winter streets were dark and dangerous. Eva wrapped her coat more closely round her, and hurried along the road, keeping her face lowered, her walk purposeful. Her eyes moved quickly from side to side, checking the people around her. If a patrol stopped her, she was going to say that she was on her way to work, on her way to the hospital.

The streets weren't empty yet. Marek had chosen a good time to meet. It was the time when people were moving between work and home, the time when people were finishing what they had to do for the day before they barred their doors against the winter cold, and against the worse things that the occupation had brought into the city.

She was near the old part of the town now. The road forked, and she turned down the smaller street. It was quieter here. There were no passers-by, nobody hurrying home to get out of the cold, to get away from the patrols and the malign eyes that watched from the shadows.

Despite herself, her feet began to move faster, past the buildings with their dark windows, past the wavering light of the street lamps, light and then dark, light and then dark. She thought she heard something. She hesitated, and looked back, but the street was deserted. Threads of mist drifted in the yellow light and vanished in the waiting shadows.

There it was again. 'Marek?' she whispered.

She could feel the hairs on her arms start to rise. Something was wrong. She turned to go back, then stopped. She was almost there. If the danger was here, then Marek would be in danger too. She had to warn him. She moved quickly now, her eyes darting from shadow to shadow. The walls closed in around her, high, cutting off the light of the moon. A voice inside her was insistent with its warning: *Get away! Get away!*

The distillery was at the far end where the roads met. It was derelict. It had been damaged in the bombing, and had been abandoned ever since. She was at the gates now, the place where she and Marek had said goodbye, over two years ago. High above her, the bear danced on the arch. There was no one there. Where was he? The road was empty in front of her. She looked back. Silence and shadows. He was near. She could almost sense him. 'Marek?' she whispered.

'Eva!' It was like a breath of silence in her ear, and he was there, tall, strong, but thinner, so much thinner, and his face . . . In the penumbral light, her brother looked old.

'Marek . . .' she said.

He put his arms round her. 'Eva!' Then he looked at her. 'You're so thin.'

So are you! she wanted to say, but there was no time. 'Marek. It isn't safe here! We've got to go. It isn't safe.'

'I know. Listen to me – someone is watching you. Someone will give your name to the police soon. They may have it already. You have to get out. Tonight.'

She felt a wash of cold flood over her . . . *give your name to the police* . . . 'Tonight? But –'

His whisper was urgent. 'Eva. You have to get out. I tried to get here sooner but I couldn't. We can get down the river, I'll –'

She hushed him. She'd heard something. A sound in the darkness behind her, in the derelict building. 'There's something wrong,' she whispered. 'Something –'

And the light was blinding her. A voice was shouting and Marek grabbed her arms and pushed her into the shadows through the gates. 'Go! Now, Eva! Go!' and she was running, weaving around piles of rubble, her feet tripping on the uneven ground, and she could hear his voice, and there were shouts and the sound of shots behind her, and then Marek's voice stopped.

Marek! She skidded round a corner, the walls of the building in front of her, walls to either side. She could hear running feet behind her. *Marek!* There was a path that ran down the side of the building, that led to the street on the other side. If she could get through, she might be able to lose them, but she'd turned the wrong way in her panic and she was trapped, no, there was a door, a door she could get through and out the other side, *Marek, Marek,* the door was blocked. She threw herself against it but it was solid. Back, she had to go back, find her way through. She spun round, but the light was shining straight into her eyes, and then she saw them, the soldiers, and they had their guns pointing at her.

Slowly, she raised her arms above her head. She could feel herself shaking. Marek? What had they done with Marek?

The soldiers relaxed now they could see her. One of them ran his hands over her, looking for a weapon. The others laughed and spoke to each other in their own language. She heard the sound of voices shouting in the night, and then a shot. Someone cried out.

She tried to run towards the sound. *Marek!* One of the soldiers swung his fist and knocked her to the ground. Something smashed into her hip and she curled up, her voice swallowed in the pain. He kicked her again then they pulled her to her feet and half marched her, half dragged her to a waiting truck.

There was no sign of Marek, but she could see on the ground as they threw her into the back of the vehicle, a pool of something that gleamed black in the moonlight.

Marek!

23

Faith woke suddenly from a restless dream in which Helen kept telling her, *You don't know what you're doing.* Finn walked away from her down a long corridor. She was awake in a dim light, and something hard was digging into her back. She struggled to sit up, completely disorientated. Her mouth was dry and her neck felt stiff.

She'd fallen asleep on the settee. The combination of fatigue and wine had been too much for her. It was almost midnight. She ought to go up to bed, but the thought of the cold darkness upstairs was chilling. And now, of course, she was wide awake. She remembered what Jake had said about his father's illness, when he couldn't sleep. *I used sit up until three in the morning smoking too much and wondering if there was any news.* She might as well find something to distract her until sleep caught up with her again.

She didn't want to look at Grandpapa's papers, not at this bleak time of the night. Her laptop was still set up on the table. She switched it on and scrolled through her files. Work was the one part of her life that was still under her control. Numbers could be trusted. Numbers were things she could handle.

She worked for an hour, the flicker from the screen

becoming soporific. The storm had blown out, the rain had stopped and the night had the silence of deep cold. Even with the heating now working, she needed the heavy sweater to keep warm. Her eyes were getting heavy, and she thought she might be able to sleep.

She leaned back in the chair, massaging her neck. It was getting on for one, time to go to bed. She decided to make herself a warm drink and was just standing up when her phone vibrated on the table beside her. She looked at the number, and picked it up. She knew what was coming.

'Miss Lange? It's Janet from the hospital. Your grand-father's taken a turn for the worse.'

Jake's mind had been working fast as he left the Lange house, trying to make sense of what he had found. When he got back to his flat, he got out the papers that Cass had given him and went through them until he found what he was looking for.

Here. This was what Faith had been talking about: Helen Kovacs had been making notes while she was working, and the investigating team had not been able to decipher them:

Ma_y _ro_ _ene_ _.

He stared at the writing blankly. It could be a coincidence. Why would Helen Kovacs have been interested in Maly Trostenets? And if she was, why was the name incomplete? There was nothing to indicate that Kovacs' murder was related to her research – it seemed to be a second string in the police investigation – but as far as he could tell, there was nothing they had found in the library that made any reference to Maly Trostenets, to Minsk or to the 1939–45 war. He went through the papers carefully a second time. There was nothing.

He could see two possibilities. The first one was straight-forward: Kovacs' notes had nothing to do with the death camp. The similarity was pure coincidence and meant nothing. The second one . . . whoever had killed Helen Kovacs would have had time to check through the papers she was studying and remove any incriminating references while Nick Garrick lay in his self-induced stupor. But the killer had missed the note – in which case it meant a great deal.

Either way, it was something the police needed to see. He had to get this to the investigating team. He picked up the phone to call Burnley, then hesitated. The notes were not in the public domain. If the information came from him, Burnley would want to know where Jake had got it, and how he knew it was significant. He wasn't stupid. He would remember that Jake had been interested and had been asking questions. He'd start hunting around and Jake knew that Cass would have been careless. Then she'd be in deep shit with the police, and with her boyfriend as well. There was no innocent explanation that would cover her passing him confidential documents.

Jake thought quickly. He could tell Ann Harley, Garrick's solicitor. It was legitimate for her to have this information. She would be aware of those notes – they'd have questioned Nick about them. He couldn't call her now – it was nearly midnight. He made a note to contact her first thing, then he sat back in his chair, letting his mind run over what he had just found. He couldn't understand how information about Maly Trostenets would be significant.

Jake was well enough informed about the Nazi death camps, but he'd never heard of it before his visit to Minsk. He knew from his recent research that it had been one of five camps, along with Belzec, Chelmno, Sobibor and Treblinka II, that had existed purely to exterminate, but unlike the other four, its name was barely known. Out of curiosity, he Googled it and came up with only a hundred references, several of which took him to the same page. Then he tried searching for the others. He got seventeen thousand hits for

Belzec and Chelmno, almost fifty thousand for Sobibor and over seventy thousand for Treblinka.

Maly Trostenets wasn't a secret – but it had been too far east, too hidden in the lands that had come under the shadow of Stalin's rule. He wondered where Helen Kovacs had come across it. He looked at the diagram he'd pinned on to his notice board, the one he'd drawn before he went away, attempting to link the disparate threads. He added Maly Trostenets and stared at it again. He linked it to Helen Kovacs' name, then drew the line across to Faith. She and Kovacs had been friends at school. Kovacs must have met Marek Lange. She was a historian. Suppose she had picked up on the Minsk connection and followed that through . . .

And now she was dead.

The direction his thoughts were taking him shook him. Lange was too frail and old to have attacked Helen Kovacs – the idea was ridiculous. He drummed his fingers on the table, suddenly uneasy.

If something were threatening to strip Lange of his good name and his freedom, then he might have enlisted help. If he had survived by switching sides, then maybe the powerful protection that still operated around ex-Nazis might have operated for him. Jake rubbed his forehead as he thought. Why would Lange have cared? For years his life had demonstrated that he didn't. He'd said as much to Jake: *What is there to lose if the gamble fails? It is only fear that stops you.* Lange had been successful because he had nothing he cared about, nothing to more lose.

Until his granddaughter was born.

He would care because of Faith. The story would impinge on Faith, on her life, even on her career. Lange would have cared about that. But even so, why murder? It would have been enough to get rid of whatever it was that Kovacs had found. So maybe murder had never been the plan, but someone had panicked. Then Lange would have a murderer on his hands.

The bits were starting to fall into place. Lange was deeply troubled about something. According to Faith, he'd been showing signs of stress since the day Jake had met him. She attributed that stress to the interview, to awakened memories, but it had taken place the morning after the murder. It was possible that Lange's distress had had nothing to do with the interview and everything to do with Kovacs' death. And now he was ill and unable to communicate.

Jake pressed his fingers against his eyes and forced himself to think. If he was right, then someone had killed Helen Kovacs to keep her from revealing something about Maly Trostenets, something she had found in the Litkin Archive, something that would hurt Marek Lange.

But if the story had come out after all these years, who was there left to care? Who was still alive to point the finger of accusation, if Helen Kovacs had brought back whatever it was that had been hidden in the archive?

And as soon as he asked the question, the answer was obvious. There was one person who would be a danger to someone with that secret, from that place, and from that time.

Sophia Yevanova slept lightly these days. Her age and her illness dictated this – she accepted it. She required Mrs Barker to settle her for the night with her pillows supporting her, her sewing and her glasses in easy reach so that she could, if necessary, make the wakeful hours useful. Many nights, she lay silently in the darkness watching the changing patterns of the shadows against her blind.

She had been unwell that evening. Antoni had persuaded her to take some Valium to ease the tics and spasms that were plaguing her, with Mrs Barker supporting his urgings: *Come now, Miss Yevanova, just one to relax you . . .* Now

334

she wished she had not given in to them. The symptoms of her illness were something she could deal with – troublesome but familiar. She didn't care for the way the drug clouded her mind, left her not completely in control of her consciousness or of her thoughts, the way it left her hovering in the wasteland that lay between sleep and wakefulness.

She made herself focus. She could hear the wind surging against the trees, she could hear the calls of the night animals – an owl calling to its mate, the cry of a fox, the scream of the small prey whose time it was to die, the sounds . . .

. . . of the forest. The trickling water of the marshland, the birds, the soft crunch of boots on pine needles, the sound of marching feet *tramp, tramp, tramp* through the city streets and the old roads that ran through the villages. The whine of bike engines and the roar of trucks, the *klop-klop* of gunfire and a hand drawing her away from the window, *Raina* . . .

Her eyes snapped open. She had been drifting into dreams, and these were not dreams she welcomed. The hand on the clock jerked forward with a heavy *tock* and the house was silent again. Only now it seemed to be full of sounds that existed just on the edge of hearing, creaks and whispers and breathing in the shadows. Breath . . .

. . . rising in a white mist from the gratings where the frost glittered on the pavement and the ice in the air bit viciously at her face as she hurried through the darkness, her feet clattering on the flags, *klop-klop* and a hand drawing her . . .

Dreams again! The fabric of the present was tearing and she was falling through to where the past was waiting. Her hands reached for the light by her bed, but they fumbled, the muscles and nerves refusing to obey her. She tried to lie still, breathing quietly, taking command of herself. Her leg twitched and jumped. She stared into the darkness, holding on to alertness. She didn't want to go to the places her mind was threatening to take her.

The sounds of the house were clearer now, as though the

antenna of her consciousness had tuned into them. The clunk of the pipes, the sound of the clock, *tick* silence *tock* silence. Sometimes its rhythms would become a voice that talked to her: *Come. Now. Come. Now.* Like Mrs Barker with her seductive Valium: *Oh, come now, Miss Yevanova . . . Come now. Come now. Come. Now. Come. Now . . .*

And a sound that was almost like an absence, or like a sensation that came to her through the fabric and the timbers, someone moving around the house, soft feet on the stairs, *pad*. Silence. Silence. *Creak.*

Come. *Now.* Come. *Now.*

And the silence was moving along the corridor, was moving towards her door. Her hand reached for the light, for the bell that would summon Mrs Barker, but her treacherous muscles spasmed again and she felt the bell-push slide to the floor where it hit the carpet with a soft thud and lay where her fingers could just brush it, as far out of reach as if it had been on the other side of the room.

She tried again for the light, and this time her hand found the switch and her face and her pillow were flooded with a soft illumination that made the room beyond even darker.

And there was movement in the darkness. A sliver of faint grey that widened and then vanished abruptly as the door opened and was closed. The spasms in her muscles grew more acute, but her mind wouldn't focus properly, it wheeled around and around, the house, the forest, the breath in the night, the gunshots, the house, the . . .

The footsteps moved closer, and she felt the softness of a pillow on her face, welcomed, for a moment, its deceptive gentleness before it was pressed firmly down.

24

Jake got up at seven. The sun rose over the water as he dressed and made himself coffee. He called Ann Harley at eight thirty but got her secretary. Miss Harley was out of the office all day. No, it wasn't possible to give Jake a contact number. Yes, she would pass on a message asking Miss Harley to contact Jake, and she would emphasize that it was urgent, but Miss Harley was in meetings all day . . .

He banged the phone down, frustrated. He couldn't wait on Ann Harley. He didn't have the names of the investigating team and didn't want to go through all the rigmarole of making contact as a member of the public. He knew from past experience that the information would take its time to trickle through the system. Burnley was now his best bet. He would recognize the importance of what Jake was telling him and get it to the right person. He'd have to warn Cass and help her devise a cover story.

Once again, he was frustrated. Burnley was out. Jake left a message asking him to make contact urgently, and then tried Cass's number. She was either in transit or not answering her phone. He left a message. There was nothing else he could do.

He checked through his post while he was waiting for

Burnley's call. There were letters from a couple of publishers expressing an interest in his book and asking him to get in touch to discuss it. *We'd like to move quickly on this one. Stalin is hot,* one letter said.

The day before, this would have been a cause for celebration. A few weeks ago when Cass had complained about the amount of time he was devoting to the project, he'd promised to take her out and buy her champagne if he got a deal. That wasn't going to happen now. He felt a moment of regret for the time when it had just been fun – an easy, uncommitted – what? Friendship? They'd never been friends, and now never would be. A relationship? It had never really been that, for him. It had been sex – that was the interest they had shared at the beginning – they'd wanted each other. He had been stupid to think that would go on being enough for her.

The message light was blinking on the phone. He pressed 'play', hoping that his message had reached Burnley, but it was from Adam, his voice faint over the international line: *I think I might have something on your people. My friend at Hrodna says he has found a reference. I'll get back to you once I have the details. I've sent you some photographs as well.*

Jake had been waiting for these. He checked the fax. Adam had sent him pictures from the site of Maly Trostenets, with a note: *I thought you might want these. As you will see, Maly Trostenets is mostly pasture and farms today. There is a memorial of a kind, but nothing remains of the camp.*

The Kurapaty Forest and Maly Trostenets. How many cities in Europe had two such sites on their outskirts? Adam had sent him another photograph as well, the picture he'd seen before, of the cousins Sophia and Raina on the cusp of adolescence. He looked at the young faces, and wondered what they would have done if they had known what the future held for them.

338

Miss Yevanova would like to see this. He'd asked Adam for a copy so that he could show it to her. He wondered how she was. Mrs Barker had said she was better, and Garrick had expressed no alarm about her condition when they'd met the other night, but her obviously failing health worried him. He wanted to see her and had no intention of letting Antoni Yevanov stop him.

He reached for the phone, then hesitated. He didn't want to tie up the line before Burnley got in touch. He picked up his mobile, then thought better of it. If Burnley called, he'd have to cut his call to the Yevanovs short, and he didn't want to do that. He'd have to wait. He checked the time. It was ten o'clock. His day was disintegrating into bits and pieces. So far, he'd achieved very little. It was going to be one of those days of hanging around and drinking coffee.

He lit a cigarette and was about to make himself another cup of coffee when the entry-phone rang. He was wary of unannounced callers. He'd used the device often enough himself to get into a secure building, ringing all the bells in the knowledge that someone would be stupid enough to buzz him in. 'Who is it?'

'It's Nick Garrick.'

Garrick. Jake's mind leaped into overdrive. Something was wrong. 'Come up,' he said, and pressed the release button. He switched on the coffee machine then went to the front door. Garrick was coming along the corridor. As he watched, Jake was reminded of the time they'd first met at the station. Garrick moved slowly, as if he was carrying a burden that was far heavier than the backpack hitched over his shoulder. He acknowledged Jake with a nod, came in to the lobby and dumped the backpack on the floor. 'I didn't know what to do,' he said.

'What's up?' Jake shoved the backpack out of the way with his foot and closed the door. He ushered Garrick into the room and waited. *If you give someone advice . . .*

Garrick's eyes shifted around the walls, came back to Jake's, then moved away again. 'She's . . .' he said. 'She . . . You don't know, do you?'

'Know what?'

'I didn't think they'd tell you.' He rubbed his hand across his eyes.

'Jesus Christ, Nick. What?' But he knew before Garrick spoke.

Sophia Yevanova was dead.

'She died in the night,' Nick said. 'They found her this morning.' He sank down into a chair and put his head in his hands.

Jake's mind was blank. He couldn't accept it. To distract himself, he went through to the kitchen and made coffee. He heaped sugar into one cup and gave it to Garrick, who looked as if he was in shock. 'What happened?' he said.

She had been old, she had been ill – but he just couldn't accept it. She was so strong and so determined. Jake had seen the translucence of her skin and the tell-tale tinge of blue around her mouth, but death seemed alien in connection with her. She would have greeted the Grim Reaper with an imperious wave of her hand and told him to await her convenience. In his mind, she was vividly alive, sitting upright in her chair refusing to acknowledge the effort it took, the jewelled colours of the icon gleaming in the shadows behind her. His eyes felt hot and heavy.

The last time they met, he had talked to her about things she found distressing. He could remember the parchment white of her face as she listened to him. He shouldn't have been so quick to tell her about the dark side of the city he had seen. He could have told her about the cafés, the boulevards, the river, drawn her a picture of the city that now stood where she had once lived. Instead, he'd told her about Kurapaty, about the war, about Maly Trostenets.

Garrick swallowed some of the hot coffee, coughed, and

swallowed again. 'I didn't see her yesterday – I went for an interview in Leicester and she was asleep when I got back. Mrs Baker found her when she went in this morning. Yevanov threw me out. I didn't know where else to go.'

. . . you are responsible for them. 'I can put you up for a couple of nights,' he said absently. 'Give you a chance to find somewhere.'

'It won't . . . I brought you something. You're the only person who . . .'

Jake wasn't listening. His mind was replaying his last encounter with Miss Yevanova. He seemed to be specializing in this – intruding into people's grief, digging around in the middens of their lives. He'd done it to Sophia Yevanova, and he'd done it to Faith.

But as he remembered his last encounter with Sophia Yevanova, he realized it was not quite as damning as he believed. She had chosen the direction of the conversation. It had stirred up some painful memories, but she'd wanted to talk about them. She'd been interested, she'd asked about Zialony Luh. The colour had returned to her face as they talked and she'd become more animated. Until . . . Until he'd told her about the museum, and he'd told her about Maly Trostenets. *That* was when she'd gone pale and breathless. She'd said, 'Of course.' He'd taken that as acknowledgement of a place she knew about all too well, but now he thought about it, it looked more like realization. *Maly Trostenets! Of course . . .* What had she realized?

And now she was dead.

Oh, *shit.*

Oh shit, oh shit, oh shit.

The hospital was at the weary end of the night shift. The ward was dimly lit, the staff at the nursing station spoke in low voices, machines beeped and hummed. In the middle of this, Grandpapa lay still, shrunken and reduced on the

341

hospital bed. He was sleeping, but his face was flushed and congested, and his breathing was laboured.

'He's got a chest infection,' the nurse told Faith. 'He's stabilized a bit since I called – the antibiotics are kicking in, but he's very ill – you understand what I'm saying?'

Faith understood. She sat by his bed and took his hand. He looked peaceful, and she was grateful for that until she remembered her own wild dreams and knew that the appearance of peace was deceptive. 'It's Faith, Grandpapa,' she said. She didn't know if he heard her or not.

Around her, the life of the ward went on. She sat with him and watched.

Jake left Nick in the living room and went into his office. The two young girls in the photo watched him as he picked up the phone and fumbled one-handed with his address book, trying to find the number. He had to contact Burnley, or failing that, one of the team investigating Helen Kovacs' death. He couldn't understand what the connection was – he just knew there was one. There was someone who didn't want the name of Maly Trostenets to be linked to . . . what? There was no one left. Sophia Yevanova was dead. Marek Lange was dying. The story was ending.

Tell me. He directed the thought like a prayer to the girl in the picture, the girl whose life was to spiral into the chaos of war, the girl who was now dead. *Tell me*. He directed the thought at the serene, doll-like face of Raina, the other child, the one whose life was to end in the horrors of the gulags.

And she answered.

Slowly, he put the phone down, then picked it up again and dialled Adam Zuygev's number. He heard the entry-phone sound, but he didn't have time for that now. The photo in front of him told its secret, and he couldn't see anything else.

R. Yevanova and S. Yevanova. The caption was there to read, obscure, because it was written in an unfamiliar alphabet. He would have seen it days ago when Adam first showed him the picture, if he'd only had his wits about him. He could remember Adam teasing him about missing an obvious detail in a photograph because he'd misread falsely familiar letters.

The scribbled caption, the names, Raina and Sophia. But in the picture, they were the other way round, Sophia and Raina. He waited impatiently until Adam picked up the phone.

'The photo,' Jake said. 'Which one is Sophia?'

'The fair-haired one,' Adam said. 'It says on the picture. You recognized her, anyway.'

He could remember their meeting in the café when Adam had shown him the picture – two girls. They were Raina and Sophia, Adam had said, but he hadn't said which was which, and nor had Jake as he looked. He hadn't seen the story the picture told.

Sophia, pretty, blonde Sophia had been the brave one – she had joined the partisans and had been betrayed by her cousin. She had ended the war in the camps.

Raina, dark-eyed, beautiful Raina, had collaborated, had worked with the fascists, and as the Red Army approached, she had fled, taking the identity of her cousin, who she must have believed dead. And she had taken as well enough valuables to set her and her child – whose child? – up with a comfortable life in the west. The icon. Whose had it been? Someone whose life had ended in the occupation? *The only thing of value . . . apart from my son.*

The initials that Helen Kovacs had jotted down, wherever they came from, they weren't the Latin symbols *P. E.* They were the Cyrillic letters *P. E.* that transliterated as *R. Ye.* Raina Yevanova.

Sophia, the real Sophia, had survived. She had lived to pay the penalty that her cousin had incurred and had died in the gulags. Had there been no one who could confirm her

343

identity? Or was there no one left? And maybe the authorities, Stalin's forces, just didn't care. There had been a collaborator, Raina Yevanova. They had a collaborator whose name was Yevanova. They had someone to punish. That was good enough.

That was a secret worth killing for.

Footsteps moved behind him and he froze as something cold touched his throat.

25

Jake turned his head very slowly, keeping his hands in view. The knife – a part of his mind that focused on trivialities recognized it as a knife from his kitchen – touched his neck. He knew that knife. One slash, and he would be choking to death on his own blood.

Nick Garrick let him turn, keeping the knife pressed against him. 'I'm sorry,' Garrick said. Jake realized that he meant it, and felt a strange urge to laugh. Garrick was apologizing. His eyes were bright with unshed tears, but the knife stayed firm. He kicked the desk chair round with his foot and gestured for Jake to sit.

Jake didn't like that – once he was in the chair, his opportunity for manoeuvre would be severely restricted – but he felt the pressure of the knife increase and a slippery feeling on his neck that told him he was bleeding. He'd interviewed dangerous people before. He had to stay calm, and he had to keep Garrick calm. He told himself that if Garrick truly wanted him dead, he would be on the floor now, bleeding out, so Garrick must want something from him. He sat.

Garrick backed away and pushed the door shut. His movements were jerky with panic. Jake could feel the adrenalin surging through him, pushing him to some kind of action, any action, but it would be suicide to try and jump Garrick now. He had to get him talking, get him to calm down, to relax his guard. 'I don't understand.'

'I brought it to you,' Garrick said. 'I thought you'd know what to do, but you called the police, didn't you? I heard you talking.'

Jake shook his head. 'I called someone in Minsk, about that photograph.' He jerked his head to indicate the picture lying on his desk. Garrick craned his neck to look at it, and Jake was reminded of the day they'd stood in the garden at the Yevanov house and talked about Sophia – *Raina* – Yevanova. Keep him talking. 'What did you bring me? What did you want me to do?'

'The diary. And the letters. That's what it was all about.' The knife pressed against Jake's throat, just over the carotid artery. He forced himself to keep still. He was the one Garrick had come to for help, he was the one who would know what to do. He mustn't show any signs of weakness or fear, though he could feel the panic under the surface, fighting to get out. He tried not to think about the knife wounds he had seen, or the agonizing, suffocating death that awaited him if his throat was cut.

He repositioned himself in his chair, moving slowly as if he was trying to get comfortable. If he could brace the chair against the desk, he might be able to . . . The knife jerked. 'Stop that!' Garrick's voice was on the edge.

Jake froze. He could feel the blood trickling down his neck. 'Okay. It's okay. My leg was cramping, that's all.' He waited a moment. 'I still don't understand. Tell me.' He tried a smile. 'I'm not going anywhere.'

'I didn't know,' Garrick said. 'You've got to believe that.'

'Okay. Tell me. Explain it to me, because I don't know what's going on here.'

Garrick hesitated, chewing his lip. His gaze went round

the room, then back to Jake, but the knife was steady in his hand. Then he began to talk.

'It was after the accident. She told me I could stay there when I came out of hospital, but Yevanov had moved in. I didn't want to be around him. So she found me a job. She talked Yevanov into letting me have it. It suited everybody. I needed the work, and I wanted somewhere to live. He didn't want me in the house. And she . . .' He looked at Jake. 'You know what she's like. You want to do things for her.'

Jake made a careful sound of assent. He could remember how easily Sophia Yevanova had talked him into nosing around the Kovacs investigation.

'She told me that there was something she'd done in the war – she wouldn't tell me what it was, but she said they all had to do things, sometimes, just to survive. This man, Gennady Litkin, had got hold of some papers that told the story . . .'

When Antoni Yevanov had agreed to take on the job as director of the Centre for European Studies, the papers had been full of articles about him. Gennady Litkin had read the articles and had remembered the old letters and the diary he had collected years before. He had contacted Sophia Yevanova, assuming she would be interested in records of her family's past. He may even have promised them to her, but then he had died.

'She wanted me to find the papers and give them to her. I knew, as soon as I saw the library that it was impossible. I told her, "No one will ever look at all this." There were boxes and boxes of papers, all mixed up, falling apart. It was junk. The archivist said so. He said it would take years to go through it all. He thought they would just store it, but I kept on looking . . .'

And then Helen Kovacs had turned up, and with the information Gennady Litkin had given her, had located them at once.

'I tried to phone Miss Yevanova,' Garrick said, 'but the signal kept cutting out. I was using a pay-as-you go phone I'd picked up in the market – it wasn't much good. She called me back on the landline, and I told her that this woman had found them. She wasn't surprised. I think she knew that Litkin had talked to someone. That's why she was so concerned. She said, "I won't have the people I care about made ashamed." And then I knew what she was going to do. She always kept the pills to hand. She hated the idea of being helpless. She said she was never going to let the illness trap her. I had to stop her. I told her to wait. I said I'd deal with it. She'd been brave when she had to be, she'd done things she didn't want to do. I could be like that too.' He looked at Jake, making sure that he understood. 'So that's what I did.'

Jake could see Miss Yevanova, making her decision. She would choose to die, rather than be disgraced. But she had confided her decision to Nick Garrick, who already felt the responsibility – however undeserved – for the death of his mother. He would do anything to avoid that again.

'I'd seen the wire in the old kitchen. I told myself I was like a partisan. I had to make a hard decision, like Miss Yevanova had when she'd done . . . whatever it was she'd done. A garrotte. It looks . . . so quick.' He closed his eyes and swallowed. 'It wasn't like that at all . . . I can't stop seeing it. I can't stop remembering. It was horrible and I couldn't stop once I'd started. And she . . . it . . . I just . . . I wanted to stop, but it was too late.

'I went back to the phone and told her what I'd done, that I'd got the notebook and the letters. I said I was going to call the police. She sounded . . .' He looked at Jake and his face was puzzled. 'It sounded as if she was crying. Just for a minute. But she can't have been. She never cried. Then she said she wasn't going to let me take the blame. She said, "This is my fault." She told me to remember that.' He shook his head. 'It wasn't true. She wasn't to blame. I was.'

348

Jake listened as Garrick outlined the plan Sophia Yevanova had made. The phone was to be his alibi. He was to get rid of the mobile and dispose of the notebook and letters. 'She said I wasn't to burn them. She wanted to see them. She told me to put them into the post box at the end of the drive.'

Miss Yevanova was to be his witness on the other end of the phone to the sound of an intruder. 'Once everything was set up, I was supposed to hang up and phone the police at once. Only . . .' Only there had been blood. It might be on him, and the police would check. 'She said I'd have to be with the body when the police arrived, that I'd have to try and move her, like I was trying to help her. I said I'd do that, but I couldn't. I rang off, and I knew I couldn't go back there. I couldn't stop seeing it. On and on. I wanted to make it stop. I wanted to make it not happen. I took all the pills, and it wouldn't go away, and I drank the whisky, and I kept thinking *I'll phone them in a minute. I'll go through, then I'll phone them* . . . But I didn't.'

The pressure of the knife increased against his throat. Jake pressed himself back in his chair and braced himself. Sideways. He'd have to go sideways and try to knock Garrick's legs out from under him.

'Then it was morning. I'd fallen asleep. Just for a minute, I thought it had been a dream. I thought it was all okay. Then I remembered. I didn't know what to do. I dialled 999 on my phone – I wanted to call the police and tell them what I'd done, but then I knew I couldn't, not without them finding out that she'd tried to help me. I had to make it work. For her. Someone answered, and I couldn't say anything. I just sat there with this voice saying, "Emergency. Which service?" I knew they could trace it. I knew I didn't have much time. I took the phone to bits and shoved them through a gap in the floorboards. I didn't think they'd take the place apart. Then I went to the library.'

There was silence, then Garrick slumped against the wall,

all the tension leaving him. 'I'm sorry,' he said. Jake tentatively reached out and took the knife from his limp fingers.

Garrick didn't seem to notice. 'Her . . . the woman's . . . watch had fallen off – that gave me the idea. I set the time and smashed it. Then I sat with her. I didn't want to leave her again. I used her phone to call the police, in case they hadn't traced the first call. I wanted to tell her I was sorry, but I felt so ill – I think I passed out. And then the police were there.'

But Miss Yevanova hadn't destroyed the papers Nick sent to her. Maybe, even after all these years, she couldn't bring herself to destroy the only memento she had of her lover. And on the night of her death, Nick had read them.

'She was the one who taught me Russian. I was good at it. All those things I couldn't do at school – history and literature – my dad thought I was stupid. But I was good at Russian.' His face twitched. 'And I used it to find out that she'd lied to me. I went to see her that night. It was late, it was after midnight. I knew I had to go to the police, but I couldn't let her face that. I couldn't let them do the things to her that they'd done to me. I had to do something to stop it.'

Now, Jake realized what it was that had pushed Garrick to this moment. 'You killed her,' he said.

Garrick's voice was muffled. 'She didn't fight me. I think she wanted it.'

Or she had been too weak to resist.

'Where are they? The diary and the letters?'

'They're in my bag.'

'Why didn't you destroy them?' With the diary and letters gone, there would be very little chance of making a case against Nick Garrick and Sophia Yevanova. It would be a hard case to make now, without Nick's confession.

The entry-phone rang. Jake remembered it ringing before, when he was dialling Adam's number. He felt cold and shaky as he pressed the door release.

'You don't understand,' Garrick said. 'People died for those. You were the one she talked to. You need to know the truth. You've got to tell the story. I don't want anyone else telling it. That's why I brought them to you before I went to the police.'

If you give someone advice . . . 'If you were going to the police, why did you attack me?'

Garrick looked at him in puzzlement. 'I didn't! I just had to make you listen. Before you called them.'

'So who's been calling me?' a voice said from the doorway.

Jake swung round. Mick Burnley was standing there, his eyes taking in the scene. 'Thought I'd call round, find out what was so important. Looks like you should have answered your door the first time, Denbigh. What's happened to you?' His gaze moved between the two men.

'Cut myself shaving,' Jake said, pushing the knife out of sight among the papers on his desk.

Burnley's eyes went to Garrick. 'Yeah?'

Garrick pushed himself to his feet. 'I'm the one you want,' he said. 'I want to make a statement.'

Burnley looked at him in silence, then interrogated Jake with his eyes. Jake kept his face expressionless. 'I'll need a statement from you as well, Denbigh,' he said.

Jake had no intention of making any kind of statement yet. He had too much to do. Burnley had no reason to take him in, though Jake could see him running the possibilities through his mind. 'I'll talk to you later,' Burnley said, making it a threat. He took out his phone and spoke quickly, giving Jake's address and arranging for a car to meet him and take Garrick in. While this was happening, Jake leaned against the wall, watching the light on the water. Once, he met Garrick's eyes and nodded to his unspoken request.

After they had gone, Garrick cuffed between two police officers, he went to the backpack that neither he nor Garrick had acknowledged, and opened it. Inside, there was a tattered envelope containing a notebook, a sheaf of letters, and sheets of paper covered with writing that scrawled across the page, jagged and uneven where the pen had dug in. The notebook and the letters were old, the writing indecipherable to his untrained eye, but the sheets of paper were new. A translation. Nick Garrick had provided him with a translation. Jake wondered if he'd done it while Sophia Yevanova lay dead in her room.

He spread the papers out on his desk and began to read.

Love letters written on thin paper, so fragile it had started to crumble along the folds. They looked as though they had been folded for a long time, the creases embedded in the structure of the paper.

The writing was fine italic, but the ink was faded. They should have been tied with a ribbon, kept with a pressed flower as letters of a doomed love are often said to be. The ribbon would be black, the flower one of those exotic blooms that flourishes in marshland and bogs and draws its prey with the reek of corruption.

My dear Captain Vienuolos
How kind of you to write. I would be delighted to
attend the ceremony welcoming the
Generalkommissar . . .

My darling . . .
On the darker days the thought of you . . . You know
that I cannot come to the command centre. People will
not understand. Please send a car . . .
* . . . tomorrow night! I am obsessed by the thought of*
it and when I leave you I will not be able to get the
memory . . . you must come to me soon . . .

The letters were written to a Lithuanian officer from his young mistress. She promised him a haven of pleasure and sweetness in middle of a dark and deadly war. She flattered and cajoled him . . . *to wear silk stockings for you. I cannot wear those ugly socks, not when we are together* . . . There was talk of gifts he had given her . . . *the necklace fits just around my waist. I will show you, next time we meet* . . . She upbraided him for his neglect, but sweetly, with promises of rewards for a swift return.

You neglect me! You say that you 'must' go to Slutsk. I am quite sure you choose to go. I will be so lonely when you are gone – what am I to do? Hurry back to me . . .

You promise and promise to take me away from Minsk . . . to Vienna, or to Berlin. I am so, so tired of this war, war, war . . .

In his last months in Minsk, the officer had been sent to work with the platoons organizing the killings in Maly Trostenets. He recorded little of what he did – his diary, translated into Russian in Gennady Litkin's copperplate hand, talked only of 'actions' and occasionally of the logistical problems and the conditions at the camp. He missed his home and his family.

Later in the week, we were given orders to clear the area. That night, they firebombed the houses and left the streets burning. I watched as the work progressed. Towards midnight, a woman with a young child in her arms ran towards the gates. She was stopped by a policeman who seized the child, who was perhaps a year old, struck it against the wall then threw it into the flames. He shot the mother dead.

I very much wish to be home.

But it seemed he truly loved his mistress: *Now I am stationed close to Minsk, I can spend more time with my Raina . . . I worry about what may happen to her* . . . He wrote about her beauty:

> *. . . think we should have a taste for Frauleins. Not me. I love my dark-eyed beauty with her delicate body and her iron will. She can wind me round her little finger and the witch knows it!*

And he knew the danger she faced, both from her own people and from his:

> *She has given up so much for me, and now they don't trust her. She has a cousin who has gone to the forests. They live like animals and they kill our men. Now the KdS are asking questions about her. If they arrest her . . . I could not bear to see my Raina hanged like a dog on the streets for the eyes of the soldiers . . .*

He had bought Raina's safety at a terrible price. The letters spoke of an informer. He lived in the city, and he sold his countrymen to the occupiers, to the *Schutzmannschaft*. He was clever – the partisans would have had him killed, but he never went near the Special Police. He took his information to the officer's mistress, and she passed it on. *Your rat has been digging in his hole again. He brought what he found to me. I do not like doing this.* But the letters were riddled with a catalogue of betrayals, small and large . . . *old woman who has hidden fugitives in her cellar . . . from the ghetto to the forests . . . . . . the girl from the hospital who has been taking messages . . . This Petr Dyakin is a disgusting man. My darling, I do not want to do this.*

Letters from the collaborator Raina Yevanova to her Nazi lover.

He wrote in his diary as well about the letters he received from his wife, and his frustration that he couldn't do anything about the increasing shortages that she complained about. He talked about having sent her gifts from looted cities. *Times are different now.*

He wrote also – and here the writing became erratic, as though he was frightened to commit the words to paper – that the war was not going well. He seemed suddenly aware that he might be brought to account for the actions he had carried out, and that there might be other ways of seeing than the one he and his compatriots had worked with through the war. And he was worried for his mistress. *Raina may pay a terrible price for siding with us against the communists.*

He outlined his plans for their escape – his, back to his wife and children in Vilna, hers, to a place beyond the reach of Soviet revenge. *She will travel under the identity of her cousin, who she believes is dead. Poor Raina. She wept when I told her. It is a small untruth. The woman will surely be hanged before the next weeks are out.* Raina, it seemed, was not entirely *au fait* with his plans: *She is so lovely as she talks about our life together when this is over. I haven't the heart to tell her I must go home.*

The diary ended abruptly with no further indication of the identity, or the fate, of the writer. It must have lain unread, with the letters he had kept, until it had come to the attention of Gennady Litkin with his desire to tell the story of the people who had suffered so terribly in the war against fascism and whose stories were the least told.

Antoni Yevanov's name had come to the fore locally when he had taken the Chair at the Centre for European Studies. And mentioned in the articles was his mother, Sophia. The partisan cousin of the collaborator Raina.

And the ghost fingers had reached out.

26

The sky was growing darker when Jake pulled up outside the Yevanov house. Antoni Yevanov opened the door. If he was surprised to see Jake, he didn't show it. He stepped back from the door, gesturing to him to come in. Jake didn't want to cross that threshold. The warmth, and the smell of flowers and polish now made him think of a charnel house where the reek of decay was imperfectly overlain by perfumes. As far as he knew, Garrick had told no one else about Sophia Yevanova's death, and in that moment before the police took him away, Jake had decided to accede to Garrick's unspoken plea. Sophia Yevanova had been mortally ill. Her illness had killed her.

Yevanov looked gaunt and hollow eyed. He took Jake into the study where the two men had talked just a few days before. He indicated a chair to Jake and sat down himself at the desk. 'Well?' his voice was indifferent.

Jake studied him. The dark eyes and the narrow, fine-boned face came from his mother. Maybe the cold demeanour came from the same source, or maybe that was a legacy from his father. Jake had spent a few hours researching the information he'd found in the diary. It wasn't much time and he hadn't tracked down Vienuolos, but he'd read about the men from the Baltic states who had supported the fascists.

He'd found a letter from Wilhelm Kube, the General-kommisar of Byelorussia to Gauleiter Lohse concerning German Jews who been sent to Minsk to be killed:

I am certainly a hard man and willing to help solve the Jewish question, but people who come from our own cultural sphere are just not the same as the brutish hordes in this place. Is the slaughter to be carried out by the Lithuanians . . . ?

Vienuolos must have been a committed Nazi to have achieved officer rank – he may even have taken German nationality after Hitler's rise to power. Such men had been consigned to the work of pacifying the civilian population behind the Nazi advance into the Soviet Union. They had participated in some of the worst atrocities, and had assisted in the destruction of Maly Trostenets as the German forces fled from the Soviet advance. One such man had been Antoni Yevanov's father.

Without speaking, Jake put the copies he'd made of the letters and the diary on the desk in front of Yevanov.

Yevanov looked at him without comment, and began to read. Jake noticed that he was looking at the original diary, not the translation that Gennady Litkin had attached. As he turned the pages over, his face became expressionless and when he finally raised his eyes to Jake's, they were unreadable. 'I think I can work out the rest of the story.' He picked up the papers in front of him and aligned the sheets before he secured them with a paper clip. They made a thin sheaf. 'It's very little to have caused such grief.'

'Did you know?' Jake said.

Yevanov's eyebrows arched. 'Mr Denbigh, you are not here to ask me questions.'

'Then why am I here?' Jake knew that if Yevanov let him through the door, then somewhere, somehow, he had a lever that would make the older man talk. He just didn't know what it was.

'As you are the visitor, I hoped you might tell me.' Yevanov picked up a paper knife and balanced it between his fingers, his eyebrows raised in polite query.

Jake wanted the link with Marek Lange. 'I don't have the whole story,' he said. 'I have just enough to know that I don't have it all.'

Yevanov's eyes measured him, but he didn't speak. Jake edged further out, aware how thin the ground was under his feet. 'The investigating team never went after Helen Kovacs' research,' he said. 'Because they didn't find anything in her records to point them in the right direction.'

'There was no mystery about her research. Mr Denbigh, I have more important things to do with my time . . .'

Jake gambled. 'They didn't find anything, because by the time they looked, the incriminating files had been removed. And I presume you devised a pretext for searching everything thoroughly to make sure you hadn't missed anything.'

Yevanov's face was indifferent, but the paper knife was now still between his fingers as he watched Jake.

'It's hard to tamper with computer records and leave no trace, but it can be done, especially if you have control of the network.'

'As you say, Mr Denbigh, if any such tampering had occurred, it would be hard to trace.'

'But not impossible – if the police technicians really took the system apart. What would they find?'

'Who knows?' Yevanov said. He sighed, and flicked through the pages that Jake had given him. 'I really had no idea about this. If I had, I would have done something, long before it brought about these tragedies. There was no need for this.'

'You must have known something,' Jake said. Enough to have removed all references to this research from Helen Kovacs' papers.

'I knew there was something in the Litkin Archive my mother was worried about. I thought – the kind of life she'd led – there had to be things she was ashamed of. The partisans, especially the women, had to do things that are hard to stomach. I didn't care what she had done.' His eyes assessed Jake dispassionately.

'And you didn't make the link with Helen Kovacs' death?'

'I thought Nicholas was responsible. I thought it was the way the police said – he was unstable, he'd attacked her. I didn't want any investigation of my mother's background. I didn't want her embarrassed or upset. She was becoming more and more frail. I knew that Helen's interest in the archive related to the Baltic states in the war, and I knew that might lead her to wartime Belarus. I erased any such references from Helen's computer as soon as I heard what had happened. I can access the network from here. As it turned out, I erased a file in error. But my mother was left in peace.' He studied his hands, frowning. 'Or she would have been, if she had not chosen to champion Garrick. I take it the police and the newspapers will soon have this story.'

'The police will get it if Garrick chooses to tell them. They won't hear it from me.'

Yevanov raised an eyebrow. 'Of course,' he said. 'Your book.'

Jake didn't bother to deny it. 'And now maybe you can tell me about Marek Lange,' he said.

Yevanov looked at him with genuine surprise. 'Faith Lange's grandfather?' He shook his head. 'I have no idea what you are talking about.'

'Lange was in Minsk as well,' Jake said.

Yevanov seemed not to hear him. 'What my mother didn't realize,' he said, 'was that I wouldn't have cared. If the story had come out, I wouldn't have cared. I doubt anyone would. It wasn't her fear of exposure that was driving her, it was her sense of guilt.'

'And Helen Kovacs?'

For the first time, Yevanov's face showed a flicker of emotion. It was quickly suppressed, but Jake thought he had seen regret. 'Maybe Helen was my mother's last victim,' he said.

Faith sat on the windowsill of the high ward. The first shadows were falling across the city as the sun set and the light began to fade. From her vantage point, she could see the patterns of the streets, the sheen of damp on the roofs and the branches of the trees.

Once upon a time, there was a forest, with birch trees that were bare in the winter and reached their fingers high up into the sky. But in summer, the leaves grew and the branches hung down in fronds. When the wind blew, the branches would wave and the leaves would dance. Then the sunlight made patterns of shadow and gold. And the tree trunks were white, like slender pillars along the paths . . .

She felt tears stinging behind her eyelids. The house in the forest, the orchard, the well. It had all gone. And Stanislau, Kristina and Eva. All dust. And soon Marek would be gone too. There would be no more stories. Grandpapa's secret. What was it, what had happened that had made him hide away from his countrymen all these years, made him give away all his money in an attempt to assuage the guilt of . . . what?

He stirred restlessly against the pillow, and she went back to the bedside. His lips moved.

She took his hand. 'Grandpapa?' she said.

His head turned and he started muttering. She could catch the occasional word. '. . . at the gate . . . Eva . . .'

Eva. 'I found a photograph of Eva. In the desk.'

His head turned from side to side, and his lips worked, but no sound emerged.

'It's over,' she said. 'It's done. Rest. Please rest.'

But his hand gripped hers, and his lips moved urgently as if he was trying to tell her something.

'What is it?' she said. 'Grandpapa?'

The sky grew darker.

Jake lit his tenth cigarette of the day and pressed 'delete'. He was working on his book. He was trying to explain the complexity of motives that drove the people caught behind the German advance. He knew what he wanted, a cool and cerebral analysis of influences that led to both heroism and craven defeat. But the words wouldn't come. This rarely happened to Jake. He stared at the blank screen, and the face of Sophia Yevanova – he could only think of her as Sophia Yevanova – looked back. *You must understand that, for some of us, the fascists came as liberators, at first.* And the crosses of Kurapaty, vanishing under the trees.

He couldn't hate her. She had lived with the reality of the Kurapaty killings for much of her life. *You must understand that, for some of us, the fascists came as liberators, at first.*

Could he hate her for her betrayal of her cousin? Sophia had been brave. She had fought, and she had finally been brought down. She had survived the prison camp only to fall into the hands of the NKVD. Had Raina known, when she stole her cousin's identity, that Sophia would pay the price for what she had done? Maybe she truly believed that the real Sophia had died in the camp to which Raina had consigned her.

He had his book. He had all the information he needed, and more. Tiredness overwhelmed him. He just wanted to lie down and sleep, but he had to work. His notes scrolled down the screen in front of him, in a mockery of what he now knew. He couldn't face it, not tonight.

Jake didn't know what to do with the evening. He didn't want to go out. He couldn't face even the anonymous crowd in a bar. He didn't want to be among other people. He switched on the television and channel-hopped for a while, then switched off in disgust.

Some stuff had come through on the fax earlier. He hadn't bothered looking at it. He knew what it was. Adam had e-mailed him earlier: *I have found your people. I have sent you what there is of the story.* The papers were waiting for him. He'd have jumped on them a couple of days ago. Maybe Adam's notes held the clue to Marek Lange's secret, but Jake wasn't sure he wanted it any more. From what he had seen, Lange's secret had tormented him far more than Raina Yevanova's secret had tormented her. Digging around in other people's pasts had brought death and chaos in its wake. Whether it was Kurapaty, collaboration, or something else, the secret could die with him.

But he didn't have anything else to do. He took the papers out of the machine and began skimming them. The papers relating to the Lange family had largely been destroyed as the Nazis fled Minsk, razing the city as they went. *Much of this was taken from the trials of the collaborators after the war*, Adam had written. Jake flicked through the pages, skim-reading. He began to frown and turned back to the beginning. This time, he read the closely written pages intently. An hour later, he sat back in his chair and stared out of the window. The text had been disjointed, patched together from different sources, but the story it told had been vivid, and he needed to take himself away from the streets of wartime Minsk, away from the story he had just pieced together.

Marek Lange's secret.

He thought about Lange's arrival as a refugee towards the end of the war. He thought about the life Lange had tried to make for himself – the marriage that had failed, the daughter he apparently couldn't love, the business that had been so successful because he had nothing else to fear and nothing else to lose. And finally his granddaughter had been born. Faith. Maybe the last years had been less tormented.

There had been an end, of a kind. He had sold everything he had to sell, given his money away to the children and grandchildren of the survivors, had stayed in the cold, comfortless house, lovingly tended his garden and tried to ensure his granddaughter's future.

And now, it was nearly over.

It wasn't quite ten. He picked up his coat. He knew what Lange's secret was, and he knew what he had to do.

He just hoped he wasn't going to be too late.

Faith was weary. The monotonous hum of the ventilation system was playing tunes in her head, and her eyes were starting to droop. The clock continued its relentless march towards midnight. The doctor had told her that Grandpapa wasn't responding to the antibiotics, and they didn't expect him to survive the night. 'Short of a miracle,' the young man had said with a tired grimace.

She'd phoned Katya at six. 'Please come,' she'd said.

'As soon as I can.' Katya had promised, but Faith knew she wouldn't be there, not until she was sure that it was all over.

Grandpapa woke and recommenced his restless search, his head shifting from side to side, his lips moving wordlessly. She took his hand. 'I'm here,' she said. He didn't seem to hear her. He was going to die, and he was going to die with his desperate search unfulfilled. A search for what? Faith couldn't help him because she didn't know.

'Grandpapa,' she said again. 'It's all right. I'm here.' She tried giving him some water, but it trickled down the side of his face and soaked into the collar of his pyjamas. She dabbed at it gently.

363

Even now, even late at night, people were coming and going. It wasn't a place of rest. She heard the clang of the lift doors, heard the echo of footsteps, heard the ward door sigh open and then creak shut. Someone was coming along the corridor now, moving quickly. She hoped it might be Katya, but Katya's footsteps were always the sharp tap of high heels moving with urgent haste. This sounded like a man. The footsteps came to the door of Grandpapa's section and then moved into the four-bed unit. She looked up.

It was Jake Denbigh. He looked exhausted. His face was grey and his eyes were shadowed with lack of sleep. She stood up slowly. 'Jake.'

'I told them I was your brother. Faith, I had to come. I got it so wrong. How is he?'

'He's worse. Much worse. Something's upsetting him. He won't rest.' Her throat was dry.

'I know what it is,' Jake said. 'I think I can help him – I was afraid I might be too late. Will he be able to hear me?'

What could anyone say that would help him now? It was over. But Jake's urgency was as convincing as Grandpapa's distress. 'If there's anything – *please*, do it.'

He moved to the bed. Grandpapa turned his head restlessly on the pillow. '. . . *the light . . . They are watching. Go. Now, Eva. Go . . .*'

Faith took his hand. 'Grandpapa,' she said.

'*Now . . . go . . .*'

Jake bent over the bed. 'Mr Lange.' Faith could hear his voice, low but clear and authoritative as he spoke to Grandpapa. 'Mr Lange. There's news from Minsk. Listen.'

Minsk! She reached out her hand to silence him, when she saw that Grandpapa's restless movement had stopped. His eyes flickered. Jake spoke again. 'That night – they lied to you to make you talk. Eva escaped, Mr Lange. She got away from them. She escaped.' He leaned closer, watching Grandpapa's face. 'Can you hear me? Do you understand?'

364

Grandpapa's eyes opened. His eyes focused on her and she could see . . . was it recognition on his face? A tear ran down on to the pillow. His mouth moved. She thought that maybe he had tried to smile. Then his eyes closed.

They sat by the bed. Jake stayed with her as the night drew on. Grandpapa sank back into unconsciousness. His breathing was harsh, and his skin became hotter and hotter. The nurses came and turned him once. Faith cooled his face with a flannel. He didn't stir.

Shortly before one, his breath started to become uneven, with a catch in his throat. The gap between each breath became longer, catch . . . and breathe, catch . . . and breathe, slower and slower. His jaw slackened, and the laboured breathing grew fainter.

And then everything was still.

The Bear at the Gate

And this is the story of how Eva died.

They kept her in the cells in Minsk for seven days. They didn't seem to care how much or how little she knew. They knew that she had gone to meet Marek. That was enough. They wouldn't tell her what they had done with him – whether he was alive or dead. She wrote to her mother from the prison:

Dear Mama
Please don't worry about me. I have not been badly
treated. Please tell the director at the hospital what has
happened. I don't want to be without work when I
leave here. Ask Larissa Moskoff in the apartment
above if you need help. She has been very good to me.
Eva

It is not known if the tone in this letter reflects Eva's true expectations about her fate, or if the information she gave her mother about her treatment was true.

It was January 1943. The tide of the war was turning. In a little over a year, Minsk would be liberated. But time can form an unbridgeable gulf. A week after Eva had been taken into custody, she left the police building where the suspects were held.

It is a grey day. It rained in the night, and the water lies in pools on the ground. Eva looks small and pale among the men who surround her. Her hands are tied behind her back with twine. It has been pulled tight and must dig into her flesh. Her eyes are fixed ahead.

She wears a blue dress her mother made for her, and a grey cardigan that another prisoner has given her against the cold. It is buttoned up to the neck. The officer leading the death squad wears a long greatcoat. The peak of his cap points down towards his nose.

They escort their captive through the streets to the entrance of the old distillery, to the gates with the arch of the dancing bear. The officer throws a rope over the crossbar and makes a loop. Someone brings a stool from inside the building. They lead Eva to the makeshift gallows.

She can see over the heads of the watching soldiers as she is lifted on to the stool. Her face is very white. Her eyes are fixed on the street, on the alleyway that runs back into the shadows, the place where she last saw her brother.

The officer puts the noose round her neck, frowning slightly in deliberation as he places it and runs the loop down the rope. Eva turns her face away, then looks back to the alley.

The officer steps down. Eva's eyelids flutter.

She is in the woods, in the shadow of the trees on a summer's day. The light seems to flicker as she hurries along the path, shade and light, shade and light. And on either side of the path, narrower paths twine away into the darkness, into the secret places of the forest. She doesn't know why she is running, not at first. She looks behind her, but the way home has gone. To either side, there is nothing but trees and shadows. And ahead of her the path vanishes under an arch of leaves.

But she can hear it now. Deep in the forest, under the darkness of the trees, she can hear it. The careful placing of a foot, and silence, and again, and silence, and again . . . closer and closer.

Baba Yaga has found her.

Time stops.

Then the executioner kicks the stool away.

27

The memorial service for Helen was held in the church near the university, six weeks after her death. The chapel of rest was full. There must have been a hundred people there. Faith saw Trish in the crowd, neatly turned out in black, and Greg Fellows, looking uncomfortable in a jacket and tie, standing unobtrusively at the back as if he was afraid someone would come and eject him. Maybe he had more cause to mourn Helen than she knew.

She looked round again and saw Jake coming down the aisle towards her. Their eyes met, and he came and stood beside her, touching her hand lightly. 'Okay?' His voice was low in her ear.

She nodded.

The morning after Grandpapa had died, he had taken her home. She'd fallen into bed and slept until the evening. When she woke, he was still there. He'd prepared food and bought wine. 'There's something I have to show you,' he said.

And later, towards midnight, he'd given her the papers he'd obtained from the archive at Hrodna where the story had lain untold since the end of the war.

That is enough, little one . . .

'He thought he'd led Eva to her death,' Jake said, when

she'd finished reading. 'He was with the partisans after the Nazis invaded. He got cut off from his platoon – it happened to a lot of Red Army soldiers. He must have kept up some kind of contact with Eva and his mother – they were in Minsk during the occupation. She was doing some minor work for the resistance and someone informed on her. He tried to get her out and they were both arrested. The S.D. – that was the secret police in the area at the time – told him that they'd followed him, that they were after him, not Eva. That's what they said, but in fact it was the other way round. They knew about Eva, and they were watching her. Getting him was a coup they didn't expect. Her offences were fairly minor – she'd probably have been sent to one of the camps. But they'd arrested her with a known partisan. He knew what that meant.'

'But he got out.'

'He was lucky, if you want to call it that. They thought he was important. They sent him to the S.D. Headquarters where the real Gestapo could work on him. The partisans blew up the railway line and the train was derailed. He got away. There was no way he could get back, and by that time Eva was dead. All he could do was try to survive. He made his way across occupied Europe to join the Allies. It was an amazing escape. But of course, by the end of the war, there was nothing left.'

'Did he know what had happened to her?'

Jake nodded. 'He must have done. The refugee organizations would have told him. But he probably never heard it from an official source, he never heard an eye-witness account. There was always that loophole for hope. And at the end, in the hospital – I think he was back there, I think he was reliving it.'

Enough . . .

It was almost time for the service to start. Faith looked round and then looked again as she saw Daniel take his place

369

in one of the pews. Finn was with him, and he gave Faith a quick smile. He had promised her that his father would be here, and he had delivered. Daniel looked across at her, and after a moment, he gave her an abrupt nod. That was the only apology she was likely to get.

Finn had told her the story, or as much of it as she needed to know. Daniel had been out the night Helen died, called out to do some emergency work at one of Lomas's clubs, and had been an unwilling witness when the car involved in the shooting turned up. Lomas had made it clear that if Daniel brought the police to his club, then he and the children would be in trouble. Daniel, knowing that he would be the first person the police looked at, had been left to concoct the best alibi he could. He had been frightened for the children, and Faith could forgive him a lot for that.

The minister stood at the lectern to greet them, and the service began. Faith let the words wash over her as she remembered Helen, the girl she had known at school, the friend through their university years, the woman who had started her life again, and lost it. She thought about Helen sitting on the rocks above Conies Dale, smiling, the light shining through her hair. She felt Jake's hand touch hers.

. . . for now, we see through a glass, darkly; but then face to face; now I know in part; but then I shall know completely, even as I have been known. But now there remains faith, hope and love, these three; and the greatest of these is love.

The colour bleached away and the bright image faded. The service was ending. Helen was gone.

She didn't see Antoni Yevanov until she was leaving the chapel. They came face to face in the aisle. 'Faith,' he said. He bowed his head in acknowledgement. His eyes flickered briefly over Jake, and she was immediately aware of the antagonism flaring up between the two men.

'Thank you for coming,' she said. He had been away since his mother's death, working in Brussels. She had heard a

370

rumour that he was planning to return there permanently, to end his connection with the Centre. She wanted to ask him about this, but now was not the time.

She walked on with Jake, and they paused by a bench in the small churchyard. There were names carved on the flagstones, memorials to people who had died centuries before. They watched Helen's friends and colleagues wander down the path in groups, then disperse into the city.

'I still don't know why he killed her,' she said. Nicholas Garrick had pleaded guilty to the charge of murder, but had given no further account of his actions. The case would come to trial later in the year, pending psychiatric reports. 'Do you think he was crazy?'

Jake's foot traced the lettering on one of the stones. 'Yes, but I don't think they'll enter that as a plea. I don't think he'll let them.'

'Do you feel sorry for him?' She felt no compassion for the man who had killed Helen and left Finn and Hannah without a mother.

He sighed. 'I feel sorry for the whole bloody mess. Maybe now there'll be an end to it.'

The sky was clear and brilliant, and a March wind blew leaves across the ground. Spring was on its way, and soon the cherry would be flowering in Grandpapa's garden. Soon, it would be time to scatter his ashes. She pushed back her hair where it had blown across her face and looked up at Jake.

'It's finished,' she said. 'It's time to go.'

The House in the Forest

This is the story of an ending.

After the war was over, only a few people came back. Many of them had vanished forever, and their stories would never be told.

The house in the forest was abandoned. There was no one to return. The seasons passed, and the house began to decay. The floors sagged and the roof fell in. The low wall around the well began to crumble and to collapse into the ground. For a few seasons the trees blossomed, the fruit ripened, the cherries and the plums, but there was no one to harvest them and they dropped from the branches and rotted on the ground, or were torn down by the summer storms.

Gradually the forest reclaimed the land, the pines and birches moving into the clearing, growing through the floor of the old house, the brambles entwining around the collapsed walls and the rusty stove. The house vanished forever into the deep glades of the forest where the trees were bare in the winter and reached their fingers high up into the sky.

But in summer, the leaves grew and the branches hung down in fronds. When the wind blew, the branches would wave and the leaves would dance. Then the sunlight made patterns of shadow and gold. And the tree trunks were white, like slender pillars along the paths.

In the forest, there was a clearing. And a man called Stanislau built a house in the clearing, a house of timber. And Stanislau and his wife Kristina lived in the house, where their first child, Marek, was born.

Stanislau planted trees in the clearing, cherry trees and plum trees, and he dug a deep well. The water that came from the well was clear like crystal, sweet and cool.

Marek grew big and strong, a happy boy with fair hair and a ready smile. And then, five years later, in the depths of winter, Eva was born. The last child, a little girl. The night of her birth, there was a storm that made the trees bend, the branches lashing through the air as the wind whooped and swirled . . .

No more stories.